ALSO BY WILLIAM WHARTON

Birdy

Dad

A Midnight Clear

SCUMBLER

SCUMBLER

WILLIAM WHARTON

Alfred A. Knopf
New York
1984

THIS IS A BORZOI BOOK
PUBLISHED BY ALFRED A. KNOPF, INC.

 Published in the United States by Alfred A. Knopf, Inc., New York, and simultaneously in Canada by Random House of Canada Limited, Toronto. Distributed by Random House, Inc., New York.

Library of Congress Cataloging in Publication Data

Wharton, William. Scumbler.

I. Title.
PS3573.H32S3 1984 813'.54 83-48864
ISBN 0-394-53574-X

Manufactured in the United States of America

FIRST EDITION

Dedicated to:

ACQUIESCENCE, WISHES . . .
DREAMS

Why? Why?
'Cause I'm
Gonna die.
That's why.

SCUMBLING: to modify the effect of a painting by overlaying parts of it with a thin application of opaque or semi-opaque color.

—American College Dictionary

SCUMBLER

I

THE RATS' NESTER

Right now, here in Paris, we have seven different nests. That's not counting our old water mill, two hundred miles from Paris. I spend half my time rousting out, fixing up, furnishing these nesting places.

Rats' nesting's what it all is; can't seem to keep myself from burrowing, digging in; always stuffing bits and pieces into one corner or another.

Even before we snuck away from California, we had four nests and forty acres; not a single one of those places there you'd call a real home: a trailer dug into the side of a hill, a tent nestled against a cave, then the shack on top of a hill we called home before it burned down. There was also that place I built with rock and cement at the edge of a streambed in a gully up on the forty.

We furnished all those nests complete to knives and forks; every one a hideout, places we could run to if things got too bad; holes where we could go to ground, wait it out, hide from the crazy ones, learn to like radioactive eggs, a purple sun over green skies, a stinking stagnating dead world.

A family man's got to think ahead these days, especially someone like me, living on the outside, ex-con, a man who had his first nest—wife, two little ones, house, everything—snatched out from under him. I'm always looking for someplace for us to hide.

In California I cadged stuff from the Salvation Army, junk shops. Here in Paris I haunt flea markets; sometimes I can fix up a whole hideout for less than fifty bucks.

A MAN FOR A WOMAN, EACH TO EACH
OTHER: MOTHERING FATHER,
FATHERING MOTHER.

We've been living in Paris more than twenty years now; I'm not sure why anymore; maybe I'm a new kind of bum, rats'-nest bum. Every New Year's morning, I check with the family, ask if they want to go back.

No, they like to stay, like being aliens.

I still think of myself as a serious artist, paint hard and heavy when I'm not caught up in nesting fevers, father juices.

Don't get me wrong. I'm not talking about masterpieces, museums; used to dream that war; just don't care so hard anymore. When the end gets closer, those kinds of crazy ideas don't mean much; everything gets sucked into the painting itself.

ONE LEG OF A ZIGZAG, MY LIFE
TACKS WINDWARD WITHOUT A LUFF.

I like to rent out our Paris hideouts to last-ditch people: students and artist types, end-of-the-line people; they appreciate my hiding places, feel safe.

One of these nests is in a quarter behind the Bastille. This part was supposed to be torn down fifty years ago. I'm nibbling around over there one day, looking for something to paint, something to fix up, something, anything; helping me delude myself into believing life makes some kind of sense, any kind.

I'm on my Honda motorcycle. I traded a painting for this Honda seven years ago; it's over ten years old now and has 160 cubic centimeters displacement with around 75 cubic centimeters of power left. About like me: plugging up, wearing thin, metal-mental fatigue, general sludgishness.

I have my box and canvas strapped on my back, they rest on the carrier. Sometimes I paint sitting ass-backwards, straddling the bike, with feet jammed on the foot pegs. At my age, the back can't take much stand-up painting without stiffening. If the back goes, I can't get out of bed in the mornings; need Kate, my wife, to give me a push up, just to get going, moving.

I'm scumbling, stippling around, in and out courtyards, all crowded with wooden sheds and shacks. They're piled tight, holding each other up. I'm ass deep in broken windows, old wet mattresses, sacks and boxes of garbage—everything smelling of mold. Rats are playing in the garbage. I'm feeling at home, in my natural place, delayed decay, festering under gray Paris skies.

There's a marble workshop in back of a court, beautiful pieces of cut marble, sliced like cheese for tabletops to make French-ugly-type furniture.

On top of the other smells is cut-wood smell, sawdust, greased tools. This is a furniture-making part of town, gradually going downhill, out of business. Factories are making modern, glue-together furniture—cheap, throw-away stuff, nobody gets bored. Change your furniture with your husbands, wives; hard come, easy go; the new life.

I stop and get talking with a great older guy—older than me, even. He's wearing a gray denim cap and could pass for Khrushchev, the Soviet shoe banger. He's built like a four-poster fire plug. I wrestle the motorcycle onto its stand and follow him into his shop. He has a mattress business, makes mattresses from the wire up. I love seeing this kind of thing, helps me enjoy sleeping in a bed.

He comes on with an exciting, long story. I can sit all day listening to a good storyteller.

Sixty years ago he jumped ship; was in the Russian Navy. He winds up in Paris alone, nineteen years old and a Jew. Fat chance.

He starts calling himself Sasha, can hardly remember his real name anymore. During WW II, he hid from the Nazi Jew hunters, French *and* German, in these very buildings. He grabs me by the arm and hustles me down a tunnel and hole he's dug into the ground under his garage.

There's a whole room carved out down there; stocked with food, rice, beans, canned food, even candles.

Sasha and I could be soul mates. He invites me to lunch with him in back of his shop: cold borscht, bread, runny cheese, warm wine.

We talk on and on for hours. He tells how he started his spring-and-mattress business, one-man operation, never hired anybody. He found himself a nice Jewish French girl, got married, had three kids; lived on top of this mattress shop thirty years.

Now the kids are grown up, have a furniture store

on the Faubourg Saint-Antoine. They're ashamed of Sasha, don't want him around their fancy store; he's too fat, too dirty, too old, smelly, too Russian, too Jewish.

WE OUTLIVE OURSELVES, BECOME TRASH,
OBSTACLES, UNWANTED. UNWANTED EVEN BY
THOSE WE LOVE, WHO LOVE US, TOO.

Last year Sasha's wife died of cancer. His eyes fill up telling me about it, whips out a greasy blue handkerchief and wipes tears away without slowing down. He tucks the handkerchief in his back pocket, looks me in the eye and tells how he has a lady friend now.

He smiles, I smile back. He says when a man has lived with a woman for fifty years he can't live without one. He's telling me?

Men are only parking spaces for women to fill. A man without a woman is a house without windows. God, I hate to think what I'd do if Kate died. It'd sure take most of the fun out of life; not all, but a big part of my reasons for living.

TO SEE IN SOMEONE ELSE'S EYES
THE CENTER OF YOUR OWN AND FEEL
LIFTED, SHUTTERING FROM THE GROUND.

The wild part is this woman friend is forty years younger than Sasha. He's proud as a rooster. His kids are going crazy, afraid he'll give her his money. His woman friend is an Arab widow; he keeps her in an apartment near the mattress shop; he's thinking of moving in with her.

Sasha laughs; says he's had everything else in life, so what if he has shit for kids.

No sense me explaining the regression to the mean, so I don't; too complicated; nobody wants to admit it anyway.

I tell him he should have more kids with the new woman, Middle Eastern peace right here in Paris, handmade. To hell with the old kids; make new ones; maybe they'll be more real, like him. He gives me a punch on the arm, a hard punch. You know, that's about the closest men come to showing love for each other, giving and taking punches. That's weird.

I LIE HERE WEEPING IN MY WIRE
SPIDER'S LAIR; DRY MOTES FLOAT
FREELY IN INSECTLESS AIR.

I ask Sasha if I can paint him. Sasha handles it in stride; wants to know how long it'll take. I knock this painting out in an hour and a half; get a good one. I do it size 20F, about eighteen inches by two feet. I do head, shoulders, full face; great head, pig eyes, putty nose. When I'm finished, I try giving it to him.

"What for?"

"Give it to your kids, make them suffer!"

Also I want to pay him back for his story, his life.

Sasha punches me again, tough, thick, ham hands. He hangs his painting on the wall between some brass springs, tells me to follow him.

He waddles along ahead of me and we go farther back up the alley. There's a three-story wooden building there. It leans out in every direction, has a tar-paper roof. It's half full of old furniture, mostly waterfall design, nineteen-twenties stuff. Everything's dirty as hell, inch-thick dust, caked and oily. Sasha says I can have any furniture I want; all this taken in on trade years ago.

I'm excited by the building; ask if he'll rent it to me. Sasha laughs. I tell him I'll turn it into a studio, have naked women in to pose. Sasha laughs louder, says wind blows through, cats crap all over, holler and fuck at night; rats eat cats' kittens, pigeons fly in through the roof. I tell him I'll feed the pigeons, train my rats to fight his cats.

FLOATING, FALLING: NOTHING UP
PEERING BLINDLY THROUGH SNOW.
MY IGNORANCE, SKETCHING ARROGANCE.
THE FINAL SCOPE OF INNOCENCE.

We make a deal right there; no papers. I pay six hundred francs every three months; that's about forty bucks a month. I promise I'll paint a portrait of his wife from a tiny photo. It's the only picture he has of her, one of those five-and-dime automat photos.

A FACE AS STILL LIFE
BUT STILL LIFE LEFT.

I get in there and clean things up. This is grim corruption. I haul most of the furniture up into the attic; chop the worst, stack it up for firewood.

First I put in big beams so the whole place won't fall down on me with a strong wind; then I cut a hole through the roof to let in light. I put plastic panels in this hole and line underneath with thin-roll plastic for insulation. I cover all the walls and ceiling with Styrofoam panels and paint the floors white.

Sasha lets me tie in to his electric line; I'll pay a set amount every month. Then I buy two potbelly stoves at the flea market, put in long pipes to radiate the heat. I haul back down some of the furniture and spread it around. The place is light, great, looks like something between a cheap whorehouse and a surgical theater.

ANOTHER NEST, NOT MY BEST
YET MEETS THE FINAL TEST.

The first thing I do there is paint the portrait of Sasha's wife. I let myself drift, float into it, hardly looking at the photo. I'm painting her as Sasha described her to me, the way he felt about her, her soul.

A FACE I DON'T KNOW, A MIND ECHOING ME.
I'M INFUSED WITH ANOTHER, MOTHER, SISTER, BROTHER.

I do this in an afternoon. Sasha says the painting looks more like his wife than the photo. He cries.

I'm a bit psychic; it's a nick of woman in me, I think. I might be part male witch. I've met two true witches in my life so far: exciting women.

A WOMAN LIVES INSIDE ME, CONTENT
TO PULL THE REINS OF MY CLUMSY CART.

Next, I rent out the ground floor to a sculptor. He's a rich young French aristocrat, pays me six hundred francs per month, cash. Everything cash. French officials are very uptight about people like me.

I keep the middle floor for myself. The stairs come straight up from the door, so I wall off my stairs and put in another door for the sculptor.

To bring water in, I run a line from the street spigot across the alley—strictly illegal. I bootleg this in at night using plastic hose going under the cobblestones.

I'm out there in the dark, working with a flashlight, digging up cobblestones, when the concierge catches me. I tell her I'm looking for some money I lost. She stares but isn't willing to call me an outright liar. The French are nice that way.

I bring water into the downstairs and up to the first-floor studio, but can't rig a drain system for the very top floor.

This third floor isn't much; the ceiling's low and it's dark. I figure I'll use it for storage. To get up there, you need to go through my studio, up a ladder and through a trap-door.

A TRAP NEST, SPIDER NEST, PULL IT
IN BEHIND YOU, HIDE AND ABIDE.

Just shows how you never know. Three months later, I have a Dutch woman in for some modeling. She has a nice body and is only charging me ten francs an hour. Great, beautiful, solid, rounded tits meant for having kids sucking on them, one kid on each tit. It gets me all hot and bothered for nothing just looking at her. I'd give anything to have big working tits like that; feel like the fountain of life. I'd rent myself out as a wet nurse and learn to eat grass—regular green grass, that is.

She starts telling how she doesn't have a place to live; hints about staying in the studio, doing free modeling—that kind of business. To turn her off, I tell her I'll rent the upstairs room for two hundred fifty francs a month.

She's one of these new, rugged, live-on-a-sewer-cover kind of wonderful women; takes me right up, moves in, money on the barrel two months in advance.

I squirm three days hoarding enough nerve to tell Kate, my wife, about it. Kate is *not* enthusiastic; knows how vulnerable I am. We have a good working relationship, Kate and I, based on respect for the way each of us is. Still, despite all, sometimes it gets hard. No two people so close could be so different. I wouldn't have it any other way myself, but *easy* it ain't sometimes.

This Traude turns out to be a neat, clean hamster of a woman; no trouble at all. I don't know she's there most of the time.

She gets herself a Primus stove, cooks her meals; invites me for lunch once in a while—very domestic. She usually stays in bed mornings on cold days till I get the fires going. Some heat *must* move up to her place, but she comes down and dresses next to the glowing stove; has a nice, round, almost heavy body, wide hips, beautiful glutes. I get some fine drawings; good deal all around. But I'm not showing these drawings to Kate; no sense pushing the edges. I've fooled myself into thinking that sometimes honesty can be a cruel hypocrisy.

. . .

The big mistake was renting to the blue-blood sculptor. First, he has the most active social life I've ever seen. He's a stone sculptor, cutting gigantic five-, six-ton blocks of marble or granite. He works hard when he gets the chance but that's not often. Most times, there are French dukes driving up the alley in limousines, tooling over to watch Claude play at being sculptor. They can't believe he's trying to work; only peasants work. They're titillated seeing Claude, sledgehammer in hand, goggled, genuine stone dust whitening his face like a clown, staggering around in piles of stone chips.

Maybe the one thing worse than not having enough money is having too much. You get caught up with rich friends and relatives. Then how the hell can you get anything done?

But my *big* problem is stone dust. Joseph P. Baloney, it gets into everything. Thin, light, like soap powder, it rises from his studio into mine. I run around with pieces of glass wool, putty, plaster, trying to plug holes. Nothing stops this dust. Mornings, it looks as if it's snowed; all day long there's a haze. It gets into my paint and into the paintings.

My way of painting involves slow-drying varnish; this floating stone dust is deadly. Altogether—with what's in the air, what settles on my eyeglasses and what's getting ground into the varnish—I'm working in deep cream of wheat. My white beard gets so white it glows.

THE BLINDING LIGHT OF NO WHITENESS
DARK LOST IN MEMORY: A DULL CLUMPING
OF FRAGMENTED IDEA. CLUTTER GROWS.

Finally I give up. I rent *my* studio to another painter, a friend of Claude's. This guy works abstractly, sort of white bumps on white flats; sometimes light purple or green squiggles over these large white canvases, different shades of white, all very subtle. He says stone dust won't matter.

He's a social type, too, won't mind dancing bear to the royalty. I sign him on at eight hundred francs a month. I tell Traude about it; she asks if he's married. It's OK with her. Traude's money almost covers my outgo and the other fourteen hundred francs a month is pure gravy. We definitely have use for the extra money. Trying to paint truly personal paintings, make some kind of a living *and* be a good husband-father, can be almost too much sometimes. All that's beside living some kind of life for yourself.

So that's the way we make it. We ourselves live in what used to be a carpenter's shop. I bought the bail, that's the lease, for five thousand, and pay eighty bucks a month rent.

It's a great place for living, eighty-seven square meters, plus a *grenier* and a *cave;* that's an attic and a cellar. When we moved in, I tore everything out except for one center support post. We redid all the windows to make the place weatherproof. Then I drew a plan on paper just as if we were building a house on a lot in Woodland Hills, California. I chalked my plan on the floor directly and started building up walls. The job took six months. Kate was a little worried at first but she likes it fine now.

We have our kids sleeping on platforms. It saves floor space and they don't have to make beds. There's a mezzanine-type balcony all around the living room. You can use it to get from one bed loft to the other. There's a place up there for trains or slot cars when they're young, stereo sets as they get older. We have a house rule, earphones only; these old nerves can't take loud music of any kind. Kate agrees, thank God!

I built a fireplace where we can climb in and warm up around the flames on cold evenings. A nest inside a nest.

It's a terrific place for us to raise a family. Every night, family dinners at a ten-foot-long table I knocked together from a single slab of three-inch-thick mahogany cut from the center of an African tree. The bark is still on the outside edges to remind us where wood comes from. I bought this piece of wood at a sawmill in the neighborhood: weighs over two hundred and fifty pounds; took four of us dragging it up our three flights of stairs. A big heavy table like that can help hold things together no matter what happens, gives some weight to life, keeps it from just flying away.

Evenings, after dishes, we do our sitting, reading, talking, homework, model building, drawing, around that table. This is one fine place to live, love. Our kitchen is smack in the center and open. When you're in that kitchen, you're in the command post, can see everything, control our family tree house. Swiss Family Robinson in the center of Paris.

. . .

There's no television, never has been in our family; that's one reason we ducked out of California. There's just that big open room for living, eating, sharing; each person in the family has a private place for sleeping and working. Peapods inside peapods; five bedrooms. The plumbing's tricky but it works most of the time.

I rent our apartment at five hundred bucks a summer to American university professors doing research in Paris. This almost pays the year's rent. We're down at our rugged, ragged stone water mill summers anyway.

That's the way it goes. Christ, if you're an artist with five kids, two already away at American universities, you have to figure something, somehow. It's how I make my rat-nesting instincts pay off; me the slum landlord of Paris.

I RAGTAG MY WAY THROUGH LIFE: BORN-AGAIN CRIPPLE: CURSED WITH SOMETHING EXTRA: A THIRD ARM GROWING BETWEEN MY EYES; BLOCKING THE VIEW; MAKING THE FEW SEEM MANY.

Now, in this crazy book it might be easy to get the wrong idea about how my life is lived.

I'm writing a lot about painting, about what happens out on the streets, but my *real* life, the one I live for, is home with Kate and our kids.

I hardly ever paint past five o'clock, even in summer, and I never paint on Sundays. Lots of Sundays we go to one of the zoos—we all love animals—or we row in the Bois de Bologne or, more often, the lake at the Parc de Vincennes.

I'm home for dinner almost every evening and while we eat we all share what we're doing. I'm just not writing much about that part of my life here, maybe another book; no, I'll never write another one, not enough time.

Remember, above all, I'm the nester and this is my home nest. Don't get confused by the flickerings or you'll never understand this book, what it's all about.

II

SELF-PORTRAIT

Raining today: Paris has too damned much weather. I clean my box and set up for a self-portrait. I do one each year, usually in midwinter; good for winter glump, cheap emotion massage, gets the neurons hopping. I'm working in what used to be Tim's bedroom before Annie went off to school and Tim took her room. It's my mini-studio. Actually, I don't need much space to paint.

Self-portraits are by far the most interesting paintings. Just look at Tintoretto, Chardin, Rembrandt, even David. Active and passive simultaneously, body with a brain seeing a brain through a body; the eye painting the eye seeing the eye. There you have it: what the painter is, what he'd like to be; the way he paints, the way he'd like to paint, all in the same place at the same time. Looking inside yourself must be the hardest—at the same time, the most rewarding—thing anyone can do.

Take Rembrandt. Cocky at first, full of feathers, bearing down, concentrating like a fool, believing in it all. Then, slowly backing off, starting to wonder, letting the brush paint for him; he begins staring in the black hole; keeps painting straight to the end, kisses the wall, falls in; emptiness, the emptiness of a full moon.

I'M SELF-UNSEEN; NEITHER HERE NOR
THERE; AN INVISIBLE BODY-SHAPED HOLE
IN SPACE; CONSTANTLY GETTING IN MY OWN WAY.

I set up my mirror and stare into it. The urge to paint is coming on like a blush, catching me up, pulling me down. I struggle to hold in there. It must be a little bit like going crazy, this urge to paint, to fall through a brush.

Actually, I love to paint *anybody.* The trouble is getting people to sit. When I ask, they act peculiar. Women think

I have something else in mind. Nobody can believe somebody else might just really want to look at, listen to, talk with another person. Everybody's alone, knowing they want something more, not knowing what it is, or how to have it. The overwhelming, final big mystery: joy.

Practically all men cross their legs, fold their arms, maybe expect me to rip at their flies.

After all, I *am* an artist. Men live such dumb lives anyway, continually defending their precious inviolability, their phony territory. Mostly they're afraid somebody might just find out nobody's home. They live in film sets like on Universal Studio lots, fancy façades, nothing behind, a front for the tourists.

Generally, people seem to be getting more and more invisible, slipping around inside their stories. Even some women are turning slightly translucent; I can see through them against certain kinds of light. Or maybe I'm going people-blind; there's hardly anybody around for me anymore. Could be I only need new glasses: thick, rose-colored; multifocal, with catalytic platinum frames.

HOW TO AVOID A VOID? FIRST THERE WAS
THE VOID, THEN THE WORD, THEN THE WORLD.
IT JUST CURLED BACK ON ITSELF!

Everything's ready now. The box and a 25F canvas in front of me; palette set with earth colors, turp, varnish. The mirror's on my left. I paint best over my left shoulder, probably because I'm right-handed.

THESE FIRST STROKES AGAINST WHITE:
LIGHT FIGHTING; A SEDUCTION TO WHAT'S GOING
TO BE. AN OVERWHELMING OF WHAT WAS.

In the mirror, I'm holding the brush in my left hand. I try to see myself as a left-handed painter, switch-painter, leadoff painter. No. That's not me; ambidextrous I'm not. I never punch singles to the opposite field. I'm always swinging for fences and mostly striking out. Mirrors lie too. Lies reflecting lies into something we can almost believe. That is, if you're a believer. We're running out of believers: I believe.

I try scrunching back on my haunches and staring. I'm a Russian sitting down before leaving on a trip; say a few prayers. Got to let this happen to me, get into the magic passive-active mood.

. . .

I'm ready. I lean forward. I let go, fall into my private craziness, the insanity that keeps me sane.

When I paint anybody, even me, I go a tiny bit berserk. I want something that can never be, probably isn't meant to be. My easel's set so I can see the model *or* the canvas, not both at once. Everything close; no secrets; we're involved in a birthing, for better or worse.

But this time the model's the mirror, *me*. And I'm wanting the impossible, to get close to myself. It's hard! I'm always twice the distance between my eye and the mirror. I know I'm there on the surface, but I seem to be in the distance. I lean close, closer, trying to see me, to crawl inside myself without touching.

In a mirror, eyes are static; they don't move. The mind blanks it out, a minor hysterical blindness. It gives self-portraits a stare, that and the painful concentration.

HOW HARD CAN ONE LOOK? DOES LOOKING
MAKE US BLIND TO SEEING?

When I paint anybody else, we're jammed close: model, me, easel; a triangle, knees touching, wrapped into each other around my paint box. We need to get close or it's only looking. And just looking is like counting, or measuring or describing—or, worse yet, estimating.

There can be no sitting still. We're not catching a moment; we're trying to paint a lifetime, two lifetimes, all lifetimes, past, future, present. This isn't a Polaroid instant camera click-whirrr-wait. We're human beings making mistakes; jumping around in our loose, confining skins trying to make mistakes real, make them ours. Somehow, life must be caught in the paint, poured, forced, squeezed, seduced, transmuted into it; hard, hard, like labor-hard. Hard labor, over forty years of it now, and nothing's really been born, only a series of miscarriages, abortions, anomalies.

IN DIVERTED LINES THOUGHTS DISGUISE
AND OPEN LANDED MINDS ARE PLOWED
BY CROWS. SOWN, EATEN, SEEDED GRAIN.

I'm drawing, trying to let it happen, at the same time doing it; establishing figure-ground relationships without thinking too much, not designing or composing. Part of what I am is how much space I take up, how and where, and I don't know what the difference is anymore. It gets harder to sustain the illusion of importance in uniqueness, individuality.

It's much easier having another human being close to me, talking, yawning, smoking, nose-picking, staring at space, smiling, frowning, lifting eyebrows, twitching, sniffing, belching, more or less hiding farts, sneaking peeks at me; or the painting. These things slip through me into the painting, give it life, life not mine. It isn't true creation but it's the best somebody with outside plumbing can manage.

It's a kind of osmosis; people filter into me. I never look and paint at the same time; I paint in a dream, absorbing my models, being absorbed by them. They become the blood, cells, chemicals, electricity in my brain. They pass around in there, mix with me, my plus and minus ions, my personal hydrocarbon chains, chemical memory banks. There's a wild churning; then it comes back down the nerves, along my arms into my fingertips and out through the brush. Out it pours, color and light being moved around by my brain, my body, my psyche, under my eyes; blurred by the model, somebody, not me, and feeding back, turning me on, symbiotic, back and forth; a bit cannibalistic, with Roman pagan feelings thrown in.

BECOME ME. COME WITH ME.
WE COME TOGETHER AND THEN
WE ARE APART; A PART OF EACH,
NEVER TO GO AGAIN.

Each portrait must be a new person. It's a new being growing from the mixing of another human with me. It's a temporary marriage consummated, and the portrait is our child, a birth, a rebirth, second mutual coming.

Compared to really having a baby, it's like one of those old-time "radio re-creations" of baseball games before television days. The announcer would thump his pencil against the mike to simulate a hit, turn up some canned crowd noise, do an excited description of slides, tags, put-outs. But it's better than nothing. I try to live with it; without this slim hope I'm dead.

SLOW-FOOTED, HEAVY-WINGED, LATE TO
STING, AUTUMN HARVEST BEE GATHERING
FOR THE WINTER COMB. AND THE SUN PASSES
LOW ACROSS THE FADING SKY.

I paint very traditionally; grind my own paints, size the linen a special way so there's a flexibility to help with the dance of my brush. For me, working on canvas board or wood is like dancing in ski boots.

I do a thin, double priming to attain just the right absorbent quality. I paint my underpainting with a personal medium, a combination of Lucite, varnish and linseed oil, then work with impasto wet-in-wet technique, followed by glazing and scumbling. I lean on all the usual tricks, plus some few I've invented myself.

OUT OF DARKENED SKIES, A BEAM CUTS
LIKE GLASS, DEFINING CLOUDS. I
CLOSE MY EYES: BETTER THE KNOWN
CONFINES OF AN EVEN DARKNESS.

In our days, it's hard to find schools teaching these things. Nobody seems to care enough. Everything's only instant gratification, a veneer of the immediate visible result, without concern for permanence or even what passes for permanence. Sometimes I seriously think we might be living in a dark age of painting.

The little I did learn as a painter I got by looking, reading or copying. Every morning for five years I went to the Louvre and climbed all over, inside, the good ones. I ate, drank Rubens, Titian, Rembrandt, Chardin, Velásquez, Goya, until they were a part of me, I was part of them. I'm closer to some of those long-dead people than I am to most of my today friends. These painters are very visible. Each was somehow desperate to *be* and struggling to become. They were part of their time but walked through it. They put themselves out into the future with everything they had. In them you find pain and joy blended into strength—real strength, not just muscle stuff. They tried to live in times not yet there.

I'm still drawing. I've got to draw through to the painting. Drawing is turning space into volume, not just making lines. There's actually no such thing as a line. Good drawing for a painter is showing where the paint must go and what it should do. It's easy to get caught in drawing for itself, then have nothing left to paint; romancing until there's no room, no space, no place for making love, an isolated unpainted unpaintable corner.

DESCRIBING MAKES SLASHES, MINOR SCRATCHES IN STEEL WALLS OF OUR SEPARATENESS. WE ONLY MAKE THE IMPOSSIBLE MORE SO.

Somebody watching me work can go mad. It's like watching a tailor working carefully, with good material and fancy stitches, sewing up a coat with one arm longer than the other or with no neckhole.

The point is, there's no sense in imitating life, or representing it; it must be invented, imagined. This does not necessarily mean abstract or nonobjective objects or theatrical distortions or strained efforts at intellectual composition either. Those are the easy ways, avoidance systems. One needs to show life the way one sees it personally, the way it is felt.

So, in the end, my own particular paintings come out a bit crooked in ten different directions. OK, so that's the way I am. I struggle to show my personal reality, the only one I know. I try to paint it carefully with full attention and much love.

GETTING LOST IN THE SPACES BETWEEN,
A GENTLE LEANING TOWARD EACH OTHER.

When I'm actually painting somebody, they see me staring, poking at the canvas with my brush, leaning in, backing off; I'm trying not to jump up and down. Once in a while I remember to smile. I want them to stay with me, not run away or disappear. Most people think I'm painting *them.* Actually, I'm painting the taste, the smell, the space they're taking up. I'm trying to paint them all the way from fetus to corpse, and all in one moment, all in one place.

They see me paint one ear too high or too red. The painting looks like Eisenhower or Uncle Jim in 1962, and they get nervous, restless. Sometimes they giggle, or laugh!

God in heaven, this is a serious business: it's a painting; I'm digging inside both of us and trying to put it in one place. We're damned close to communication, a serious effort to glue things together.

By the end of a painting I'm sweating down to my shoes, toes are squishing around in sweat pools. Did Rembrandt paint Hendrikje Stoffels the way she looked? Hell, in five different paintings she looks like five different people. She probably was, and he loved all of her. It's the all of things that's beautiful; a painter's got to paint past the flickers, somehow. Or at least convince himself and a few other people that he has.

BLEND A HUSHED WHISPER, A SKITTERING
IN ONE CORNER; THE TASTE OF SMELL.

I stand; go to the toilet. I sit down again and stare into the mirror some more. Haven't actually been looking at myself enough lately; been looking at a memory. I know I'm a vain bastard but I never really look close except when I paint me. It's as if I'm only checking my watch, checking to see how long it is till something, not looking to see what time it actually is; how much time I've spent, how much I might have left.

I look at the old "visage." It's aging faster. There's more sag in the eye sockets and dark purple-blue smudges, more veins breaking out in the cheeks. I look like a fatal terminal all right. It's about time. God it's hard to know when to give up and let yourself start dying.

There's practically no hair on top and the beard's almost pure white. I rub some yellow ochre and black into the beard; gives about the right color. That looks better. A beard hides most of the ordinary muscle sag; terrific advantage. I wonder why women don't have beards. Probably men needed them to absorb hard punches; men've been living the physical dominance stupidity a long time, women have maybe learned to take those socks and keep on with it. No hairy hidings.

One thing, if women did grow beards, they sure as hell wouldn't shave them off. They'd make something beautiful of them, the way they have with tits.

I'M TRUE, SO ARE YOU AND SO WE
LIE. BECAUSE, TO TELL THE
TRUTH, WE BOTH LIE, YOU AND I.

I get to work on the underpainting; transparents. I'm working fast with a big brush. It's terrific doing self-portraits; only posing when I'm looking, nothing wasted. I'm into it.

He twists his head, stares out the corners of his eyes: suspicious-looking bastard; gazes out as if he doesn't want to look anymore; getting harder all the time. Put that in there, Scum, get that. If you're not honest here, you're nothing. But remember, always distrust professed honesty. It's the ultimate con job.

I'm laying me in down to the waist; maybe I'll do the hands, put the brush in my right hand. I tone ground with burnt sienna, use a cloth for wiping in the main forms; work up shading and volume.

> FIRST IN EARTH, THEN AERATED. WE'RE
> CARELESSLY CREATED TO FIGHT THROUGH
> TIME AND SPACE TO OUR PROPER PLACE,
> TO DIRT.

It's time to thicken the medium; build up my darks. I start brushing in cool colors, beginning movements from the light side; pushing colors in under where the impasto's going to be.

Look at those stupid eyes; they're staring back with such intensity, as if it matters. Get that, too, Scum! Work that in! Boar's whiskers, you really love yourself you broken-down fart; what else, who else. All painters love themselves or they wouldn't do it; writers too, probably; I think old Camus even said it once.

I start mucking in the background; moving out there some of what's happening inside. Now grab that kink around the nose and make it show again up here in the right corner. I'm happy, juggling two, three dimensions simultaneously. It's enough to make one want to stay alive. It's all lies, one bigger than the other. OK, make the hard one truer; paint it louder.

I squeeze gobs of opaque paint on the palette: titanium white, all the cadmiums. STOP! Careful with those cadmiums, Scum; use burnt umber, more raw sienna, yellow ochre, our kind of colors, cheap colors. I'm the earth-color man; Scum of the earth. Let's not forget!

> CAN WE EVER BE FORGIVEN
> THE MOMENTS OF OUR BLISS:
> THE TINY CRACKS IN LIFE
> THAT AREN'T JUST LIKE THIS?

Now we're backing in. Picking out the highest points with light. Fan the white bleeding away into rolls of color and darkness across the forehead and into the penumbra. Make it live! I'm alive now, breathing through my brushes; color like blood, light like oxygen.

We need to keep my brush in close; laying it in carefully, deeply, with strong tenderness. Yellow next to orange and then together. Make it stand up. Light! Light it!

Goddamn Scum! Now drift back with the highs fading away. Gently scumble. Scumble, you scum; pearl away, fade back but still keep it close; help those sharp edges move together. Birth the lie into li*f*e; squeeze in that missing "f." Only a word, but first was the word. No, first and last is the void.

I smell myself: part oil, part sweat, all horseshit. Here I am, laughing at me laughing at myself and crying at the laughing. I wasted valuable years trying to be a serious Dostoevski type, a latter-day van Gogh. Then I buttered myself deep with Middle European suffering, *Sturm und Drang;* after that, I experimented with nineteenth-century melodrama. Now I'm cried out, dried out. All I ask is something to make some reason—now, before it's too late. How dumb can you get?

LISTLESS LISTENING, CRYING, SCREAMING,
ALL WATER ON WATER. AN ENDLESS FLOWING.
ANOTHER PROOF OF OUR NOT KNOWING?

I lean in tighter. Get the stinginess, the meanness, the fear, Scum. It's in the lips; frothed with hair but it's there; you know, you live with it.

Over sixty years with this same face, this same body. I've watched it grow bigger, harder, softer, sadder, hairier. Now I even grow tufts like foxtails inside my ears. I'm falling, failing from the effects of gravity, cell deterioration, laughter, weeping and plain boredom. Watch the cracks deepen, the flesh putty out, slowly turning into aged meat. Put that all in, Scum; make it visible. Death's stalking just around one of these hours. Maybe yesterday.

I finish off the blue jacket; decide to leave out the hands, after all. Darkness is pushing me down, pinning me. I can't believe it; here I've been painting over four hours; actually painting some of the time, blubbering, yammering the rest. The family will be home soon.

I lean back and look. It's not a bad painting; still too much self-pity. I'm like one of those donors jammed into the bottom corner of a medieval painting. Only I'm all alone in the center of this canvas, begging to nobody, everybody; praying for everybody, nobody. Definitely obscene, in the deepest sense, unbearable, not to be seen.

I clean up; pack away the box. I need new pig's bristles; the ivory black's almost gone again, too. I use too much black in my painting. I can't catch myself doing it, but the paint's going somewhere; I'm not eating it. I'd better watch that.

EATING BLACK: CONCENTRATED SEARCH FOR COLOR,
OR, PERHAPS, THE LACK OF LIGHT IN WHICH TO
BURY THE NIGHT. BUT NIGHT IS ONLY A LACKEY;
COLD AS NO HEAT, SLOW MOLECULES. I FACE
BACK TO BLACK, NO ONE, NOWHERE.

III

SLUM LANDLORD

I work outside today, Saint Valentine's Day. It's cold but I'll take any sunshine I can get. I feel all cramped up painting inside, as if I'm cut off from life. I'm happiest out in streets, fighting crowds, cursing cars, yakking with people; it all gets into the work.

My painting's got to be part of life, not just about it anyway. I'm OK inside for a while, sharpening up my personal carving knives, digging into myself, getting close, but then I've got to break out and muck around. In some strange way, I have the feeling I'm most alive when I'm painting, as if the other time is a kind of waiting. I don't know what I'm waiting for but that's the way it feels.

I'm working down on the Rue Princesse in the Latin Quarter. I've just started on a woodworker's shop, *menuiserie-ébéniste*. The owner of the place comes out. We get into some standard everyday talk about "lost-artisanship-craftsmanship, world-going-to-hell," all that tired jabbering. He asks me to put his name on his sign; it's weathered off. I think he wants me to climb up over his door and do some actual, honest-to-God painting up there, but he means *in* the painting; that's fine with me.

The painting's going to be mostly browns and some dark blue-grays, with a light bulb hanging inside, lighting raw wood and sawdust; yellow-ochre hollow spaces. I'm doing the place almost face on, slight angle left. There's a big old carved doorway on the left I want to finagle in somehow.

The door's closed when I do the drawing. Halfway through my underpainting, the concierge comes out, jams this door open.

She's an old gal, new face painted on. New face has nothing to do with her real face; hair cut gaminé, bright red. She looks terrific, like a clown. There's still a good body there too; moves easily, holds herself straight; thin freckled legs. Nobody with freckles is ever old. She's maybe seventy and packing some fifty pounds of libido; comes on and chums me with "Oh-la-la" old-fashioned-girl-style press; hands all over me. I love it.

I ask if she'll stand in the doorway so I can paint her into my picture. She runs her fingers through the red straw hair; bony, bent fingers. She leans in the doorway, arm cocked against the wall. She's wearing a blue-flowered dress. I paint it orange, need an orange accent. I gussy the dress up and make her about forty. Wish I could do that for myself, for everybody. No, there's a time for each of us.

EACH TO A TIME A TIME FOR EACH—
WE WADE THROUGH OUR LIVES, THROUGH
MINUTES, HOURS, DAYS, MONTHS, YEARS
TILL WE GASP FOR AIR, DROWN IN TEARS.

She can't believe it when I'm finished; a thing like this takes me maybe five minutes. One thing, I really *can* paint: good, fast, powerful. I might just not have enough aesthetic, or maybe too much—somewhere in there. I can spin around, fall down and begin painting anything in front of me, wouldn't shift my eyes. I love it all, can paint everything; no damned discrimination. There are fifty paintings within a hundred yards of anywhere I'm standing. I know it. I could spend the rest of my life painting self-portraits, or stone walls; I might just do that.

Take my milk pots. I've painted sixteen milk-pot paintings already this winter. Who the hell wants paintings of milk pots? Thank the Good Lord our weather's getting better; get me away from those pots. I'm beginning to smell sour milk on my nostril hairs all the time. It's like when I was painting fish and they kept rotting on me. I get to be manic about these things, find myself falling into them, out of control. It's unreasonable.

THE ONLY FINDING OF SELF
IS LOSING IT SOMEHOW.

This old gal's looking at my painting and crying. Her face is beginning to run off into the street, makes me want to take my brush and touch her up. I'm also afraid she's going to ask the price. I've sold more paintings for less than canvas cost because people want them and have no idea what's involved. Rich people should pay me five thousand dollars apiece for paintings; make up for the ones I sold at ten. Only trouble is rich people don't usually like my paintings, remind them of a whole bunch of things they want to forget. This gal slips a five-franc coin into the paint box; makes me feel like a real turd.

LACK OF TRUST
SPIRITUAL RUST.

An American's been standing behind me. He's watching the whole show, smiling, very catlike, very dignified. He's young but there's much dignity there. His clothes are old: worn cuffs, bed-pressed pants, very neat; carries an umbrella on a sunny day.

The concierge goes away. I start painting seriously again, trying to forget those five francs.

"That was really nice, man."

I knew he was American all the way, even with the umbrella and all the dignity. He has swimmy blue blinking eyes; contact lenses. He tells me he likes my painting; stands in the sunshine watching me paint; not much talk.

I'm up on the sidewalk leaning against the Hôtel Princesse; painting's coming along fine; beautiful shadows falling across the wall. I'm painting a GAZ box now; lovely things those GAZ boxes, especially in early, almost spring morning, clear light.

The American comes up beside my paint box, wants to get something with the five francs. What do I care? Five francs; if he wants them, OK. I nod, smile, trying not to break the magic; I'm deep in the middle of things; I'm lost, floating in light and air, thinking and dreaming at the same time. But I might have to wipe out the old gal after all, too sharp and the top right feels blank. I'll work on it; try to save her. The American's disappeared with the francs.

Then he goes past with flowers, yellow daisies; slinks into the concierge's doorway; comes back without flowers, very catlike. He's a cat all right—big one, has all the marks. I like cats, usually; dangerous, but something. Wolves and dogs like me can usually make it with cats. We're different but we respect each other.

I SLINK THROUGH MY PRIVATE FOREST,
SNIFFING TRACES, SEARCHING PLACES
TO HIDE MY KNOWINGS, LUSTING FEAR.

Next, the concierge comes gliding out with the flowers in a vase. She perches them on the back of my box, next to the turpentine. She's probably some kind of small cat, too; clean little feet, sure sign. Here I am, surrounded by cats, trying to paint. Holy God!

A FEINT AT DEATH:
LAST BREATH. I PAINT.

The American invites us both for coffee. What the hell; I hate losing light but it's OK; this is what my painting's about, being close with people. We go into a small café next to the hotel.

The bartender here used to be a bullfighter. Every tiny Spaniard I've ever met in Paris is an ex-bullfighter the way all big Americans are ex-football players or boxers. No, that's not true anymore. Today they're all black-belt judo or karate or kung fu experts. Times change, stories change, but men's stupid lies about themselves don't change much.

We have coffee, then a cognac. The concierge—her name is Blanche—is turned on. She's about ready to lock both of us between those skinny thighs of hers. Probably be wonderful. Ben Franklin knew what he was talking about; one of my all-time heroes. He was seventy years old when the Revolutionary War started, and they couldn't've won it without him. But he never fired a shot. I wonder what kind of pictures Ben'd've painted if he'd turned his fantastic mind that way?

LOST BODIES, LOVING SOULS:
WE SPRING FROM NOW TO WHERE
BELLS TOLL FOR THE LIVING.

The painting's standing out there in the sunshine alone. There's maybe an hour more before the light shifts. Light's important when I'm leaning into impasto. This time of year I can't afford to let any light get away; I'm running out of time no matter how fast I run.

I go out. My American and the concierge stay in the café and talk; his name is Matthew, calls himself Matt. I get by without telling my name.

I work madly. I want to paint in the rough impasto, then let it dry a few days. Afterward, I'll work on glazes, scumbling and accent some lights. Painting has a rhythm of its own; I just follow it. I'm only a man chasing after a magic Pied Piper who's playing haunting tunes, tunes I can just barely hear.

A TINGLING, CLANKING OF MULTICOLORED WHITE;
THE COWBELL RINGING OF MOURNING IN THE NIGHT.

An hour later I stop. The American's standing behind me; he could've been there all the time; he invites me to lunch. I'm beat but I say OK. I'm beginning to think he's one of those rich Americans playing hooky in Paris, checking out French language, French cooking, French living, French loving, French potatoes, French dry cleaning.

We eat in a little *friterie* around the corner. I've never tried this place before. It's good, cheap. We feast on aubergines, pork, wine and tart for twenty-two francs. I find out he's not rich; poor, living on less than a hundred and fifty bucks a month. He's in a fifteen-franc-a-day hotel; does without heat to save a franc; that's rock bottom. He's studying at the Sorbonne; doing a master's about some 1870 Socialist named Jean Jaurès. To live, he teaches English to French businessmen at IBM.

We begin talking motorcycles. He has a 1950 Ariel; now that's a truly vintage bike. He takes me up onto the Place Saint-Sulpice to see it. It's covered with a black tarp. We unwrap and this bike's beautiful enough to bring on tears. A good well-cared-for thought-out machine like that is a delight. I'd love to paint just one painting as perfect as this machine. We check oil, set magneto and turn her over. Two kicks and a lovely deep sound.

He bought it from a woman in Versailles for only five hundred francs. It'd been sitting on blocks in a garage for twenty-five years. She'd talked her husband out of driving it thirty years ago because it was too dangerous. He died ten years later of diabetes.

It's marked in miles and has a grand total of 6,021. There are saddlebags and two old-style helmets. I guess the old guy even thought he'd get his wife to ride with him sometimes. There's a high-mounted back seat so a passenger can see over the driver's head. In those days riding a motorcycle was supposed to be a pleasure.

He takes me for a nice, slow tour around the Place; I'm sitting up high with a great view, no helmet. Matt says he never goes over thirty; in no hurry at all. It's rare to find a young person, especially a man, so smart about those things. If you go fast, you can't see anything; if you can't see anything, why go? We park the bike, carefully cover it again and shake hands.

A RACE THROUGH LIFE, QUICK
GATHERING OF FOOD, SHELTER,
WIFE, CHILDREN: ALL THE SPACES
CLUTTERED: SOME FACES, A BITE OF
SONG, ONE LONG LAST TRICK.

I'm late. I pack my paints and drop in at Lotte's, just around the corner. I need to fix her heater. It's an electric job, the kind that heats oil in a radiator; gives fine heat but expensive, big electric bills. I always keep a tool kit in my bike. I unpack it, go through the courtyard on Mabillon and into her place.

Lotte's not happy. I was supposed to eat lunch with her today and forgot. I could kick myself. She's an Austrian woman and can really cook. She gets great food from home, like weisswurst and stollen.

Lotte's very quiet, wears mostly black; about thirty-five, teaches German at a French lycée. Smart woman, sensitive; loves paintings, one of those people you have in mind when you paint, someone to paint *to,* like my Kate.

I met her in the street; she stood behind me the way the American did today. She has quiet eyes, Egyptian eyes, green. She tells me, in French, how she likes my painting. I start playing "mad artist." There's something challenging in her old-maid look. She listens. I spread more crapola in my personal, fractured French. I'm romancing; definitely not seducing. Most people don't understand the difference. One's for fun, the other's serious business, distinctly not for clowns like me. She nods and looks into my eyes.

"You may speak in English."

Not much accent. I'm painting in front of Chardin's house on the Rue Princesse, just up from where I worked today, nearer Rue Canettes.

I enjoy feeling the lonely master Chardin peering over my shoulder while I'm painting in that street. He lived at number 13. It sort of kills time, talking to a lovely young woman and having him there too. It sort of kills time not in the meaning of wasting it but really killing it, making the seeming reality of it go away.

I invite her for a cup of coffee. She says no, leaves. I figure that's the end of it; just as well, back to work: balancing light, space, the illusion of objects. I'm communing with Jean-Baptiste Chardin, an almost ignored master in his time.

LEVELING TIME, MY MENTAL SHOVEL
LABORS TIGHT BETWEEN GOD AND DEVIL.

I'm just packing up my box, dead tired, when she comes back, invites me for a cup of coffee at her place. I'm out of the painting enough now to catch the great overwhelming black waves of sadness she's giving off. I follow. Am I being seduced? No, it's mutual induction like electric current. Probably nobody's ever really seduced or seduces anybody. Seduces are only excuses.

Her place is a little attic room on the Rue Buci, two streets away. The room is neat as a pin; clean, more Austrian than French. There are two beds and a small room cut off for a kitchen; john's in the kitchen, curtained off. Old building, thick walls, sun coming in through a window, flowers in the window.

We eat some tasty home-baked cakes with coffee. She makes good coffee, not instant: filtered. We talk about Chardin, reincarnation, death, vibrations. This is a serious woman, nothing of sex here at all. I can relax, just enjoy.

Then we're talking about something else—I don't remember what—and she's crying. Just like that, from talking to crying, no bridges.

TEARS BURIED IN EACH
OF US; WELLING UP UNBIDDEN.
TO TAP THIS SOURCE IS, FOR
ME, THE LAST RESOURCE.

My motherly juices begin flowing. I move my chair closer, take her in my arms. She fades into me, cries harder, sobbing now. Says she's sorry, been walking around all day trying not to think, working on some painless way to kill herself. My maternal glands are in full operation, but I'm wary. I've been fooled by too many women with this "kill myself" business, but this time it's important; this woman wants tender, loving care: love, not sex. I hold on and let her cry. I'm running out of even simple ordinary love lately, and there's hardly enough sex left to fill a hummingbird's nest.

Finally, she pushes away. She goes into the kitchen and comes back with more cakes. She's beginning to watch me as if I might jump up and rape her.

There's not much experience with trust here. She sits down and begins telling how she has to get out of this place. The French guy she's been living with is kicking her out; that's why she's going to kill herself; not so much losing her apartment but the Frenchman dumping her like that. She really cares, still thinks she loves him.

I start feeling sorry. Here's a nice domestic mother type with no man and now no nest either. I feel like a pig with all my places, all my family. I tell her about one nest I've got. It's not far from where she is now. I can let her have it for seven hundred francs a month; that's less than she's paying the Frenchman. This place has terrific potential; I've been using it as a studio sometimes, a place to store my box when I'm painting over here. It's not quite finished, but I can whip it into shape in a week.

I found this space last fall when I was painting in a courtyard off the Rue Mabillon. It's on a deep court; you actually go through almost like a tunnel and come out in the court, away from traffic noises. In back is an *ébéniste,* Monsieur Moro. I painted the inside of his shop on a large, 50P canvas. Painted it like a still life: all the saws and lathes and equipment quiet in the feeling of wood. I'd come home nights smelling almost as much of wood and sawdust as I did of turpentine. Kate asked if I'd given up painting and taken to carpenter work. Could be; my dad was a carpenter.

I talk a lot with Monsieur Moro. He's a peculiar character: lives alone; part queer but doesn't like it. His wife divorced him ten years ago. She's remarried, has children. He goes Sundays to play with her kids; another natural mother with the wrong plumbing. I try to tell him about my good friend Ben Franklin who was such a fine mother, but he doesn't understand.

Moro has a huge room where he stores wood; he hardly uses this space at all. I talk him into letting me build a mezzanine storage deal for his wood, then close off the underneath part. I tell him I'll rent that bottom section from him for two hundred francs a month. After a lot of wiggling and niggling he agrees and I cut myself out that space, build him a staircase using his great tools.

The space I hack out has its own door and windows along one side. The building's an old carriage house for the church of Saint-Germain-des-Prés. I get fifty square meters; it's only two meters high but a great location, right on the *rez-de-chaussée,* opening directly onto the courtyard.

I find an old stove and fridge. I build in a toilet with one of those garbage-disposal units to grind the shit and paper so it can go out a water pipe. I put in a portable shower and buy a used *chauffe-eau* water heater. I find the oil-electric space heater at a flea market in Montreuil for eighty francs. My whole investment is under four hundred bucks. I could probably rent this hole for a thousand francs. I'm letting her have it at seven hundred. Lord, I need a keeper.

I'm a sucker for damsels in distress; I should learn to distrust distress. Getting involved in other people's distress only leads to stress for me and stress is probably what's going to kill me in the long run; or short.

I MUDDLE IN OTHER PEOPLE'S
PUDDLES, THEN FIND IT'S ALL
ONE BIG, LONESOME OCEAN.

Lotte moves in the next week. She *does* appreciate the place, a true homemaker. I begin going over once in a while for lunch. She loves to cook and is good at it. She plays a little harpsichord, plays it well, a real artist. There's no sex or even vibrations. We're like brother and sister or father and daughter.

That Frenchman made a big mistake; this is a natural wife. I think she'd make a great mother, too, only she doesn't want to. Says she wouldn't bring anybody into this mean, vicious world; people dangling nuclear bombs in the air, underground and in the oceans.

That's the kind of talk breaks this old Scumbler heart. What the hell else is there except life? Sure we have to be afraid of the crazies with the bomb, fight them with all we've got; but we've also got to love and be loved, or we'll get to be like them. They don't know about love, so they don't know how to fear; that's the real trouble.

I fix the heater. Oil's leaking out one of the elements. Lotte warms up the meal I missed. I don't have the heart to tell her I've already eaten. I can always eat anyway; should probably be a fat guy, might be one yet if I live long enough. The painting knocks five pounds off me every day. I come home nights sweating as if I've been running a marathon. It takes two showers a day just for people to be able to live near me.

We finish off with Steinhager and Bauern shenken. Then I sit under the pale, struggling spring sun falling softly through her window while she plays and sings a few of those German lieder. It's healing time for my beat-up, turpentine-shriveled, Y-chromosome-cursed soul.

PUTTING TOGETHER AGAIN WEATHERED
WOOD, RUSTED NAILS, PITTED STONE,
TO BUILD ANEW THIS DWELLING CALLED
ME. PERHAPS A CAVE—OR A TREE HOUSE?

IV

RIDING EASY

Today, still sunny, cold. I paint more on the Rue Princesse *ébéniste* painting. There's good light in the morning but it starts falling off by noon. I get some glazing in, some scumbling on the walls and over the door. My American comes while I'm working. His last name is Sweik, better name, more a cat name. We have lunch at the same place, then go up to his room for a nip of Grand Marnier.

This is some room; falling-down, peeling-faced hotel; Hôtel Isis. There are long, dark halls, no lights. The steps used to have rugs but they're all torn up; catch your feet in rug strings; smell of dust when you trip. Burlap bags are tacked on the walls and ceiling to catch falling plaster; these are hanging, sagging bulges full of broken plaster.

Sweik's room's on the second floor. And this is a great room: light; looks out on the street. His fireplace is blocked, plastered up. There's a double bed on one side, sink in the corner, collapsible bidet under the sink. The green wallpaper has twisting, crawling flowers with stains running down; there's a big beam across the center of the room, small light hanging from the beam. Terrific place, something to paint. I can definitely leave the planet through this room, free-fly in my mind.

The sun comes out again. I sit in the window, back to sun; sip Grand Marnier from a miniature bottle; tingling taste of oranges on a cold day in the sunshine. There are sounds of people walking below. I look out his window into Madame Boyer's café-charbon across the street. Sun comes deep into Sweik's room. I'll paint it from the window looking in, inside, enclosed, with air at my back; then from the door looking *out* the window, a rabbit view from his burrow into free light.

His old-time motorcycle saddlebags, helmets are hanging by the door. They're brown leather and well oiled. Sweik says he keeps his clothes in those saddlebags. There's nothing of his spread around the room; all very neat, cat; says he only has enough stuff to fill those bags, nothing extra. Heavenly beans, so different from the way I live: my guts, my life spread all over the landscape.

The walls are covered with drawings, charts of French political history, some Goya bullfight prints. Sweik says he likes bullfights. I can't make it myself, nerves won't stand it; wind up feeling sorry for everybody, despising them at the same time; rips me up.

Sweik says it'll be OK for me to paint his room. He'll leave the key under his doormat, he's gone most of the day. I make arrangements for tomorrow. I'm hot, bubbling to get into this; drink, suck this room into me; make it real, my real, stop it from changing. We also agree to get together with some friends of Sweik's that night; go to the Bastille and look at motorcycles. Probably Kate won't want to come but she won't mind my going. Kate and I have a lot in common but our pleasures are different.

SIMULTANEOUS ALTERING;
ON THE ALTAR FOR WHAT?

We meet at Sweik's place around nine o'clock. Most of the motorcycles in Paris cruise to the Bastille on Friday nights; everybody checking everybody else out. Motorcycle cops are sitting around waiting for trouble. There are some old bikes; and even more crazy people. It's the ultimate macho machine orgy.

I meet rare individuals at Sweik's. One's named Lubar, Brooklyn Jew married to and separated from a French lawyer; he runs English classes for the French at IBM. Sweik works with him. Another, Tompkins, is a physicist-poet; brings a woman friend named Donna along. He's here on a grant from Berkeley, supposed to be working at the Sorbonne in solid-state physics but spends all his time writing poetry. Duncan, a tall, thin man, has a Triumph 500 and doesn't say much. Lubar has a BMW 750. Tompkins is riding on the back of Lubar's bike, Donna on Duncan's.

Sweik gets his machine from up on the Place and

we tune it in front of his hotel on the Rue Guisarde. This makes an awful racket with the close walls. A man throws water out his third-story window; can't blame him. I turn off my bike. Lubar pees on the side of the wall; yells up in street French, no Brooklyn accent. The man throws out a pail of *hot* water this time. Lubar is drenched; laughing, he starts a jig in the street singing a song about a fucking machine—in English, thank God. More people come out, laugh at Lubar, who's putting on a show.

Finally, we roar off, down to the river and over onto the Right Bank and along the quais. We're not going fast, only riding easy on a coolish springlike night. Sweik and I bring up the rear; my tired 160 sounds like an organ grinder and I'm the monkey.

THE SWELLING OF DECAY, A SPONGY
POROUSNESS, FESTERING AS A BLIGHT;
BLISTERING INCANDESCENCE OUT OF SIGHT.

We hang around the Bastille an hour or so; there are some handsome machines. There's a new Kawasaki, and more cross bikes every time. Some leather-covered character offers Sweik ten thousand francs for the Ariel. Sweik only smiles, says no, politely. We swing around the Bastille column a few times with the mob. Then head down Roquette to the Rue de Lappe.

We park and work our way into the Belajo, an old-time French dance hall. There are coveys of Algerians and black guys; some tired-looking middle-aged women; a fair sprinkling of whores, both sexes. We find a table under a balcony; the orchestra is up on the balcony.

Donna stops by the women's room to pee; bike riding joggles kidneys some when you aren't used to it. Lubar moves an Algerian or Tunisian guy's coat to make a place for Donna when she comes back. This Arab gets all excited, slams his coat back on the seat. Lubar jumps up and throws the coat onto the floor.

Here we go, we're off again. The bouncers begin drifting close. Lubar pushes up the sleeve of his jacket and shakes his fist in the Arab's face. I'm slipping under the table, easing my helmet onto this old bald head. I'm ready to crawl out of there on my hands and knees.

Donna comes back, sits in the chair and smiles. The Arab smiles, backs off, apologizes to Donna as if Lubar doesn't exist. Everybody settles down; bouncers drift away. Another little dumb male scenario has been worked out. It's worse than watching belly dancers or bunnies at a Playboy club.

We order beers, start scanning the scene. There are more men than women, about two to one. Most are simple working stiffs, Arabs, other Africans, Spanish, Portuguese; mostly they don't dance. They're here in Paris with no women; they come hoping for a contact. Lonesome men, cut off from women, are dangerous.

The music starts again; everybody's hustling. Lubar's still looking for a fight. He keeps going up, tapping men on the shoulder, cutting in—that kind of dumbness. A little guy like him, failed athlete, is never finished. He's liable to wind up growing a short-handled blade between his shoulder blades.

I dance with one woman, almost my age, wearing a wig; stiff-backed type, likes to dip and twirl but keeps pushing me away with her skinny, sinewy arms. There's a big, old-time crystal ball going around over the dance floor. It throws lights on the walls and floors in different colors. If you concentrate on the lights, you feel as if you're turning upside down.

The next one I get pushes *her* sagging belly into *mine.* Her breath would burn if you struck a match; blend of booze, garlic and sewer gas. I stagger back to our table.

We stick through two beers. Lubar drags over a pale girl, wearing a tiny miniskirt, with incredibly thin legs; she starts quoting the price structure and we decide to skip the whole deal, too sad. We go out, charge up our bikes again and head for Contrescarpe.

There we check in at Cinq Billards. This is a little café with four good tables. Lubar, Duncan are sharks; they chalk up. Tompkins and Donna watch. Sweik and I play Ping-Pong in back behind a string net. He has a strong forehand, some good spins but an ordinary serve and nothing on the backhand. I keep playing to his bad side and picking up on his serve. I've got a sneaky drop serve but no backhand either.

We come out even: good games, good fun. Sweik and I are both players, not sportsmen; we laugh too much. And God, I tire out fast; can you imagine, tiring out from Ping-Pong!

DEATH IS A CUP OF COFFEE, OR A DAWN, OR ORGASM, ALL THE GOOD THAT COMES IN LIFE, AND THE BAD. THAT'S LIFE, THAT'S DEATH.

It's getting late, time for this old man to go home. I drift downhill beside the Jardin des Plantes, past the morgue and Jussieu, the science part of the Sorbonne. It's where the Halles aux Vins used to be; I think that represents progress. I cut over the bridge across the back of l'Ile Saint-Louis and up Henri-IV to the Bastille again. The motorcycles are gone and it's quiet.

I cruise down Rue Charenton, avoiding the Faubourg Saint-Antoine. I can't take all the crappy furniture in the windows. It's a long street pretending things that aren't and never should be. Poor people walk up and down that street Sundays when the stores are closed; they stare into the windows practically genuflecting.

At the end of Charenton, I see a man lying in the street. He's under a streetlight with his head propped on the curb. There's thick blood. I stop. Nobody's around; it's quiet. The gutter is full of blood. I yell but nobody opens any windows. I get down; his hands and face are cold, white; there's no breathing. I jump on my bike and speed up to the Marché Aligre where there's a police station.

Two flics are standing spread-legged on the corner. I explain. I know I'm getting myself in trouble. One flic surprises me by jumping on back of my bike while the other phones in. We head back to Charenton. When we get there, my flic leans over the poor blood-drained bastard. People are looking out windows now. The flic asks my name and looks at my passport. I figure I'm set for a night in the pokey.

He takes off his cloak and covers the dead one, head and all. It's a damned nice thing to do; it's not exactly warm. He says I can take off. He's written my name, address and passport number in his little notebook. I figure I'll hear from the cops, but don't; you never know in France.

I roll the few blocks home. The door's locked but I

have a key. I try to slip into bed quietly. No good. I wake up Kate and snuggle against her. It feels great, spoon tucking, warm body, warm bed feeling. There's nothing better than sleeping wrapped up with a wife. It's awful to be dead out there on a street like that, nobody even opening a window to peek out.

Kate rolls over, looks at me just as I'm drifting into sleep.

"Dear, you really can't stay up late like this and get your work done. It's almost three o'clock and it doesn't make sense. You're not a kid anymore, you know."

I don't feel much like answering but Kate deserves to know.

"Yeah, you're right, I know; but sometimes a painter works without a brush in his hand, Kate."

It's quiet, I should leave it there. I've sworn I'll never argue with anyone, especially with Kate. Everybody loses every argument. But I'm so upset by that dead man in the street I can't keep my mouth shut. Mostly I want to tell her, to spread out my fear.

"On the way home, I found a corpse stretched out in the Rue Charenton. I called the police, and that flic even got on my bike with me and rode back. I thought for a while there I might spend the night in the hoosegow. You know, Kate, I'd've called you if something like that happened."

I leave it. This kind of thing unhooks me, maybe even more than dead people. I'm probably afraid of becoming one more of the living dead, living all my life's time for some kind of postmortem postpartum expectation or justification; defensive living. Most people wear out their shoulders from looking over them.

TORRENTS TRIGGER ENDLESS FAULTS
WITHIN THIS AMPLITUDE OF WELL-FINGERED
FAILURE. IN PAINTED ILLUSION TRUST DECLINES.

V

THE PEOPLE'S PAINTER

Today I begin my painting of Sweik's place. Sweik *did* leave his key under the doormat. It's cold but sunny when I step into the room. There's strong slanted sun pushing in through his window, but this place smells musty even with that window wide open.

I stop there in the doorway and set up my easel. I want it just this way; maybe later, I'll get Sweik to sit under the sunshine, casting unpredictable shadows.

There's not so much cat-look in the room. Books, pipe, wine bottle out; pants hanging over a chair; clock crooked on the mantel; little things. Sweik might be a bear or a bear cat; Himalayan bear; hibernating type. I'll have to find out if he eats honey and berries. Bears tend to gorge on honey, berries, fruit and meat, almost's omnivorous as men.

This room desperately needs paintings to cover those water stains on the walls; I'll bring over some sunny Spanish wall paintings. I did them two years ago, when we went down to southern Spain for Easter holidays; never managed to sell even one. Nobody believed them; that can be a problem with paintings or anything else. People don't seem to want to believe the beautiful hard things.

I do a fine layout; stand-up view; looking across the table and over his bed; almost one-point perspective. The wall, fireplace, books, a mirror fill up my right side. The window's dead center. Outside, across the street, there's an old wall in the shade. The room's so full of trapped sunlight you can almost wade in it.

It'd be terrific having Sweik in front reading; alone like a bear; definitely bear. How could I've thought cat? His hands, feet are too big. Big soft-moving mountain bear or bear cat; he even lifts his head up every once in a while, sniffs, looks around, the way all bears do—definitely bear.

RESTING DARKLY IN A MOLDERING CAVE
A SLAVE TO ALL SEASONS, YET BLESSED.

First, ultramarine blue, ochre, burnt sienna for the underpainting. No real drawing yet; I'll get my drawing in the painting. I'm inside the forms and light now; splicing places where walls meet. I'll use that sagging beam in the ceiling against the rug and light on floor tiles. Leitmotif: yellows, yellow-browns against dark green.

EATING AIR, RACING LIGHT, FLIGHT
THROUGH SPACE AND EYES THAT BITE.

I'm a kind of dog myself. I'd like to be a wolf. Kate's a full-blooded wolf. Dogs need to be liked; bark a lot; whine. Dogs care. Wolves never give anything away; are very loyal, very uptight about the nest, kids, full of pride; possessive. My first wife was a wolf, too. She brought on the pack and they destroyed me. Sometimes I even think she enjoyed it; I keep trying to wipe that thought out of my mind but it won't go away.

THE HOWLING OF AIR IN A CHIMNEY,
THE CALL OF A WOLVERINE FOR HER CUB:
I'M EMPTY WITHOUT FIRE.

I want as much room as I can get in the painting, so I blow out the perspective to a wide-angle-eye distortion. The problem with four major converging forces like walls is they can confuse the point of focus.

Now I'm drawing over my underpainting. The light's moving across the room, falling left to right. I'm moving with it, tilted at an angle in my mind, leaning on photons.

I've just put on the first licks of impasto when Sweik comes. He agrees to sit in front of the window; has some studying to do. He sits in his chair, rocks back with a foot on the rail of his bed. It's quiet. We're both working hard. I can hear my brushes on the canvas.

I'm feeling and letting it happen. I'm out there and the room is flowing through me. I don't even know *how* it's happening. I'm watching the painting from far away, like watching God create the world. I drift on the brushes that way an hour or two, controlled falling, skiing on light.

But that light's dropping off now. Sweik rocks down and stretches. We decide to eat here in his room. There's a half bottle of wine; the wine's in the foreground of my painting on the table. That wine can never be drunk completely; it's there in the painting forever, or at least what passes as short time forever.

We chip in ten francs each. Sweik goes out to buy. I pack up my box feeling empty. I flop on his bed and listen. The painting's on the mantel; another day pinned down. I turn it over, can't look at it; more real than real; can't get out of it. It's so easy to get lost, to lose your bearings, not know what's real anymore.

Sweik comes back. He has warm baguette, Camembert, some tomatoes. These're the first good-looking tomatoes of the year, Moroccan. I cut the bread down its length, spread Camembert and hunks of tomato. We slice into the sandwich some sausage that's hanging over the sink in my painting. Here we are in the waning sunshine eating immortal sausage washed down by immortal wine. Downright immoral.

THE TEMPORARY ARREST. THE OBJECT
OR PAPER TO ATTEST TO WHAT IS, OR
WAS, OR MIGHT HAVE BEEN.

I sit on the floor; Sweik's on the bed. Now our sun's bouncing against that wall across the street not fifteen feet away. The reflected light is warm. I pour wine into a glass, toothbrush glass; Sweik drinks out of the bottle. It's blanc de blanc, cheap, dry, good with cheese.

We spend all afternoon shab-rapping. Sweik has no idea what he's doing. Feels he has no big talents, no strong drives; refuses to live just an automatic life. He likes living around, traveling; likes women, sex, but has a hard time getting anyone up the front hall with the sagging burlap bags and rug strings. He'd like to find some important, serious woman he could live with for a while.

I tell him about Lotte's place. I might be able to work out something there. That nest's too big for only one person; holy heaven, fifty squares. That's almost as much as I've got at home with five people. I'll divide off a room for Sweik. It'll be cheaper than the hotel. He can share john, kitchen, maybe bed, with Lotte. It'll be good for her. A guy like Sweik'd be good for her soul: scrape it up a bit; loosen some of those icebergs left over from the disappearing Frenchman. Sweik's soul's so big she can't put any hooks into it either; big bear soul. Lotte could sure use some careless loving.

Yes sir, Lotte needs a bumbling bear to muck around with her, smell things up. She'd be happier with Sweik; give some sense to things, put some surprises in her life. Sweik'd have something to fill his empty space, too. It's a bad habit living only with things you already know.

AUTOMATIC LIVING, SPIRITUAL, PSYCHIC
OXYGEN TENTS, IV, CATHETER TUBES PUMPING.
WE KEEP ALIVE IN A KEEP, LUBRICATING
OUR PATH TO THE GRAVE, SAVING NOTHING.

Before leaving, I arrange to come paint some more next day. I go out, hop on my bike and ride over to the Marais. Marais's the old Jewish quarter of Paris. There are good bakeries with bagels and pumpernickel; delicatessens with pastrami; Yiddish in the streets. You see kids with black hats and schoolbags going to the "shul." Uplifting smells, beautiful small streets, all crooked.

I sit on my bike and start some sketches. I'm laying out an idea for a whole series: thirty or forty paintings at least. I've been working on this idea for a month and I'm almost ready to start.

The people here are great; ask all kinds of crazy questions. The first one is usually if I'm Jewish. Sometimes I say yes, sometimes no; see if it makes any difference. I can't notice any.

CATHOLIC, PROTESTANT, HINDU,
MUSLIM, ORTHODOX JEW;
BUT *WHO* THE HELL ARE YOU?
NOT WHAT!

I always try to paint in series, want to give the whole idea of a quarter. Any *single* painting is only like a man with a stiff neck: nice view so long as you don't move. I pick good spots, then turn slowly, painting in all directions, one painting ending about where the other begins.

I'm sure the future for painting is video-cassette tapes. I'll tell what I'm thinking about while I'm painting, tour all over my painting with a video camera, show it happening. People can see things the way I see: completely subjective;

my Paris, nothing real to get in the way; just glorious, personal lies. Everybody'll have video-cassette players soon; full-wall color cathode screens. That's the future for paintings, all right; the only trouble is, I'll be dead.

Museums are mummy shows, nobody goes. Private collections are money tombs, cut off from the world. Hell, I'm the people's painter! I paint the way most people'd like to paint if they could. People in the streets like my paintings, like to *watch* me paint. They drift along with my mind through my eyes, and the more they know about what I'm painting the better they like my work. For me it's a good part of what makes the whole thing worthwhile.

What bugs me is I always have to break up these series, sell them in bits and pieces. I can't seem to find anybody rich enough to buy a whole set intact.

I try keeping track of the work, someday maybe put them together again; but it's hard, probably impossible, definitely improbable.

OUR EFFORTS, DREAMS, IDEALS, IDEAS
DISSIPATE, DISPERSE, LEAVING US
LIKE CHILDREN. COULD BE WORSE.

I'm coming near the end of my Canettes series. I've been into the houses, up and down the streets. I've painted portraits, straight-on façades, peeped in windows, painting, sniffing around generally. I've got just about all of it. Now I'll need to cut it up; like slicing salami or cheese.

My new series will be the Marais. Best way to forget paintings is to start new ones. I'd sure like to try living down there. I even found an apartment for rent; this Jew's going to Israel for his kids' sake. But I can't move into *every* painting. Kate says she'll *never* move again, anywhere; can't blame her. We've really played a lot of gypsy in our lives, and without violin music either. She deserves a regular sit-down nest now for sure. Thank God we overlap some, both like being aliens, living outside; but my restlessness can be too much for her sometimes.

A HOME OF HER OWN.
WALLS, HALLS, A TOILET
AND A BED WITHOUT LUMPS.
IT CAN'T BE ALL BAD.

So I'm sitting on the bike, sketching away, creating space with a pencil, when a woman comes up to me. She's about forty-five or fifty: nice face, hair cut short, bit dikey somehow, in a nice way. She speaks to me in English: reasonable English, French accent. She knows I'm American because I have California license plates; avoid French taxes, French tickets that way.

Says she's a painter and looks into my eyes. She has the most amazingly dirty eyes I've ever seen. They make me want to reach up and wipe my own. She tilts her head and gets close; little alky smell there, too; bacteria shit, human vomit. She turns her soft, dirty eyes onto my drawing. Then she puts her hand on my hand while I'm trying to draw. She smiles at me; I can't keep on drawing like that!

She asks me to join her for a drink. Sure, maybe she'll go away if I buy her a drink. She takes me to a place around the corner, we sit in back. I'm tired; I don't really even know how I got here.

We've just sat down when she reaches over and puts her hand in my crotch. Nothing serious, I think; only keeping her hand warm. She orders a marc for each of us. That's the end of drawing for the day. She starts telling me her life story; some people think artists are priests. Maybe I should have a portable confessional, wear a stole. Maybe I can steal one.

THE SOFTEST BOULDER IS A
SHOULDER, BUT BE CAREFUL
IT DOESN'T BECOME A LANDSLIDE.

Turns out she's the daughter of a famous artist. Her father and mother died when she was a baby. I think I can see him in her eyes; maybe only alcohol, maybe drugs; dried-skin look, more than age. She paints, sells father's drawings, sells authentications.

She's just back from Switzerland. Tears start filling her dirty eyes; I look for mud to run down her cheeks; story's getting expensive. While she's in Switzerland, her daughter runs away, gets pregnant. So what's so awful about that? Wish I could get pregnant. Probably we all want what we can't have; part of being human.

Now her head is down on the table next to her hand holding the drink. It's all very Lautrec. She's crying like a mad Russian; men around the bar turn their heads away.

I want to get out. This is developing into something too scary for me. She's asking me to come visit her place, see her work and her father's drawings. She's getting lovey; insists on paying for the drinks; pulls a thick folded wad of hundred-franc bills from her purse. I should've packed up and driven away in the first place.

We leave the café; I have no desire to go with her but I don't want to hurt her feelings either. I lie, tell her I'll finish the drawing, come over later. She points, gives me directions; one street away. She wobbles off. I hustle back to my box, pack it up, jump on the bike and roll, drifting downhill a ways before kicking over the motor, sneaking away.

I can't face a sad sex scene with a drunk. I can be an awful coward; I'm not strong enough to help when things are really bad; my nerves aren't up to it. I only hope she bombs out and forgets she ever saw me.

I'm not ready to waste my time either: scarce stuff, coming to the bottom of the barrel. It's terrible to feel you're running down like an eight-day clock and you've lost the key. I don't even keep correct time anymore, always slightly behind.

VI

NOTES FROM THE UNDERGROUND

Wednesday I finish the painting of Sweik's room, the one looking in from the door. I also bring over some sunny paintings to take the curse off his walls.

Thursday I start a new painting, this time looking from his window toward the door. There's a large French wardrobe with a mirror next to Sweik's bed. In French hotels, you almost always find a mirror beside the bed. I paint Sweik's motorcycle bags and helmet hanging against the back wall by the door. On the other side, I paint the sink and bidet, working up all the French plumbing details.

Sweik's in bed. He hurt his back carrying a Danish woman up these stairs. He says they were both half looped and he was trying to make it sound like one pair of feet going past the concierge. He tripped on the rug strings, twisted his back and dropped the woman.

Sweik's really racked; the Dane stayed overnight but he was useless to her. She left in the early morning: one set of feet going down.

THE JOY OF SEX,
OUR FAVORITE TOY.
THE PLOY OF SEX,
A SHARP KNIFE IN
A STEEL TRAP.

When I finish the drawing, I help Sweik struggle out of bed to wash up. His back's so bad he can't sit in a chair; just rolls out onto his knees on the floor. Kneeling there, he really looks like a shot-down old bear. I pull the sheets and blankets from the bed. I put the sheets back on upside down and the other way around; thin, gray, dirty sheets, no sex-juice marks.

Using his Primus stove, I warm some water. He's in

deep pain. I help him off the floor back to the edge of his bed. He sits there and lathers himself. A bear cat like Sweik suffers deeply when he can't keep clean. I almost expect him to begin licking his paws and grooming. Beautiful as this room is for painting, it could be depressing as hell if you were sick and forced to stay in all day.

I try talking Sweik into cutting out for Lotte's place. I'll wall off a room, hunt up a flat board, a piece of foam rubber and make a bed. That's the best thing for a back like his. This ditch he's sleeping in has a permanent body dent in the center: worst thing possible.

WE SLEEP CURVED TO THE EARTH
AND FOR WHAT IT'S WORTH,
WE DREAM.

Meanwhile, my painting's coming along fine. I paint my own paintings in the painting. I paint paintings reflected in the mirror in my painting. I even paint one painting reflected in a mirror reflecting in a mirror in my painting. Now that's what I call outright, fourth-dimensional lying; good honest lying to tell the truth, whatever that might be. My mind is spinning again about time in paintings. I'm sure foreground is present and background is past. I'm beginning to think middle ground is future; it's where we take what we know from the past and then, in the present, make guesses about what's going to happen. Yep, future is probably middle ground.

After Sweik's back in bed, we get talking. We start on how hard it is for men to be friends; how it all gets pissed away with "camaraderie," buddy-buddy kinds of shit: softball leagues, bowling clubs and poker parties. I tell how I'm convinced men are afraid of each other, circling with hackles up all the time.

We both know we're feeling each other out, trying to let down walls but feeling vulnerable. It's so hard breaking through. Men're forced into competing, fighting each other so young it's almost impossible to make contact. Sweik arches, groans, talks through his teeth.

"You know, a guy's finally cornered so he's allowed one close friend in the world; out of four billion, he gets one!"

I look at him, stop painting. He smiles, grits his teeth.

"You know, I'm actually scared to get married. After a

guy's married, he's only supposed to be close with that one woman. Since all men are already out, that leaves a total of one."

He rolls and winces. He'd be better off sleeping on the floor than in this eggcup of a bed. I change brushes, add some turp to the varnish.

"Same thing for women, though, right? If people are stupid enough to run their lives that way, then that's what they get."

Sweik stares at the ceiling, arches his back again. I think maybe he didn't hear me. He looks over, almost in a wrestler's bridge, his teeth clamped together.

"I don't know; it's different. Women have each other; they're closer."

I keep my mouth shut but I don't believe it. Sisterhood and brotherhood are for real sisters and brothers only—and even then, rarely.

WHEN YOU'RE ALL WET,
HOW CLOSE CAN YOU GET?

We gab away that afternoon. It's good talking at this part of a painting. It's nice having Sweik there in bed. We bullshit some more about what's wrong with men's lives. For a young guy he's figured out a lot of things.

I even tell about World War II and me. Sweik had a student deferment from the Vietnam mess.

Sometimes I can get to feeling guilty, knowing everything we know now. If there ever was anybody worth fighting a war with, I guess it had to be those Nazis. My trouble was I just didn't want to be a part of any killing—still don't. Even killing people who are killing other people doesn't make sense to me. How can it end? I hate being part of anything really stupid. But my own life sure got screwed up; I'll say that.

A LINE OF EATERS, EATING
EACH OTHER TO THE END.
WHAT BEAUTIFUL FLOWER
IS THIS WE NOW DEVOUR?

Then, somehow, I don't know how we get started, but we begin working on the idea of a fantasy motorcycle club here in Paris. We're going to mock up a super-macho Warlock or Hell's Angels Paris pack; only with practically no real bikes, a totally phony affair.

Sweik gets to laughing so hard tears slide down his cheeks from the back pain. We'll write to the biggest motorcycle club in America and request a charter for our Paris-American Motorcycle Club. We'll invent stories of way-out trips and races; send off reports of these hokey events; create a completely ersatz motor scene.

Sweik laughs and hurts; probably the best thing for his back, relax the muscles. I get some paper from his table and Sweik, propped up there in bed, writes out our letter. We get off a very good maniac missive, with baroque and arabesque flourishes.

THE LAST CURE (BEFORE CURARE)
A SURE, PURE UNCARING,
UNBARTERED BURST OF LAUGHTER.

Later, just as I'm finishing for the day, Lubar, Duncan and Tompkins stop by to see how Sweik's doing. They can't believe the letter. Lubar thinks it's for real. Duncan goes out to buy wine. Lubar runs down and brings up some stolen IBM stationery from his saddlebag. We rewrite the letter with more embellishment yet. This letter's turning into a narrative poem. We describe the kinds of motorcycles we're supposed to have, developing the most outlandish rare bikes and combinations of machines anybody ever heard of. We're having a real old-fashioned tribal male-camaraderie scene. Kate would probably vomit if she could see us. No, she'd shift into her cool, above-it-all mode and make us feel like damned fools. Kate doesn't have much tolerance for tomfoolery. But I think at the bottom of all art is some taint of foolery—Tom, Dick or Harriette. But she could be right; maybe all this nonsense uses up, wastes whatever creativity is. I don't really know.

It takes two days to finish the painting. Sweik's feeling better but he's still in bed. I find a board, smuggle it up those stringy stairs, beneath sagging burlap, past the concierge, and put it under his mattress. The bed's still not much good but it's better. I also sneak out the sheets and run them through a laundromat around the corner. Poor Sweik's developing bedsores; says he thinks he'll never be up and walking around again.

IN THE BEGINNING THERE WAS AN
END AND THAT'S THE BEGINNING.

Meanwhile, over at Lotte's, I'm building a partition to cut out a room for Sweik when he gets well enough to move. Lotte's griping because I'm dividing her place; she doesn't want to share. I tell her she can leave if she wants. She doesn't want to leave, just wants all that space for herself; *Lebensraum!*

Lotte's a true cat, little cat: minx, maybe, or a small leopard. She likes everything neat, carefully wiped. She actually listens to hear if I've washed my hands after I take a leak. Maybe old blunderpuss isn't much anymore but it's the cleanest thing I've got. He rarely even touches air, all swathed in elastic supports. It's my *hands* get dirty handling money and crappy things like that. I should wash my hands *before* I pee. If I'm not careful, maybe I might even get paint on the master brush; give some unlikely, lucky woman a cobalt-blue clit. Ah, fantasy; takes some edge off the bitter dawn. I don't even *use* cobalt blue: too expensive, not permanent enough.

So I'm drilling a hole to mount a baseplate for the partition, when I go through the floor! I pull up a flat stone like a paving block; it opens onto a big hole! I pull more blocks out. There's a tremendous empty space. Lotte's having catfits; raving about rats, then about graves. It smells like graves all right; black, wet, old; dead smell. I ask Lotte for a candle. I stare into the hole but a draft blows up and snuffs out my candle. I almost scream right there and then; expect Dracula to come swooping up out of the darkness.

I dash off for a flashlight and come back. Lotte's spread a rug over the hole and she's crying on the bed. I'm all excited; staring into that dank hole has me turned on. I'm confused about where I want to do my cave exploring. I think of somebody coming in and stepping on that rug. I start laughing. Lotte cries harder; I'm probably not doing Sweik any favor.

This hole is deep. I rig a ladder with the wood for my partition and lower it into the darkness. It's about eight feet to some kind of surface. I climb down slowly. Lotte's running around in circles. Maybe she'll pull my ladder, slide her rug back over the hole; save herself paying rent.

I get to the bottom and look around with my flashlight. There's a long tunnel. It goes off under Moro's and is arched with cut-stone vaulting, high enough to walk up straight but just clearing my head.

I go in about a hundred feet, one careful step at a time; creepy, spooky and it gets darker. Then I look behind me. I can't see the hole where I came in. She did it!

Panic strikes! I scamper back till I see the hole again; the tunnel curved and blocked my view. I climb out and up the ladder. I'll go ask Sweik to help. I'll get a rope, more flashlights; more nerve. It's better I don't mention anything about this to Kate; she'd be sure it was bad for my blood pressure, only another way for me to be wasting time when I should concentrate on painting. But, Holy God, think of it, tunnels under Paris, I feel like Jean Gabin-*cum*-Jean Valjean in *Les Misérables.*

GROUNDED AS WITH ELECTRICITY,
OR AS A PILOT. I'M STUCK TO THIS
EARTH, BURROWING BLINDLY THROUGH IT,
OUR ULTIMATE HOME NEST.

That afternoon I tell Sweik about the tunnel. He's moving around some; still being careful, dragging his feet like a prostate case, but moving. He says he'll help but can't go down any ladder. That's OK. I buy some string, some rope, three flashlights, extra batteries, a compass and a detailed map of central Paris. I'm planning a big operation; figure tomorrow I'm into the Paris secret underground world.

WHEELER'S WORMHOLES, PASSPORTS
TO AN ETERNAL INFINITY. I PEEK
IN AND FEEL LIGHT RUSHING PAST
MY EARS—HEARING NOTHING!

I do finishing touches on both paintings of the room. Sweik and I get to drinking wine, so I'm slightly drunk when I leave. I shouldn't drive that damned bike when I've been drinking. The trouble is, it's hard as hell carrying my box and a wet canvas in the Métro or on a bus. I keep smearing people. It's not good for paintings and very tough on people. An old lady hit me on the head with a book once. I'd given her a hand-painted back-of-coat. That coat will be worth a fortune someday but definitely not appreciated now. I really felt sorry, tried to give her twenty francs for dry cleaning. That's when she hit me over the head.

I weave home on my bike. Kate is *not* happy. I've missed dinner and I'm drunk; how wrong can you get? I show her the paintings and it's OK again. My wife knows what's important.

She saved my life once when it counted, knows I'm hers. She kisses me, really looks at the paintings; kisses me again and warms up dinner. I eat and we go to bed. It's hard trying to be an artist, a husband and a father all at the same time. Each one requires a full lifetime and I've only got one, probably a short one at that. I don't know how much I can ask of Kate and still live with myself. She doesn't want to ask any more of me than she has to, but sometimes I know it's hard.

Sweik says the difference between a Dane and a Swede is you go down the hole with a Dane and leave the Swede to hold your rope up top. Nobody should ever leave me holding any rope, anytime.

THE THIN LINE OF LIFE; A ROPE
OF WOVEN HOPES, RAVELED, WORN,
WE HANG BY IT TILL DEATH.

Next day, I take Sweik over to meet Lotte and help with the tunnel. Sweik goes into his very reserved, well-mannered role. Sweik is handsome in a nineteenth-century-sailor kind of way. He and Lotte will be in bed soon's his back's better. I can tell he's surprised with the way she looks. Lotte looks as if she's going to correct your grammar, straighten your tie or light a candle for your soul. I know he thinks I'm sleeping with her. Let him think, good for the imagination. I can't say I'd really mind, but it's too complicated; I need to conserve what little energy I have left. Besides, I don't think Lotte's exactly hot for this old man's flabby body.

My idea is to map the tunnel, find out where it goes. We'll use a string to make measurements and a compass to measure directions. I'll mark it on the map as we go. I tape two flashlights onto my motorcycle helmet to keep my hands free. Sweik gives me a pellet gun to shoot rats. Where the hell did he get a pellet gun? I'm feeling like Tom Sawyer but I'm not shooting any rats if I can help it. After all, it's *their* tunnel.

. . .

I climb down the ladder and start counting out on my string. I go in about two hundred feet and come to a crossroad. I see my first rat: big bastard, big as a cat; he stares at me, ruby-eyed, then scampers off.

I go back, mark measurements and compass reading on the map with Sweik. One arm of the crossroad goes toward the church of Saint-Germain-des-Prés across the boulevard; the other arm toward Saint-Sulpice. I'll try the one to Saint-Germain.

Lotte's already leaning all over Sweik. Women are marvelous, have a nose for something valuable. She'll have him in her sack soon enough, back or no back. She'll get Sweik all fat with Salzburg cooking. Damn, I'm going to miss the weisswurst. Maybe I'll raise the rent next month. No, I can't do that. Maybe I can bargain something for a once-a-month meal. I have a hard time letting go. I've got so many strings hanging from me I'm like a three-year-old Christmas tree somebody forgot to take down.

HOLDING ON, HOLDING BACK, HOLDING UP;
ROBBERY, BREAKING IN, BRAKING.
THE PAST BECOMES HEAVY; THE FUTURE
FURTHER AWAY AND I CAN'T LET GO.

I inch along the tunnel toward Saint-Germain. It starts dropping sharply. Maybe I'll get the bends; should've brought along my canary, like a coal miner, in case of gas. I can hear traffic rumbling overhead; a Métro goes by, rattling the stones.

Panic's surging; I stop a minute to get my bearings. I take slow, deep breaths; whip out the old mantra for a couple of quick Kee Rings; try to think of something else except where I am. What're they doing up there?

Sticky cobwebs keep brushing against my face; there can't actually be spiders in all this dark; these must be left over from the Middle Ages. Maybe secret mystic masses were held down here: Ignatius Loyola and his fighting Jesuits.

I flash my light around; don't see anything except more tunnel. There's water running over the stones, and dirt's caught in the spiderwebs. It's warmer down here than outside. "OK, get on with it Scum, stop diddling." I reach the end of my string, a hundred meters. I check my compass, mark the spot and go back.

I sneak up the ladder. They're sitting on her bed. Never trust a Swede at the hole! I climb out and we work over the map again. I'm up to Boulevard Saint-Germain, now; be crossing under the church next.

I go back down and in. I find my mark, drive in a stake and tie the string to my stake. Maybe I should be dropping bread crumbs as I go along; feed the rats. I move on. The tunnel begins rising and turns to the left. There, at the turn, is a big wooden door with iron hinges and a bolt. I give the door a strong pull; it budges and dirt falls. I try two more tugs and the bolt snaps off. The door swings open on its own; the middle hinge is broken, but there are three hinges, so it holds.

I flash my light on four steps down. Now I'm into Ali Baba's cave. I go down slowly into a big room with cut-stone paving. I flash my light around. There are tall boxes standing against the walls. I start pacing to get the size; this room must have two hundred squares, at least.

Holy mackerel! Those are coffins standing against the walls! Right then, one of my flashlights blinks out and I let myself sink slowly to the ground; time for a little more deep breathing; I need to take a leak, too—mostly just nervous, probably.

The rats'-nester-scumbler mind is spinning. What a great place I could make out of this, a *real* rat's nest, burrows and all. Nobody could ever find me, not even the FBI. I turn my head slowly, the flashlight cutting through the dark. There're maybe twenty coffins around the walls. There's also something in one corner made of wooden poles and rotted cloth.

It might be tough renting with all the coffins; like one of those French apartments you buy already occupied—only occupied this time by a few dozen corpses.

There's another door in the wall to my right. I get up, go over, try it. This one's locked tight; probably leads up to the church, straight into the tabernacle. Hey, maybe I could rent this nest to a religious freak. He'd be the first one to early mass mornings; beat the sexton, the priest, maybe even God himself. I take my leak against the wall while I'm over there.

INSIDE, UNDER, BEHIND; I BURROW
OUT OF LIGHT, OUT OF MIND. I DRILL
INTO A CAST CORE OF CARBIDE HARDNESS.
NEVER MIND.

I go around checking coffins. They're nailed tight; square-headed nails; wood rotten but holding. Nobody's going to get out from any of those boxes. I'm beginning to have a hard time breathing again; too much excitement for an old man; ticker's pounding wildly, skipping beats like a Caribbean marimba player.

About halfway back along the string, I see something moving in the tunnel. I hit the floor without even knowing it.

It's Sweik; he borrowed a flashlight from Lotte. He got to worrying what the hell happened; thought maybe the rats had wrestled me to the ground. I take him back and show him the room. He comes in behind me and keeps saying, "Jesus, man!" "Shit, man!" "Holy fuck." We both try that other door but it's locked tight. I put my flash onto the ceiling. It's a high-arched vault, no bats, no vampires. We check measurements and head back out to the map.

It feels wonderful being outside in light, clean air. We calculate that room to be directly under the altar of Saint-Germain-des-Prés, one of the oldest churches in Paris.

I'm covered with cobwebs and dirt, so I take a shower in Lotte's little stall shower. She's not making any noises at all about not wanting to share now.

DESIRE WASHES AWAY RELUCTANCE,
REFURBISHES TIRED, SWAYING BONES.
WE ATONE WITH ELECTRIC ATTENTION.

We spend the next day exploring. There are tunnels under the whole Left Bank. They go up to Montparnasse and down to the river. We don't find any more big rooms like the first one but we do find ways to come up in different cellars all over the quarter.

We invade the cellar of a high-class restaurant and snitch a few bottles of wine. That's a kind of wet dream, direct access to a wine cellar.

I think of getting a Velosolex, one of those little French bikes with a motor on the front wheel; use it to run around down in those tunnels, my own private Métro. But I don't. I know I'll use that tunnel somehow, someday, but now I only want to think about it; let my mind play with the idea of deep tunnels and nests under the city.

Sweik tells me he thinks he'll stay on at the Isis; leave the place for Lotte. I don't know whose idea this is but I think it's Sweik's. He's no fool.

EGYPTIAN MUFFLED TUNNELS. NO SKY,
NOTHING OPEN, A CAREFUL PREPARATION
FOR AN UNENDING NOTHINGNESS.

VII

CHICKEN

It's Saturday and one of those spring days we often get in Paris when there's a constipated heavy sky trying to rain and thick hemorrhoidal clouds listlessly drifting.

I go down into the Marais, ready to start the first painting of my new series. I figure Sabbath's the best day, not so much traffic. I don't figure on old ladies.

I'm setting up my box when the first one comes over to me.

"A nice boy like you shouldn't work on the Sabbath," says she.

"Not work, my pleasure," says I, smiling. Haven't been called a boy in about thirty years or more.

"All the same," says she, then hobbles on down the street, shaking her head.

I get the box set up. I'm painting the façade of a broken-down old kosher poultry store. It's the kind of place where they bleed chickens live, old-style; makes me think of South Street in Philly. There they used to keep all the live pigeons and chickens in wooden cages right out in the windows. No birds in the window here, but the same smell.

This place is a terrific mess: smeared cracked windows, dirty white marble tables inside. There's chicken shit, blood and guts all over; probably the chickens are out of the window for Sabbath.

I'm doing it straight on. I dig in with the underpainting; mostly dark browns and yellows, with some blue for inside. I'm concentrating and flying; this will be a good one. This whole series is going to be wonderful: interesting people, real places, trapped space, good twisting light.

CUTTING LIGHT DOWN AND STILL STAYING TRANSPARENT: ANOTHER FACE OF REALITY, FUTILE FANTASY. I DRIFT

ON TRANSITIONS TILL WE TOUCH EARTH
IN DARK STILLNESS.

Another old lady comes up. Skinny hag; hair all whichway. No teeth; bottom lip almost touches her nose. The toes are cut out of her shoes; big bunions bulging out. She pushes me away from the box, good strong push.

"You got permission to paint my store?"

Face right up to me.

"No, lady, didn't know I needed permission. May I paint your store?"

"No!"

I look down at her, trying to figure if she's only crazy.

"I'm going to paint your store anyway, lady. Don't need permission; street's a public place. Artist's got some rights."

She stomps her bunioned foot.

"I do not give permission!"

She stares at me wetly. Her eyes have Velásquez lower lids, red, watery. She stomps again and goes away.

I get to work; probably isn't crazy, we're just not communicating.

Five minutes later she's back. She looks at the painting for a while. I smile at her, hoping for a convert.

"I'll let you paint my store for twenty francs."

"I'm sorry, lady; I'm not going to pay. Artist has rights."

She watches me for a while. She's not acting mad or pushing now, just watching.

"There should be chickens in the window."

"Don't need any chickens."

"For ten francs, I'll put chickens in the window."

"Don't need any chickens."

I prove this by painting a few quick chicken strokes into the window. She still stands there watching me. I try to keep working. There's a long pause; then she pushes between me and the painting.

"Why are you painting my store? Why don't you go paint Notre Dame or some church for the tourists?"

She's beginning to bug me. I stare down at her. I can see her scalp through thin gray hair. She'd make a fine painting. When I'm mad or drunk, I speak my best French.

"Look, lady! I'm a world-famous collector of ugliness. I have a terrible passion for ugly things. I paint pictures of ugly things I can't buy and move to my castle in Texas. I have a whole museum filled with paintings of the most ugly places in the world. They're from China, Timbuktu and Cucamonga."

She's paying attention now.

"This chicken-shit place of yours is my greatest discovery. I've never, in twenty years' searching, found anything more ugly than your store. I'm going to paint it and put this painting at the top of my collection!"

Her mouth is open. I can see bumpy, hardened ridge where her bottom teeth used to be. She's staring at me through the whole speech. One eye is slowly dropping to half-mast, like a dead woman's wink; her eyes are runny cataractal blue. I smile at her. She looks across the street at her store. It's probably the first time in thirty years she's actually looked at it. Practically nobody ever looks at anything.

Her place is truly beautiful, beautiful for a painter. It all runs together; the dirt makes everything fit. The old lady stares at me.

"Maybe it's dirty, sir; but it's not ugly."

She backs off, turns and walks up the street. You never know when and where you'll meet a kindred soul.

WE TOUCH IN A CAULDRON, TWISTING
MISSES OF CONCURRENT THOUGHT IN A
MORASS, A BOILING SOUP. WE'RE ALL
BETROTHED IN THE SAME BROTH-BREATH.

Two men in black hats and beards are standing behind me. I've been listening with one corner of my mind and they've been discussing the painting like connoisseurs. They're into a long discourse on my use of warm and cool colors to penetrate the plane and establish an illusion of space. They've got all the baloney together, very impressive. They both have rosy cheeks, bright eyes and a very healthy look. They look like grown-up altar boys. I reach down to get some more medium. One of these guys speaks in perfect English.

"Pay no attention to her. She is a *dir*-ty woman."

I look back at him. He has long curly sideburns and a fine fat-cat look.

"She's a *dir*-ty woman and her shop is *not* kosher. We tell our people never to buy here."

"Not kosher?"

I take a cloth and wipe the word "CASHER" off the window in the painting. They laugh. I get to working again.

The other guy leans closer; maybe I'll give him a quick dab.

"Why do you paint pictures, sir? Do you paint them for money?"

"It's the way I try to feed my family."

"Yes, but do you get joy from it?"

What the hell, nobody ever asked me that. I do. I certainly do; boy, do I ever get joy out of it.

"Yes, much joy!"

"But, what is the joy in painting buildings?"

This creep's right there.

"Nothing much. Only the joy of making them mine, of having things pass through me; the joy of playing God, screwing some details and chewing up, spitting out others. I enjoy the joy in the great delusion of being alive."

I'm into it. I go on and on, painting away, slashing and picking at the color, wet-in-wet. The world is forming under my hands. I'm taking things from out there, bringing them in and pushing them out again, like breathing, panting.

"Painting's the joy of kissing, sleeping, sunlight, breathing; and it's all in this work. I get inside, the outside-inness of an exploding wish. It's more than joy, more than ecstasy; it's a soft gliding and turning in midair with complete control."

Holy bloomers, I go on and on. I'm making a total ass of myself, bleeding emotion all over the street. I keep thinking they'll get embarrassed and go away, or laugh, or maybe call the police. I'm not trying to put them on, just turned on myself. What a great question: "Is painting joy?"

Finally I run down, lean further into the painting. Maybe they've already gone; I don't look back. Then one of them puts his hand on my shoulder.

"You might well be a religious man, Monsieur le peintre."

The two of them walk away up the street. What a wild thing to say; probably means I'm some kind of maniac. That's for sure. I guess being a maniac and liking it has to be the greatest insult going for all the sane people in the world.

A WHITE CRY TO THE BRIGHT, SILVER-LINED
CAPE OF MEANING. A BLACK EDGING TO MAKE
IT VISIBLE. BUT IT'S BUTTONED TIGHT,
SMOTHERED BY BONE BUTTONS AGAINST COLD.

I work on. I want to get the impasto finished. It's a perfect surface for dragging now. I drag to peel paint off the wood horizontally, then wipe it down with dirt, black, vertically. It's the battle of man versus gravity, energy versus entropy. All art is basically anti-entropic, that is to say, foolhardy; it takes hardy fools.

The inside light's getting brighter and brighter; pale bright like a morgue light. The chickens look like corpses. They *are* corpses. It'd scare hell out of some thinking, live chicken; Dachau of the chicken world.

ONE MAN'S FEAST, BANQUET,
ANOTHER'S GROSS INIQUITY.
NOTHING IS FOR NOTHING.

Later, a thin girl slinks up behind me. She squeezes into a doorway. This door is closed; only a very thin person could fit in that doorway. I keep working away. I can't tell if she's thirteen or thirty; blond stringy hair. She smiles; I smile back.

"J'aime beaucoup votre tableau, Monsieur."

"Merci."

That's enough. I've the world's strongest American accent in French. I can't even say a simple "*merci*" without giving myself away. She switches into English.

"I also am an artist. I study at the school of decoration."

"That's nice."

I'm not too interested in womankind or any kind right at that moment. It's no insult or anything; I'm not interested in anything else much when I'm deep in painting.

"Would you like to drink some coffee with me?"

Oh, sure, here we go: coffee, cigarettes, eye wrestling. I stop, take a good look at her. She seems like a fine, sensitive young woman, maybe twenty-five. I *would* like to know her, talk about painting. What I can't figure is why she wants to take time talking to a worn-out old bozo like me.

"OK. Come back in half an hour; I'll be finished then."

She slides away, I figure I'm rid of her. I dig myself back into the work. What do young girls like that want? I know there's no natural father love in humans, it's something we have to learn, but it can't be all that bad. God, if it's only sex, pick on one of these young bucks stomping around, unbound dongs dangling loose against their knees.

There's something about a picture painter turns a certain kind of women roundheeled. But why should I knock it? Maybe I need a shot of vitamin E, need to eat more parsley, oysters, hot peppers. Then again, this young woman might really need or want to talk with another artist. I'm definitely getting too cynical in my old age. I'll have to watch that. I think I'm mostly afraid, been hurt too often, love-punch drunk, can't take it anymore.

I work another half hour and there she is. I'm still not quite finished. I squeeze off a little smile and work on. She lights a cigarette and offers me one already lit. I shake my head, tell her I don't smoke. She takes both those cigarettes between the fingers of one hand and smokes them at once. I never saw that before. She smokes Greta Garbo–style, hollow-cheeked deep drag. There's much of Garbo there: blond straight hair, thin; Garbo except for the part about wanting to be alone.

I stop painting. I'm finished enough so it needs drying for a while. I pack up, we walk down the street to a café. I'm shooting quick looks around to avoid the scary daughter-of-the-painter, woman. I order a beer. I'm still too excited from the work to take coffee. When I'm up, high with painting, coffee turns me into shatters.

I listen to her, feel myself unwinding. She tells how she's living with an older married man. He has her put up in a room near here. He comes every afternoon to extract his pound of vaginal, not so virginal flesh. He gives her money so she can go to school; probably proud of her work like a father. Not much original there.

Halfway through the beer, she tells me she *won't* take me to her room, very ethical. I didn't *ask!* I sip the rest of my beer; I'm flattening out. Then, straight from the blue, no prelims, she volunteers to go to a hotel with me. Now she's looking into my eyes, feeling for the tongue of my soul. This can usually give me a lift but I've nowhere to go. I'm going down fast, irreversible.

I try to stay with her, but it's impossible. She must see me shrinking before her eyes. I feel any minute I might slip under the table and disappear into a small spot of emulsified linseed oil.

I tell her I'll be painting around the quarter and I'll see her another day. I'm fading. She sees it, smart, sensitive woman. There's some little hurt, disappointment; but nothing world-shaking. She's an artist, she must understand.

TRIAL, TRIBULATIONS AND LOST EXPECTATION,
NO TENDERNESS CAN SOFTEN SOME BLOWS.
THE TOUCH OF A FEATHER WITH THE STING
OF A WHIP; SOMETIMES TOUCH AND GO.

We need women like her for the bad times. They can crawl out from under atom bombs and start having new babies: two-headed, eight-armed babies with maybe no hair and yellow eyes—all kinds of exciting possibilities. Maybe we can even mutate ourselves out of males, put human beings back together again. It's an ill wind that blows no good, even if it's radioactive.

I say goodbye and leave her sitting in the café. I strap the box on my back, check to see the painting's on tight and mount my bike. The traffic's a horror and I don't roll into the house until after five. There are visitors from the States, some spring-tide travelers. I'd like to flop dead but I need to play host, might sell a painting or two, souvenirs of Paris.

Sometimes I think there's too much of the accidental in my life. Or maybe life is only an accident itself—sometimes just a fender bender, other times a "total."

CHAOS, AN ABYSS OF INDELIBLE
NOTHING. WHY TELL OF IT? WHY LISTEN?
BUT WITHOUT, THERE IS NO MASS, NO
MOMENTUM, NO GRAVITY—NO LEVITY.

VIII

MOUTH-TO-MOUTH

At our place, I'm the homekeeper. Every morning, Kate and the kids go off to school. Kate likes teaching kindergarten, hates housework; probably did it too long; anything gets boring sooner or later. I like everything to do with nesting; but I don't much care for the words "homemaking" or "housekeeping." To me, you *make* a house and *keep* a *home.* I love to be in a house I made, a home I can keep.

Usually, I stay in bed mornings, out of the way, while the mob is jamming our jerry-rigged bathroom; the shower's up on a platform three feet high to give some drainage.

After that first scramble, I jump up, make breakfast and we eat together. Then everybody's off by seven-thirty. Four months of the year it's still dark in Paris at seven-thirty in the morning. I give myself an hour and a half to wrestle our home in shape again after they're gone; best workout anybody could ever think up.

First I make our bed, everything off, shaken out and tucked back on—under two minutes, just warming up. I strip off my pajamas; do all the homekeeping bare-ass. I like to air my old body; sweat like a pig.

We turn the heat down nights. Kate fires it back up mornings to take off the chill. I turn it off again; gas and electricity cost a fortune in France—state-controlled, no real stimulation to be efficient, no incentive. I've got to keep moving.

I run hot water into the kitchen sink; dash around gathering dishes from the table, slipping them in the water; let them soak; most times I save dinner dishes for mornings. I wash glasses first, rinse with clean hot water to make them shine.

I start the washing-machine water running and begin picking up. Goddamned piles're like cancer; once begun, they keep growing, every one malignant. Operate! Surgery! Pilectomy. Takes five minutes to break up a typical pile. The secret is stopping the first thing from being put down. That's impossible in our house; we're all great putter-downers.

Our little one, Tim, leaves toys all over the house. I gather these, stuff them in his closet. His bed's just a mattress on the floor; he's afraid he'll fall out of a real bed. The other two kids are up on the platforms. I check those beds: everything OK.

I let our canary out. He knows me; started calling soon as I came into the room. I prop open the cage door with an old paintbrush. He's eaten almost all the hairs off that brush. He flies out right away; does a couple of quick reconnaissance flights, then goes down to visit the goldfish.

I'm into the other kids' rooms now. If they're not picked up, I don't dust or sweep; just close the door and lock it; open it again for sleeping only. I'm a mean bastard here. Ecology begins with hanging up your clothes, making your bed and keeping your private nest livable.

ALL IS ONE AND I AM ONE SO
I AM ALL. I*M*U*U*R*I.
WE LIVE IN OUR ENTIRETY OR
WE EXIST IN A CLOVEN SPACE.

Now I'm dusting, moving fast. I jump up and down, keep the heart muscles pumping. I never know whether to dust first or sweep first. I hate vacuum cleaners; crummy humming sound and a big loaded dirt bag to drag around. I'm the mad sweeper, sweep in every corner. I'm moving furniture; reaching under things I can't move; wear out three brooms a year.

I throw dirty clothes, soap in the washer, turn it on. I move into the kitchen; got to be thorough about this part. There's no saving little things; no ends of tomatoes, no bits of grease from the bacon, no rinds from cheese. Out with it all; just piles up in our refrigerator till it smells like a garbage can.

My canary's eating the calendulas I bought Sunday at the Marché Aligre. They make a pretty combination. I jog in place and watch, listening to my heart beat, feeling the pulse in my neck; feels OK to me.

This is the kind of scene I can't bring myself to paint. I wish somebody would; not sentimental mush, but the same colors, one a flower, the other a bird; one still, the other moving. It could be good; only I can't do it; maybe Chardin; too bad he's dead. God I miss him, even though we passed each other by a couple of hundred years; so many private painting secrets I'd like to ask about.

I finish the dishes; scrub bottoms of copper pots and hang them. It's easy if you do it every day, kind of thing the mind doesn't want to believe, have to discover yourself. Same with windows. Every Tuesday I wipe windows inside and out with a dry cloth. That way I keep crud from starting; no big window-washing scene.

I'm rolling sweat now. I slip on a jockstrap for my janglers, and then my sweat suit so I won't catch chill. It's still not nine o'clock. I pull wet wash from the washer and hang it around the heater; turn heater back on. Our crummy dryer's kaput; no money for a new one. I wouldn't know how to get that busted dryer out of the bathroom anyway; built the bathroom around it.

I start my Yoga; been doing it for ten years, since we got pregnant last time. I was over fifty then and Kate pushing forty; knew I had to last out in the streets till seventy-five somehow. Won't make it, but worth trying—who wants to be old anyhow? I also run every other day around this apartment. I run for an hour; that's about ten kilometers the speed I can go. I have fifteen different ten-kilometer routes I take in my mind, through different parts of Paris. I have my Marais run, my Latin Quarter run, my Bois de Boulogne run, my Bois de Vincennes run, my down-the-Champs-and-through-the-Tuileries run; I'm jogging round the living-room table, into the bedrooms, through the kitchen, but in my mind I'm on one of my runs, watching the leaves fall, listening to the river flow; I really think I see more of Paris with my eyes half shut than I would really running through the city, dodging people, dog shit and stinking automobiles.

I run to keep alive, strong enough to be a stand-up painter. Painting's a hard business, especially the way I do it; I've got to be strong enough to stand up in the middle of everything and concentrate. Running helps keep the damned blood pressure down, too. Blood pressure's going to burst every single blood vessel in the back of my eyes if I'm not careful. And what's an artist without eyes?

. . .

After running and Yoga, I put new seed, water, a piece of apple in the canary cage. That's the signal and he flies back in; no problem at all. Most of us go back in our cage no matter how much fun it is flying around.

CROUCHING IN TWILIGHT,
POUNCE AT THE DAWN.

Well, this morning, just after I've run, yogaed and gotten the bird in his cage, and I'm about to shower, I hear a tremendous scream out on the landing; really a whopper. Then a deep sob and a yell for help. The only other people on our landing are Monsieur and Madame Costanzo. They have a little cabinetmaking atelier; very quiet people, been in the same place over forty years; work together, man-and-wife woodworking team.

I dash out our door in my sweaty sweat suit. The door to Monsieur Costanzo's place is open; he's bent over something just inside the door, hollering and crying. The Costanzos aren't French; Italian. I don't think any Frenchman could ever make the kind of scene Monsieur Costanzo is making. He's yelling and waving his hands like an operatic tenor or soprano.

Monsieur Costanzo has big hands, soft as clouds. Usually he and I do the French handshake once a week. My hand's smothered in his, like a fitted fisted pillow. The concierge says Monsieur Costanzo beats his wife but I don't believe it; concierges only say those things—intrinsic part of the job. He couldn't hurt anybody with those hands; they're too soft.

It's his wife there on the floor. He stands, bent over, looking at me: tears in his eyes, white-faced, big hands open. He tells me his wife came through the door, put down a shopping bag and fell over.

I stare down at her. She's jammed against a Louis XIV bureau and she looks empty. I pick her up, carry her into the room; she's not heavy, more like the way a bird is, mostly feathers.

The Costanzos don't live in the atelier—strictly a workshop. There's no couch or bed or even a chair with a seat on it. I stretch her out in the sawdust and wood shavings on the floor. A cabinetmaker's atelier has a patina of light wood dust that blends everything into a wooden haze.

There's no breath and she's a banana-yellow color. I can't find a pulse; nothing. When I picked her up, she let out a long sigh, but nothing now. I tell Monsieur Costanzo to phone for a doctor and an ambulance. I assume he'll just go into my place, the door's open. I don't know where he goes.

I'm alone with Madame Costanzo. The dead are so vulnerable. I'm convinced she's dead now, but I know I ought to do something. I start external heart massage, thumping poor Madame Costanzo's shriveled little titties with my painter's palms.

I'm trying to hit hard enough but not break anything. Up till now, we've only discussed the weather and her grandchildren; no more grandchildren stories, no more weather. Madame Costanzo's daughter makes the grandchildren sit at the table until they eat everything, sometimes for hours. Madame Costanzo cried when she told me this.

Her eyes are stuck half open, not looking at me. I close them. It's something I can't take, like looking into a dry well.

I start mouth-to-mouth resuscitation. Here I am French-kissing a seventy-five-year-old corpse on an early-spring morning; and she's not even French.

There's no response except her false teeth get dislodged. I take them out. What the hell would her husband think; maybe I'm some kind of vampire or necrophile. I stop the mouth-to-mouth; nothing there. I try fitting the teeth back in; can't get them quite right; the jaw won't close and stay closed. I tie it shut with a piece of cord. What the hell can be keeping Monsieur Costanzo?

Just then, Monsieur and Madame Bellini from upstairs come in. They're Italian too; longtime friends of the Costanzos, both over eighty. They used to do some babysitting for us. When they see Madame Costanzo, they turn green and waver on their feet; we're going to have a mass grave.

Pushing behind them comes Monsieur Costanzo at last. He drops to his knees, heavily, beside his wife. Somebody has to say it and I want to say it right. I'd been thinking out the phrase while I was mouth-to-mouth breathing, pondering the grammar for something to keep my mind away.

"Monsieur Costanzo, je crois que votre femme est mort," I say.

I forget to put the verb in agreement with the subject, so I say it wrong, and it's probably subjunctive anyway.

Monsieur Costanzo says he's called the *pompiers,* the French fire department rescue squad.

The young couple beneath, the LeClercs, upholsterers, come up. Madame LeClerc is very effective. She gets the name of Monsieur Costanzo's daughter and goes to phone at my place. Monsieur Costanzo lies down on his floor, in the sawdust and shavings, beside his wife. He puts his arm across her. It's a very smart thing to do. He'll never get to sleep with her again; officialdom'll soon arrive. After that, Madame Costanzo is an administrative problem; Monsieur Costanzo loses all rights. He can never kiss her, make love to her, bop her again. It's all over.

I dress, go downstairs; tell our concierge so she can direct the *pompiers*. She, too, is a longtime, maybe forty-year, friend of Madame Costanzo. I try to remember how they do it in movies, but it doesn't come off right. She sits flat down and turns green like the Bellinis; she asks me to get her heart medicine from her little bathroom. Accidentally, in there, I look up into the mirror. Some guy with a white beard and a green face looks back at me.

The concierge chews on her medicine; keeps repeating how it can't be true. Madame Costanzo'd just picked up mail for the Bellinis and taken it to them. There were eighty centimes postage due; she promised to bring the money back down.

Then the concierge remembers she has money for me: *allocation familiale* has arrived; this is four hundred francs the French government gives us back every month because we have three kids still at home.

She carefully counts out the money and I give her a tip. It's so goddamned mundane after all the reality upstairs. Already we're trying to pretend it didn't happen; that death isn't there waiting for us all the time.

HOW DOES GOD LAUGH?
WITH A BANG OR A WHIMPER?

That day and the next, I have a hard time getting myself convinced it's worthwhile doing anything. It's especially hard working up an excitement over something as far removed from life and death as painting. But then finally, when I get back working, the momentum of living catches me and I get on with it.

You've got to do something; you can't stand around waiting with your hands empty and your mouth open.

DREAM IN CIRCLES, DANCE TO THE SILENT,
INTERNAL BEAT OF LIFE, DROWN IN UNSLAKED
THIRST. BUT KEEP MOVING! DON'T STOP
OR YOU CAN'T HEAR THE MUSIC.

IX

ACCIDENT-PRONE

It'd be great to paint everybody in the motorcycle club; sort of Americans in Paris. The trouble is it'd be just more time, paint, canvas down the drain, no cash return.

Yesterday we took a picture for the motor magazine in America. Our club hung around the police station at Saint-Sulpice where they park their big Triumph 500s. A friend of Duncan's has a good camera with a telephoto lens. We casually strolled over and stood by the bikes. The cops lounging in the doorway can't figure what's going on. Duncan's friend is behind a tree shooting away.

We pose beside the bikes. It's planned to the last nickel. We're in and out from behind those bikes in less than thirty seconds. No running; camera clicking away.

Finally, those two cops start over. We take off at a quick walk across the Place and into the church. We gather in the Delacroix Chapel for a short chorus of the "California Drinking Song." Saint-Sulpice has great acoustics, I'm sure old Eugène enjoyed it; I hope God got a laugh, too. That church is a great place for singing.

MAYBE GOD DOESN'T LAUGH;
MIGHT NOT EVEN KNOW HOW.

Sweik and I write a story about a motor-club outing to go with the picture. We tell about a race from Paris to Chartres. The race ends with two turns around the outer aisle of the cathedral. We put in a big award ceremony, with us all standing in front of the altar, stained-glass-window light flowing in. Very poetic. I wonder if they'll believe it. They'll want to, that's for sure.

ANY TALE UNTELLABLE IS BELIEVED AS
UNBELIEVABLE AND BECOMES LEGEND.
LEG-END IS WHERE TOES AND TAILS BEGIN.

Today I'm painting on the Rue Guisarde; painting Madame Boyer's place; that's across from Sweik's hotel. Looking out his window gave me the idea. I keep thinking I'm finished with that Canettes series but something new is always coming up.

Madame Boyer has a nice little café. It's a café-charbon-auvergne place. Local old alkie women hang out there. Some of them buy burning alcohol and strain it through charcoal, then drink it. But most of them are social drinkers, heavy social drinkers. They lurk around the café to watch the men who carry the coal and wood. These are big brutes, covered with black coal dust all day. They wear filthy undershirts and caps, have burlap bags over their shoulders to keep skin from rubbing raw. Very dirty, smelly, crude, nice guys. It's fine for the old women who only have cats and not enough money to keep a big dog. There're all kinds of jokes and full half-assed passes.

Madame Boyer's a fine woman, about forty. Her old man is the dirtiest, biggest, crudest of them all. He weighs three hundred at least. Poor Madame Boyer must about suffocate when they go the course.

TWO DOVES FLUTTER IN HEAVY AIR,
STRUGGLE FOR RELEASE, THEN SETTLE
AT LAST TO GROUNDING PULSATION.

I'm standing across the street painting in a doorway to keep from getting run over by cars. Guisarde's a very narrow street. A gorgeous slick-type woman squeezes in behind me; sort of like the one in the Marais, only this woman has gigantic boobs pushing into my back. I'm thinking maybe I should stand in doorways more often; maybe there's something magic, symbolic about doorways. I can feel the points of her tits through a layer of flannel, a layer of wool and a layer of cotton. That's not counting what she's wearing, which isn't much. Probably that's why they're so hard; she's freezing to death. She sure as hell can't be turned on pushing her tits into a turpentine-and-sweat-soaked smelly old man like me.

She steps back a touch and offers me a cigarette. It's enough to make me wish I smoked more often. I shake my head, keep painting. My concentration's shot; I'm only going through the motions. I peek. She's wearing a little checkered cap on the back of her head and a short-sleeved tight red sweater. This can make some women look little-girl but not this one with these boobs; she looks almost round-shouldered. She's wearing one of those blanket kind of skirts with fringe, held together by a giant gold pin. I haven't seen anything like that in years. Her shoes are patent leather, high heels, thin soles, definitely not good for walking through all the dog shit on Rue Guisarde. She talks in French. I won't write it out that way, probably can't.

"I like your painting, Mr. Painter."

She looks into me, not the painting.

"I like it too."

Brilliant remark. I sneak another stare. Deep blue eyes you could backflip into. She pulls off two muted slow-rolling grinds. I'm hoping some of the old women across the street are catching this; give me some status around Madame Boyer's.

I try to concentrate again on the painting; being very professional. Yes sir, we professionals out there doing our thing. We're at "check" like that for maybe two minutes. I'm only dinking around with the brush.

"I can give you a *jolie heure* for that painting, Mister Painter."

Right on. One pro to another; it's out now. I've got about four hours so far in the painting and eighty francs in materials; not exactly a good deal for only one pretty hour. I'm not really interested anyhow, just the idea excites me. I wonder what café she's working from; where's the *maquereau;* how's he going to come out in a deal like that? Do they cut the painting in half? I stop and smile at her.

"Thank you, Mademoiselle, but the painting is not finished. Also, I need the money; a painter is never rich."

"Yes."

She says it with an intake of breath, a statement, a question, a condemnation, a promise—all in one word. She takes another long, quiet look at the painting, then ducks into the door. Here I am standing in *her* doorway. Probably she wasn't rubbing her tits into me at all; only trying to get enough room to open the door.

Somehow, too, she didn't quite come off as a pro. She had on the right costume but it didn't come off. That's an accidental joke; I'm accident-prone.

She seemed too young; having too much fun with

me; too much humor there. I've never yet met a whore with much sense of humor; all very serious types; serious work, no nonsense. Only humorous whores I've ever met were in Henry Miller's books. Maybe there are different whores now, different everything else.

Later in the afternoon, two French businessmen types push past me. These lads are completely unrelated to the scene. One has dusted white hair and a deep tan. The other is more the accountant-data-processor breed. They almost knock me down in their hurry through that door. I figure my little friend might have something to do with the rush. Behind me is a plumbing-supply shop; I don't believe they have the kind of plumbing these fellows are looking for, and in the apartments above there are mostly old women. I don't think any of them would claim motherhood to either of these two.

One of these wonderful old gals upstairs has more than twenty little Pekingese dogs. When there's a downdraft, it smells like a kennel in this doorway.

These two jockos never come down while I'm painting and I quit at about four-thirty. I'm sure they don't live there. Maybe there's some other exit, some secret way out devised by a medieval queen to get errant knights into her bedroom without anybody knowing. Maybe there's even a private entrance into my tunnels.

STANDING IN A DOORWAY, FACING IN OR
FACING OUT—ENTERING OR LEAVING?
WALKING BACKWARD OUT?

The next day she comes back. I've been half waiting for her all morning. We chitchat about five minutes, the length of a cigarette; then she invites me upstairs for lunch. You see, fantasies do come true.

My painting's almost finished. I'm only edging it along, looking for those little loopholes where I can make what I'm trying to say more visible. I'm always afraid of tickling a painting to death; I've done it too often. It's easy to do if you're not careful. You're going along, adding here, subtracting there, building this up, cutting that down, sacrificing this for that, and then, suddenly, right under your eyes, the painting starts to fade. And once it gets going there's nothing you can do. It's almost as if the life of the painting is siphoned up your brush, up your arm and back into you again; nothing left but pigment and cloth; ex post facto birth control, like abortion, or putting babies out on rocks or ice floes to die. There's nothing for it but cover the canvas with a sheet and chant a few soulful Te Deums.

She asks me to bring the painting with me. She's got her hooks into it all right, or maybe the painting's got its hooks into her. It doesn't matter. We're being very wary today. I'm thinking I might even get a look at the merchandise; maybe we can make some kind of deal for posing.

There I go, dreaming again. Dreaming can't hurt—much. I tell myself I can always paint the painting again; but that's not true. It's never the same. I could paint the same thing a hundred times; be different every time. Everything's always changing all the time, especially me.

DRIFTWOOD WOULD DRIFT.

Third floor. She opens the door and tells me to take off my shoes. I put down the box in a little curtained-off alcove. She comes back with an honest-to-God golden robe. It's the kind of thing Japanese princes or wrestlers wear; gold brocade with a golden silk lining.

Naturally, I'm dirty; painting's a dirty business. But, aside from that, I'm something of a slob anyway, careless about things. I peel off my painting jacket: a red sweat shirt with a hood. It's streaked with paint; smelly and dirty, body or neck dirt, all around the top. I slip the golden robe over my shoulders like Jersey Joe Walcott waiting for the decision after a close fight. She drops to her knees on the soft, thick rug and starts taking off my shoes, dirty, paint-splattered canvas boots with many-knotted, broken shoelaces, carelessly strung. There are holes in my socks, toe and heel, both feet; socks not matching.

She slides the whole mess off and fits little slippers on my tootsies, golden like the coat.

Then she touches me on the thigh. Stiff. The thigh of the pants, that is. I wipe my brush off there on the front of my pants all the time. It's a bad habit but handy. The pants get stiff with varnish, will practically stand by themselves. She reaches for my belt buckle.

This is getting *very* embarrassing. Most of the time I don't notice how really sloppy-looking I am; it doesn't matter. I put my hands over hers and slide down my pants: old jeans with jagged patched holes in the knees.

I'm wearing trapdoored, olive-drab, army-surplus long johns. What the hell, it's cold out in the streets this time of year. Just then, another woman comes into the room. She's wearing the same kind of golden costume. Maybe I'm involved with a pair of Hari Krishnas, luxury edition. I wrap the golden bathrobe around myself. Both the girls start giggling. I don't know what to do; never expected *two* of them. I decide I'll act as if standing there in long johns and a gold brocade bathrobe is the most natural thing in the world; grin back at them, look around.

The room is beautiful. There's a deep soft brown woolen rug on the floor, wall to wall, like one giant bed. There's fine Louis XV furniture, brocade-and-velvet walls, deep, golden-yellow drapes on the window. She leads me by the hand across the room to a bathroom. A bathroom is the last thing I'd've expected in one of these old places.

I lock myself in and wash my hands. There's a nail-brush; I try to scrub off some of the varnish. There's nothing to do with my nails: the cuticles are deep split and the dirt's driven down in. At home I use 23 Skidoo hand cleaner. It's the only thing I import from America; it's the only thing I know that works on my hands.

I reach inside the long johns and freshen up. There's some fancy spray deodorant on a shelf; I decide to sacrifice a tiny chunk of the ozone layer and give myself a few squirts. I take a piss; not much. It's a typical woman house: cover on the toilet lid so it won't stay up unless you hold it.

SMALL MOVEMENTS OF THE MIND,
UNKIND THOUGHTS BUILT-IN, LIKE
CABINETS IN A RENTED HOUSE
SAY, WHO BUILT THIS PLACE?

When I come out, they're *both* dressed like rich Buddhist monks in gold silk kimonos. I can't tell how much they're wearing under, but they look very sexy. First girl does the introductions. They call themselves Colette and Colline. I call myself Bob. The French are nuts for the American name Bob; say it like "snob," short and in the nose.

There's a table set by the window with real china

dishes and silverware, even crystal goblets. We sit down and they take turns serving the meal and entertaining me. What a meal they bring out! It begins with moules farcies, then truite meunière, followed by paupiettes and pommes dauphines. It's all perfectly cooked and served. For a serious eater like me it's a dream.

It turns out these women have a great little business going. They serve a luncheon for one or two men every noon, with a nice easy screw or whatever after. It's all very high class, nothing vulgar. The tab is a thousand francs for two, lunch and the works—a good deal for everybody. They have their regulars and work five afternoons a week. They take two months off in the summer; go stay on a small Greek island where they own a house. They're saving their money and hope to retire in five years. They love each other.

LOVE IN A CIRCLE
THE TRUE HONEYMOON.
FULL THAT IS.

They're both seriously interested in the painting. The regular customers for this day are no-show. They pull out the note with two five-hundred-franc bills. Private unemployment insurance. They begin by offering the thousand. I only smile and shake my head.

These girls are like French geishas; seem to get their jollies together, working it off on men. They're playing to each other, using me. It's a wonderful lift for my sagging libido, at the same time a bit tough on the old ego.

WE PLAY AND I'M THE BALL
NOT SO BAD, AFTER ALL.

We finish with a flaming Norwegian. The painting is standing on top of a small piano against the wall. I wonder which of them plays it, or is it only decoration? I'd love to hear them play a duet on that little thing, music wrapping itself around me in my golden robe. Maybe I'll be a Buddhist monk in the next life.

They both speak reasonably good painting talk; have an idea of what's going on, ask good questions. They really want the painting. God, I hate talking money about a painting while it's still hot in my mind. After a painting's finished and I'm into something else, OK; but not while I'm still painting.

To tell the truth, I paint every painting for myself. Only later, when we've grown a bit apart, can I let go. So I'm uncomfortable. They have good antennae and feel it, but keep after me. I'd actually like them to own my painting. It'd be exciting having one of my paintings, part of me, staring down from a wall here, watching the action, displaced voyeurism; even from the grave. But this one belongs to the Canettes series; who knows, maybe I'll meet some millionaire and he'll buy the whole bunch. See, I really am hopelessly hopeful.

I AM WHAT I CREATE AND I
CREATE WHAT I AM. ONE
MORE CIRCLE.

They begin working on me, promising a wonderful afternoon. They're on both sides, stroking, petting. They keep darting looks at each other. Colette is definitely the leader. She begins talking in that pursed-lip French way Simone Simon used to use.

"What can an American man know about what a really good French woman can do for him? Have you ever made love with two girls together; two girls who love each other? We can have a festival of passion."

That's an exact translation of the phrase she uses in French. I'm sinking fast. It's almost too much; I don't have vast reserves of resistance in these areas. I also don't have vast reserves, period!

The thing that's bothering me almost as much as the painting is maybe I'll bomb. It's bad enough when there's one woman, but with two to share the joke, I'm not sure my fading flicker of masculinity could survive. I don't know if it's age or whatever, but sometimes lately, at the critical moment, I can get to thinking of how ridiculous it all must look and how monotonous it is; then, bump, London Bridge falls down. Poor Kate tries not to take it personally but it's the kind of thing that's hard to talk about. A catastrophe under these conditions might eliminate the old libido for good and all.

Finally, I tighten the strings on my golden bathrobe and tell them I can't sell it now. Maybe later when I'm into something else, but not yet. I tell them I'll be working in the quarter and they can always find me. They're not happy but they simmer down, let me off the hook.

MY PROSTATE IS PROSTRATE,
MY COCK IS UN—OR, MAYBE
THE SAFETY'S STILL ON.

It turns out they met each other in the conservatory of music. One plays piano, the other violin.

We finish the afternoon off with a Brahms concerto for piano and violin. They're really good. I have to ask, how great can life get anyway? I could sure use more of it but I can't find any for sale or barter. Hey, Mephistopheles, give me a chance, huh? I won't even dicker the price.

MAKE A DEAL WITH THE DEVIL.
DEVIL DEAR, HOW DEAR ARE YOU?

X

THE NEW YORK BUYER

We usually keep the paintings I'm working on hanging all over our place; like to live with the whole thing. My Canettes series is more than forty paintings now. We've got paintings everywhere, even in the bathroom; one for standing, another for sitting down. We have them stacked around the living room three high. It looks like the reserve downstairs at the V. and A. Museum. That reserve must be the most discouraging place in the world for a painter. The rooms are filled floor to ceiling with paintings, some bad but mostly good. They're down there in the dark, suffocating, no air, no eyes; canned vomit, victims of changing times.

The Canettes series is built around five streets between Saint-Sulpice and the Rue du Four. Two of my nests are right there; I can work, keep things up and collect rent money in one trip. It's an incredible place for painting. There are carpenters, tinkers, plumbers—all mixed in with fancy boîtes and boutiques. The buildings lean toward each other, trying to hold up under the press of time.

I've concentrated on the Rue Saint-Sulpice, Rue Guisarde, Rue Princesse, the Rue des Canettes and some of the Rue Mabillon. I've painted straight on at façades; I've painted inside courtyards; painted people in streets and in bars; painted inside rooms like Sweik's; painted portraits of the people. I even painted a dog that hangs outside an Italian restaurant on the Rue des Canettes: Mafia or Corsican dog, bites *and* barks.

A series like this says something about Paris by getting up close to a small part. It also says something about me, my unreal aspirations and nit-picking desire to tell all; to burrow into things like some kind of magic tick.

PULLING IN THE WORLD AROUND ME, SOUNDING DEPTHS TO THE SINGED CORE. I NEED TO SCRAPE FOR MORE, THE EDGE TO SIDES OF ENDINGS.

A few nights ago, I decided it's complete. I pushed all the paintings around under a light. I put them up chronologically. I put them up according to street, then according to subject. I spent four hours wallowing around in my own filth. God, it's hard to let go but this series is definitely finished. The last paintings are beginning to smell afterbirthy.

I hate like hell breaking them up. I'll probably never see them all together like this again, but we've got to eat. The painting money isn't big but we need it anyway. Five kids cost money, especially with those enormous American university fees; greatest way I can think to spend money, but tough to keep up with.

We eat meat every night in our house. For me, not eating meat is like not getting a night's sleep; I'm a real dog. Hamburger costs seven bucks a kilo in this town; that's about three-fifty a pound. And then there's my own personal time running out on me and my forty acres slipping away. I'm needing income.

TIME QUAGMIRE, SLIPPERY AND
LIKE QUICK-MUD, SUCKING DOWN.

I've broken up other series before, but it's always painful. It's a chunk of my life; every painting's wrapped with good experience. Looking at them is like hearing an old song, or smelling a smell and having a space of time come to life again. They represent the prime part of a year in my life, a vintage year.

Yesterday, I'm down working in the Marais. The Marais's different, different from Canettes, different from me. Either I'll change it or it'll change me. Something's got to give, probably the old Scum.

Goddamned kids there drive me to the wall. They want to know about everything. Why do I do this, or that; how much does the canvas cost, the paint; how much do I get for a painting? I tell them they cost five thousand dollars apiece. Shock. Two men come over; street men of the Marais, well dressed; they change money illegally, any kind of money.

"Do your paintings really cost five thousand American dollars each?"

"Yes, but I'll let you have this one for only three thousand Canadian dollars because I don't like it."

I come home tired. I've been laying in a whole street down the Rue des Rosiers from the corner of Ferdinand Duval. Duval used to be called Jew Street. Rue des Rosiers comes from when the whores had red flowers, roses, in the windows. Everybody's priming me with gratuitous information about everything.

I'm building up a large complicated painting and it knocks me out. I'm worn down from trying to hold all my ideas in one place and see them at the same time. I'm making space out of nothing from an abstraction of something. It's hard keeping the faith when there isn't much to go on yet; I keep falling back onto the canvas. The deal is I've got to stay inside it, not on it.

HOLDING TIGHT WITH BOTH HANDS, SCRABBLING
TO STAY IN THERE, MAKING THE SEEMING SEEMLY,
A DREAM SEWN WITH INVISIBLE SEAMS.

I come home and there're guests. Just what *we* need. I put down the box, smile around and duck into our bathroom to wash up. I take my time; I'm dying for a good hot soaking bath. I hold my head as long as I can in a full sink of cold water. Maybe I'll slip into oxygen conservation and it'll all go away. I can't make it. I dry off; comb my few hairs; pull them into a thin pigtail; brush my Santa Claus beard out fluffy and put on my salesman smile. I go back to the living room.

These people look more interesting than the usual creeps who come visiting us. Mostly, it's some old friends from the States with tight assholes and loose mouths. Or, worse yet, their kids with loose assholes and tight mouths. The kids hate us because we're friends of their parents and because they want something from us. They want to sleep in our house, or borrow money, or both. Sometimes they want me to tell them in fifteen minutes how they can sell their work and start making fifty grand a year beginning next week. Most often the "work" is an outgrowth to an "art project" they learned in junior high school. When I try telling something of the realities, they hate me even more. I don't like being hated.

Their parents usually hate *us* because *our* assholes aren't sufficiently bunged up yet and we refuse to play pecking-order games. They give out reams of hooey about how *lucky* we are to live this wonderful *free* life while Jack's staring into dirty mouths all day at his Beverly Hills dental office, or Walter is forced to teach eight hours of class a week and is so underpaid at thirty or forty thou a year.

I'm tired of hearing it; maybe *that's* why they hate me.

But these people look different: loose, breezy, Kate's age, quite a bit younger than me; in the saddle and with a good grip. They look like Fitzgerald people, could be the Gerald Murphys. The man has gray, wavy hair, white-blue eyes, smooth tan; he's tall. More like Dick Diver. Right on, Dick Diver, living, breathing there in front of me. The woman's almost as tall, boyish-looking, powerful arms, tennis or swimming arms; powerful. These look like exciting people, worth getting close to.

It turns out Kate met this woman in the Luxembourg Gardens, where the kids sail boats. They have a kid the same age as Tim. I tell you, second families are fun—thirds, too, in my case. This woman's name is Jan; does sculpture, she says; has big enough hands but they're not dented up. For sure it's not stone or wood sculpture.

The husband's named Bert. He's not saying much. He's walking around looking at the wall-to-wall paintings. He stays and looks at each one quite a while. He gets up close; knows how to look.

People should look at paintings from arm's length, not across a hat-hung-far-flung room. They should look from the distance the artist painted them. These are subjects, not objects. This man's doing it that way; having a private conversation with my work.

It's amazing how some people don't see paintings. They can walk in and not even look at the walls. There could be dead people hanging in every corner and they wouldn't notice. They live in private tunnels; only use their eyes to keep from bumping into things, the way bats use sonar.

Other people come in and scan the whole room but don't pick up paintings. Maybe they'll remark on the nice drapes, or how clean the windows are, or notice some spider's building a web in one corner.

Others come in, look briefly at my paintings, the way they would at a pile of carrots or potatoes, and say, "Oh, you paint?"

"No, Goddamn it, I cut them out of soap!"

Or they put one finger against their chin or hold out an index finger like a measuring worm, or start boxing a painting between their hands, squinting down one arm and saying things like "Hmmmm," or "Lovely," or "Do you use acrylics?"

A curse on them all.

THE CURSE OF INSENSITIVE KINDNESS,
A BLUSH OF AN INGRATIATING HUSH,
I SLINK INTO A CORNER UNDER THE STAIR.

But I love this man; the man with wavy gray hair, a man who looks like Dick Diver and is called Bert. He's truly looking. I have the feeling he's both taking them apart and putting them together with himself in his own mind. I begin sneaking around behind him. Even with a good viewer, it's a crummy position to be in. I'm so deep into my own work, no matter what anybody says, it's never enough.

Finally he stops and I follow him back to the big table where Kate's serving tea. She and Jan are gabbing away. Jan's been watching Bert, I think, and looking at the paintings a bit, too. Bert sits down.

"You see, Jan, these are what you could call subjective reality. They're more than real; true surrealism."

I stare at him. Holy cow, it's like listening to myself! I'm ready to jump on the damned table and do a wild dance!

Instead, I start talking. I talk about everything I'm trying to do. I tell how I want to be the people's painter, trying to be a part of life, making living things, trying to make life seem more worth living. I tell how I want to let people know how close they are to experience, open up their stuffed emotion passages with sharp, clean breaths of beautiful images, break the first or second commandment depending on whether you're Jew, Protestant or Catholic. I roll on and on. I'm not even thinking of selling paintings; just so damned excited having somebody who can listen and understand. I even begin to feel *she's* listening. Artists hardly ever listen to each other: too much static.

We have a fine time—at least I do. We invite them to stay on for dinner but they can't. We agree we'll get together soon. I go to bed that night feeling warm, inside thoughts.

Today, I come home by accident. I forgot to bring money and then got hungry. I left the box at Goldenberg's and biked home to raid our refrigerator, best and cheapest place to eat in Paris.

I'm going upstairs when I see Jan coming down. She's a bit embarrassed; says she wants to see the paintings again. Sure, come up and see my itchings, young lady.

Maybe I won't get back to painting this afternoon. The box is safe at Goldenberg's. Everybody down there's convinced I'm a big American painter doing twenty paintings of the Marais on commission for a rich American Jew who's going to donate them to the Guggenheim. It stops the crazy questions; gives me big-man status, the new Messiah; going to make real-estate values shoot up.

I'm having all these fun kinds of rootless fantasies while I'm following Jan up the stairs. My mind can just run away with me sometimes. I think I have a slipping clutch somewhere in there; gets worse every year, silent erosion. Jan's walking ahead of me. She's wearing jogging shoes and those little socks with tiny pom-poms sticking out the heel.

I open our door and we go in. I walk into the kitchen, put on water for tea, turn on the heater. I peek in our fridge. I'm not usually so hungry at lunch, because I eat liver, orange juice and parsley for breakfast. But there was no liver this morning.

Jan's walking around staring at my paintings now. I almost expect her to put a finger to her chin. She rocks back on one foot.

"Bert really likes your things, you know. He talked about them last night at dinner and then some more in bed. I thought he'd never shut up and let me sleep. I've never seen him so crazy about paintings. Psychiatrists don't usually get turned on by art; Freudians don't, anyway. They think artists have no choice, that kind of crap."

She's talking away, I'm listening, wondering. Is she doing a put-down on the old man? That's almost always a come-on. Most American women give the high sign by running down the husband. I'm starting to figure how I can get out of this without embarrassing anybody, especially me.

I bring out tea, some radishes and leftover pizza; slim pickings. She's already eaten. I still don't feel anything of sex. Holy mackerel, maybe she's actually interested in paintings. It sure would help the cause if I could sell one; haven't sold anything for too long. The rent's coming up on our place in ten days; comes every three months. It'd be great to sell a painting.

"I'd like to buy Bert something for his birthday. It's terribly hard finding anything for him. If I bought a painting, could I keep it here till October?"

Could she ever keep it here? Wow! Sure she could. I'd have the rent money and still hold the series intact a little longer. I try not smiling too much.

Then we start the choosing process. Stand this one here, that one there. I can't take it. We move this one into the reject pile, that one into the "good" pile. It's going to take all day. I've gone through this hundreds of times but still can't handle it; baby slave auction. Finally, she gets down to seven paintings in the "good" pile. I take a deep breath, preparing myself for the last, long stretch.

"I'll take these," she says.

Jesus! We haven't even talked price!

"You mean all seven?"

"That's right."

Then I notice the rock on her finger. I don't know if she was wearing it all the time or not. Maybe she kept it in her pocket and slipped it on just now to show me she can really pay out that kind of money. The thing runs about halfway down her finger, greenish color, but a diamond sure enough; not big as the Ritz but big as the rich all right.

WEALTH, THE BRACE OF STANCE TO THIS
STEALTH: IT WASHES AWAY SO MUCH WITH IT.

I try out a price of three hundred bucks per painting; hold my breath, and look to see if she'll faint. That's over two thousand bucks by a quick stand-up calculation. She rips out her leatherbound checkbook, verifies the spelling of my name and writes a check on one of those California picture checks. She writes it with a real ink fountain pen, right out to the last zero. She blows on the wet ink and hands it to me. I try looking as if I'm paying attention but my brain is short-circuited.

We sit there and drink cold tea; best damned cold tea I ever tasted. I try to tell her what I'm doing down in the Marais. She's not much interested; just bought a birthday present for her husband, everyday affair, ho hum. She asks me not to let Bert know she's bought the paintings; it's a surprise.

She stands up and packs the checkbook back in her small purse. I go down with her. I didn't even eat any pizza. A big money earner like me should eat cold pizza? I leave the stuff on our table. I'm not usually so sloppy, being the homekeeper, but *twenty-one hundred dollars,* just like that, in an afternoon; it goes to my head. I pick fifty francs from our hiding place behind the mirror and roll back to the Marais on my bike in a rosy haze.

I recoup my box at Goldenberg's. I'm wearing a two-mile-wide grin all over my face; I'm actually beginning to *look* like a guy who's painting a series of twenty paintings for the Guggenheim. Nothing succeeds like success. Goddamn, I just sold seven paintings; things're looking up! The scumming slum landlord of Paris is breaking out.

LUCK IN A BUCKET, WITHOUT HOLES,
CHANGING ROLES IN ONE STINKING BLINK.

I set up the box. I hassle a guy into moving his truck. I talk to a little fellow who runs a grocery store on the corner. He's a Middle Eastern Jew, low man on the totem pole around here. The top Jews came in the twelfth century, sealed into the Marais by the French. "Marais" means swamp. These first ones made something of their swamp; live in swamp palaces now. Middle Eastern Jews moved in mostly after Suez. They have their own foods, own storefront synagogues, own stores, a ghetto inside the ghetto.

BOXES INSIDE BOXES, WALLS TO DEFEND
AGAINST WALLS. WE LOCK OURSELVES OUT
BY LOCKING OTHERS IN.

I'm deep into my painting, looking down a street, trying to make a bright red stay back there, when I see the Bert man running *up* the street, almost as if he's coming straight out of my painting. He's wearing an eager, serious look on his face.

I catch on right away; the wife's a nut and he's found out she wrote a twenty-one-hundred-dollar check on the old joint account. Dick Diver chases Nicole through the streets of Paris. It was nice while it lasted; I should've cashed the check immediately. I'm glad to see him anyway; I'm used to this kind of thing—story of my life.

"Boy, you sure are tough to find," he says, breathing hard. "Jan said you were down here somewhere today but I've never been here before."

"Yeah, Bert. Great place, isn't it?"

I'll let him bring it up. I'm not going to fight, but I'm not going to roll over on my back either.

"In the office this morning, I got to thinking about your paintings. They're really important; shouldn't be broken up. That series should be kept intact."

Very nice way out; very nice guy. I try to keep on painting; can't even get up a proper mad about it. I have the check in my wallet; I'll give it to him when he asks. I'm a lousy businessman. I'm terrific at nickel-diming, fighting for remnants, putting together broken-down nests, but at the big moment I'm a pushover.

I have a feeling these thoughts are getting into the painting, so I stop. I'll give him a chance to get it over with. He's looking at the painting. He lights a cigarette, offers me one. I take it; what the hell. I smoke six cigarettes a year, one on my birthday, one on New Year's Eve and four over the rest of the year on special occasions. This looks like a *very* special occasion, the day I *didn't* sell seven paintings.

"What would you charge for the whole series?"

He takes a deep inhale and blows smoke out his noseholes. I *usually* choke on the first puff of a cigarette anyway, but I almost strangle this time. I cough and choke around in a circle. I stop, stare at him.

"You mean the *whole* Canettes series? There're forty of them, you know. I can't sell them for nothing."

I still can't tell if this man is serious. I can see in his eyes that *he* thinks he's serious.

"Forty-two."

"What?"

"Forty-two, there're forty-two of them. I counted."

"Oh."

How do you deal with a nut like this? I try to take a drag on my cigarette. My hand's already shaking so I almost shake off the light. No, he can't be serious; he can't have any idea.

"I could never pay what they're worth," says he, "but if you can give me a reasonable price, I'd like very much to buy them."

Joseph O. Baloney! Did his wife tell him she'd paid three hundred bucks apiece? No. She said it was a surprise. Maybe he has no idea what paintings cost. But he's a psychiatrist, not an industrialist hick or something.

Sucking sow! Just then I remember I don't own the whole series anymore! I sold seven of them this morning to his sculptor-woman wife. This'll probably screw up the deal. I have to tell him.

"Bad news, Bert. I sold seven of the series this morning to a buyer from New York."

His face almost drops off his head. I feel like some creep working out of Windy Folly's Gallery on the Right Bank, turning paintings over like flapjacks. He drops his cigarette and stamps it out.

"Christ, I knew it! I should've come back last night. I told Jan they couldn't last; too good. I'm a psychiatrist, I should know enough to trust my feelings!"

I'm listening to him and I can't believe it. This whole scenario sounds like the kind of ego trip I make up when my mind's drifting, stretching canvases. I'm having a hard time keeping the decaying brain from spinning off on its own again.

"Which ones did he take? Did he take the one with the inside of an apartment and the little old lady?"

"Nope."

"He must be an idiot!"

He goes through three or four others, two of which his wife had bought. It reminds me of some far-out Bingo game. He stands there, frustration leaking out the seams. I'm trying to think my way around it. Maybe I could play double agent: put on a raincoat, buy a dagger; stab his old lady, hide her body. He lights another cigarette.

"Could you give me the name of the buyer in New York?"

I have to play it by ear.

"Sorry, Bert, this guy buys confidentially for his clients and I'm sworn to secrecy; professional ethics, tax dodges and all that. You know how the art business is."

He seems to go for it. I'm standing, developing cramps from trying not to kick myself in the pants. He's looking some more at the painting on the easel.

"OK, I'll take the rest of them then, including this one if it's for sale."

He looks almost apologetic. I still can't figure how to handle it. He's got to be a nut. I haven't even given him a price. He looks sound enough but he must have some hidden screw loose.

Psychiatrists are usually crazy anyway. I read somewhere they kill themselves ten times more frequently than doctors, and doctors do it ten times more than the rest of the population. Ten times ten, a hundred to one. God, dying's so easy, so hard to avoid, especially when you *don't* want to.

DEATH AS INDIAN GIFT, TO BE
LOOKED AT IN THE MOUTH, LIKE A HORSE.

How the hell would a psychiatrist have that kind of money anyway? Sure they get a hundred bucks an hour, but how many hours do they work? This could all be some kind of complicated con game. Maybe he really is Dick Diver. When last heard from, Diver was in the Finger Lakes district of New York, but that's over fifty years ago. My mind's burning out relays all right. Somebody'll be changing my Pampers and spoon-feeding me soon.

"Bert, I haven't even told you how much they cost yet; how can you say you'll buy them?"

"That's right. How much are they?"

No concern, only brushing gnats out of his eyes. He *must* be a loon. But I figure I'll treat it seriously and see how it comes out. I can't give his wife one price and him another; I tell him the paintings are three hundred apiece but maybe we can make a volume deal. He looks through me with those mad blue psychiatrist eyes.

"You're a fool." He smiles. "I'd've paid a thousand apiece or even more."

I *am* a fool, the happiest Goddamned fool in the world. I'm glad I'm selling them to him for three hundred, more than they're worth to me, and he's getting them feeling they're worth a thousand. All business should be that way. I'm exploding inside, like holding back waiting for somebody else's orgasm.

He drops his cigarette after two puffs and stamps it out.

"Let's find someplace for a glass of wine and we'll work it out so I can write you a check. Boy, Jan'll really be surprised; I haven't enjoyed buying anything so much in years. I could shoot myself I didn't get the other seven. Those paintings should all be together; one painting leads to the other like a set of symptoms in a classic case study."

That's right, let's find a place, get them sold and the check written before the mad psychiatrist shoots himself. We go into Goldenberg's; I order some pastrami sandwiches on me. Rather, on rye. I'm a rich man; on paper. I used to be rich in oil; now rich in money. Yippee!

Pastrami's called *Pickelfleisch* here. You ask for pastrami and you get tongue. Bert takes out a pen, real ink pen again, and we work it out. Thirty-six paintings, counting the one on the easel, times three hundred; harder than ten times ten but we work it out to ten thousand eight hundred dollars. I try to even it off at ten thousand but Bert insists on making it eleven. Like statistics, he says, over five it goes up. I feel as if we're playing with Monopoly money. Yeah, I'll buy St. Charles Place and Saint-Sulpice.

Being Scum the scumbler, I have to ask.

"Bert, how in the hell does a psychiatrist squirrel enough money to buy eleven thousand dollars' worth of paintings in one 'swell foop'?"

He laughs, says he isn't a psychiatrist anymore, does brain research; besides, the money isn't his, it's Jan's. She's deep rich, three generations rich. She likes making money, has a guilt feeling about having so much unless she keeps using it, keeps making more money. Bert seems to think it's all vaguely amusing.

We drink another beer. I can see my easel up the street; kids're getting out from school, hanging around. If one of them touches that painting, I'll break his arm. That's three hundred unfinished U.S. bucks sitting out there.

We finish; Bert has an appointment. I insist on paying, paying with his money. I'm over thirteen thousand dollars richer than I was yesterday. Hot dawg! Here I am doing something I want to do, *have* to do, and making money at it. How good can things be?

Before he leaves, Bert asks about frames. He wants to hang the paintings all over his apartment here in Paris the way we have them at our place. We agree to get together and I'll take him to a frame place. He gives me their phone number. He says we'll hire a couple taxis and move the paintings to his place, soon.

I'VE BEEN FAMED, DEFAMED,
FRAMED, DEFRAMED. MY IDEAS
ARE LOCKED IN WOOD.

I go up the street to a little *tabac;* buy a genuine Cuban cigar in a metal holder with a piece of thin wood wrapped around it. I take a ten-franc bill in the change and twist it as I'm walking back to the painting. There's a big crowd, mostly kids but all kinds. I go up to the easel, smile around like Al Jolson and pull out my cigar. I take it from the casket, toss the casket over my shoulder, throw the piece of wood after the casket. Kids fight each other to pick them up. I sniff the cigar and snip off the end with my palette knife.

I take out the ten-franc note I've twisted and light it. I get it burning fine. The crowd steps back in hushed shock. I light the end of my cigar and take a few good puffs. The ten francs is blazing away in my hand. I throw it, still burning, on the ground under my easel and get to work. The French are phasing out ten-franc notes anyhow; have a ten-franc coin now, encourages inflation. The hot-dog painter of the Marais is at work. Nobody's bothering the big man now.

I work away for maybe fifteen minutes. I didn't think I could bear down again with all the excitement but I'm doing great. I throw away the cigar after a few puffs; makes my head spin, too strong for me.

I'm putting in a critical light, letting the sky move down through the buildings where my focus of distance is, when somebody taps me on the shoulder. It's a flic. There are two of them. One has the burnt remnant of my ten-franc bill.

A real sacrilege has been committed in the streets. I raped money. He asks if it's mine. I say no; I threw it away. I ask if it's his. No smile, no sympathy, no humor. He asks if I burnt the money. I tell him I used it to light my cigar; I point to the cigar in the street. The other cop leans over and picks it up. Evidence? Wants it for himself?

I try ignoring them, get back to the painting. The flic leans forward, between me and the painting. He salutes. He salutes the insinuating way a French flic salutes when he wants you to give him your full attention so he can chew off your ear.

"Monsieur, it is against the French law to destroy the French money."

"I'm sorry, I didn't know that."

I put down my brush and reach for my wallet. I take out another ten-franc bill. I hold it out to him.

"Here, replace it with this one."

He won't take it, so I put this ten-franc bill on the tray of my paint box and get back to work. Both cops close in some more. The crowd's beginning to thicken; there's muttering, some laughs. I can't tell if they're with me or the cops. I pretend to work; pretend the bastards aren't even there.

Big conversations are breaking out through the crowd. Some of them start arguing with the cop, some with each other. Absentmindedly, I wipe my brush off on that ten-franc note. The flic leans over and picks up the bill by its corner. Here, more evidence! I must say it looks fine, lovely colors, some ultramarine and a little yellow ochre.

"Monsieur, you have done it again!"

He's quivering with outrage. I dip my biggest brush in some turpentine and begin brushing off the bill while he holds it. He's holding it by one corner and backing off to keep his uniform clean. I dab at it with my brush. I'm talking about *nettoyage,* cleaning; splashing turpentine around. He's backing off and I'm following him. I'm into being Charlie Chaplin now. The crowd's definitely with me. People are hanging out windows. The flic finally drops the bill.

I go back to my easel; I figure they're not going to shoot me but I'm expecting the worst. I'm enjoying myself so much I'm not really scared as I should be. You never know with the French police; they can be real mean. Those cops have a conference and then leave. I figure they've gone for the paddy wagon. Everybody's worried for me; nobody picks that ten-franc bill up from the street. There it is, a genuine hand-painted ten-franc bill, lying there in the street of the Marais and nobody picks it up. That's impressive.

IGNORANCE IGNORED, INTOLERANCE TOLERATED,
WE ALL FLAIL ABOUT IN FRUSTRATED FAILURE.

People begin touching me on the arm and saying "*Vite, vite.*" One even translates, "Hurry, hurry, sir." I start packing up. Little boys are guarding at the corner to warn me when the cops come back.

I stop packing. What the hell, I'm not running away; I have a painting to finish. Let them come; first things first. I turn around in front of my easel and wave both hands in the air à la de Gaulle.

"*Liberté, fraternité, égalité; je reste!*"

Everybody's shocked. They stare at me. I decide to top it off right.

"*Vive Israel!*"

The crowd shouts "*Vive Israel!*" in response, like a prayer.

We do that back and forth about five times; then I try getting on with the work. But there's no chance. Somebody brings out a bottle of wine and some glasses from a café. We pour and toast to another "*Vive Israel.*" It's sort of a liquid condemned man's last meal. We wait for the cops but they never come. It's just as well. I'm sure those cops got back to the station and told the other cops about the *salopard* in the Marais. Nobody wants to tangle with a *real* crazy; they're afraid they'll find they're crazy themselves. They're crazy not to be having more of a good time with their lives. That's *really* crazy, if you think about it.

XI

TIME OUT OF MIND

Now we have some money, I send off five thousand dollars to the Los Angeles County tax man. That'll keep him from selling the forty acres out from under me for a few years; another nightmare-maker parked quietly in reserve. With that out of the way for a while, I feel I should be able to relax.

I'm ready to tear into that Marais series. I buy a roll of good Belgian canvas, enough for at least twenty paintings. I get some dammar crystals, do my witches'-brew trick and build up my stock of paints. I even replace all my brushes; some of them were worn clear down to the ferule.

But I can't paint! Whatever it takes to bear down, concentrate, ignore the normal passage of time, is gone. I get bored. I do one truly crappy painting and it's pain all the way. My mind is racing, not staying in there with the paint. It's a really treacherous line one walks as an artist. The cusp of defiance is blended with grateful acceptance in some magic melting alchemy. When, for some reason, the balance is lost, the fall to the normal, ordinary progressions is almost unbearable. I'm on the edge staring into a more than imaginary black hole.

WHY CRY ABOUT IT? WE TEAR INTO EACH
OTHER'S TEARS. TYRANNY THROUGH
INTERMINABLE YEARS.

Maybe I've been painting in the streets too long. A person gets tired painting the same kinds of things all the time. I'm feeling overwhelmed by shutters and cobblestones. Also I'm being asphyxiated by automobiles. I've got about a hundred excuses going.

I move back into my studio, the one I got from Sasha. The white-on-white painter has left. He's run off with a famous rich French gay painter for the aristocracy, a friend of Claude's. They're touring Italy together.

I start sitting around in the studio, alone, spinning wheels, hours slipping by unnoticed; I'm caught on a snag. I have this weird idea clawing at the back of my mind and can't let go of it. Whenever I begin to paint, it drifts in and fills my entire foreground so I can't see anymore, can't paint.

WHAT IS ANYTHING IF YOU CAN'T TOUCH IT?
HOW TO KNOW A REAL OBVIOUS UNREALITY?

I'm hung on the possibility of painting my way through time. There's something strange happens whenever I paint, and I'm thinking I can use it to break my way right out of time sequence into time the way I'm sure it really is: continuous.

I'm convinced our perception of time is warped because we're part of it, locked in. Space and time have much in common, but space we can handle. We move around in space, sideways, up and down; we can know something about it, experience it. But time is different.

With time we're the way a tree is in space; a tree can't know space except in a very limited sense. A tree takes up a certain amount of space and moves through "it" slowly as it grows, that's all. We're the same with time. We're hooked into a certain section and use up a bit of it as we grow, but that's all.

A tree can't walk across the field or hop a jet from Paris to Los Angeles, just as we can't move into yesterday or tomorrow, or two hundred years from now. We're locked into our limited progression of time. Space is probably as much a mystery to a tree as time is to us.

I want to uproot myself in time, as we might uproot a tree and move it across a field. I want to be unhitched from my particular little niche in sequential time and move easily along the bands of continuous time. And I think I might have actually found a way to do this.

All these thoughts almost convince me I'm bonkers, but they won't go away, get back in the background where they belong, let me get on with my life, my painting.

A CATCH IN THE EYE, A MOTE IN THE MIND,
TEMPTATION TO SURRENDER, PRETEND KINDNESS.

When I paint, especially a portrait, there's a magic moment just when the painting is finished. Till that last stroke of my brush, the painting has been continuously changing while the model and I, the painter, have seemed stationary. Then, suddenly, everything is reversed. The painting is finished, static, while the model and I go on, strapped into our personal relentless time bands. The painting remains virtually the same, for centuries, millennia; but the model and I will decay, rot, be burned or buried.

I'm fascinated with that precise second when this change occurs. It's like the surf on a beach. The water rolls up onto the sand, a culmination of ocean movements; waves, winds and currents traveling thousands of miles. Then it climbs the tilt of a beach to a certain point and falls back, sliding under the surface. A new set of vectors carries it off to other beaches in other times. This moment is like that somehow.

I feel if I can catch this moment, I'll have a handle on elapsing time and can perhaps lift myself out, be detached; for a brief space participate in the true nature of time, be part of it, not merely a fixed point or intersecting by-product.

A CEASELESS TWIRLING, TWISTING WHIRLS IN VAIN,
THE CEMENT CAVITIES MELT THROUGH MY BRAIN.

I'm going to reach for this through a self-portrait. There should be no outside deterrent or interference. I must lean completely into myself, get as close as possible, penetrate to the last layers of temporality and dig for my essence, the immortal timelessness of true identity which I'm sure is there, just beyond grasp.

I know my entire field must be filled by the canvas. So I stretch a 120F and stand it vertically; it's more than six feet high and four feet wide. I don't want to violate any of the perceptual reality; there can be no distortion in size; I'll paint exactly life size, and all of me from head to toe.

The only distortions will be those necessary to create a three-dimensional world on a two-dimensional space. This time I must believe my eyes, my brain; distrust my mind. There can be no shortcuts, no exaggerations, no trimming to fit preconceived ideas of the way a painting "ought" to look. I've got to paint straight. I try for this in all my paintings, but whatever I am always gets in the way, muddles things. But not this time.

WHITE HOLLOWS ECHO IN A VACUUM.
BLACK SOLIDS STILL IN THE DARK,
THE SAME.

The relationship between the second and third dimension is also at the bottom of my idea. I want to break through to the fourth dimension, time. I've already learned how to see in three dimensions, see in space; then create on an object in two dimensions the illusion of a third. This seeming three-dimensional, yet two-dimensioned object then, in turn, exists in a three-dimensional world.

Is it illogical to think that perhaps in this illusory third dimension I might leapfrog to a *real* third dimension? From there, I could perhaps slip through into an illusion of the fourth! Could it be possible to do a metaphysical backflip, penetrate one illusion to the awareness of another, a psychic Möbius twist? Mightn't I then break the seemingly immutable barriers of sequential, clock-locked time and enter into the open plains of real, continuous time? I'm ready to try. I'm ready to sacrifice all—sanity, life itself—to make this jump.

SEE, BE, IN LINE WITH MYSELF, A
POLARIZED VIEW, LINEAL PERSPECTIVE.

To start, I lock the door of my studio. Traude has an early class, so she's gone every morning by eight o'clock. Claude's off to cut more marble in Carrara and then to investigate some dark blue granite in the Midi. I have total privacy.

I set up a big mirror I bought last month in the flea market. I was looking for clocks and found this absolutely flawless mirror for seventy-five francs. It's six feet tall and three feet wide, beveled on the edges where it goes into the wood. There's something of beveling in my idea of time.

I stand this mirror on the floor at a forty-five-degree angle to the windows. The window light falls on me, plus there's reflected light on my dark side from the mirror. I glow in super three dimensions. I'll stay with this mirror image, not try to reverse it; I'll stay left-handed, it's part of the warp, the bevel. I'll use my lap-landed twin brother to help with my leapfrog jump.

WE LIST MUTUALLY ON OUR PERSONAL
INCLINED PLANES. TO DECLINE IS SANITY.

The first day, I don't do anything but stand there and stare. I look at the all of me and at the parts. I watch myself breathing; try to catch myself swallowing, blinking. I want to see myself aging, like watching the hour hand on a clock. I'm looking for the little differences, second by second, minute by minute, hour by hour, day by day. A life seems only so many of those units; I must penetrate that lie by acute observation. If I can actually see myself happening in time, real time, not sun, clocks or calendars, then I've made a beginning.

By the middle of the second day, I begin to see myself changing, some subtle changes in coloring, in the hang of my flesh. I'm watching a slow-motion Dorian Gray right before my eyes. "Death, where is thy sting?" Easy. It's around you, inside you, every day you breathe. The end is in the beginning as the beginning might be at the end, if you believe in beginnings and ends. I'm not sure I do anymore.

On the third day, I start projecting myself onto the canvas. I stare at the mirror without turning my eyes, trying not to blink, staring until my own image is registered, burned onto my retinas. Then I close my eyes, shift my head, line up with the blank canvas, eyes still closed, then open them suddenly, casting the afterimage from my eyeballs onto the canvas. I do this over and over, time and time again, time hammering, sinking the nail of identity deep into the wood of life. Finally, I know just where each part of me should be on that blank canvas; all the canvas space has been apportioned, involved with my image.

THERE I AM; I AM THERE!
WHERE? THERE! THAT'S WHERE!

When I start drawing, it's almost as if I'm following a drawing that is already drawn. I'm doing me and my easel, the canvas, my paint box, the part of my studio behind me in the mirror. I rarely look back at the mirror to verify a location or a relationship. It's flowing through me onto the canvas, my hand tracing out the projection of my mind into lines to define me. It all flows so easily, so calmly, that the days pass almost unnoticed.

I draw for three days. I'm drifting over the surface of the canvas, entering into the confines of this illusion till the two dimensions no longer exist. I spend hours staring at the drawing, going back to the mirror, drifting between the two, meandering in space and time, losing myself, forgetting that I, as physical flesh-and-blood reality, am the true stimulus, the first source.

Instead, I'm feeling how the reality of the mirror and my drawing are taking over. Especially the drawing is gradually assuming a much greater substance as I cumulate, synthesize, concentrate and elaborate this identity to the suppression of the necessarily momentary image of the mirror. I'm getting to the moment for painting.

LOSING TO FIND, A DRIFT INTO A
LIFTING PYRAMID; INTERLOCKING
EQUILATERAL TRIANGLES ON A SQUARE.
THAT'S WHERE!

The terrible part about this whole experience is that at home I'm almost invisible. Even when I'm away from the studio, I'm back there with the mirror, the canvas. I don't want to talk, to break the completion of my involvement. Kate knows and is resentful but resigned; she leaves me alone. Even my kids more or less understand from long experience and give me room.

In my dreams, I'm sometimes the mirror, sometimes the drawing, sometimes sitting watching myself watch, feeling the stroke of the pencil on my body. I'm scared, spooked out, but I don't want to back off; this is something I must carry through to the end.

I WATCH MYSELF WATCHING ME, WATCHING ME.
I NEED NO WATCH, THIS WATCH. WATCH OUT!!
THAT'S ALL.

I start to paint. I develop the underpainting with great care. I'm thinking like a sculptor; I'm cutting away the fullness of the white with my brush as knife, as chisel, subtracting the reflective quality of the canvas differentially, regulating, measuring, modulating, mirroring my mirror. The imagery flows easily through me. I'm painting in thin layers with short strokes, hacking, continually overlapping, carving interrelationships of planes, feeling the glow of white from the canvas fight against my mutilation, my light slashing. I'm producing the illusion beyond vision.

I paint in a delirium, and four more days pass. As I come out of it, what I see is more than real, more than surreal; it approaches an ultimate reality, verges on the intrinsic.

I feel I'm not doing this myself anymore. I've been taken in hand and I'm being led to truths beyond knowing. Now I'm really scared, rat scared; but this is what I've been asking for. There's no going back; even if I want to, a part of me won't.

HOLDING BACK, NOT BACKING UP, BUT
STANDING THERE, LISTING FOR RETREAT.

When I begin the impasto, there's the eerie feeling it isn't paint on my brush, on my palette, but flesh, cloth, hair, air. I squeeze the usual pigments, load my brush, the old well-known way, approach the canvas as I've always done it, but the ordinary magic I've lived with for more than forty years, the magic of living in the painting, the space of the canvas becoming real to me, is so magnified my brain can't absorb it. My mind is being absorbed itself; I've become a technician to another act, beyond painting, beyond thinking. I'm transcended, not only in time, not just a question of space dislocation, but with some complex blend of the two.

I paint, or apparently go through the motions of what I've always called painting, and another thing is happening. I'm on the edge of a new-dug well, seeing myself reflected at the bottom, and I'm falling in. Something is holding me back, but another pressure from behind, within, gently eases me forward. I can sense my lack of real control, the gracious glide by which the difference between mirror, painting and self can disappear. Then where would I be? Would I be? I become so frightened I have no volition to move. But I *am* moving, sliding as if between stars, free-gliding without desire, a willing victim of forces beyond gravity, direction, place or time.

BETWEEN IMMUTABLE FORCES TORN, QUARTERED
BY FOUR HORSES: FEAR, DESIRE, IDEA, INERTIA.

Then, suddenly, all is quiet. The air around me is incredibly clear. There's an enormous stillness in my heart. The restlessness around which I've lived my life is gone, raked smooth.

I look out at a circumscribed world and as I look, the painting starts to move. I stare, transfixed. The "me" in the painting is reaching into the paint box I painted and picking up one of the tubes I painted and squeezing paint onto the painted palette. Then it leans forward and strokes gently—carefully, softly, with love and concern, with my brush—*my* shoulder.

It's the next thing I was to do. The painting is painting me; it's like having love made to you when you are finished, have nowhere to go anymore; passively enjoying being somebody else's continuation, anticipating, participating in the other's joy by not moving, not responding.

I watch, I feel, I don't move, I don't breathe. Then I know. I'm *not* breathing. I can't move. I'm not *me* anymore. That's *me,* out there! I'm watching "me" out there painting, painting a portrait of me and I'm the *portrait!* I've stepped through, out of my body, out of space, out of the third dimension and into time, real time; I've become the painting!

I know this and I'm calm. A swift feeling of separateness, of flatness, of wide emptiness and no emotion pervades me. I watch and know the time of him, the old me, moving out there is not my time; I'm not locked into it anymore; I'm time-drifting, as an astronaut drifts in space. I'm free of time-gravity, time-direction.

I also know how, with another effort, an effort not much stronger than that necessary to leave my body, I can now move out of this "time" into what would be called the future or past for the "me" out there; that "me," staring into the mirror, staring at me, as portrait. What will happen?

I concentrate. Some mindlike but physical shifting occurs, and I move. I move slowly without friction and the room darkens. I stop and it is night. In the dim light I see "me" sprawled on the floor. The mirror is twisted. I panic and lean backward, back in time to where I was. There's light again; "he" is still staring into my eyes. I frantically juggle time back and forth, parking a car in a tight space, trying to get back to where I was. Did I really push ahead in time, was that the way it is, will be? And why was I stretched out on the floor? If I leave, must my body die? What will happen if I, as him, leave here without me, going home, moving in space? Or what if I leave, go two years or three centuries forward or backward, or only into yesterday or tomorrow?

WITHOUT TIME, LIFE IS A TRAGIC MIME. A
MOVEMENT OF EMOTION STRIPPED OF MOTION. E.

And what would I be to Kate and our kids? That body *can't* be *me* anymore. It *can't* be having the thoughts I'm having. Can he have a future without me, even within his time; my old time? Is all I know, all I call my past, still registered in the folds of *his* cerebral cortex? And if so, what is it I have?

THE HOLLOW OF ZERO,
THE IMPRESSION OF NOTHING.

I then realize I can no longer move in space. By releasing myself from time, I've locked myself into space. Perhaps the old me, out there, is locked in this space too, or perhaps normal time will no longer happen to him, a moving robot. Perhaps that's what he was doing on the floor, a deep, timeless sleep; or maybe death.

TIME WARPS
TODAY'S CORPSE.

I want to go back. I want to put myself together again in space and regulated time. I know it can only be done through the mirror. The mirror is turned so I see him reflected, but I cannot see myself. I broke through to here through that mirror and it must be the only way back. Without the mirror, I'm doomed to wander through time in this place. Whatever forever is, I'm there and from now on space can only move through me, I never through it.

I'm feeling claustrophobic, not in the sense of space, but of time. I feel too much time around me.

It's then I know that the passing of time through us is part of our genetic expectation. I don't feel *alive* anymore. Perhaps *this* is death; I want to feel warm again inside the movement of time, sense the familiar glide of entropy, growth and decay. Time without participation is a raft in an ocean without drinking water and I'm deeply thirsty.

A GREEN BLANKNESS, THE GREEN AT THE
EDGE OF A BEVELED MIRROR—
SILICONED PALENESS.

Somehow I must contact me out there. Now I watch me packing up the paints, closing the jars of turpentine and varnish. Is he really me? Is there space and time for me out there? Or have we separated irrevocably as in a new form of osmotic miosis?

I must make him turn the mirror so I can see myself in it. Is it still possible to move his mind with mine; is there still enough of me in him for this? I concentrate. I pressure him to stay in my field of vision, in front of me, the portrait. I try to captivate him to me, hold him from moving away, leaving the room, abandoning me.

I bring all I have of life to bear on him with the one thought: "Turn the mirror."

He comes close, stares into my eyes. I project, penetrate his mind. Slowly he moves, clasps his hands on the sides of the mirror, then stops; stares again into the mirror, looks back at me, perplexed. I bring to force all I am and watch as he tightens his knees, flexes and gradually twists the mirror till I see myself, see myself as portrait in the mirror and, at the same time, see him as me, frozen, frightened, caught in the fusion of time and space. He stares. For the first time he's seeing me as he is, not as I am, and in this second there's a great roar, a sound of ripping and all is black.

THE SKY IS A HOLE, THE EARTH A DAGGER.
I TREMBLE, STAGGERING ON THIS ILLUSION OF
A GLOBE, HOPELESS, BUT GLAD TO BE WHAT WE
CALL ALIVE; AT HALF PAST THREE—
    OR QUARTER TO FIVE.

It's dark in the room when I come to. I'm on the floor. I lie there for several minutes afraid to look, afraid to know what's happened. My heart is pounding sluggishly in my ears, my head is spinning. I feel sick, and throw up.

I struggle to my knees and look through the dimness to the mirror and the painting. I look away quickly; it's like mental quicksand; I'm still too close. I search on the floor and find my glasses; both lenses are cracked, crazed webs like shatterproof glass at the scene of an automobile accident. I slide my glasses back on. I pull myself onto my chair and try putting myself together.

Finally, I have enough strength to turn the mirror completely away from the painting. I look in the mirror through my crazed glasses and see a large bruise on my forehead where I hit the floor. I go over and turn on the lights. The fluorescent glare makes it all seem grim. I scoop up and wash away my vomit. It's so real I almost enjoy doing this. It's wonderful to be in normal, in-step, sequential time again, to live around it, through it, wallow in it, die of it. Time in its passing is as essential to life as food or love. Even more so, because without time there is food but no eating, love but no loving.

I stand in front of the painting and open my box. I take up my brushes. Carefully, without using the mirror, I paint the bruise onto my head and then, with meticulous detail, paint in the shattered lenses of my glasses, scumbling my eyes with white for the reflection on the glass. Then, at last, I feel completely inside myself again. I've pinned that painting, *me,* to a moment in time, a moment from which I can again spring off in regulated time participation.

CASTING, THRUSTING AWAY ALL CHANCE OF IMMORTALITY
ALLOWS FOR THE JOY OF MORTALITY, MORTAL SIN,
MORTAL PLAY—COME AGAIN ANOTHER DAY.

I leave the paints and lock up the room. I ride home slowly on my motorcycle, drinking the Paris evening air. I deeply enjoy my dinner and rejoice in the ordinary kinds of happenings, conversations going on at home. Everybody's glad to see me back, glad to see me smiling. Maybe I'm smiling too much, idiot smile, but any smile is better than having the world's champion grouch slumping around. I hug, hold on to Kate and listen to the clock tick, listen to the chimes and feel blessed by time going by. I'm deeply immersed in continuity, the volume and presence of time, being part of life again with my loved ones. Lazarus must have felt like this.

The ticking, the chiming of our clock is the baton of a conductor before a symphonic orchestra. It isn't music he's playing but it's what measures and defines the music.

TICKERS, TIMERS, DIALS AND CLOCKS,
DRIPPING WATER, EATING ROCKS.

As I'm going to sleep that night, cuddled up behind Kate, I realize how close to death I've been. It could even have been a heart attack or a stroke. Dr. Jones warned me to expect it. Falling unconscious on the floor like that must mean something; it certainly can't be a good sign. I know I don't want to go back into the American Hospital, so I don't say anything about it to Kate. I've too much to do. I also know I don't want to tell her all the things that happened to me with that painting; it'd only worry her for nothing. I'll have to live alone with this one.

SECRET HOLES, TRAPDOORS TO
MOVE FROM FLOOR TO FLOOR.

The next day, when I go back to the studio, I take down that mirror and put it upstairs in Traude's room; it'll be a nice surprise for her. Then I go back downstairs and look at my painting. It seems so tortured, there's no fantasy in it; it's virtually faultless. I didn't allow myself to make the mistakes which give life to painting; I tried to deny the faults and schisms that result from time lapse, breaks in concentration and the complexities of bioptic vision.

It's simply *not* a work of art, only an exercise of the mind, the hand and, yes, something else too. I can't deny it. I know this painting is dangerous. I think of painting over it, destroying it, but can't. I don't really know, either, how much of me is still in that paint.

I carry the painting home surreptitiously and hide it in the farthest-back dark corner of the attic. Nobody will ever look up there, at least until I'm dead. Maybe I'll even burn it before then. That painting is definitely treacherous, like the San Andreas fault in California, a fault in time.

Then, after all this, I don't know why, but I *still* can't get started with real painting again. Whatever it is that drives me, makes me go from one painting to another without too much thought, is kaput. I don't see any reason for doing it anymore. My desire, *need* to pull things together out there, induce, seduce, reduce them into me, make it all mine, then design it to my private dream is gone. I don't want to waste my time in futile smearing of paint on canvas. Something's missing in the old Scumbler. The scum is sinking to the bottom instead of rising to the surface.

OUT OF A MURKING OBSCURITY THE SKIN MOTHER LURKS, A MEMBRANE FORMED ON THE SURFACE AND SINKING INTO SLIME.

XII

FULL OF SHIT

Now the thoughts that keep me from painting aren't all wrong. It's as if I'm only missing one important idea. I've forgotten something and I'm not sure what it is. I can even *remember* myself getting maniac, cross-eyed, excited about painting but I can't do it anymore.

It's the same way with remembering almost anything these days. Sometimes I'll be about to do something and be interrupted; or, more often, I'll be having a conversation with someone, and then, while I'm waiting for them to finish, I forget what I wanted to say. I remember *wanting* to remember but it's gone. There's an empty space.

This drives me nuts. My memory banks seem to be failing me; I can't put anything on "hold" anymore; another slipping gear.

NEURONS HOPSCOTCHING, SKIPPING LINES
SLIDING GENTLY AWAY, MEMORY A BLESSING
OR A CURSE, BUT TRANSGRESSINGLY TEMPORARY.

I finally quit completely; lock up the studio. I'm going to find out what's happening with painting, see if it's me or the whole stinking mess. I visit every show in town, trying to look at things like a client, a buyer, a consumer; as if I have no ideas of my own, have never painted. I pretend I'm a man from another planet making a sociological, anthropological, archaeological study on the nature of man and his artifacts. What the hell's it all about? Why do humans do this?

I'm having some of the same alienated feelings I had when I couldn't get myself to register for the draft. When that FBI man came to get me, I told him to do whatever it was he had to do; I wasn't dodging or running away or anything. Whatever the American people thought should be done to somebody who wouldn't go kill other people for them should be done. And since I wouldn't take the job of somebody else to kill for me, either, they locked me in federal prison at Danbury for three years.

I'm having a little of those same separated feelings.

IN A CAGE, THE LUXURY OF BARS, NO NEED TO CREATE THEM. SO NOW I THRASH ABOUT LOOKING FOR VICTIMS UPON WHOM TO CAST MY BLAME.

I go to all the museums in Paris. I look at every hotshot object they have to show me. I really look; wear myself out; lose ten pounds, flesh melting off me, nervous, no appetite.

I even go through the Musée Guimet. I stare carefully, blankly into the jaws of howling Chinese dragons and vases. I go to Arts Décoratifs; concentrate on costumes, bits of buttons and braid for Napoleon. I'm truly looking, trying to see these things as important.

I take a train up to Amsterdam, bear down on Rembrandt and van Gogh till the paintings fade before my eyes. Was it worth it to them, all the life they didn't live so they could make those objects? Is it worth it to us, to me?

Then, back in Paris, I hunt up every painter or sculptor, young or old, I can find. I listen. It's the first time anybody's ever listened to most of them. I look at their work; try to imagine I've just finished these art objects; try to get inside them. I imagine each one's the last remnant of man on earth, saved from the holocaust by being wrapped in a lead balloon or a platinum blanket.

I waste a week doing this. My eyes are sticking out of my head; poor Kate's pushing me to go into the American Hospital again. I must have something else terribly wrong with me: cirrhosis of the liver, Hodgkin's disease, mental derangement. I have all those things but they're lodged in my soul.

I tell Kate I'm making a big decision and please leave me alone for a while. She asks if I've fallen in love with somebody else. Good question; Kate always asks good questions. It's not what I've fallen *in* love with; it's what I've fallen *out* of love with—all the way out. I try to tell her this but can't. Soon as I start talking, I fill up; my voice breaks and I can't go on. I'm a candidate for the looney bin all right.

. . .

I go down to the Beaux-Arts School here in Paris. I want to talk with young French people just starting, getting immersed in the whole swing of it. I want to find what *they* think makes it worth doing.

I can't find anybody there! I walk through the whole building, a complete hulking city block in the center of Paris, four stories high. I go into every last room, at least fifty of them. I find seven people in the entire building, two of them janitors. Maybe there's a strike, a war, no school, something. I go down to the concierge, ask if school's open, if there's anybody around. The school's open all right, over eight thousand students enrolled.

"Where the hell are they?"

I walk back upstairs. The walls are covered with graffiti, poorly executed graffiti, not an original idea, neither in content nor technique; the kind of thing you find in any public toilet. There are windows broken out; the floors are packed with mashed bits of paper, chunks of food.

I find a huge assembly hall: chairs, tables scattered around. There are paintings on the walls, monstrous affairs, mostly commemorative, not very impressive, but *somebody's* stab at communication; they sure as hell can't defend themselves now. There are gaping holes ripped in these canvases; people, probably artists, have thrown rocks or wine bottles through them. Along the walls are statues. These are chipped off and scribbled on, ends of dongs painted red, paper airplanes stuck in hands.

I'm wondering what kind of people do this. Can these be artists who work here? What's happened to us? Are artists only the inept, the ignorant, stupid, arrogant kids of the wealthy; put to pasture, tucked out of the mainstream?

"Get thee to an art class!"

I don't see myself that way; can't live with it. If I can't grab on to some real reason for doing my work, I'll figure another—any other—way to spend what's left of my life. I know I sure as hell don't want to be classed with most of the hangers-on I know who call themselves artists.

MOSTLY EATERS OF GARBAGE, MAULERS OF
SECONDHAND IDEAS, PRESENTERS, PERFORMERS.
HOW CAN THE HIGHEST USUALLY BE SO LOW?
BE-LOW?

As a last-ditch measure, I decide to go visit artist friends of ours who live in Spain. I need some rubbing up against true working artists; find out why they do it.

These are Swedish friends, living in southern Spain. They're a whole family of redheads: Sture, Anna, three kids. They wear high wooden Swedish shoes, stalk around towering over tiny Spaniards like praying mantises—praying, not preying. I think.

We met them twenty years ago at the beach in Torremolinos. Their kids had dug a deep hole with a shovel and then sat in the shade of that hole reading. Sture and Anna wore huge flopping sun hats. These people live in Spain but stay out of the sun; classic alien behavior.

TIPTOEING, TOP-HATTED WITH WILTING FLOWERS.
COUNTING YEARS AS HOURS AND HARDLY EVEN
NOTICING. PUTTING A LID ON THE SUN, HANGING
ONE-HANDED ON CRUMBLING SANDBANKS, HAND DUG.

I stop by in my vague wanderings and tell Sweik I've had it; I'm going down to Spain. Sweik's been watching me mope around for a month. Sometimes I'd go over to his place and just sit there staring out his window. One time I almost told him about my time trip—stopped myself just in time. If he knew about that, he'd think I've finally gone over the line, completely cuckoo.

"Spain! Sounds great to me, Scum. Get yourself out from under these Paris gray skies; an artist needs light. Man, I wish *I* could go, watch some of those first bullfights, *novilladas,* under clear bright yellow Spanish sun."

He's rubbing saddle soap into his shoes, actually into the hiking boots he wears as shoes. He's just finished working some into his bags for the bike.

We walk up to the Place Saint-Sulpice. Sweik's carrying his bags with him. When we get there, he pulls the cover off his bike, folds it into one of the saddlebags, then attaches the bags to the bike. He works more saddle soap into the seat and even into that leather handle for the passenger.

From his other bag, he takes out the two helmets. They've been saddle-soaped till they glisten. This bike smells more like the park guard stable in Cobb's Creek Park than a gasoline combustion engine.

Sweik kicks once and the motor turns over easily; the machine *wants* to start. He stands beside the bike, carefully twisting the accelerator handle, slowly gunning the motor lightly into easy life, warming it up, gradually letting off the choke, adjusting the magneto.

"Here, Scum, take a helmet, let's ride up to the pad where Lubar's staying these days. He's holed in with two women named Sandy and Dale. I'm not sure he even knows which one he's chasing; I don't think they do either; probably don't care; closed-circuit situation there."

I figure, what the hell, why not? My own bike's not running at all. I checked all the easy things first; spark, carb, timing, but it's the engine itself. I pulled off the head and there's enough slop space between the pistons and cylinder; I could slip a match between them. The rings are shot. I can get the cylinders reamed out here, but I'll need somebody to bring in some oversized pistons from the States; then I'll have real power. Be sort of like a bypass surgery.

"Sure, Sweik, take me up to the den of iniquity. I'm ready for anything."

He laughs, puts on his helmet, hands me the other, swings his leg over the bike, pushes it down from its stand, kicks loose the two rear foot pegs.

"Come on, it'll blow some of the dry rot and cobwebs out from under your vaultings."

KEYSTONES PRESSING RELENTLESSLY OUTWARD
AGAINST SLOWLY CRUMBLING BUTTRESSES.

So we take off. Sweik tells me this place we're going is way up in the twentieth arrondissement behind Les Buttes Chaumont. It's a studio for an older American woman who does stained glass. She's off installing some of her work at a church near Lyon, so she's letting the girls use it while she's gone. She and Dale, one of the girls, have a special relationship.

I, personally, can't figure why Lubar hangs around up there when he could have his own house in the west suburbs, a smart wife and a little son. According to Sweik, neither Dale nor Sandy has much room in her life for Lubar —at least not so long as they have each other. Maybe he's a pointer or football in a private game. I have a harder time keeping up with these things as I get older; it used to seem so much simpler, but then maybe people just weren't talking as much about real relationships thirty, forty years ago.

We stop out by Strasbourg Saint-Denis to buy food. It'll be lunchtime when we get there. We buy two liter bottles of beer, a baguette and a Camembert. It's Saturday, so they won't be at work.

My own family's out picnicking at Saint-Germain-en-Laye; I couldn't get myself to do it; they didn't exactly knock themselves out encouraging me either; can't blame them. Right now, I'm the sick albatross.

Lubar's gotten jobs for both the girls, talking English in a conversation class with the French IBM executives. Maybe that's why they let him hang around.

A FIFTH WHEEL IS A SPARE
YOU ONLY NEED KEEP IT FILLED WITH AIR.

We climb a steep hill and just before we reach the top, Sweik pulls into a curb. This place looks like an abandoned factory. The building's two stories high and the part they're living in is at ground-floor level opening off a courtyard. We knock on a door that's at least ten feet high. A young woman, practically a girl, swings it open and stands back. With a smile she motions us inside.

Lubar's rolled his BMW right into the studio and has it propped up on its stand in the middle of the floor. The front wheel is off; tools and pieces are spread all over the place. There's another woman squatting beside Lubar, watching him. Actually, she's in a Yoga Lotus position with bare feet; and this on a cold cement floor. If she thinks she's going to learn much about mechanics watching Lubar, she's in for a shock.

He looks up as we come in. He has grease all over his face, arms and hands. His goggles are on his forehead. He's wearing black twill pants so you can't tell, but they're probably grease-smeared, too. There can't be much grease left on the bike; you'd swear he was doing some kind of major overhaul from the mess he's made.

"Shit, Sweik, I took these brake disks off because they were squealing; now I can't get the fuckers lined up again."

He's straddled the front of his bike. He's sitting on the floor with the wheel loose between his spread legs. There's sweat running down his face and the T-shirt he's wearing, besides being streaked with grease, is soaking wet sweat. Sweik and I squat beside him. I'm strictly superfluous. When it comes to mechanical skills, Lubar and I are probably about a photo finish for last.

Sweik figures it out in minutes. He has those plates aligned and for the next while we're all tightening bolts under his direction. I swear he doesn't even get his hands dirty; just the master surgeon directing his assistant and nurses in closing after a minor surgery.

When it's done and adjusted to Sweik's satisfaction, Lubar pulls on his leather jacket, slips down his goggles, then rolls the bike out that huge door, through the courtyard and into the street. From inside, we hear him turn over the bike, roar off.

The one who let us in, Sandy, is wearing a checkered shirt, men's buttons; Levi cords with a button fly; she closes the door behind him.

"You two like a cup of java? It's the least we can do. I'd begun to think maybe we'd have that machine all in parts, parked there in the middle of the floor like a piece of junk sculpture. Maybelle'd have two fits. She's real down on motorcycles and that macho shit anyway. She'd just throw us all out, fast."

Sandy's pouring water into a teakettle. I'd personally rather have tea, even herb tea, but maybe the old nerves are strong enough for one cup of pure caffeine. Sweik opens our beer, bread, Camembert. Sandy sets salt, pepper, two tomatoes, some butter on a little side table.

"I'll put out a cup for Lubar, he might be back. He's got the hots for Dale here, but she's scared to ride on back of that bike with him. I keep telling her he drives better than he fixes, but it doesn't help."

She gives Dale a loving, understanding look. Maybe Lubar likes it this way: no wins, no losses, just a lot of ties. Sweik settles onto a lumpy couch. I carefully balance myself in an armchair with one wobbly leg. Sandy's just pouring hot water through the coffee-filled filter when Lubar comes back. He still has his jacket open, zippers flaring. He's pushed his goggles up onto his balding forehead again.

"Man, it works like new, really holds without grabbing and that squeal's disappeared."

He kneels down and begins gathering up his tools. He has top-quality tools and keeps them neatly in a manydrawered, metal toolbox. He's the kind of poor workman who can't blame his tools; I'm the other kind. He gets them all gathered and even wipes the floor with a grease rag. He stores the tools by the door and pulls off his sweaty, dirty T-shirt. He steps into a little room built under a balcony.

"You guys start with the coffee. I'll be right out."

Sandy pours around in the mugs. I put three spoonfuls of sugar in mine. I really don't like the taste of coffee, I guess, but I love sugar. We all break off bits of bread, use knives to cut the cheese, tomatoes. I make myself a small sandwich. As I said, food isn't meaning much to me these days.

Sweik starts telling about my taking off for Spain. Sandy comes over, surprises me by putting her arms around my neck, rubbing her hand over my bald head.

"Wouldn't you like somebody to carry your bags, help keep you warm at night, wash out your socks and underwear?"

I must admit I would, but then I wouldn't. I'm deep under my black cloud over Toledo. I can't get my mind around her coming on so fast; she must be kidding, maybe trying to work me into the game. I can be the goalposts.

I put my hand on top of hers on my chest. My hands look so old, so veined, so thick-knuckled, so blotched with liver spots against the slim, smooth white, almost bluish, marble-like hands of Sandy. I notice she bites her nails; they're bitten so deeply into the quick one of them is bleeding. Gosh, you think someone might be leading the life they want, no hang-ups; then you see something like that. It's the kind of little vulnerability brings me to tears these days. Sandy takes her hand away.

Lubar yells from the bathroom:

"Spain! Hell, that's what we all should do, just take off and get under some of that mainline sun. We could tool down there on the bikes, taking pictures the whole way, and have something real to send off to that fucking AMA magazine."

Sweik is sipping the hot coffee. It's still too hot for my mouth. I'm blowing into it and stirring. Sweik cradles his cup in both hands to warm them; this place has such high ceilings it must be impossible to heat; I only see one little gas heater in a corner.

"You're the boss, Lubar. I'm ready to take off anytime

you are. Maybe we can get IBM to forget about English lessons for a few weeks."

Lubar sticks his head out from what must be the bathroom. He's drying off his face and hands. He has on a clean T-shirt.

"That's not a bad idea. I'll bet I could get Bouvier to cancel classes for that long; hell, I haven't had a vacation in over six months."

He comes on out. The two girls are watching back and forth. Dale speaks up for the first time.

"Wow, would I ever love to get someplace where it's warm. But I can't afford it and I could never ride on the back of a motorcycle that far. I get scared just going around Paris."

Sweik gives her a look. It's definitely derision, but mostly "Who invited you?"

Sandy jumps up, reaches for the high ceiling, brings her arms down fast.

"Go ahead, Dale, you'd love it. If *you* won't, I'd sure as hell love to hang in there if Lubar'd let me. I'm really sick of rain."

I try the coffee again; at last it's cool enough to get past my lips. I peer at Sandy over my mug; she's full of beans all right.

"Well, ladies, personally I'm going down on the train. My kidneys couldn't hold out for that long a trip. I'd get down there with all my organs huddled in a sodden bunch around my ass fighting for space with my hemorrhoids."

A LOW SKY, MOUNDS OF DIRT PILED HIGH,
MY EYES ARE LOST EVEN TO SOUND. CAN'T
EVEN ASK WHY ANYMORE.

Despite everything, they keep talking about this crazy trip. Sandy gets out maps and they plan a way through Tours to Bordeaux across the border to Burgos and down by Madrid. It's not much different from the train route. They even work out where they'll stop each night. It's about time to get out the trusty pen and compose one of our masterpieces for the AMA magazine. Hell's Angels of Paris strike again. Lubar looks up from the map at me.

"Where in Spain you actually going?"

"A little place near Torremolinos, up in the hills. I have Swedish friends there."

"You think they could put us up if we came down?"

Holy Lord! I think of my privacy-conscious Sture and Anna. They'd die if this bunch of bandits rolled into their little world.

"No, they only have a small place. I don't even know if they can put *me* up. I'm just taking a chance they'll *be* there. I haven't written."

"When you taking off?"

I hadn't gotten that far. I'm in such a state of drift I don't know what I'm doing, where I'm going.

"I'll probably take the eleven-o'clock train from the Gare d'Austerlitz tomorrow night."

"That's Sunday, right?"

"Yeah, I guess so."

He's striding up and down the room now. He's still in his T-shirt, he must be freezing. I have my jacket open but haven't taken it off; neither has Sweik.

"If we leave tomorrow morning early, we could make it in five days. Let's say we meet you there."

He looks over at me, his little bird eyes glistening in excitement, challenge. He's playing at Napoleon, laying out the campaign. He stops.

"I was down in Torremolinos with my ex-to-be wife three years ago. There's a bar right in the center of town—the oldest bar around, I guess—called the Bar Central. It's where the bus from Málaga used to stop. We'll meet you on the terrace outside, Thursday morning at ten o'clock. If we aren't there by noon, you'll know we couldn't make it."

At least he gave himself an out; maybe he isn't Napoleon. Sweik is watching to see just how serious he is. It sounds crazy but Lubar's acting serious.

"God, Sweik, think of it, we can roll along through those hills and the farther south we go, the warmer it'll get. We'll go right over those Sierra Nevada Mountains."

"I'm not sure my old Ariel is up to a long trip like that, Lubar. The farthest I've ever pushed it was to Amsterdam once, and I had a stiff back for a week when I got home."

Sandy goes over to Sweik, flops down on the couch beside him, puts her hands on his knees.

"I'd be happy to hold on and squeeze against you, keeping that bad back in place. You can't know how much I'd like getting to someplace warm and dry."

. . .

And so that's the way we leave it. There's more map talk, calculating how much they can do in a day stopping every two hours. Sweik's getting caught up in the whole insanity of it. He's bringing up bullfights again. I listen along, convinced it's all make-believe, another way to fight off a grim, gray rainy day.

But I can't make it with them. The fantasy part of my mind isn't working; in fact, none of my mind is active in any way. I'm like a piece of film or a pile of mud; I only take the prints, don't feel or do anything, only register.

SILVER PLATE REFLECTING,
NOT EVEN A FINGERPRINT OR THE
FOG OF BREATH. SPIRITUAL DEATH.

After a couple of hours Sweik and I leave. We get on his bike and I think of Sandy holding on up high there for maybe eight hundred miles. She's a tough young lady; she'd be just the one to do it and smile, laugh all the way. There's something in her between not seeming to care and caring so much she could try anything and maybe really hurt herself. I can't help but be glad she isn't my daughter.

On the Place Saint-Sulpice we cover the bike. Sweik's unhooked his bags and put the helmets in them. He stands a minute looking at the covered bike.

"You know this machine probably *could* make it."

A SIMPLE TOOL WITH
WHICH TO FOOL SIMPLY.

The next night, I get out an old Eurailpass a friend gave me. I've changed the name and used my magic French three-fluid ink remover to change the dates. There's a date on the back, the stamp's overdue but it's hard to change stamps. Nobody ever looks at the back anyway. I pack myself a change of socks and underwear but I'm only going through the motions.

Kate hovers over me like a mother hen. She doesn't want me to travel on a bogus Eurailpass, but I can't justify spending money that way. She doesn't want me to go *anywhere,* but she knows Sture and Anna might just be the thing for whatever ails me.

She drives me down to the Gare d'Austerlitz at 11 p.m. The kids are asleep. I know she's worried but there's nothing to do. I spent the whole day cleaning house, getting in everyone's way. I want to have it in perfect shape, like an Irish family cleaning house for a wake, but actually I feel like an old bull elephant heading off for the burial ground.

I climb up into the train and take over a whole first-class compartment. Eurailpasses are first class. First-class people don't usually sit in train seats at night; they buy Pullman berths. I pull the seats together, stuff my handbag into the space, take off my shoes, put the Eurailpass on top of my passport and sack out.

I sleep better than I have in a month; wake up in Bordeaux. It's seven-thirty in the morning. My Eurailpass and passport are in the same place; didn't even hear the conductor come in—maybe he didn't.

I look out the window as French civilization breaks down kilometer by kilometer till we're at Irún, the Spanish border. Suddenly, there's instant poverty. People's eyes have a resentful begging look; never find that look on a Frenchman.

Everybody out. Time to go through Spanish customs. Surly bastards, don't believe I only have my little handbag with jockey shorts, T-shirt, towel, bathing suit and socks. I think for a minute they're going to make me strip, but they pass me on as I'm unbuckling my pants. Why is it everybody's supposed to love Santa Claus but when they see a real old man with a genuine white beard, blue eyes and a nose like a cherry, paranoia strikes?

WE WEAR OURSELVES INSIDE OUT
TRYING TO BRING THE OUTSIDE IN.

I look around for the train to Madrid: TALGO EXPRESS. Usually you pay extra but it's free on a Eurailpass. Friends warned me about using my phony pass in Spain. What the hell, I couldn't care less. I've been in jail before; one more time can't hurt. I jump into a shiny red-and-silver round-topped train. I can already feel the south winds; it's turning into a beautiful day. The trees are in bloom on a scraggly hill out the window. I settle down.

The train starts. They're playing Spanish-style Muzak, like a Los Angeles Rexall drugstore. I get out my book; reading *Borstal Boy,* seems appropriate, gives me some nerve. Would an Irishman be nervous? Hell no! He'd probably have a bomb in his briefcase; hand it to the conductor, ask him to keep it in the refrigerator; get off the train just before it started. There's definitely not enough Irish blood in me; I worry too much.

There are some impressive, fancy folk on this train. Good-looking, tight-twatted women with pearls, matched; bullet-eyed men. They all look bored; all look disgusted with me in bushy white beard and scraggy pigtail. Maybe I'll tell them I'm a retired American bullfighter, friend of Ernesto.

The train's so smooth I hardly feel it, icy-smooth rails; acceleration like an airplane. The air conditioning is humming away. I ease out my pass and look at it: really blotchy —boy, are they going to get me! OK for night traveling in France but I must be crazy here in the bright day with Spaniards. Maybe I should pull the emergency brake, step off this train, say I forgot my toothbrush back in Irún.

The conductor sneaks up behind me. I hold out my pass expecting the worst; pretend I'm concentrating on my book. He doesn't take the pass; I look up. He has a pad in his hand. He's *not* the conductor, only a waiter taking orders for breakfast. Ho ho!

I order eggs and fruit juice, ham, coffee; another last meal. The train is humming on at about a hundred miles an hour through rolling green hills. The windows are tinged blue at top so it looks like deep blue, high-mountain sky. I dip my head down to look out through untinted glass; it's really only a flat, light blue sky; a painted sky like California.

The waiter comes back with my breakfast. He hooks it on back of the seat in front of me and it costs three hundred pesetas. I give him a fifty-peseta tip, get him on my side. They're bound to find me out.

I eat heartily. The train's vibrating some now; tiny little circular ripples in my coffee cup. The real conductor has started at the head of our car and is looking at tickets. I try concentrating on my reading again. I put my little packet with passport and pass on the tray beside my eggs. He backs his way to me; has a nice little word or two for each passenger. I can't see his face yet but he has a mean-looking back. He makes clicking sounds as he punches holes in tickets. Some of those tickets are two yards long. Maybe I ought to just say I lost my ticket and pay. Hell, I can't. I don't have that much money with me. I'm never going to get back home. Courage, Scum, old boy; hang in there.

I put on my best smile when he stops beside me. I pretend I'm holding the coffee down while I hand up the ticket. He takes it and looks, really looks. He turns it over, looks inside. I'm dead! I concentrate harder on the coffee. Actually, I'm holding myself from bolting down the length of that train, taking over the engine and driving us back to France.

"Señor," says he, smiling, leaning over, still being nice, pointing at the date on the inside, "*no es bueno.*"

He's got me. I pretend I don't understand. Something inside me is turning to ice. I take the pass from him and look at it. I try acting as if it's *his* pass and I'm giving it the final once-over. He stands there. I stare at the pass: really crappy-looking. I turn it over, answer him in English.

"*No comprendo,*" says he.

"You don't speak English on an international train?" says I, in English, putting on the outraged face. I'm getting into the feel of things.

"I want to speak with someone who understands English."

I put the pass in my passport. I slip both into my pocket. He stares at me.

"*No es bueno, Señor,*" he repeats. Probably a very nice guy just doing his job.

A fat, tan, bald Spaniard leans across the aisle; very prosperous-looking.

"He says your ticket is not good, Señor."

He speaks slightly accented, money-thick, English English.

"Thank you, Señor," I say, and wish him right on through the window into the bushes whooshing by.

I take the ticket out again. I remember then that there's something in small-print English on the back about this ticket being refunded except for ten percent if it's surrendered within the year. The stamp is within the year, just, but within, I point out this line to the conductor. Naturally he doesn't understand. I share it with my unwelcome benefactor across the aisle. He says something to the conductor about one year. The conductor glares down at me and gives me back my pass.

Then he goes for the fat guy's ticket. This is at least three yards long and in four different colors. What a terrific chance to wield the old ticket punch. Punch-punch-punch-punch-punch, Technicolor snow, little round bits drifting to the floor of the train.

I *know* I get by on the impressiveness of that bald, tan Spaniard's ticket. But I'm not sure I'm actually through yet; the conductor could come back with reinforcements, maybe a translator. Every stop till Madrid, I expect *guardia civil* to step on the train and pull me off. They stare into the windows with their submachine guns looking for me. I hide behind *Borstal Boy.* I don't really want jail again: *doing* time is losing it. Kate's right; an old guy like me, getting close to retirement age, shouldn't be sweating this kind of hassle. I'm past the end of a part of my life, a good part, but I can't get my head to live with it. That's the trouble with having too good a life.

THE DIVIDING LINE IS SO FINE, SO
HARD TO SEE, NOT BETWEEN LIFE AND
DEATH; THAT'S EASY; BUT BETWEEN
LIVING AND NOT; THAT'S HARD.

We roll into Madrid about two o'clock. I stay in mid-crowd getting off the train. They're not going to open fire into a crowd. There are no *guardia civil* at the door, nobody on the platform. I duck out the train station and jump into a taxi.

"Prado, *por favor!*" I look out the back window. Nobody. "You made it again, Scum; you lucky bastard!"

The taxi takes off madly, swerving around streetcars, between bare, peeling, new apartment buildings set right down in red dirt. It looks like somebody's badly worked out dream. I figure I should have two hours in the Prado before they close. I haven't been there in five years; that's five years without Goya, Velásquez, Bosch. You really only find these babies in the Prado; I'm hungry for them. Maybe I'll find the old spark in the dark moldy corners of this Spanish palace for kings.

Two hours later, I come out depressed as hell. There's Goya taking all his talent, his fantasy, to design tapestries for the king's slop room. He's frantically painting Cheshire-cat grins on the faces of Bourbons, trying to hide the mad ball-twisting minds behind painted masks and not quite making it. And then the violent deaf madness he painted for himself in his own dining room; more agony than any man should have to live with. There he was, a genius of his time, lackey to a packet of morons.

Velásquez, same thing. How he must've despised those vacuous Hapsburg blue eyes and equine lantern jaws. I'll bet he could paint them blindfolded: acres of stupid-looking little girls, bare open spaces between their eyes; each little ribbon and frill painted carefully in place.

And how many horses' asses did Velásquez paint? Not just the kings, or queens; *real* horses' asses Velásquez, master of the horse's ass. Something true he could paint. There's great love when he attaches the strong muscle of a tail; luxurious flow of tail hairs barely hiding private parts. He stroked those tremendous bulging muscles into life, carefully modulating surfaces of burnt sienna and yellow ochre. Pure mastery.

Such beautiful painting, such a tremendous person. He's the one who did the painting of the princess with the dwarf. The dwarf has his foot on a giant dog in the foreground. I can hear the king telling Velásquez what to do.

"Diego, I want this big painting for that space over between those windows. I want little Theresa here in front, with her maids dressing her. Use the new dress we just got from Paris, put in all the details. Beside her I want old Jocko, the dwarf, with this here gun I got from the Pope and with one foot up on the dog like he just shot it. The Queen of England gave me that dog; sort of symbolic, you know. Got that?

"Then, off in the back, I want an open door, and, standing with light coming in behind us, I want me and the wife, as if we just came in unexpectedly on this nice domestic scene. You know what I mean, Diego? You could even paint yourself in the corner, not blocking anything but real natural-like; maybe you could be painting this picture in the painting. Get it? You do this right, Diego, and I'll order three, one for the Queen of England and one for the Pope. Show them how much we like the things they gave us. Be good for diplomatic relations. Stick with me, Diego, you'll be an international star."

So there it is in the Prado, with a big whorey mirror on the other wall to show all the people what it really looked like because Velásquez was painting in a mirror. He had to be; he's in the picture himself, right? One good thing about being a painter is you usually die before you see what some moronic museum director is going to do with your work.

Then, there's Hieronymus Bosch painting wet dreams for the monks. Only a very sane man could have painted those things. He sure knew the sick mind inside and out. A real sick mind only knows the inside; can't write or paint or anything about it, just lives it. Bosch flowed this specially canned erotica for the religious. Holy heaven, but he knew his clientele.

"Put down your whip, Brother Adrian, take off your hair shirt, Brother Damien, drop your cock, Brother Xavier; come see what Jerry's painted for us this time—a real tribute to the marvels of God's will."

Shock, wiggling and giggling.

"Oh, you nasty thing, Jerry. Look, teeheeheehee, that one's got flowers growing out of his seater. Teeheeheeheehee!"

One crappy way to make a living. Imagine, this impressive mind with his magnificent skills doing a medieval version of *Playboy.* Freud, Jung—all those guys were only playing games compared to Bosch. It could make a person vomit, the kinds of things an artist has to do, just getting by. And nothing seems to change. All the L.A. and New York artists are doing the same thing, only instead of brownnosing kings and queens, it's a bunch of rich widows and bored daughters to rich millionaire crooks. These gals open galleries as happy hunting grounds and the artists are their pimps.

Now, I know I'm putting all this down a bit hard up there, but it's the way I'm thinking when I come out of the Prado. I have stupid missionary feelings about painting and it breaks my heart seeing this kind of sacrilege.

I mope across the street and sit in a chair along a wide boulevard. I drink a Spanish version of absinthe, hoping it will make the heart grow fonder. The train for Málaga is at ten o'clock. I figure the night train is best: flash my pass in the dark. I'll even try turning the light down in the compartment, not enough so the conductor will notice, just enough to blend out my blotchy pass.

I watch people walking past. There are tiny women all dressed up, flicking their asses around, and tiny men larking along behind them. Beautiful to watch. They're all so small. The farther south you go, the bigger you get, like Gulliver.

I catch the train and there are two other people in the compartment. The whole train's crowded. One guy has a big black hard cardboard sample case. It fills up the knee space completely. The conductor comes in, switches on the bright lights, looks at my pass then gives it back without a word. I can put up with a lot of discomfort.

I go to sleep and don't wake till we're coming down out of the mountains onto the coastal plain. It's like early summer here: everything green, trees in flower. I climb over the snoring bastard with the suitcase; he sleeps, his nose tucked under a fedora hat.

Out in the corridor, I wait in line to take my morning crap. There are four ahead of me, two women. Each takes too long for just a piss; the Spanish must be regular. The john smells like Spain already; cold air blows up the hole. I look down at the railroad ties whizzing by but can't make it. I've been having troubles that way—not like me at all. By nature, I'm more the diarrhea type.

I go out and stand in the corridor to watch the scenery. Small white adobe houses are in clusters along the track and up sides of hills. People stop work to watch us go by.

I get off in Málaga and take a bus to Torremolinos. When Kate and I first came here, this was a town with two bars and a bodega; now it's Babylon, an incredible mixture of Moorish and Nordic. The whole place a kind of Stockholm or Essen transplanted into the sun. Long-legged blondes in bright colors and tight jeans march to the hard thumping beat of flamenco and tiny Spanish men. Pure heaven for everybody; the Mediterranean shimmering just down winding steps from the village.

I walk through town and out the road toward Benalmádena. Sture and Annastina Dahlstrom live about two miles up this dirt road into the mountains. I know I can find their place by gigantic palm trees Sture stole from the botanical gardens in Málaga.

He and his eldest son, Per, drove up in work suits and started digging. It took all day; people stood around and watched but nobody stopped them. They hoisted the trees on top of their old Volvo station wagon and drove off up into the hills with palm fronds dragging the ground behind them; planted the trees in their front yard. Sture says the average Swede has a soft spot in his heart for palm trees; part of the great tropical dream for the frozen ones.

WE DECORATE OUR INNER SCENERY
WITH DREAMS: MOSSES, FERNS AND
OTHER TENDER SUNLESS GREENERY.

I get to their place; knock on the door. Nobody comes. I peer into a window. Annastina is peering out at me. Both Sture and Anna are paranoid, convinced the world is trying to get them—probably true.

Annastina throws open the door talking Swedish, little bubbles and all. She puts her strong arms around me; that I understand. I lift her off the ground; surprisingly light for a strong, tall woman. She hasn't changed at all, even more beautiful. Sture comes around from back. We grab one another by the shoulders and hop in circles, shouting, hollering and shaking hands. We poop ourselves out, both breathing hard; like some kind of sumo wrestling match—too much for a pair of old guys.

They switch into English. Both speak English fluently with a lilting singing accent. Sture even *writes* in English sometimes. I call it Swinglish; he makes up words that ought to be there, carves them out of Swedish words curved to sound like English—lovely words.

Inside, they give me some of their presweetened coffee; it's always brewing on the back burner. I tell them how everybody is, except me. They tell me about their kids. We pause; they're waiting. What the hell am I doing all the way down in Spain? I don't want to tell them yet. They aren't pressing, know it will come.

I could actually stay a week and go back without saying a word. These people know what privacy means. My experience is the only people who respect privacy are those who want it for themselves. Most people can't even understand the idea, want to live in beehives under spotlights on TV. Annastina's getting a bed ready for me; no question about my staying.

A PLACE WHERE YOU ARE IN
OTHERS' HEARTS, WHERE YOU BELONG
NO MATTER HOW LONG YOU'VE BEEN GONE.

Then, right off, before I know what I'm doing, I'm into my whole tale of woe with Sture. He listens, bright blue eyes hooded with fine red eyelashes; thin lips smothered in bushes of red beard. He's hmming and uhhuhing in Swinglish. Annastina's listening from the kitchen. She comes in now and then to cock her head and listen closer. Sometimes she shakes her head up and down so hard her hair bounces. I can feel the confusion melting off me as I talk. I'm having a hard time reminding myself why I came. I know I still don't actually want to paint, but it doesn't matter so much. Finally I wind it up.

LETTING LOOSE, TEETH OUT, HAIR DOWN;
MUD SLIDING GENTLY ACROSS A GRANITE FACE.

Sture leans forward.

"And that's it?"

I nod.

"You're just full of *shit,* man!"

I stare at him; it's not what I expected.

"You've got a galloping case of artist's constipation!"

Annastina leans over close to me, takes me in her arms, kisses my bald head.

"He forgot to hold out his cup, Sture, darling. He smells like someone who's been reaching."

They nod together, hair and beard shaking. I feel my bowels turning over. What a hell of a time to have to take a crap.

I know they're right. Everything's seemed full of shit lately. Here I am, me the old genital gentle gentile, reverting. I'm trying to listen but the pressure is building up. I'm bent over, holding off cramps. I can feel myself sweating. Sture stares at me.

"You sick or something?"

I break out in a smile; it spreads so wide across my face I can hardly get my mouth around it. I stand up bent over.

"No, Sture, just full of shit; please tell me in a hurry, where's the crapper around here!"

We start laughing. I laugh so hard I can hardly hold it in. I'm in misery and laughing to kill myself. I'm going to have a hateal fart attack. Annastina takes me by the arm and leads me, bent over, to the bathroom; pushes me in.

I just about get my pants down. Bam, splash, whoosh, fizz, bam, splash. I'm falling apart. Sture and Annastina are laughing outside. I'm sure people can hear me in Torremolinos, think they're having an earthquake, *terremoto.* I'm afraid I've cracked the toilet bowl at least.

The storm is finally over. I stand up; feel weak. It looks like a bucket of black snakes in there, purple black. I can't believe all that was inside me. And, Lord, it stinks to hell. I push open a window. Flush. Let the tank fill up; flush again. The water's still brown. I feel a thousand percent better already; probably all this agonizing was only something not ticking with my tired gall bladder. There's enough bile in that bowl for two or three years.

I hang around in their bathroom, half fainting from the smell, waiting till it gets better. I'm afraid if I open the door they'll need to have the whole house fumigated, repainted. I'd expect the paint would peel off the walls. Speaking of walls, I haven't even looked at Annastina's new work. I walked right in, saw there were new paintings and started with my private bitch. I was sick all right.

I go out. They're both backing off with bandanas wrapped around their faces, looking like the James brothers, laughing. I tell them about the black snakes in the bowl. Sture says he'll sue me if they block his septic tank; most likely poison his fermentation.

"Built-up artist constipation like that, concentrated shit from paintings not painted, books not written, is the most corrosive, destructive matter known to man. Just look at Adolf Hitler."

PLUGGED UP, MY LUG WRENCHES RUSTED:
STREAMS DAMNED AND DAMMED, PATHS BLOCKED:
I WIND AGAIN MY BROKEN CLOCKS.

We talk for two days. We talk about Annastina's paintings, which are wonderful. Anna was blind for two years after an attack of spinal meningitis. During that time, she experienced other worlds, other beings. When she miraculously got her sight back, she started painting what she'd seen, what she could remember. She's deep inside herself and won't talk about it. She'll only paint it; lets me talk. Me, the big talker, turned on; just imagine.

Then we get on Sture's new book. It's about a guy who sets up an élite artificial-insemination business for wives of sterile or impotent men. He advertises his stable of human stallions; makes up all kinds of imaginative stuff about their being from the best bloodlines: generals, leaders, athletes—no artists, sculptors, writers. Actually, he's the whole stable himself, dresses differently for each situation. He's written some of the funniest seduction scenes I've ever read. Of course, nothing will do for the anesthetic but champagne. For the insemination he talks about direct versus indirect transportation; recommends direct as more practical, most sure. I read it that night in bed: hilarious. For a man, there's probably nothing better than laughing with a hard-on.

Next day, I keep asking for reasons why I should paint. It gets to be the big joke. No matter what they say, I answer, "Not good enough."

NOTHING MATTERS AND
MATTER'S NOTHING.

The third morning when I wake up, Annastina is sitting in the coolish kitchen. Sture's down milking the goat.

She looks up at me when I come in, stays sitting at the table.

"I know why you should paint."

She's serious; measuring me with her glacier eyes, not glacial; glacier, big, wide, deep and so cold they're warm from strong inside pressures.

"It is because you're a Saturn man; Kronos, child of Uranus. That's why you get so full of shit, why you can have black moods, black bile. That's why you get so worried about time; Kronos is almost the same as the Greek word *chronos,* for time. You're the sower, the nester, eating his own children, your paintings, so a god can be produced. You sow madness, genius and suicide; that's the way you are, an old-style artist, out of the ancient past, a shadow of our ancestors."

She's staring right through me, seeing my innermost parts at the same time not seeing me, seeing something else.

"But that's not all of it either. Sure; Scum, you must paint because it's your life, what you *must* do, what you are. Painting *is* you; you are your paintings."

I look at her, shock leaking out of my eyes. She's

right. That's good enough. I was even coming to it myself. Almost everybody has nothing inside or they don't know how to get at it. They need to scramble for outside things like money or status to keep from thinking, staring into some black hole. Anybody with something welling up from inside should grab on to it.

Forget the society, time, immortality, the perfect painting, aesthetics, birth, creation, ethics, making a million bucks. Balls, ovaries, scrotums, fallopian tubes to all that. I'll keep on painting for the sheer hell of it, because it's what my life is.

When Sture comes in, we're drinking the coffee with dollops of Spanish cognac in it. Tastes terrible. We all get hysterical, start dancing around in the garden, between rows of new-grown corn, holding our cups high, shouting to the gods.

XIII

WOMAN TO WOMAN

By Thursday, I feel Anna and Sture are ready to get on with their work. I'm also interested in seeing if the Paris contingent has actually made it down from the frozen north. Much to Anna and Sture's consternation, I've been sunning in their garden. They're convinced sun causes cancer and melting of brain cells.

After breakfast I tell them I'm going into town, that some friends from Paris might arrive and I could stay with them for a while. I leave my stuff there with them, figuring I'll be back that evening, but tell them not to worry if I don't make it till the next day. Anna gives me a look, but I know they're both more than ready to get back to work; playtime is over.

It's about half an hour's walk along the dusty twisting road. The smells of spring flowers, dust, and of sewers not quite functioning, come to me as I work my way downhill. I cross the main *carretero* and head for that Bar Central. Kate and I used to enjoy ourselves here in the old days when we'd come for winter sun. That was before kids' schooling got in the way of our lives. We taught them ourselves then.

The bar hasn't changed much. The awnings are rolled back and it's a beautiful day. I go down a few steps and find a sunny table sheltered from the slight breeze. It isn't a swimming day yet, but it could be by two o'clock for anyone who doesn't mind water under sixty degrees Fahrenheit, and I don't. I actually prefer it.

It's nine-thirty when I settle in for my wait. I'm not exactly waiting, because I'm sure there's no chance they'll try such a long trip. Crazy they are, but not that crazy. I order a glass of white wine, some tapas, then slouch down and try pretending I'm Spanish, watching all the pretty Nordic girls parade by.

At half past eleven I'm ready to pay my bill and take a walk down the *bajandillo* along the beach, when sure enough, here they come, cruising up on those two motorcycles with the girls behind them. They're covered with dust and look like the first WW II German motorcycle patrols rolling into Paris: the marauding huns.

They have sleeping bags and mounds of junk piled up behind them. Lubar stops, and flips up his goggles. He's sand-dirt brown all over except for his eyes and these're rimmed white from his goggles, pale blue-gray bird eyes staring out and smiling, glistening at me.

Sweik stops behind him, unhooks his helmet and turns off his motor. Sandy is waving crazily, and, just as I figured, smiling. She pushes her hand on Sweik's shoulder to swing her leg up and over the pile stacked behind her. It's hard to believe they ever got through those mountains with all that weight. She jumps down, brushes her pants.

"Well, here's the old man himself. I bet he never thought we'd make it."

She vaults the low wall, comes over, plants a nice open, thin-lipped, cool kiss on my mouth. The whole terrace is watching. This is a place to watch from and here's something worth watching.

I'm really glad to see they're not spread over a mountain pass somewhere, sanded down to bloody stumps and human hamburger. Lubar's got his bike pulled up on its stand and helps Dale off. She stumbles when she tries to walk. I don't know if it's because her legs are asleep or she's still that scared.

I'm also not so sure they can actually park the bikes right here; the bus pulls in from Málaga almost every half hour and the bikes are blocking the bus stop totally. Some *guardia civil* with a Thompson machine gun will come over and get them to move soon enough.

I stand and shake hands with Lubar, then Sweik. We pound each other on the back, man-style, but nothing like the crazy dance Sture and I did. Dale gives me a hug and sisterly kiss. She's cold and her whole body's shaking, even her hands. When I hold them, they seem to give off vibrations like touching a low-voltage wire, something around six or twelve volts and low ampere; it's a physical hum.

We sit in the sun. Lubar's proud as a peacock; it's as if he's hauled them over the whole trip himself. He spreads his legs and scrunches down in the chair. I order Spanish cognac and tapas around. They all look as if some kind of pick-me-up might help. Sweik has his jacket open, his shirt top button's open and he's tilting his face up to the sun.

"Do you know anybody wants to buy a perfectly wonderful 1950 Ariel? I love that machine but I'll never get it all the way back over those hills to Paris again."

Lubar straightens. The drinks and tapas arrive. He takes a sip of the cognac.

"Come on, Sweik; it wasn't that bad. OK, so you swung out on that curve between Burgos and Madrid trying to avoid a pothole, but that could've happened anywhere. We have worse holes than that on the Connecticut Thruway back home."

"Let me tell you something, Lubar: this last stretch from Cordova, over those mountains down to Málaga, was more than I can ever manage again. You've got a low center of gravity on that monster of yours, but each of those curves was a life-and-death affair for us. I'm pooped, and my back hurts. I'd be better off *walking* home."

Sandy and Dale are sitting next to each other. Sandy puts her arm over the back of Dale's chair, looks over at Sweik.

"Honest, man, I could ride like that the rest of my life; but I'm sure as hell glad I didn't know you were scared. Matt, I thought you were in full control the whole way."

Sweik smiles.

"About twice there, Sandy, I was ready to give you the choice of getting off and hitchhiking or else letting me show you how to drive the damned bike and *I'd* hitch. Or maybe I'd move into one of those little towns with the orange trees and settle for life. God, I was tired *and* scared. That is one miserable combination."

I know Sweik. He's exaggerating some but he's talking truth. I'm glad I wasn't with them; the whole phony Eurail thing was bad but it wasn't life and death.

We order another round of drinks. The plan is, they're going to spend a few days lolling around on the beaches. They're even hoping to find someplace down there to sleep. After that, Lubar wants to explore the foothills just in from the coast. Sweik has entirely other things in mind.

"Listen, Lubar, I'm not going anywhere. I just want to

sack out in this sun. I've had enough bike riding for at least a year; my rear end's so sore it feels as if I'm sitting on one giant festering boil."

He shifts back and forth from one haunch to the other in the chair. I tell them about some caves I know cut under a promontory sticking out into the sea between Torremolinos and Carregheula. In the old days, there used to be a wonderful simple old-fashioned hotel built on top called the Santa Clara. Now the point's been developed with fancy motels and condominiums. Still, some of those old caves might be left, and it's right next to the best, most protected beach around.

I show them how to get the motorcycles as near to the beach as possible. We make arrangements at a small hotel down there in the *bajandillo,* where the original village was, to keep the bikes behind the hotel, against a stone hill, almost a cliff. There are still some simple fishermen living here but mostly it's taken up with bars, fancy pensions or small hotels.

We slog across the beach and, sure enough, even though the beach is cleaner than I remember, more tended, cared for—with even some beach umbrellas and beach chairs to rent—those old caves are still there. They smell damp, with an aroma of piss and shit, but not too bad. Everybody seems happy with the spot but we can't leave the bags and things here; they'll get stolen for sure; also the local *guardia civil* would be tipped off.

We go back up to the hotel where we're keeping the bikes. It's a place called Casa Suezia. I try negotiating for a place to store the bags and stuff.

This is a bit too much for the hotel man, but he finally agrees to let us store in a small room he'll rent me for only ten dollars a night. I'm eager to get out from under the feet of Sture and Anna, I'm beginning to get a slight whiff of three-day-old fish, so I say I'll take it. I'm not about to sleep on the beach, but after the mob's come all the way down, I want to spend some time with them.

Everybody agrees to pitch in a buck a night, so it's only costing me six, a good deal for everybody. Then too, they'll have a place to come for a wash-up, or shit, or whatever, and to change.

Sweik suggests we head back to the beach. The

Casa Suezia is built as little cabañas piled helter-skelter, one on top of the other, at all angles, with courtyards where you wouldn't expect them. There's a small deck on top of our room where I can see miles up and down the coast.

Dale and Sandy change first; then we do. We descend some steps to a small street running along the beach. I'm wearing my bathing suit as underwear, because I was heading for the beach anyway, even if they didn't come. I have a towel, too. Sandy and Dale carry along their sleeping bags to open up on the sand. Sandy's wearing a red bikini and has a lovely body. It's nice seeing an American girl without wobble ass and cottage-cheese legs. She's been living away from TV and cheap ice cream long enough, I guess. She's satin smooth, practically hairless, no sign of shaving and already the beginning of a good tan from somewhere. She's probably been sunbathing during the trip down. Whatever it is, she's a wonderful sight; I'd only seen her in jeans before. My old-fashioned dirty old mind would love seeing her in a skirt with stockings and medium-high heels, all the trimmings.

We decide on a place close to the water, just over the tidal hump. There are very few people at the beach, though it's definitely warming up to a sunbathing day. The little breeze has either died down or is blocked by the projecting promontory. Sandy spreads her sleeping bag, opened out, and invites me to share it with her. I'm feeling very saggy-fleshed; I look at my wrinkling flab in contrast to these young people; takes getting used to.

Dale has her bag opened and the other three settle on it. I'm being treated to some kind of special "daddyo" treatment, maybe because I put out for the room. It's uncomfortable, but then that's where I am in life, uncomfortable. None of these young people, except maybe Lubar, can be even half my age; I'm older than most of their parents. It's hard to believe sometimes; how did it happen? I stretch out, close my eyes, feel the sun and pretend I'm only forty.

It's revitalizing; hot sun is beating on my eyelids, the heat sinks into me. I hear, feel, Sandy turn over. She puts her arm across my chest. I'm surprised, pleased, but it's within the range of "daddyoness." God, I could probably be her grandfather or great-uncle; she can't be much more than twenty. I stretch out, let myself absorb the perfume of her, her body, her hair. I *think* too goddamned much.

Then she starts working one cool little finger round one of my nipples, gently pushing aside the hair and baring it, lightly turning round and round, bringing it up, making it hard. I feel a tingling, almost electric sensation behind my ear on that side. Wow, this is more than playing up to daddyo; she's playing with *me*; playing with the old Scumbler bod; Holy Moses, save me! What could be bringing this on? I snatch a quick look to see if the others are watching. They're not noticing.

I turn my head and look at Sandy; she has her eyes open, staring into me; she smiles a pseudo-Greek archaic smile, a slight momentary turning up of her lips. She winks slowly, then closes both eyes, making me feel as if I've gone blind. What the hell's going on? Is she just practicing nipple diddling to help her get Dale back?

She shifts her finger to the other nipple, softly pushing away the hair again, starting the slow turning of her finger, her nail-bitten finger around the small inadequate volcano tip of my old brown nipple.

BANKED FIRES, INTEREST FREE,
THE TIGHT HEDGE OF BANKRUPTCY.

Watch out, Scum! You get into something like this and it can blow up your whole life. You can't move in and out of feelings the way young people can.

I don't think I ever could. And, in the end, I'm the one who's going to get hurt, along with a whole clutch of fine people I love.

If I lose this nest, that's the end of me. The first time almost did me in; I got so I didn't care about anything: life, painting, loving; none of it made sense.

BEYOND WORDS, A GULF
OF EMPTINESS UNBRIDLED.

Poor Jane just couldn't handle having a draft-dodging jailbird for a husband. And I could never make her understand *my* feelings either. I believed, and still believe, that in time of danger a father should be home protecting his children, not off killing strangers, maybe even fathers to other children.

So they put me in jail. I found myself in jail with a passel of guys who *wanted* to kill people, some of them already had. Some of them definitely wanted to kill *me,* the Jap and Nazi lover. I still don't know how I got through those first six months. Just going to the cafeteria and eating was a very dangerous business.

So Jane got her divorce, our house and total custody of our kids without any question. I wasn't even allowed to write, let alone visit when I got out. It's then I found out fathers *aren't* real parents; society only allows them to pretend; that is, if they do as they are told.

WITHOUT A SENSE OF PLACE, WE CAN'T
FACE CHANGE: TIME, LIFE, DEATH, BIRTH.

Lubar goes up into town to buy beer and sandwiches. He's the only one of us not in a bathing suit. He's stripped to Levi's and they're rolled up over his knees. Even with all the biking, he still isn't tan at all, only pink and peeling. For someone like him, the Sture and Anna theory is probably right: he *should* stay out of the sun.

When he comes back, he says his asthma's acting up, so I show him how to do a Yoga shoulder stand; it seems to help. The rest of the day, whenever he starts sneezing or coughing, he's up on his shoulders in the sand.

After we eat, I stretch out again. I think Sweik actually goes to sleep; at least he's lightly snoring. That trip on his bike must have been hell. Sandy cuddles up next to me. I don't know how to handle this; I'm excited but I'm scared; I'm also not sure if she's making fun of me to give the others a laugh.

She reaches down, takes my hand, pulls it under her and inside the top of her bikini. I feel her hard little nipple with my pinkie. She's on her stomach and lifts slightly on her elbows so I have rubbing room.

Hell, this is the Scumbler and we're in Spain! I look around; nobody's noticing but I'm getting hot and sweaty over nothing. I struggle myself up and pull Sandy with me. We walk down to the water and she keeps hold of my hand. It's glaring hot now, almost's hot as summer, and biting clear.

The water pushes loose stones around. We walk in carefully; the water's cold but not impossible. I take a flop into the shallows and Sandy comes in behind me. After the first shock, it's wonderful.

I strike out with my modified Australian crawl; I'm not much of a swimmer. Sandy's in and out of the water like a dolphin, the water making her shine as if she's been varnished. She doesn't swim much on top but is constantly ducking under, twisting, turning, rolling, almost like dancing. The water's so clear I can easily see my shadow on the bottom and it must be twenty feet deep already. Sandy's hair's cut short and she has a small head, small features, a tight, light body. I roll over on my back, back-paddle and enjoy watching her.

She swims toward me, little bubbles coming out of her mouth, just a foot underwater. She swims right on top of me, pushes my head under and grasps my head by both ears, then plants, digs, a kiss in my mouth underwater!

It's a very salty affair; I come up coughing, gasping for air. We tread water, face to face; she's laughing, taking water in her mouth and spouting onto me. Sandy's a dolphin all right, somehow got caught up on land. Gradually I recover; she's swimming around me as I turn to keep her in view; I don't want to be ducked again.

She goes underwater, swims toward me; then, Mother of God, she reaches her hand inside my bathing suit. She finds it, not that hard to find; hard, even in this coldish water, but easy to find if you look in the right place. I keep treading water, trying not to drown.

She holds on, pulling me along behind and beside her. She's towing me, like a tug, laughing all the time, turning and flipping hair, water out of her eyes, spouting at me. I'm beginning to think she'll pull me out by the roots; my roots are kind of loose as it is.

When, finally, she lets go, I tuck the rubbery old hose carefully back in my trunks and spout once or twice at her. She begins swimming away. We're about thirty yards out from shore. I switch to my usual dependable but slow sidestroke and swim along behind her. I didn't know hands could shake uncontrollably in the water.

I'm definitely not fish, not even reptile. But Sandy's doing everything: crawl, backstroke, breaststroke, underwater, overwater, butterfly; she keeps waiting up for me. But I'm never going to catch her, I'm totally pooped. I start swimming toward the beach before I sink. Sandy turns in and races, a quick neat crawl, ahead of me.

She stands at the edge of the water with hands on hips. I float to her, belly down like a piece of flotsam or jetsam, more flotsam. I crawl on my hands and knees, potbelly sagging, blubber, a beached whale. We get to laughing and giggling so I can hardly stand up. Sandy gives me a hand, then practically hauls me up the beach.

. . .

It takes ten minutes to get my wind back, and she's not even breathing hard; holy death, the worst disease known to man is time; absolutely terminal; but then, without it, there doesn't seem to be anything else. And there's not much of it left for me, not much chance to play with a lovely young creature like Sandy; I should make the most of it but I won't.

DRIFTING SEEDS, LIKE DANDELION FEATHERS:
MEN FLOAT, SLIP, AIMLESSLY TO EARTH.

The next day, while everybody goes into Málaga to buy bullfight tickets, I walk back up into the foothills to Sture and Anna's house. I tell them my friends have arrived from Paris after all, and we're staying at the Casa Suezia. Anna throws back her head and laughs.

"Moving from one Swedish house to the other, huh? Have you got a pretty young Swedish girl down there to keep you warm nights? What's the matter, tired of us old folks?"

I'm not one of the world's best blushers, but I blush. I can feel it spreading out from behind my eyes. They both laugh. I tell how I've taken a room and the others are storing their stuff in it, sleeping inside the caves down by the beach. Sture's shocked.

"You mean in those stinking shit holes down there? God, I wouldn't even take a piss on one of those places, let alone sleep."

Sture's staring in my eyes, amazement clouding his face. I smile.

"Sture, let me tell you; that air smells good after the car pollution of Paris. But don't worry, I'm not sleeping there myself. I'm too old for that."

"No, he's sleeping in a soft Swedish bed with a nice young lady from Malmö or Stockholm, aren't you now?"

"That'd be nice, Anna, but I'm too afraid. And, besides, Kate would kill me."

LAST LAMENTS TO A TORMENT OF DESIRE.
YESTERDAY'S FIRES STILL ASH WARM.

I pack my things and promise I'll stop back before I leave. I've interrupted their work; Anna has on her smock and Sture was typing when I walked in. They're so incredibly kind and, at the same time, involved with their work, interesting, it's an almost impossible combination.

I carry my light bag down to our hotel. The gang won't be back yet but the sun is high. I put on my bathing suit, get my towel and then head for the beach. It's hard to believe it's still dark and gray in Paris, that the leaves aren't even showing green on the trees. I walk along the *bajandillo* and listen to a woman singing flamenco out one window and Frank Sinatra singing "Chicago" through a radio out another.

I find a spot, spread my towel and flop out on it. I must drop right off to sleep, because the next thing I know, I feel something on the bottom of my feet; it's Sandy tickling me. The rest are settling in and are dressed for the beach, except Lubar. I'd left the key under the doormat at our hotel room. Sweik is walking back up from the water; his hands and feet are wet.

"That's *cold,* man. I don't know how you two could take it yesterday. By the way, we got some good tickets for the bullfight tomorrow; they're in the sun close down to the barrios."

I hope they didn't get one for me, but I'm sure they did. OK, I'll give it one more try.

They've brought back baskets of food from Málaga; they shopped in the big open market there. There's bread, cheese, tomatoes, lettuce, apples, oranges. We make ourselves quite a meal. Then we spend the rest of the afternoon sopping up that sun. Lubar rigs a kind of football by rolling his T-shirt in his belt and he plays catch with Sweik and Dale.

Sandy doesn't make any overt moves but by some general understanding we're together; Sweik's backed out of the whole thing, the way he did with Lotte.

I can't tell what Sandy's thinking but she gives me a couple of long looks; she's probably wondering why I didn't invite her to share that nice bed in the hotel last night. Maybe she isn't thinking that at all; this could only be my worry.

We go bar hopping in the evening and end up eating pizza at an Italian place. It's the cheapest and best-looking deal in town. The Spanish cognac is cheap, too, and we all drink more than we should; nobody's weaving drunk but we're louder. We walk down to the *bajandillo* roaring off a chorus of Lubar's fucking-machine song. I don't know if there are that many real lyrics or if Lubar makes them up as he goes along; maybe he made up the whole song.

They pick up their things at the hotel room and head out. I'm pooped. The last to leave is Sandy. She turns as she goes out the door and gives me another long look. Gosh, a young, easy-moving girl like her can make a man my age feel old; it's cruel. But then I *am* old; what the hell.

A BOUNCE IN GRACE, A FLOUNCING OF
THE NATURAL; WITHOUT A TRACE.

The hotel has a small red neon sign outside the window. I can just pick up the change in color against a whitewashed wall as it flashes on and off. One minute in my imagination I see us, red devils, slipping over each other; next it's dark, green-dark in after-color. It's like a 1920 porno movie or the kind you turn yourself in an old-time penny arcade. I make it go slow, sometimes, then fast; I begin to think I'll never get to sleep.

I'm almost wishing they hadn't come down; it's pushing things for me. I'm only just coming out of a deep hole and I can't take this kind of excitement. I'm feeling fragile and this is edging the blood pressure up for sure, going to blow out those retinas. Hell, I'm a painter and I'm missing work time. That's the real world for me; this one's too much. Finally, I manage a dry, restless, thin-eyed sleep.

SLEEP WITHOUT REST, DREAMS
THAT TIRE: AT BEST: STILLNESS.

Next day, we beach in the morning. Sure enough, they've bought a ticket for me and they won't even let me pay for it—definitely some more "daddyo" treatment. They're going in on the bikes but I'll take the bus.

Sandy volunteers to bus it with me, keep me company. Sweik isn't exactly fighting the idea; it can't be much fun having somebody high up over your shoulder like that while threading your way along a crowded Spanish road, past donkey carts and huge trucks.

During the bus ride, Sandy slips her hand into mine and pulls it onto her lap. It's a wonderful, calm, almost warm, sunny afternoon. The sun comes through the bus window and warms my hand there between her legs. I'm feeling shy somehow, afraid to look in her eyes.

She's wearing a dress and sandals, almost as if she'd read my mind. Why should that be more sexy than jeans? I don't know; maybe, just as with everyone, I'm caught up in my own past, old hang-ups. But it feels wonderful having her dry, coolish thumb caressing me slowly in the joint between my thumb and palm. The dress she's wearing is soft, silky, one of those dresses you just twist and pack so it comes out wrinkled in one direction and looks as if it's supposed to be that way. I can feel her thighs; hard, slippery under the cloth; no slip.

We find the bullring; the others are waiting at the entrance gate for us. They're excited by the crowd, the sounds, the street vendors, the prospect of the corrida. Sweik says it's only a *novillada,* so it probably won't be the best of bullfighting, but he hasn't seen one in over two years so anything will do. Sandy's never seen one before and neither has Dale. I think they're somewhat anxious. I know I am. My stomach's twisted, curled in knots.

I'm remembering the first bullfight I ever saw, where the ribs of the bullfighter were ripped out like a clamshell by a hooking horn. He kept trying to stand up, holding himself in, blood over everything, and the bull knocking him down time and again while the other bullfighters danced around yelling, waving capes, trying to catch the bull's attention.

Then, after they dragged the poor kid screaming out of the ring, they got an older bullfighter to kill the bull. He himself was just coming back from a bad goring, and was so scared he couldn't get the damned sword to stick in the bull's neck. He must have tried to stab it six times and the whole crowd was hollering and hooting, whistling, throwing paper and pillows into the ring. I walked out not knowing for whom I felt more sorry, the bull, the bullfighter or all the sad, hostile, hopelessly incapable men in the stands.

I read in the papers the boy died that night; he was nineteen years old. So I'm not looking forward to a bullfight, no sir.

"Sandy, I don't know whether I'll be able to make this. The last one I saw was awful. I couldn't eat meat for a week. I could hardly get anything at all to stay down, even chicken soup. So if I walk out, I'll wait for you outside by the gate or you can ride back with Sweik, OK?"

"OK. But wait for me, huh? I'd rather go home with you

on the bus. I'm not so hot with this kind of stuff either. Once I fainted at a boxing match on TV."

The seats are about twenty rows up and the sun's directly in our eyes. We're with the real Spanish fans. They're drinking beer or swigging wine, and most of them already seem half drunk. Sandy and Dale are some of the only women in this section.

I don't even like all the theater part of a bullfight: the trumpets, bugles, drums—everything they use to start it off. It sounds too much like sad, scared bragging to me, something close to Fourth of July military parades or the Anschluss. Then that first black bull comes tearing out of his gate, stops in the middle of the ring, lifts his head up and down, pawing the sand, so beautiful, so powerful, so dangerous.

After only the third pass, with the crowd already roaring quietly, I'm ready to go. I've put myself on the end seat and everybody's concentrated so I don't make much fuss. A few Spanish men give me disgusted looks. I guess it's like walking out with the count three and two on the first batter at a baseball game.

I'm glad to get down the worn, splintered wooden stairs and outside. Inside, there's music again and the crowd's undulating roar plays against it. This part reminds me of being late for an American football game and hurrying when you know that first big yell is the kickoff. Only this is the opposite; I'm running *away,* not rushing to get inside. Maybe I'm just too American to be a bullfight aficionado.

I find a seat in a small bar across the street and order a beer. Even the noise from here makes me nervous. After I've finished my beer, I might walk down to Málaga's botanical garden where the Dahlstroms stole their tree. The whole town is quiet except for the stadium. It's as if there's an execution going on and everybody's holding their breath. There is.

I sit there and wonder what happened in those bullfighters' lives or even the lives of these screaming people in the stands that didn't happen in mine so I'm out here drinking beer and they're in there enjoying a bull being killed.

I'm paying for my beer when I see Sandy come

out the gate. Two Spanish men who've been loitering at the door move toward her. I don't blame them; she looks tender and vulnerable in her dress, crossing that wide street in the bright sun. I wave but she's already seen me. There aren't many people except vendors; I'm the only one sitting at the café.

She runs across the street. There's something of a junior-high-school high jumper in the way she moves; when she runs, she lopes as if she's about to put all her force into one grand leap against the sky.

"Oh God, Scum! I couldn't handle that. I felt sorry for the bull, the bullfighter, then that whole damned crowd of horny, roaring men. Do you know what they do to that bull? And they use horses; I love horses."

"Yeah, I know. It worries me so many people enjoy that crap, Sandy. Sometimes I think they could want me to be the bull for them. They always ask men at one time or another to play bull or bullfighter. In a way, war is a gigantic bullfight, a phony proving ground for when people aren't sure of themselves. Watching a bullfight makes it hard to stay an optimist."

Sandy says she doesn't want a beer. I tell her about the botanical garden and she wants to go there.

"I need something clean and beautiful to get the feeling of sand, spit and blood out of me."

We walk hand in hand into Málaga. It's like a grandfather with his grown-up fifteen-year-old granddaughter. I could have a granddaughter this age by my first kids; maybe I do. It feels nice. We talk when we want but most of the time we don't; we only look at the flowers and enjoy the peace, the shade, the green of grass in this dry town.

CONTRAST IN TIME, TWO ENDS OF A DISTRIBUTION
MOVING TOWARD EACH OTHER, SLOWLY, HASTELESSLY,
WITHOUT WASTE: YET WE YEARN FOR RETRIBUTION.

When we get back to the bullring, the fights still aren't over. Sandy and I walk around the ring outside to the accompaniment of hysterical shouts, yells, moans, screams interspersed with music, like circus music, DA———DAAA! In back we find a pair of dark red-painted doors partially closed. There's a small crowd of old people, cripples, children looking in. We peer through the crowd and see two of the dead bulls stretched on yellow sand bleeding from the mouth: red, thick blood against black fur, blue muscles. One is hoisted on a butcher's hook.

Four butchers are working frantically, skinning the bull on the hook. Skins of earlier bulls, horns and all, are piled in one corner. Before the skin is fully off, one butcher cuts away a hindquarter and carries it, bleeding warm, to the butcher bench where two others are cutting it into meat-sized chunks. These in turn are wrapped with newspaper and brought to the opening in the door. The next person in line shows some kind of identification, presents a colored slip of paper and receives the cut of meat. It's done with the efficiency and dispatch of long experience. We turn away. I look at Sandy.

"Well, the matadors might get ears or tails or hoofs or balls, or whatever they cut off a bull for awards, but these people get the best parts. Bullfighting isn't all bad after all. You know 'matador' means butcher or killer in Spanish. The whole thing's only a complicated, dangerous way to kill and butcher some beef."

When the others come out, they're excited. It seems one of the bullfighters felt the bull he'd fought wasn't good enough, so he bought, with his own money, a seventh bull to be killed so he could show how good he really was. He then did the job in great style, was awarded two ears. It was like an extra-inning ball game, or when you go to a movie and find out they're having a sneak preview in addition to the feature film. I wonder if they still do that in L.A.

We agree to meet at the Bar Central. On the bus, on the way home, I hold out my hand, palm up, and Sandy puts her hand in it. We don't say much. But it will definitely go down as the nicest bullfight I ever didn't watch.

WE CALM EACH OTHER MUTUALLY, GIVE BRACE
TO OUR GRACELESS EFFORT: A BALM THAT EMBALMS.

That night we ride up into the hills to see what's supposed to be genuine gypsy flamenco dancing. Lubar takes Dale up there first, then comes back to get me. Some ride! No wonder Dale's scared; I'd be a blithering idiot. Lubar likes to go *through* things—ditches, bumps—at high speed rather than avoid them; it makes for nervous riding. He drives with his shoulders hunched forward and his head tucked down between his shoulders as if he's driving through a snowstorm.

Maybe there actually aren't any genuine gypsies and there definitely isn't much genuine about flamenco dancing, but it's fun. A real tourist kind of thing, with swinging blue-black straight hair flinging a flower into the audience. Lubar catches one and puts it between his teeth. There's much breast heaving, breath holding, loud yelling, along with hard heel stomping and good guitar playing. Sandy puts her hand on my thigh under the table. I put my hand on top of hers. This way, flamenco dancing is really exciting: having a good-looking, vital, young girl's hand on your thigh; edging its way slowly up to your crotch.

Is this wrong? How far out of line am I? Maybe I don't care enough. There's some kind of hole in my head. Kate accused me once of being able to compartmentalize my mind, close off parts of it. She said it might only be a thing all men do. She could be right.

I know Kate knows what just about everybody we know—especially our kids—is doing all the time, no matter how far away they might be; right through time zones, even. She must write five letters and ten postcards a day. I tend to live my whole life only about three yards around me. I don't think I write ten letters a year. I'm definitely short-minded the way some people are shortsighted.

We buy a bottle of cognac when we get back into town, then we all go up to the room. We spread out on sleeping bags and pass the bottle around. Lubar is still pressing everybody to make a tour along the foothills. He bought a detailed map in Málaga and he's worked out routes on dirt paths from one mountain village to the other. Sweik passes the bottle to Dale.

"Look, Lubar. We don't have enough bikes. And I refuse to do any dirt riding with my antique machine and somebody on back. It's not built for that kind of thing. Besides, my back won't take it. I can feel it's about ready to go out again."

Lubar takes the bottle from Dale, drinks, wipes his mouth.

"I saw a place outside town where they *rent* bikes. I'll bet the old man here can rent a bike good enough for those hills and Sandy could ride on back with him."

We talk about it more, poring over the map; as we get drunker the better it sounds. Sweik agrees if I can rent a bike and Sandy rides on it, he'll go along.

"But I'm telling you, Lubar, if I hurt my back I'll haunt you into your grave."

They all leave except Sandy. She's stretched out on her side, with her hands clasped under her cheek on her sleeping bag, pretending she's asleep. After the door's closed, she opens one eye and looks at me. She's one of those people who can give a full double whammy with one eye—sideways.

"Do you want me to go?"

"Not if you don't want to."

"Do you want me to sleep here in my bag on the floor?"

"If that's what you want."

She doesn't move. She opens the other eye.

"I'd like to sleep in that big bed with you."

I sit on one end of the bed, take off my shoes. I feel as if I've gotten caught up in a porno flick, as if everything we're doing is being filmed or written down somewhere.

"I didn't think men meant much to you, Sandy."

None of us has ever come out in the open, talked about this part of things, but I'm in a very faded-away mood, partly drunk, excited and at the same time tired. Sandy gets up, comes over, stands between my legs, kisses the top of my skin-bared head. I look up at her.

"Oh, you're so old you don't count. I just want to sleep with you, OK?"

"Tired of the damp shit and piss smell already?"

"Yeah, and tired of listening to Lubar and Dale humping away beside me, too."

"Jealous?"

"Two ways, bi-jealousy; simultaneous agitation."

And suddenly, she seems so vulnerable, so intensely young and somehow jaded, overused. I put my arms around her and she falls onto me on the bed. She runs her hand over my face. I hook my heels on the edge of the bedspring to push my head farther back onto the pillow. She kisses me softly just above my beard, then on the end of my nose, then brushes her tongue across my lips.

"I'd like to cuddle and kiss, huddle and hug with you. There's nothing so bad about that is there? I'm feeling awfully alone."

I roll her off me so we lie side by side holding each other. She's tucked her hand up under my beard against my neck. I run my hand down her back feeling the tight stringy muscles, the little pebbled mounds of her spine.

"I'm a deeply married man, Sandy. I have five kids; I love my wife. I don't want to hurt anybody, including you and me."

I pause. Shit, it all sounds so mundane, so much like things people have said too often for too long. Boredom for me is the greatest torture. But I'm not bored right now, quite the contrary; but what I'm hearing myself saying sure as hell sounds boring.

"Sandy, I'd love to cuddle, hug, hold and kiss with you. Something inside me *always* feels alone; it's a private disease. I hate sleeping by myself, in any case, at any time."

She pushes herself away, gets up on her knees beside me, sitting back on her heels, her hands between her thighs.

"OK, then. So what're we waiting for? It isn't going to kill anybody if we curl up together and go to sleep, is it? You probably couldn't find a woman within five miles you'd be safer with; I promise, cross my heart, I *won't* rape you."

She smiles. I take her hands where they're clasped, holding each other tight in her crotch.

"Now, since we're out of that goddamned cold water, I'm unrapeable, lady. Not only that; I probably couldn't rape anybody myself, even if they wanted me to."

She reaches up, unbuttons the top button on her shirt, then crosses her arms in front of her breasts, grabs hold of the shirt and sweater on opposite sides and lifts the whole thing over her head. She isn't wearing a bra and has beautiful, firm, small tits, with very pink nipples. She cups them each in a hand.

"How you like them apples, buddy?"

I sit up, lean forward; the temptation to kiss each gently with open lips is almost overwhelming.

"Remember, Sandy. Kiss, cuddle, hold and hug only; that's the deal. Right?"

"Right," she says, and we proceed to undress quickly in the cold room.

I'm surprised to find that although I don't exactly have an erection, the devil's advocate is taking up a bit more space than he should. Sandy's under the covers before I am. I keep my back to her as I pull my jeans over my feet so she won't see my mini-erection. Leave it to my prick to double-cross me every time, one way or another.

We do curl into each other, face to face, add snuggle to cuddle, hug, kiss, hold and huddle. We snuggle. Her body is silken smooth and hard. There doesn't seem to be any layer of fat. Sandy puts her face against mine, then comes down on me with her mouth, hard, fast-moving slippery tongue. She slides her tongue between my front teeth. I can hardly get my breath. I push my butt out to keep the devil from giving me away. Now he's at full mast. What's the connection between my tongue and my cock? There must be at least one. The light's still on in the room and the switch is over by the door. I manage to free my mouth from the all-enclosing, penetrating power of Sandy.

"I'd better turn the light out maybe."

Already I'm breathing hard, my heart's beating, skipping, jumping around in my breast as if it wants to escape.

"OK, if you're bashful. Sleeping in the dark's best anyway."

Now I've got to figure how to get around the bed, across the room, to that light and back without showing this ridiculous hard-on that won't go away. I swing my feet out of bed on my side, give the old devil a good whack with my middle finger cocked by my thumb, the way you'd scoot a bee or fly off a piece of bread. It stings but the damned thing won't go away. I run fast, barefoot, round the end of our bed to the light, flick it out. Now the room's dark enough so I can slip back in without too much visible stiff dangling. The red neon light is flipping on and off and I remember last night. That doesn't help.

MEMORIES OF IMAGININGS
SLIDE SILENTLY INTO VIEW.

When I climb in bed, Sandy's crying. Her face is in the pillow and she's shaking the whole bed with what seems like racking sobs.

The devil goes down to the nether regions. I ease

myself under the covers and take Sandy in my arms. She pulls her face out of the pillow. She's giggling, laughing. She holds my head by the ears again, pushes her tongue through my lips past my teeth into my mouth. When she lifts back, I can see by red neon-light flashes her face is wet. She stares into my eyes in the flickering dark.

"Boy, Scum, you really are a nut. Raping you would be the easiest thing in the world, but honest I'm not going to. You don't have to be afraid. And so what if I did. You could just tell your wife you got raped. You're not going to get pregnant or anything, you know; it doesn't work that way."

Then I'm laughing with her. She reaches down to grab hold of what she thinks is going to be a nice stiff joystick and finds a limpish bit of German weisswurst. My organ seems to have given its little concerto for the evening. Organ, hell, it's not even much good as a mouth organ.

We cuddle, kiss, hold, hug, stroke, huddle, squeeze but nothing more happens.

"What's the matter, Scum? Spirit willing, flesh weak?"

"If I have to be honest, Sandy, I think it's the reverse. Flesh willing, spirit weak; nothing personal."

She gives me a long deepening look in the dark, then puts her cheek against mine and begins licking my neck, behind my ear; she shoves her pointed strong tongue into my ear through the foxtails and all, wetting it, blocking it sometimes so I feel half deaf. My body's quivering, my mind's spinning. Is it possible to feel this sensually, physically excited and not feel anything sexual? That's what's happening. It's a new experience for me. It's like seeing very clearly, but not recognizing, knowing, anything you see; it's all new.

I put my hand up to the back of Sandy's neck, pull her away softly by the hair.

"I won't be much good for you as a man tonight, Sandy. How about teaching me to love you as a woman?"

She pushes away, turns me on my back, straddles my stomach, leans her hands against my shoulders, pressing them into the bed, pinning me.

"Boy, you really are weird. Do you mean that?"

"Sure, why not. I'd like to try. Something in me has always wanted to be a woman anyway. I think I'd like loving you that way."

. . .

And so we spend most of that night being as close together as two women can be, or at least as close as a woman and a man pretending he's a woman. We don't do anything I've never done with another woman, but Sandy shows me how to do these things properly, carefully, with intensity, concentration; slowly, tenderly, at a proper pace, as if it's happening to me at the same time, feeling her joy, her pleasure. It's a soft falling in and out of each other, somehow more than sex; we're *becoming* each other so I *do* almost feel like a woman. It's as if we're painting portraits of each other simultaneously, creating each other and being created at the same time.

And then, as Sandy reaches raptures of sensuality, the devil decides on a return engagement. It's some kind of sympathetic arousal; I don't feel it as my own sex at all; male sex feelings can so easily get in the way of deep sensuality. He's up and yearning as a part of our mutual excitement.

Sandy feels it happening, reaches down and holds on; she grabs him in both hands, not moving; holding him tight. It's this way, then, when she flies into her own highest place, leaving me, as my mouth, my tongue tastes her. Vicariously I experience her release, her ecstasy.

Then, as she relaxes, melts into me, pulsates against my body into almost sleep with me, she slides against me from my neck to my nipples with her tongue, opens her mouth licking me down one side then the other, making love to me with her mouth, without rush, without hurry, fear or expectations. She licks as if she has a strawberry ice-cream cone she's eating slowly, trying to make it last. Then she drinks from *my* fountain. I feel as if I have breasts and am giving milk. My own little nipples are hard and I feel them cool, still wet in the night.

SEX AS MIRAGE, A FLESH GARAGE WHERE
WE PARK OUR IDENTITY, INTEGRITY, AS
HUMANS AND THEN CLOSE THE DOORS.

Sandy comes back up to me, slowly, the way she went down, lingering on my breasts, running her tongue in the hairs of my armpits. I'm drifting, lost, away in another world. She tucks her face close to mine.

She pushes her nose under my ear; I'm almost asleep as she whispers,

"I've never been able to do that. I've never wanted to. You wonderful old man, I love everything about you: your feel, your smell, your taste; the way you feel my feelings; you could even make me learn to like men, maybe."

I think that's what she says; I'm past remembering. I'm sinking into a velvet violet place of peace.

AWAY IN ANOTHER PLACE, FACE TO
FACE WITH JOY, A FADING HAPPINESS
THE OTHER SIDE OF ECSTASY.

I wake before Sandy. I lie there still not believing what's happened. Technically, we did not have sex together; in reality I can't remember being more aroused, having experienced such depths of life. At the same time, as one part of me is feeling complete, integral, another part is shattered, guilty. I lie quiet, Sandy breathing against me, her face huddled under my arm. It's still there, the grandfather-granddaughter part, even now. I almost feel as if I should wake her and tell a story, a bedtime story. But we did tell each other a bedtime story, most of the night; and it wasn't avuncular or grandfather-granddaughter; it was two humans giving each other comfort, pleasure, a strong feeling of belonging, being alive, without regard to sex, age or any of the other divisions which keep us all apart.

But I'd hate like hell trying to explain this to my Kate. It's not in her dictionary, what she considers normal behavior; it's hardly in mine.

I also realize I can't handle, can't afford any more of this kind of relationship; not at this time in my life. It's what I must tell Sandy when she wakes; that's the bedtime story Grandfather needs to tell.

So I do and, she *laughs!*

"God, you're too serious, Scum. We're OK. I love you but I'm not *in* love with you. Relax. There's a big difference. I'm *in* love with Dale."

She stops, looks into my eyes.

"Or, at least, I was; I think."

I get another of her fourth-century Greek smiles.

XIV

A MARRIAGE

At ten o'clock we meet with the others at the Bar Central. The three of them act as if nothing's happened. Lubar wants me to go with him to check the motorcycle rental place.

After breakfast rolls and coffee, I reluctantly get on the back of his bike and we drive out to the edge of town. I wonder if Sandy will say anything to Dale about last night. I don't think so, I hope not; it was a very strong and private experience; I can't believe she'll want to take away any of the magic, but then I'm from another generation, two generations removed. What to me might be violation could just be loving sharing to Sandy.

Renting the bike is easier and less expensive than I thought it would be. My French driver's license and American passport are all that's necessary—that and a deposit. I take the daily rate; we don't figure on being gone more than two days. The mob needs to hurry back to teach and I want to be home for a rest before Easter vacation at the mill.

The bike I rent is a little Honda 125 CB. It's a bike I know, because Mike, my second son, has one like it down at the mill. It's a single-cylinder, four-stroke engine and practically nothing can go wrong with it. It's big enough to carry two but the going had better not get too rough. Trail bike it is not.

Lubar and I roll up to the Bar Central. Sandy, Dale, Sweik stand up and cheer. We sit down and Lubar pulls out his map again.

PLAN PLANS! LOOK AHEAD! DON'T GET BEHIND!
YOU NEVER KNOW WHAT'S AROUND THE NEXT BEND.
CERTAINLY WE DO—OR SHOULD—THE END.

We'll keep the hotel room and leave most everything there, even the sleeping bags. We hope to find small hotels in the villages. Sandy will ride with me. If the going gets too tough, we'll turn around and come back. Sweik says he isn't going to be doing any rough riding either. He's distinctly moving as if his back is giving him trouble. Sleeping on the ground in that damp cave can't help much. If anybody should be sleeping in my bed at the hotel, he's the one; probably he's the one who should be with Sandy, too—either he or Dale. I'm feeling like some kind of placebo, or a one-man control group. It's not exactly comfortable.

First we'll be heading up to a town called Mijas. We'll go past Sture and Anna's, through a town called Benalmádena, and across to Mijas. We're going to Mijas because there's an old-time bullring right in that little town beside the church.

A TEMPORARY NEST ON THE SIDE OF A HILL. I GROPE STILL FOR THE SKY, EVEN NOW WHEN I SWIM IN IT. HI DIDDLY DOO!

We're off and riding by noon. It's nice having Sandy behind me; she holds her hands tight, one on each of my shoulders, and we ride as one.

We go past Sture and Anna's. I don't see anybody but they must be looking out. I wave. Anna will be sure she was right about my little Swedish girl.

The road starts to get steep as it goes up toward Benalmádena and I shift down to third. We're at the tail end, with Lubar leading. He's bursting ahead, then slowing down to wait. Sweik refuses to be pushed and I know there's no way I'll go faster than thirty miles an hour. Actually, I'm doing about twenty on this hill and with these curves.

Mijas is a disappointment, pretty much of a tourist trap. But there *is* a bullring, all white, not more than thirty yards from the church. The church is uninteresting but the graveyard is fascinating. The graves are built aboveground, in tiers three high. On the other side of the bullring, past the church and graveyard, is an old mine. There are deep shafts and tunnels. From the debris at the mouth of the mine it looks as if they might have been pulling out quartz. It also looks as if nobody's been working the mine for at least ten years.

The road out of Mijas goes farther up into the hills and generally down the coast; it's gravel and dirt. I go along behind, staying out of Sweik's dust and still less than fifteen miles an hour. The going's so rough I need to hold my eyes on the road and can't see much. Sandy keeps telling me to look at this or that as we go around tight curves but I need to concentrate. She kisses me on the neck, behind the ears; takes one ear in her mouth. I feel myself melting; she didn't listen carefully enough to Grandfather's story. How much can an old man take? She doesn't seem to realize, or even care.

"We're in no hurry, Scum. When there's something interesting, let's just stop and look."

So that's what we do. Sandy gives me an extra squeeze when there's something she thinks I'd like to see; then I pull over, put my feet down and shift into neutral. We stay straddling the bike but at least I get to see some of the really incredible natural beauty: the rock formations, the upland greens and wild flowers. I guess Sweik's keeping an eye on us in his rearview mirror, because he stops whenever we do. Lubar's probably driving around in circles. But this way I can actually enjoy the trip without being scared half to death.

Just as the sun's going down, we get to the town where we intend to spend the night. It's called something El Grande but it isn't very grand. It's big enough to have a hotel, though, and we rent two rooms for under ten dollars. Lubar and Dale take the smaller room, with one bed. There's a double bed and a single in the other. Sweik, gallantly, flops out on the small bed.

"God, I don't know if my back can survive this. It's almost going out all the time, like a worn universal joint."

He arches the way he did in that Paris hotel bed, grits his teeth.

"Do you two mind if I take this bed for myself? I could never make it in a bed with someone else."

I don't know if this is only a nice ploy on Sweik's part because he thinks Sandy and I want the big bed, but I suspect he's speaking truth. His face is white and there are beads of sweat across his forehead. I look over at Sandy; she winks.

"Well, looks as if you're stuck with me again."

She turns to Sweik.

"This old man's sure I'm going to rape him, destroy his virginal purity."

Sweik's trying to reach down and take off his boots. He can't reach that far. I go over, unlace, pull them off carefully. Sweik settles back on the pillow.

"Thanks. Don't worry, Scum; just scream and I'll crawl across the room to save you."

Sandy seems to become aware for the first time of how much pain Sweik is in; she goes over to him, kneels beside his bed.

"Gees, Matt, you're in a bad way. I thought you were exaggerating. Roll over and I'll give you a massage. I'm really good at it, I have strong hands."

"No, I'll be OK if I can only lie out still here, stop the spasms. You guys go eat, bring something back for me."

We leave the room and Lubar is waiting with Dale for us down in the town center beside a fountain. There are orange trees growing around the outside edge of the plaza. There are two restaurants in the town; mostly they're bars but they serve a single meal, no menu. We go in one and drink good, soft white wine. Except for tapas, they don't start serving food until ten o'clock and it's only seven-thirty.

We go outside. There's a crowd of kids around the motorcycles. One kid's even mounted on Lubar's bike and is making motorcycle noises. Lubar dashes up and the kid runs away. Lubar chases him across the plaza and throws his helmet. He comes back.

"Goddamned kids! We've got to find a place for these bikes or they'll be gone in the morning."

Sweik speaks the best Spanish in our group but he's not available. I'm second best in a very slow race. I go back to our hotel and ask the man who runs it if we can store our motorcycles somewhere. I somehow get across what I mean, because he takes a key and comes outside. He opens a door to a small courtyard and points. We roll the bikes in; it's costing twenty pesetas for the night.

At ten o'clock they serve a good paella in one of the restaurants. I don't know how they get the fish up those roads from the sea; no car or truck could ever make it. There's not a car to be seen in town. The fish must come in on donkeyback. Driving up here, we saw trains of donkeys with baskets. We buy an extra serving for Sweik and two bottles of wine. It's almost eleven o'clock now and I'm feeling tired; Sandy and I didn't get much sleep.

We put all the pillows behind Sweik's back and prop him up so he can eat. He says he feels a lot better. He has his heels pulled up to his crotch and his knees spread, claims that's the way it feels best. When he's finished, I take the dishes down to the restaurant. I stop on the way back and look up at the stars. There are virtually no lights in town and up here in the mountains the stars are close, filling the sky edge to edge. The ridges of the highest mountains are cut tight against the sky, sharp, clear. Kate would love this; while I was in prison, she was secretary of the astronomy department at Yale; says she spent most of her time dusting meteorites, dusting stardust—perfect job.

THE UNIVERSE ON INTIMATE TERMS, A HEAVY METEORITE, A LIGHT-YEAR. SO FAR AND YET SO NEAR.

Upstairs, Sandy has gotten Sweik out of bed onto his stomach on the floor, with one pillow under his head and another under his hips. She's loosened his pants and pulled them down past his butt. She's massaging two-handed with the hams of her hands into his lower back. Sweik is grunting and groaning.

"Stop her, Scum, she's killing me."

"God, this bucko's so tight he's just one lump of knotted muscle down here."

She leans back and perspiration is dripping from her nose. I kneel on the other side of Sweik. There are tears running down his face.

"Let me take a try at this, Sandy. I have a back problem myself, same place, sacroiliac; it's a very tricky business."

Sandy stands up and moves aside. I straddle Sweik. I put my hands on both sides of his spine. Gently, closing my eyes, I try feeling for the tightness.

"Just relax, now; I won't do anything to hurt. I'm only feeling for what's wrong."

Sweik lets out a breath. I search with my fingers down his spine almost to the coccyx. On the left side there's a hard bunching of muscle. When I press my thumb into the muscle running along the third vertebra up from the bottom, Sweik grunts. I lean, arms straight, and stroke away from the spine out toward his hip above the gluteus maximus. He moans with each press. He's got something pinched all right, and the whole area is spasming. He'll need a week in bed, or more. I can't see how he's going to get that bike down out of these hills, let alone back to Paris. I decide I'll keep this opinion to myself; a part of back trouble can be mental.

"You've got a spasm there all right, Sweik, old buddy. No kind of massage is going to help and I wouldn't try manipulating either. Even if I knew what I were doing, it'd probably do more harm than good. I think you've got a ruptured disk; it's swelled and pushing against a nerve. Here, hold out your hand, let me help you back into bed."

Sweik rolls over onto his back while Sandy and I carefully pull him to his feet. We sit him on the edge of the bed. While he's sitting there, he starts unbuttoning his shirt, hands trembling.

"I'm going to undress and sack out. Would somebody see if there's a pharmacy or a witch doctor in this town where we can get some painkiller? Maybe a good night's sleep in a real bed, zonked out, will relax the damned thing."

We help him off with the rest of his clothes down to his underwear. Sandy pulls off both socks and swings his feet up while I lower his back onto the bed.

"That's right, lie out on your back with your knees up, keeping that spine flat on the bed. We'll go look for something but probably everything's already closed."

Sandy nods her head toward the door. She and I go out in the hall.

She whispers, "I know Dale has some Midol; that should help. A cramp is like a sort of spasm, isn't it?"

"Good idea. I don't think we'll find anything else here. Would you go ask her? Knock hard on the door before you go in. No more bi-sexual, simultaneous jealousy, please."

Sandy puts her arms around me, kisses me on the nose.

"I couldn't care less; I'm cured. The object of my affection is old, wrinkled, scared and unavailable. I'm not really complaining, though, honest; I understand."

She turns and leaves me standing there alone in the narrow whitewashed hall. I go back to our room. Sweik's staring at the ceiling. He's more relaxed. I stand over him, then pull a chair across and sit by his bed.

"Sandy's convinced Dale has something that will help. The main thing is getting a good night's sleep."

"That Sandy's really something else, isn't she? Coming

over those hills on the bike, she never made a false move. It's kind of a shame she's hung up on women. She's the kind of person a guy could live with and not feel guilty or responsible about all the time."

"I'm not so sure she's all that hung up on women, Sweik. I think she's still only trying to sort it out. We men can get all uptight when women love each other; we're so afraid we can't really make it with them ourselves."

Sweik looks up at me with his eyes, not moving his head. When you have a bad back, even turning your head can cause a twinge. He smiles. Just then, Sandy comes in the door; she has two pills and a glass of water. I help hold Sweik's head up so he can swallow.

"You guys could be poisoning me. What kind of pills are these, anyway?"

Sandy laughs. Looks over at me.

"Well, if you've been bleeding, or are about to bleed, these should make you feel better."

Sweik lowers his head back on the pillow.

"Oh shit! Lydia Pinkham strikes again."

"No, Midol. Stronger; relax those muscles so you'll feel like a new woman."

OUR BODIES AS ONE, THE MOON AND THE
SUN, INTERTWINING SATELLITES TO
SATELLITES, TO SATELLITES, TO SATELLITES.

It's past midnight, Sweik closes his eyes and I turn out the light. Sandy and I undress in the dark. We climb into bed and curl into each other. This time it's peace and closeness all the way; we hold on to each other without tension and I think we're both asleep in five minutes or less. It's like the best part of being married to someone you love: deep mutual trust, a feeling of safety. I've been missing it; I'll be glad getting back to Kate.

WRAPPED IN WARMNESS, SMELLS, TWITCHES,
ITCHES, ALL TOGETHER, TOGETHER.

In the morning, Sweik is awake before we are. He's flat in bed, except for his cocked knees, staring at the ceiling again. I go over.

"You know, Scum, I don't think I can get up. I'm afraid to move."

"How does it feel?"

"It doesn't hurt as long as I stay like this."

"Well, let's give it a try; you can't stay here. I think we ought to tell Lubar we're going back. You shouldn't be on a bike with a back like that. I also think you should drive my bike down. It's lighter, closer to the ground and the suspension's softer. I'll take yours, with Sandy on back."

I reach down and pull with both hands so he can sit on the edge of his bed. He winces. Sandy is looking on from the big bed, covers tucked under her arms, her bare shoulders beautiful in the morning light.

I hand Sweik his clothes one at a time and he dresses. When he stands to pull on his pants, he can't straighten up. He sits back again. I slide his socks and shoes on. In the meantime, Sandy has gotten dressed. She comes close, runs her hand across my head.

"I'll go tell Lubar we're going back down. You see if you can help Sweik out to the café for some coffee. We'll meet you there."

We make it out to the café but Sweik is suffering. When Sandy comes back, she has two more of the Midol. Sweik washes them down with his coffee. Lubar and Dale join us.

"What's the matter, man, you copping out on the old Paris-American Motorcycle Club?"

"I'm in deep pain, Lubar. I just hope to hell I can get down this damned hill and back to some kind of real bed."

Lubar looks at Sandy and me.

"Jesus, he's really bad. How'll he ever make it back up to Paris?"

"First, let's just get him back to Torremolinos, huh? We'll check in with a doctor there. In the meantime, he's taking my bike down; it's light and has good soft shocks. I'll take Sandy on Sweik's bike."

We finish breakfast and as the Midol begins to take effect, we maneuver the motorcycles out of the courtyard and into the street. We pay for the rooms, the bike storage. Sweik has driven a little Honda like mine before, so that's no problem. He gives me instructions on how to start the Ariel and I get it going. The kick start has quite a kickback. I climb into the saddle, then try a few tours up and down some little streets, around the plaza and fountain, to get the feel. It's like riding a big Percheron stallion after riding a quarter horse, but it feels good, tight. I ease up beside Sweik and stop.

"I think I'm on to it, you think you can make it?"

"I've got to, right?"

Lubar turns over his bike, Dale climbs behind him. He foot-pushes back beside us.

"I've figured a way on the map we can drop directly down to the coast road. We'll be on smooth highway in less than five miles."

We nod. He starts off. I put the Ariel up on its stand, go over and kick-start the Honda for Sweik. He shifts into first and rolls out after Lubar. I get back on his bike; Sandy swings herself up behind me, grabs tight and we go off trailing Sweik.

I don't know how he sticks it out, but we make it all the way to Torremolinos without stopping. I must admit, riding that Ariel is a great experience. The machine has so much dignity it's like Sweik. I feel as if I'm a king reviewing his troops. It *is* a bit hard maneuvering in rough parts with Sandy up back, but while we're on the highway it's like flying.

When we get to the hotel, we literally lift Sweik off the bike. He can't swing his leg over and he can't lift himself up enough to slide off the back. He can't even push the kickstand down. Sandy holds the bike while Lubar and I lift him up, one on each side, and move him into the hotel room. We undress and slide him onto the bed. I go down to the registration desk and ask where I can find a doctor. I try explaining with my rotten Spanish that my friend has a hurt back but I can't remember the word for back. I just keep saying "doctor" and *"mucho dolor."* He writes out an address and a name. I walk into town and find the place; it's a small clinic. The doctor says he'll come *"muy pronto."* He speaks a little English, about as much as I speak Spanish.

The upshot of it all is the doctor says what we knew. Sweik has a *ciática* and must remain in bed for two weeks. Definitely no riding a motorcycle, maybe never. He gives Sweik a prescription for some real painkiller, which I buy at the *farmacia.* It's loaded with codeine. At least he won't suffer.

We meet downstairs and walk up to the Bar Central. Lubar says he can cover Sweik's classes for a week or two. We chip in and find we have enough spare money to pay the hotel. It turns out Sandy has some spare cash stashed away, more than enough to buy the train fare. She also volunteers to stay down and take care of Sweik if Lubar will cover her classes, too. Lubar nods.

The big trouble is the bike. We can't leave it here and it'd be a shame to sell it. Old things don't have much value in Spain, where everything's old anyhow.

I find myself volunteering to drive it back. I say I won't go with Lubar and Dale, because I'll be taking it easy; I'll take off tomorrow and give myself at least six days to make the trip, stopping regularly on the hour for a rest, resting both my old body and that old bike.

A JOURNEY, UNPLANNED, UNEXPECTED, UNWANTED:
A REMINDER. OF WHAT? OF THE EVENTUAL *TRIP!*

We go back upstairs to tell Sweik our plans. He listens through, looking back and forth at us.

"God, I feel like such a shit. I'll pay you back, I promise, soon as I get some money. Sandy, you don't need to stay. I can get somebody to send food up."

"Hell, I want to stay, I like it here. I'll give you some more of my expert massages, make you good as new in no time."

He looks over at me. He shakes his head, smiles, half laughs, half cries.

"And you, old man. You'll *never* make it over those goddamned hills with that bike. There's forever between here and Paris, one long twisting snake of a road cluttered with stinking trucks all the way to the border. Leave the bike; maybe I can advertise, find somebody to buy it. You heard the doctor—said I shouldn't ride a bike anymore anyway."

"What's a Spanish doctor know? Probably bought his medical degree from his uncle in Madrid. You'll be back on that bike in a month. Look, I'm just going to cruise softly across those hills, drift in the sun, take it easy. If it rains, I'll pull over, stay at an inn. I won't have any heavy stuff and nobody up on back. That bike of yours is a joy to drive. We could never leave it down here; it'd be treachery. Don't you worry, Sweik, we two old farts will burp and belch our way straight to the Place Saint-Sulpice. We'll be there long before you will."

A PRIVATE CHAUTAUQUA, RACING, PACING MY
OWN LIFE, OVER SPACE, THROUGH TIME AGAIN.

So it's settled. I'm running out of time if I'm going to make it home for Easter vacation. I've been looking forward to some good time down at the mill with my family. I start packing the saddlebags. I borrow one of Sweik's heavy sweaters and his leather jacket, because he says it gets cold as hell on top of those hills. I roll up to Sture and Anna's to say goodbye. I tell them I borrowed the bike; I don't tell them I'm driving it to Paris. They'd jump me, hold me down, put me in a straitjacket. That's probably where I belong. But this is some kind of ultimate challenge. It can be the final purge to all my black thoughts, the sense of failure, emptiness. If I can't make it, I'll leave the bike in a garage somewhere and take a train the rest of the way. To be honest, I think I'd rather chance it on the bike than with those Spanish railway conductors and my blotchy pass.

Sandy and I spend the night in her sleeping bag on the floor. Sweik absolutely needs the bed. We softly, passively give each other comfort; no sex, only soft stroking, and some quiet tears and deep sleep.

BRIGHT, SOFT SEEDS OF LOVE HOVER INTENTLY
WAITING IN GREEN BUDDINGS, THE LIGHT OF
UNBIDDEN QUEST.

I'm awake early the next morning. My plan is to drive only in the daylight. This time of year it doesn't get too hot, so I can drive straight through the day. Sweik said the best time is from noon till three, while the truck drivers are off the roads having lunch and a siesta. I'll concentrate my serious travel during that time.

Sandy comes with me outside. I roll Sweik's motorcycle out of the court. It turns over on the second kick. I sure hope this machine has some idea of how much I'm counting on it to keep going without any trouble. There are tools but if anything serious goes wrong, I'm a goner.

Also, there's something psychological involved. I'm wed to that machine for this trip, the ultimate trip.

I straddle the bike. Sandy leans against me, turns my head with her hand pulling on my beard and looks into my eyes. She winks. For just an instant, I wish she were coming with me, but I'd never make it with the two of us; neither the bike nor I am strong enough; besides, Sweik needs her now. I think she needs Sweik, too.

"Have good days, Sandy. Sop up plenty of sun and help Sweik work that back in shape."

"Think of me sometimes, OK, Scum? Think of me on those long steep curves."

She steps back. I tighten the worn leather strap on the tiny brown leather helmet and shift into first. I look at her once more and gently let out the clutch to move along the quiet street and on the road to Málaga.

I TRY RIDING AGAIN, CYTHEREAN, BLOWING
UNHURT THROUGH CANYONS OF UNENDING
CONFIDENCE. I CAN'T BUY IT BACK, THE
PRICE IS TOO MUCH BY ANY ACCOUNT.

I find a station open just outside Málaga and fill the bike with gas, check the oil. Everything seems fine. If I don't ask too much of this machine or myself, we'll be all right.

Soon, five kilometers from Málaga, the road starts going up. It's a good road, well kept and not much traffic going my way. The sun is rising and as different hills get in the way, I watch at least five different sunrises and sunsets. The motor is purring away. I could go by way of Linares, but the Cordova road is better. I head up that direction.

As I climb higher, turning, leaning into each of the curves, keeping in third most of the time, it's almost hypnotic. I watch the vegetation change. I ride past little towns, dirt, white buildings with black painted around the bottoms, women in black. Kids run out at me from some of the towns. It's a weekday and I wonder why at ten o'clock in the morning they aren't in school.

I'm way up in the mountains when I take my first break. I'm not particularly tired but the bike feels hot under me from so much uphill pulling. I find a nice place beside the road, stretch out and gnaw on a piece of roll I saved from breakfast. I'll drive until eleven-thirty, then take a good rest before my twelve-to-three marathon run. Sweik's right, the worst part of the trip so far has been getting around trucks. They go about twenty miles an hour up the hills, are diesel and stink to heaven. With the tight curves, it's tough finding safe passing places.

I get to Cordova at about four in the afternoon. It's

been years since I've visited the cathedral, so I head for there as soon as I've gotten a room.

There are practically no tourists. The vast courtyard is haunted with echoes of sandaled Moslems in djellabas. The dark interior is a forest of thick barber-pole-like stone columns, nothing to do with a Christian church. It's too bad a trade can't be made with Santa Sophia where the Moslems have a Christian church being used as a mosque, mosaics whitewashed over. The whole thing's an accident in time and space.

I walk along smelling the mold, the age, the deep mystery of eternal aspirations. It makes a nice way to finish off my first day, a day doused in the high sky and dust from the road.

I wander through back streets and eat as soon as I find a restaurant open; this isn't till nine o'clock. I wonder how things are back in Torremolinos. I'm in bed by ten-thirty and hope to get out and riding with sunrise.

REMEMBERING BACK, STILLED YEARNING,
PRETTY DAMNED OLD BUT STILL LEARNING.

The next leg is a long one. I'm trying for Madrid in a day. I put in three hours straight, from early light until about ten. I rest half an hour, then drive till noon. The riding's easier because I'm out from the worst of the mountains. The motor's running smoothly. I filled up in Cordova but I'll need more gas before I reach Madrid. On the twelve-to-three sprint, I go fifty kilometers looking for a gas station. I finally find one open when I have less than an eighth of a tankful left.

I pull in to Madrid at seven in the evening. This time I'm dead beat. I'm beginning to understand what Sweik meant. It's tough concentrating, knowing your life is on the line all the time. There are so many things to watch for: bumps in the road, holes, trucks, fast Mercedes coming up behind, every vehicle throwing dust, pebbles.

My mind's tired but my body's even tireder. I don't exactly have a bad back but it's stiff. I rent a room near the Prado and spend half an hour doing various Yoga positions to help stretch and loosen up. I could use one of Sandy's massages. I try not thinking of her.

I go out and walk around the Puerta de Sol for half an hour, stop in a bar, have some fried clams with two glasses of wine, then back to bed. I sleep like a dead man.

. . .

The next day I head toward Burgos. It has one of my favorite cathedrals, a cathedral with a wonderful quality of spatial openness, airiness, yet with mysterious deep purple and blue windows. It's one of the more religious-feeling churches I know.

The driving isn't too bad, but it's colder and I've lost that beautiful blue sky. I don't push so hard and take a break every hour, as I promised myself, except for the midday press. As I've gone north, the traffic has picked up and the land has flattened out. This is not sunny Spain; this is more Europe, but somehow still scraggly. I rarely go over forty miles an hour, so there are trucks, cars passing me all the time. Twice I get good-sized pebbles thrown up against my face. One strikes the goggles and actually leaves a mark on it. After that one, I pull over and rethink the whole project; it all looks pretty stupid and I almost give up right there. But I'm deep into it now and want to finish, so I charge on. I don't quite know what I'm trying to prove, but it's something I'd hate like hell trying to explain to Kate or any sensible person, anyone not struggling for life itself.

When I roll into Burgos, I have just half an hour before they close. I park in front of the cathedral and walk down the main aisle, letting the peace and calm sink into me. I'm needing it. There seemed to be a lot of hostility out there on the road today.

The cathedral's all transparent shadows and shades of blues, purples, violets against muticolored gray stone. I kneel at the altar and say a little private prayer to whomever the "powers that be" might be, *if* they are. I ask them to help this *old* man with this *old* bike in this *old* church to get through three more days. I thank them for the last three days. After that, I find a room, do my Yoga, then go out and treat myself to a good meal in a fancy restaurant. That pebble in the face reinforced my joy in just being alive. I want to celebrate it.

WHEN DID THE LUXURY OF EXPANSION CEASE?
IN WHICH SEARCH FOR PEACE DID I LOSE
FLEXIBILITY? I'M LIKE A DRIED AND
SEGMENTED UNUSED RUBBER BAND.

The trip to San Sebastian isn't bad at all. The powers must have some power. I get there at about one in the afternoon. I park, walk along the promenade and out onto the beach. The weather has even improved some but it's not swimming weather. I walk close to the edge of the water, windmilling my arms, getting some circulation back, also now and then doing hand-assisted deep knee bends. I watch some kids playing soccer on the beach; God, they have energy to burn and I'm just a flickering spark.

FROM INSIDE SOME KIND OF MENTAL CAVE, I
PEER OUT AT BLINDING LIGHT; MOVEMENTS IN
QUICKSILVER, SOMNOLENT BRILLIANCE. I
CLOSE DOWN AND FALL BACK TO STILLNESS.

I'm back on the bike at two and decide I'll press for Tours. I figure if I don't make it, I can always stop at some little place along the way.

The border crossing is easy. I have all Sweik's papers for the bike and a note giving me permission to ride it. Nobody looks at the note on either side of the border. That's how unimpressive a dirty old bike can be to people who don't know. Since it's lunchtime, there's no lineup and the customs guards are relaxed and belching.

It's a wonderful feeling being back in France. Saint-Jean-de-Luz looks like the modern world after these past few days. I push along beautiful crowned roads lined on both sides by sycamores. These trees are murderous in case of an accident but so beautiful it's almost worth it. I feel sometimes as if I'm driving through a wooden tunnel. There's just the start of green in the leaves.

I drag into Tours at seven-thirty. I've been pushing it fairly hard. The bike is running as if it's brand new. I keep checking all the little things that can go wrong: brake cable, gas cable, clutch cable. Each night I've been unscrewing the spark plugs and cleaning them. I'm more and more impressed with the machine—also, more and more impressed with myself. I'm less tired after this longest day than on any day before. I begin to understand Sandy's feeling some, too; the joy of being on the road. Sure, I'll be glad to arrive, finally, in Paris, to walk on two feet again, but sitting that bike, eating up miles, is not all bad. Could be only I'm getting close to home. I even think of taking a detour along the Loire, look at some of the châteaux; but that'd be tempting fate. No sense *challenging* the powers.

WE GUESS AT GODS AND HOPE THEY WILL
BLESS US IN THE BOG OF OUR FAILURE.

I know of a small hotel near the cathedral here, and they have a room. It's great traveling off season. I also know of a wonderful little restaurant with specialties of the Touraine. I go there and eat my first French food in almost two weeks. It's worth going away.

After eating, I walk around outside the closed cathedral. It's always seemed a shame to close churches at night. It's in the night, or even sometimes at three o'clock in the morning, when a person can best use a church. I imagine they're afraid of thieves. But then a religious person shouldn't be too upset if somebody poor takes something. Just think of the church as a gigantic poor box—have cots for the poor to sleep—now that'd be truly religious.

I don't do any praying or any Yoga. At nine o'clock I sack out; I'll be driving through heavy traffic into Paris the next day.

I wake at about 5 a.m. perfectly refreshed. I decide to take right off. It's cold, so I button Sweik's jacket tight. It's dark and the streetlights are on; there's practically no one in the streets. I get on the main road north; I've decided to stay off autoroutes, that would be thumbing my nose at the gods. The trip is uneventful and I'm full of adrenaline looking forward to seeing my family; I hardly take any breaks at all. I pull into the Place Saint-Sulpice just as the church bells are ringing and thumping the sun-filled joy of noon.

Sweik gave me the key to his room. I take off the saddlebags, the helmets, and walk down there. In his room, I find the tarp where he said it would be, come back and cover the bike. I feel as if I'm saying goodbye to an old friend, as if I'm divorcing a friendly, supportive wife. I'd like to do something for that machine, something to keep it from rusting, wearing out, being junked.

Somehow I'm married to myself again, too, now. I feel all together, whole. I had all the requisites: something old, me; something new, Sandy; something borrowed, the Ariel, and that blue sky most of the way.

I pack my things in my little bag, take the Métro and get home before everybody comes in from school. I flop out on the bed and go right to sleep.

. . .

Kate wakes me with a kiss and hug; I pull her down on top of me and hold her tight. I feel as if I've been a million miles away. They tell me it's been raining in Paris practically the whole time I've been gone and they're impressed with my tan. Kate says it looks as if I've lost at least ten pounds, look ten years younger and it's sure nice to see me smiling again.

I tell her about Sture and Anna. I tell how my friends from Paris came down. I don't tell her anything particular about Sandy. I don't tell about driving that motorcycle back up. Maybe some other day.

That night, I shuffle my way through the paintings I've finished so far of the Marais series.

I'm really charged up. I'm feeling reborn, like a new person.

XV

NATURE NEST

The next day, I spend packing our car for the mill. We'll leave directly from school when Kate and the kids get out; we zoom right out at three-twenty; beat the traffic.

We bought this mill ten years ago. It was the ruin of an old water mill south and east of Paris. It's in an area called the Morvan, a northeast extension of the Massif Central. This is a beautiful part of France but poor: thin soil, no industry, sort of a French Appalachia. We got this ruin twelve years ago for two thousand bucks, a deal the old Scumbler just couldn't resist.

The mill was almost three hundred years old, and on the verge of collapse when we bought it. I had fun piling rocks and cementing them in place, putting on a new used-slate roof, piping in water, installing plumbing, electricity. I did the whole Scumbler thing. Now we spend Christmas, Easter and summers there. It's the one place we never rent out; sort of the home nest, our ultimate hideout.

We do great holidays down there. Our own private Easter bunny makes the best damned chocolate-covered, coconut-filled, hand-decorated eggs in the world. We have joyous fun Easter morning, rain, shine or snow, hiding eggs and baskets all around the millpond.

We have our own special treatment for *each* holiday. At Christmas we hand-cut our tree, fourteen-foot job, decorate it with real candles, then leave it up till Easter. The mill's so damp when we're away it stays fresh and green.

Good Friday we light it a last time, then take it down. Taking down a Christmas tree must be one of the saddest things going, so it's fitting. It also gives a new beginning of freshness for Easter.

All our holidays are more pagan than anything. Since

I'm a witch man, I love Halloween. We do lots of super-spooky, scary things with wild costumes.

Fourth of July and July 14th, Bastille Day, are both celebrated with fireworks shot over the pond: beautiful reflections, reverberations. The whole village joins us for those.

I'm in a wonderful pagan mood for Easter.

LEAPING WITH NEW LEAVES, SUCKING IN THE
FRESH CLEAR SUN: I GIVE MY SOUL TO LIFE.
BIRTH AND NEW BEGINNINGS, THE CLEANNESS OF
NATURE REKINDLE MY TIRED BLOOD, MY ACHING
HEART.

But first let's go back to last Christmas. It was then I got talking with Madame Mathilde in our village. She's eighty-six years old; her husband died three years ago at ninety-two. Now she lives by herself, still keeps a garden, still walks up the hill every morning to mass.

She raised a family of her own, four kids; then at fifty, when those first ones grew up and left home, she got lonesome, so she took on a second family of three orphans. The last of this batch left home when she was almost seventy. She insists her second family loves her more than the first. She was probably a better parent second time around, knew more about life and what's important.

I didn't really get to check myself out completely with my first family, never had a chance, but I've sure enjoyed the nest I got to stay with.

There's a long tradition of orphans in the Morvan. In the nineteenth century, the Morvan was known for wet nurses. The young girls would get themselves freshened by a local stud, leave their babies, then scoot up to Paris and play cow for the babies of the stylish ladies in the haut monde. Fun for everyone except the babies left behind.

EASY TO OVERLOOK, A CRY
THAT STOPS NOTHING, BUT
IS EASILY STOPPED. LIFE,
THE PUNCTUATION OF EXISTENCE.

Well, last Christmas I'm rigging electricity over at Madame Mathilde's place to run an electric blanket we bought her. Mathilde has rheumatism in her hands and knees; lives in a damp hollow near the stream coming from the millpond. We thought maybe some dry heat in winter might help. We give her the blanket and she wraps herself in it; doesn't plug it in; says it helps. American magic.

There's only one light in her house, no outlets. I run a line down to her bed from a high switchbox. The room smells like old lady; not enough light to see what she's doing. She doesn't care too much anymore; can't see well even with light; has stuff piled all around. Her husband's clothes are laid out and folded on a chair ready for him to wear, been there for three years I know of, kept clean, pressed, ready. Time gets confusing as you grow older; it's confusing enough when you're young—or even middle old, like me.

Finally I have the outlet rigged and her blanket plugged in. I point out the tiny light in the control box and explain how to regulate it. She nods. I know she isn't catching on. I spread that blanket over the mountain of covers on her bed. It really should go under the covers but I'd just as soon lift her petticoats as unpile those covers. Never know what's under all that; maybe keeps her old dead husband there, the way Faulkner's Emily did. No, I went to Mathilde's husband's funeral; I'm sure he was in the box. I helped fill in the grave, too.

The blanket starts getting warm. I tell her to touch it. She pulls her hand away quickly; looks at me, shock in her old milky eyes.

"Mais, Monsieur, c'est vivant!"

It's alive, says she. I know right away I've blown it. She'll never get under that blanket now. I go through the motions of explaining how to plug it in, adjust it; suggest she put it under the covers. She listens politely, eyes glued on the blanket. Unholy witchcraft! Foreign magic!

I notice her clock isn't working. It's a grandfather job. I take off the pendulum, pull out the works; nothing can really go wrong with these big babies. They're my favorite toys. I blow out some dust, bend a catch for one of the cogs that's gotten out of line. Madame Mathilde is watching me, nodding her head, muttering. She tells me this clock ran without stopping since her husband came home from the war. "Thirty-five years," I say. "Oh no!" She laughs. "More than that." It turns out to be the *First* World War she's talking about. The clock stopped again the week after he died; hasn't run since; a kind of local miracle. Nobody there to wind it.

I get the clock running. It's a pull-cord, weight-winding system. I explain to Mathilde how to wind the clock and chimes. She forgives me the hanky-panky with the blanket. I ask how she heats her place and she shows me the wood stove for heating and cooking; says she used to get wood from the *bois* but now buys it from Monsieur Périchon.

She explains how a *petit bois,* a small wood, came with every house in the old days. Most of these woods aren't used anymore; everybody's switched to oil, butane or electricity. She doesn't even know where her *bois* is. Of course, the rat nester's whiskers start quivering.

I offer to buy Madame Mathilde's *bois*. She says it's mine; she gives it to me. I tell her I want to buy her *bois* if I can find it. This sounds like fun; just my kind of thing—mysterious property deep in the woods.

SCURRYING IN THE WOODS, SCRATCHING
IN EARTH, SMELLING OLD ROOTS, WORMS;
HEFTING ROCK AND LOAM, WHAT ELSE
IS LEFT? I KNOW I'M BACK HOME.

The next day, I go up to the Mairie; that's our local mayor's office. Madame Calvert, another neighbor, is secretary there. She points to a wall plugged with hundreds of oblong cardboard boxes. There are dates and letters like H–L 1858 on them. The dates go back to 1814. I've no idea how I can find anything; neither does Madame Calvert. I roll downhill and try to get a specific date of purchase from Mathilde. All she knows is they bought their place three years after they were married and she was married sixty-three years when the Monsieur died. That's her husband. She always talks about him as if he's the boss away on vacation.

I go back to the Mairie. I figure it had to be about sixty years ago. Name LeCerbe. I go through the J–M boxes for 1921; old moldy-paper smell, brown ragged edges cracking off the paper; nothing. I find what I want in 1920, the year I was born. There's a description of the property; gives the location of Mathilde's wood. I get all the surveying markers. They're things like: "from the large elm, east to the flat rock." I'm disappointed there isn't any skeleton pointing north with an outstretched finger. I drive Mike's motorcycle to Nevers, our nearest big town, and buy geological survey maps.

The wood is up behind the Rousseau place. After about half a day's hunt, I find what looks like an old benchmark. I measure with rope and a couple of sticks, using a pair of binoculars tied fast to one of the sticks. I get the approximate boundaries. It's a good size; long, pie-shaped. It goes down the side of a hill to nip a small stream at the bottom. There's heavy second, third growth; nobody's cut wood in here for over thirty years, at least. All together there are just under five thousand square meters, about an acre. It's perfect for what I have in mind. There's even an overgrown path going to within fifty meters of the place.

I stake everything out and go back to Mathilde; tell her I've found her *bois.* She waves it away to me. I tell her I want to buy it; she shrugs.

I offer a thousand francs, about two hundred bucks. Madame Calvert writes the offer out for me in reasonable French. I don't think Mathilde ever had so much money at one time in her life. She still doesn't quite understand why I'm giving her money. I explain over and over, feeling like the Pilgrims buying land from the Indians; next thing, I'll be pushing beads off on her.

Of course, everything has to go through a *notaire;* that bastard takes fourteen percent for nothing. There are robbers every way you turn, no matter where you are. Handlers take everything, do nothing.

SHAVING EDGES, CONFABULATING HEDGES,
NIBBLING AWAY AT THE CORE OF THINGS.
THESE ARE THE REAL WHORES IN OUR LIVES,
TITHING TO THEMSELVES WITHOUT WORTH,
DRIVING HARD WORKERS TO THE EARTH.

So now we're back to Easter vacation after my trip to Spain. We've got some little tucks and seams showing in our tale here. Nothing like a tuck in your tail, like Dagwood's dog, Daisy.

IT'S NOT ALL AN EVEN BROADCLOTH.
MAYBE LIFE CAN BE A MÖBIUS STRIP,
A TWIRLING TRIP; BUT I CAN'T SEEM
TO FIND JUST THE RIGHT TWIST.

By Easter, the deal is closed; I own that little wood. Kate thinks I'm crazy but laughs; she's used to my crackpot ideas; even learns to like some of them. I'm going to build a hut, a wild nest, for nature freaks.

I keep hearing ragged-looking, spaced-out slobs, my friends' children, who eat nothing but brown rice, granola and cashew nuts, talk about how they want to live in nature, unpolluted nature. They sit blowing cigarette smoke in my face, complaining how the industrialist bastards are polluting the face of our beautiful planet.

The Scumbler will build them an ideal place to live, a place where nobody's even walked for maybe thirty years. It's not going to be in Afghanistan, or on the tea hills of Sri Lanka either, but right in the center of civilization, la belle France.

This place will be built with natural things: natural rocks, natural wood, natural dirt. Then the Scum's going to rent it for natural dark green money.

I'm going to have great fun building this place, too. I'm all charged up from my Spanish trip, ready to paint; I'll use some of that excess energy to build. I'm also still trying to work Sandy out of my mind; give this old psyche some peace.

I tie a shovel, a pick and lunch on back of Mike's Honda. He keeps it down here, says it's too dangerous driving a motorcycle in Paris. He's right, but how else could I get around with my paint box? I work my way up into the place. His machine's not a cross bike, but it's good enough with careful driving to get in there. The old nesting juices are flowing madly. I'm building one more of my hiding places. I think all my paintings are probably hideouts, too. I make up my own world, crawl in, then invite people to join me. This book is something like that, when I come to think about it. Look around, how do you like it here, inside my head? A bit messy, isn't it.

WE INVADE EACH OTHER, ENTWINE
OUR HEARTS AND MINDS IN A PLACE
WHERE WE ARE NOT. COULD BE THE
GREATEST MIRACLE OR A LOT OF ROT.

I dig a hole twelve feet by eighteen—nice proportion. I dig down about five feet on the high side and three feet on the low. There's one hell of a lot of rock; I save them.

There're tons of rocks in this country; makes for lousy agriculture. The houses around here are all built of rock; most of them don't even have mortar, just mix dirt with lime and pile rocks up carefully. My mill's built that way and it's almost three hundred years old. Jet sonic boom from the military air base in Dijon most likely will shake it down if the government doesn't get smart soon: houses, barns falling in all the time.

It takes four days to dig and level the hole. I feel my gut tightening up. I always like to do hard physical work on vacations. Kate does most of the homekeeping on these long vacations when she's not teaching. Digging holes, cement work—that kind of thing keeps my thick old blood flowing just right, maybe keep me living a couple extra years or so.

I've decided to build this house the way the ancient Gauls did.

I hunt around for straight trees to shape into poles. I find some small pines; cut out about twenty poles, leaving the bark on them—everything natural.

Next day, I haul out a sack of cement, fifty kilos, a hundred ten pounds. It's rough maneuvering the bike but I get it in there; trailbreak those last fifty yards. The practice I got beating Sweik's Ariel up from Spain comes in handy.

It's amazing how these little Frenchmen around here can handle heavy weights; they throw these cement sacks around like medicine balls. The men in the Morvan are all about five feet tall: old worn Celtic blood; not enough to eat for generations; brutally hard work. They're tough, hard-handed little guys. Most of them drink too much, usually dead at fifty. The women live forever. Old Monsieur LeCerbe, Mathilde's husband, was the startling exception. Now he's dead, too. I'm the only man in our village: cock of the coop, me and a bunch of strong old ladies. They can get together and bury me in the cemetery up on the hill: nice view.

> MY CEMETERY PLOT HAS A VIEW—FOR YOU. COME SEE ME. BUT I WON'T BE THERE FOR LONG. HOWEVER, COME ANYWAY: SING A SONG IN OUR HONOR; LOOK OUT AT THE ROLLING HILLS AND KNOW I'M PART OF THEM NOW. YOU'RE REALLY SEEING ME-US. DO YOU HEAR ME?

I start mixing cement with the sand and dirt in the bottom of my hole. I just stir it around dry, then pour in water

I haul from the stream. I do about a square yard at a time; takes me two days to lay the slab. I let it dry one day, Easter Sunday. I eat our Easter eggs till I'm almost sick, part of the family tradition.

Next day, feeling sluggish, I start with rocks, building up sides. I fit rocks and butter the spaces with cement. I haul a new bag of cement every time I come in; getting better at it. The kids are helping now, making a clubhouse sort of thing with me, honing their nesting instincts. Mike's good at cement work, a fine thing for a young person to know. Tim and Sara are mixing the mortar, hauling water up from the stream. We've got a real team going.

I run our walls up a foot higher than ground level; line them with plastic on the outside to run water off downhill. I shove dirt against those walls to hide the plastic; can't put off my nature folk with nasty plastic.

Now the place looks like the cellar of a house that got blown away in a tornado. I've left a hole in the center of the slab. I set up and cement in place a center pole. This pole is about ten feet tall. I lash our roof poles out from this center pole to ground level, resting them on the edge of our wall all around and extending them two or three feet beyond the wall. Sara helps with this; she has an eye as accurate as a plumb level and knows how to use her body for shifting and holding heavy weights. I try not to force the kids too much with this building mania of mine but I'm convinced it gives them a security and life meaning they'll need later on. Even Tim, at eleven, can drive an eightpenny nail into dry oak without bending it.

This job is like building a tepee, but permanent. We anchor the ends of the poles in cement and rock. The whole thing is solid; the kids have great fun climbing over it, like a jungle gym. I cut the poles off short on the downhill side to give some window space and a place for a door opening. It's going to be a Hobbit kind of door anyway, only about four feet high. I build and hang the door, then rough in three steps down to level.

I use extra slate left over the roof job on our mill. We hang it on lath I get in Château-Chinon. The slate I bought secondhand from a scavenging mason. It was only fifty centimes a slate, so I bought all he had. This is real hand-cut old Savoyard-style slate, almost impossible to find now.

I leave one hole on the back wall for the chimney opening. We work like wild people and have that chimney built and ready to burn in one day. We build it from rock and now we're gathering rock from all over. By the time we're finished, there isn't a reasonable-sized stone within a hundred yards.

The next day, I rig the windows with heavy-duty transparent plastic. Real glass is too expensive and would be a bitch to transport in on the bike. My nature folk will have to put up with this plastic, better than having wind and rain blow in, better than total darkness. I make the windows double and tight, each rolling up for good weather.

Mike and I cut down tree branches to improve our view out toward the stream. We use these branches to build furniture. We make rustic kinds of porch-type chairs and stools. Sara designs them, Mike cuts them out while Tim and I do the nailing and fitting. They're crude but comfortable.

I haul in a piece of foam rubber from the mill for a bed, and build a small platform beside the fire on which to put it. We hustle up some extra knives, forks, spoons and a few plates. We find an old cracked pitcher and a bowl for washing up. I bring out a butane stove we don't use anymore and a butane tank. We dig a john about twenty yards downhill toward the stream on the path to water. A little bit of pollution can't hurt. Mike builds a one-holer and shields it with a barricade of branches. The roof isn't much but there's a fine view of the stars. Sara even puts in a roll of toilet paper, hinges a slate over it to keep off the rain—all the comforts of home.

Our nature nesters can haul water up from the stream, use candles or oil lamps for light, cook on the stove and have the fireplace for heat. A real nature person could live here in great style. When it's time to head back for Paris, we all hate to leave.

Sara and Mike want to keep Tim with them and stay on a few weeks more, but their school would blow a gasket. They're already upset with us because we let the kids stay home when they want to. There's a true kind of sickness we call *mal d'école,* sick of school, and the best cure for it is a day in bed reading. Feeling a prisoner in school takes all the joy out of learning or thinking. The headmaster is one of those types who spends more time checking to see that all the "inmates" are locked in than that they're learning anything; should get himself a job somewhere as a warden.

We get our whole hut done for under a hundred and fifty bucks. It's the kind of nest that's really fun to make. We'll rent it for fifty a month. I know there'll be a high turnover; kids won't stick it out; we'll just insist on three months in advance, minimum. Actually be doing them a favor, helping them find their true profile, what they can realistically handle; might even come up with a modern-day Thoreau; that'd be nice.

A CHANCE FOR LEARNING STEPS TO THE DANCE
OF LIFE; TO STRIDE OUT ON THE BALLROOM FLOOR
UNDER STEADY STARS AND CURVED BRANCHES.
THE WIND IS THE MUSIC AND ALL LIVING THINGS
ARE YOUR PARTNER. READY? ONE—TWO—THREE!

We're not more than a week back in Paris when a son of friends in America comes for one of those late, spring-fever springtime visits. He has a woman friend with him; she's wearing white overalls and a beaded headband, looks like an Algonquin carpenter.

He starts off by complaining because we're using detergent to wash our dishes. He doesn't volunteer to wash dishes himself, with or without detergents, but he's an impressive expert on how detergents pollute the streams and rivers. We talk. They both wallow in non-language: "Like, you know what I mean—like, real beautiful—how come—right on, man—" It's hard having a conversation, getting them to say something. They only roll over the same set pet phrases.

It turns out he's "deep into" how he wants to find a completely "unspoiled" corner of the world where "human beings can live like human beings." That's a direct quote. The girl friend has her spaced-out, wraparound eyes pinned on him.

I tell about this place I have. It's in tune with nature: nothing disturbs the natural forest; everything made from nature, the indigenous materials.

"And there's a clear, clean unpolluted stream flowing right by, not a detergent within ten miles."

He sits back behind his fifty-dollar handmade Indian shirt and thick leather belt. He pulls at his two-hundred-dollar Universe boots. He squirms. The girl friend's excited in an underwater way.

"Beautiful! This is what we've been looking for, Dyn."

What the hell could Dyn stand for? They're both packed to the eyeballs with traveler's checks, from seven banks in five countries. They don't want to be caught in any dollar devaluation; prepared for anything. They have a thousand dollars in camping gear, which, incidentally, they dropped right off their backs as they walked through our apartment door. THAT'S pollution.

They have tents that roll up to fit in a pack of cigarettes; sleeping bags made out of Reynolds aluminum and hummingbird feathers, tested by astronauts on the moon; compasses with built-in computers; a stove the size of a flashlight; solar flashlights that will burn a thousand hours.

While we're talking, Mike and Sara come home from play practice at school. We're having pizza for dinner, so they were supposed to pick up some dough from the baker around the corner. In French it's called *pâte,* said like a combination of "pat" as in patty-cake and "pot" as in pots and pans. Mike puts his books in his room, comes out with the paper package of pâte. He hands it to Kate.

"I could only get a kilo of pâte, Mom. That's all they had."

Our guests are electrified. It takes me a few seconds to figure what's the matter. I pick it up.

"But, Mike, we have guests, a kilo won't be enough. Try the guy on Basfroi."

"He'll never sell us pâte, Dad, he saves it for his Algerian customers. It'd be a waste of time!"

They've actually turned green, with shock or envy I'm not sure. No sense having any heart attacks on the premises so I tell them about French pâte. We all laugh and they giggle nervously, Dyn fingering his pouch and papers.

TOXIC FLIGHT, AFRAID TO FACE THE
PANIC GLORY OF WHITE NIGHTS.

That weekend I drive them down and we hike out to the place. Dyn lies on the bed; she sits cross-legged on the floor—getting vibes, she says. I build a fire. I walk them down to the stream; show the john.

"Very organic," he says.

"Beautiful, far out!" says she. I get them to pay three months' rent before they know what's happened. I help them buy a secondhand motorbike in Château-Chinon, so they can get in and out, do some shopping. It just might be the greatest experience of their lives.

He's going to write a book. He has a black leather folder and about twenty sharpened pencils with his name on them in gold. He won't say what it's about except it has to do with youth looking for reality in a false world; "A sort of modern-day Don Quixote," he says. He says it "quick shot"; took me a while to figure what he meant; I've always said it something like "coyote."

She's going to make her own loom, weave. The whole deal turns out so well I search up six more woods and buy the batch for under fifteen hundred bucks. I'm going to fix and build more nature nests in the summer with the kids helping me. It'll be a sort of private summer camp for American overprivileged overaged teenagers.

On the drive up to Paris, spring really shows itself; the closer we get, the greener everything is. The chestnut trees are just coming into blossom. I'm dying to start painting; it seems I haven't had a paintbrush in my hand for years.

THE PAINT HAS BEEN LEAN IN MY BLOOD,
BLEACHED OUT BY FEAR AND PSYCHIC PANIC.
BUT NOW IT THICKENS, THROBBING IN MY TEMPLES.
THIS OLD TEMPLE OF THE HOLY GHOST-RESURRECTED.

XVI

CRS = SS

When we get settled in Paris, I roll on back into the Marais. I'm planning a painting of a façade with a little grocery in front, the shop door open; there's a courtyard in the background and I'll build that in, too. It's going to take a big canvas, a 50F. The paint box is stored at Goldenberg's, so I'm hauling the canvas down there roped on my back. I've done it plenty of times before, like sailing a small boat in a squall.

It's on the edge of rain, so I'm wearing my crummy fake black leather jacket I bought in the flea market for three bucks. I'm also wearing my helmet with my name printed on it. This helmet nobody's going to steal it's so old, especially with my weird name painted on it in acrylic paint. I hate carrying the damned thing and, worse yet, I despise locking it to the bike. I just leave it on the seat. Nobody's going to steal that old bike or that old helmet. One of the ways to feel safe is not having anything anybody else could want enough to steal.

IF YOU CAN'T GIVE IT AWAY,
YOU SHOULDN'T OWN IT.
IF YOU'D DIE FOR IT, THEN
YOU CAN'T LIVE WITH IT.

I prefer not wearing any helmet at all, but the cops are getting very touchy about people on motorcycles without helmets. The French now have a mandatory helmet law. It's not going to cut down on accidents; in fact, it'll probably increase them. You can't hear or see as well and you get a false sense of security, take more chances.

If I'm willing to have my head broken open, that should be *my* choice. I *know* I'm safer without a helmet. You start out a government to help people and the next thing you know they're running your life.

MOM AND DAD ARE BIOLOGY. BUT
YOU'RE MOST LIKELY SICK IF YOU
GET YOUR KICKS FROM POLITICS.
WEAN YOURSELF NOW, CLEAN YOUR
OWN DIAPERS. WATCH OUT FOR
SHOE TIERS AND NOSE WIPERS.

Anyway, I'm cruising along Boulevard Saint-Germain on the bike in my jacket and helmet, with the canvas strapped on my back. I'm completely legal. I'm just turning there in front of the bridge over the river where it turns in to Henri-IV when two CRS police bastards jump out in front of me with submachine guns. I stop. Of course I stop, and these jerks pull me off the bike before I can even get the kickstand down. The bike falls over and when I reach to pick it up, they pull me away. They're being very tough while my gasoline at three dollars a gallon is pouring into the street. It could cause a fire or an explosion.

They drag me over to one of their gray wagons. I have to struggle out of my canvas just getting through the door. A 50F canvas is over three feet by four feet. I lean it against the wagon; go up a few steps and inside.

A very mean-looking creep is sitting behind a little desk in back. The wagon smells of spit and sweaty leather. I have my helmet off and tucked under my arm. The little flic behind the desk points at it.

"Qu'est-ce qu'il signifie ça, monsieur?"

What's that mean? he says. I look down at the helmet.

"C'est un casque!" says I.

"Ça, ça!"

He leans forward and points at my name on the helmet. I look down. I tell him in French that it's my name, my family name. He looks very cynical; maybe that's skeptical, maybe it's both. My name could maybe be a peace slogan in French. He probably thinks I'm advocating love not war or something. I am. I definitely am, but not by walking around with slogans on my motorcycle helmet!

He asks for my passport. I give it to him. He stares at it several minutes, turning all the pages. He's pissed because it really is my name. Then he asks why I'm wearing the leather jacket. I tell him I thought it was going to rain. I'm trying my damnedest to be nice. Now he asks my why I'm *bouclié.* He kind of jumps forward and springs this on me. I don't quite understand the word in French but figure it out. He means, why am I carrying a shield.

Things are getting ridiculous and I can't stop a small smile from sneaking into the corners of my mouth. This is a big mistake; you can laugh at a French cop but never even half smile at the CRS. They're the French equivalent of the Gestapo: really vicious cats, with the male sickness and too much power.

I tell him I'm a tourist painter and my "shield" is a canvas I'm taking to paint on. One of the goons in the truck behind me thinks this is funny, snickers. He's *not* helping.

The little guy asks why I've come to France just now to paint. I tell him I'm painting the area around where Les Halles used to be. I'm not going to say where I'm really painting. I've already done a lovely series on Les Halles before the idiots ripped it down and built the stupid Forum and Pompidou Center. It took me most of a year, thirty giant paintings all done at night or in the early morning. I have them stored in my attic; still trying to sell the whole thing or make one of those video cassettes I was talking about.

I tell him I'm painting way over there, so if he sends any snooper-troopers they won't find me. I'm getting more paranoid all the time.

A totalitarian society does it to you. The secret of a totalitarian state is to make so many goddamned rules and taxes nobody can possibly obey the rules, pay the taxes and survive. Then they administer these rules and taxes to favor friends and screw the rest. Communists or Fascists, it's the same; just different names for the same bunch of crooks. France is into this scene big. There were huge changes during those ten years with de Gaulle. He really screwed up a lovely country.

The cop gives me back my passport and tells one of the goons to take me away. This jerk lines me up on the side of the wagon with three other victims. They all look scared; *I'm* scared. I try talking to one of them but the guard lowers his tommy gun on us. This is serious! A crowd's standing back at a respectable distance. I notice gray CRS trucks in a row clear across the bridge. I can never figure whether they do this because of some tip or they're trying to start something. Just *seeing* all those brutes in uniforms, paratrooper boots and helmets with plastic covers, shields and those tommy guns can *make* trouble happen. Paris is getting to be an occupied city.

CITY OF LOVE AND LIGHT NOW
DIMMED BY A BLINDING BLIGHT.

So here I am a prisoner of the CRS, torn between being scared shitless and pissed off. I'm trying to figure how I can get word to somebody about where I am. People are disappearing all the time in Paris, especially foreigners. They sometimes question suspects by dunking them in the river; no marks. I'm too old for this crap; I only want to paint my pictures.

I look into the crowd, catch the eye of a young woman. I run my finger over my name on the helmet. She pretends not to notice; probably a collaborator. I try it with an old man and another lady; they don't seem to catch on, act afraid. Maybe the French left all their guts in the mud during WW I.

Time passes; we've been there more than an hour. Two other goons get out of the truck; they go over to the guard on the left. The one on the right passes in front of us; it's the changing of the guard. Now's my best chance.

I take four steps forward into the crowd and turn around! I'm half expecting to be cut in half by tommy guns. I'm hoping they won't shoot into the crowd. I stand there. I'm afraid some fink will denounce me, give me away. Nothing. The new guards take their places; first goons get into the wagon. Now inertia's in *my* favor; I keep moving back slowly till I come out the other side of the crowd. An old guy gives me a wink, maybe a survivor from Verdun. I'm almost free.

I have to decide whether I'll abandon the motorcycle and canvas. I decide to take what's mine; the hell with them. The canvas is still leaning against the truck. I come up from the blind side, grab it and rope it on my back again. My hands are shaking so they get in each other's way.

I move slowly toward my motorcycle. Nobody's guarding it. It's still on its side. I pick it up. Gasoline's spilled all over, melting tar in the road. One foot peg's bent and the clutch handle's twisted. I'll fix them later. I roll out of the gas puddle: blowing up's no fun either. It takes four kicks to turn over. Good old bike, but it make one hell of a noise. Now's when they mow me down for the amusement of the people.

I drive slowly till I turn a corner, then cut out like a madman, heading north. I twist through all the side streets of the Marais. I get to Goldenberg's. I'm not much good for painting. I store the new canvas with my box and put down two good shots of slivovitz. My stomach's flipping; I'm going to have the shits for three days, at least.

I roll home, tell Kate and the kids what happened. They won't believe me; they figure I'm only fantasizing, romanticizing again, trying to make life more interesting than it really is. I practically get myself killed pulling off a semi-heroic escape and they won't believe me. They're right; I don't want to believe it myself. I decide to pretend it didn't happen.

CRAWLING LIKE VERMIN IN THE DARK ARE
THE MAGGOTS OF FEAR: WAITING ONLY THE
GARBAGE OF VIOLENCE TO HATCH, DRY, FLY,
SPREAD SPIRITUAL-MENTAL LOSS. DIS-EASE.

After dinner I flop out on the living-room floor, dead to the world. I wake up at three in the morning and start going over the whole thing. I get so mad I can't sleep anymore. I take a Valium, take a diuretic; got to keep the blood pressure under control; got to plan revenge.

Generally, I'm against revenge of all kinds. It might be sweet but usually, in the long run, it rots your teeth. I do some deep breathing, try to stop the blood pounding in my head. I bring on the Kee Ring-Kee Rings; picture birds flying loosely with control against a blue sky. No good; I can't get those CRS bastards out of my head. I haven't licked the male sickness in me yet, not by a long shot.

The next day I go down to Goldenberg's, pick up the box and canvas. I roll back to the studio and paint a huge picture of violence, with CRS goons clubbing students, boys, girls, old ladies. There are burning buildings behind them in the night, cars turned over, blood flowing at their feet in the street. I paint them blue, Prussian blue, in helmets and visors, cowering behind their shields. I spend three days painting this crazy thing.

I think maybe I'll do twenty of these big violence paintings, hire a gallery, call the show CRS=SS. I wallow in this idea while I'm painting.

Then I stop. "Shit, hell no! I'm not going to do anything stupid like that!" I don't care enough to spend my time that way. Also, I'd like to stay in France. If the French officials ever get mad and look closely into the way I live my life, I'm a dead duck.

OUTSIDE THE BOUNDARIES. OUTLAW.
I'M INLAW TO MY WIFE'S SISTER,
BUT OUTLAW TO ALL WHO TRY RUNNING
MY LIFE: INCLUDING MY WIFE *AND*
HER SISTER.

Then I think about my tunnels. I'll get the motorcycle club together. We'll operate out of the tunnels, buy gallons of paint, come up everywhere on the Left Bank simultaneously, spray, paint, carve CRS = SS on all the walls. We'll call the whole caper the "Gruyère Affaire." James Bond hits Paris.

Hell, I'm not going to do that either. I'm not going to write anything on those lovely walls. It feels good just knowing I'm not going to do anything.

Deep inside myself I know *that* kind of stupidity isn't worth it. There's no sense going back to jungle ways. This human animal has evolved; our fingernails, teeth aren't designed for clawing, biting; our arms have shortened, become more flexible, sensitive to handle tools not only weapons. Physiologically we've evolved; emotionally we should move on, too.

All that physical-dominance horseshit has to be discouraged. We need to be part of life; living with, not against; getting along; not just getting by, or getting ahead. There's no hurry anyway; we're all headed for the same place.

GIVE IN, GIVE WAY, GIVE UP. GIVE
TO HAVE TIME FOR LIVING WITHOUT STRIFE.
DOING ANYTHING SERIOUS, LIKE PAINTING
IS HARD ENOUGH, WHY MAKE IT ROUGHER?

I go back and dig into the Marais again. It feels great. Those walls, those people give off fine vibes of continuity, life support.

But something *did* happen to me. I was violated deeply, psychically raped. Violence to body and spirit like that always leaves a mark. It's as if we're each a sort of running balance, registering the good, kind things people do for us along with the mean, violent things. How much we can trust, how much we can love, is in that balance.

I used to think I had a shit-heavy load on the wrong side. But I'm working on it; nicer and nicer things happen to me every day. By the time I'm dead, I might almost be able to live with myself. At thirty, I was the most angry animal breathing air. I was so bad I couldn't even trust myself to sleep.

COMING OUT FROM UNDER PERSONAL CLOUDS
WITHOUT DOUBT. TRYING TO FIGURE WHAT
IT'S ALL ABOUT WITHOUT WINDING UP IN A
SHROUD TOO SOON. TELEPHONE? WHO?
AL CAPONE??!!

XVII

UGLY ORGY

The idea of painting the motorcycle club is still bubbling in my mind. I'll make it a big group portrait, like Rembrandt or Hals; the "Night Watch" of motorcycles. I want something to fill the entire visual field, big as a mural but designed as an easel painting. Maybe it'll be another way to help everything seem to mean something, hold together. It'd also be a way to immortalize temporarily that wonderful bike of Sweik's, put off oblivion for a while.

The white-on-white painter in the Bastille studio never came back. I settle myself in there; don't need the rent money right now. The French blue-blood sculptor downstairs is still off in Carrara again cutting fat white stone. Maybe he got tired of all the perfumed creeps hanging over his shoulder, breathing in sculpture dust. He'll be gone for three or four months, so I have a two-story studio.

Traude is still upstairs. She's turned her attic into a fine nest. The whole place is covered with mattresses, so it's one big bed with that mirror on one end. You have to take your shoes off when you visit her. She has drapes hanging over the ugly parts, and a little samovar Sasha gave her standing in one corner. She hands me a big handleless cup of tea whenever I come. It's nice, relaxing with her; feel cut off from the hard world.

She tells me she's doing examinations for the fifth degree at the Alliance Francaise; wants to get a job when she's finished; doesn't want to go home. She can type, speaks English and German, as well as Dutch and French. She'll get a job OK. I can't help imagining what a terrific wife she'd make: bright, sensitive, strong—a real nest-maker. It's getting harder and harder to find women like her. The world's churning out propaganda against nest-making for men *or* women; considered low-class, degrading, bourgeois, unimportant. But what a fine mother she'd be! I'm jealous, I know. It's rotten enough being male but it's impossible being an old male; got to get used to it.

I buy a roll of canvas, two meters twenty high by twenty meters long. Costs seven hundred francs. I unroll eight meters. It's the longest I can fit in my studio. I spread this on the floor. I get wood from Dubois & Duclos, a lumberyard. I make a gigantic stretcher with the French equivalent of two-by-fours. It takes a whole day, plus a quarter kilo of tacks, getting the beast stretched without wrinkles. I do a double gesso ground and stand it up. Wow! It's like going snow-blind. I build a small stepladder so I can reach the top. I'll be running back and forth to paint.

I spend a week making sketches. I finally settle on one with Sandy and Sweik working on Sweik's Ariel, Lubar's tools spread out in the foreground. I'll do it with a Parrish kind of detail, every sprocket and reflection; tribute to that wonderful machine. I'll have Lubar and Dale sitting on the bike. Tompkins and Donna will be standing in the left foreground just behind the front wheel, watching. Duncan and Pierrette will be behind the rear wheel, to the right of Dale, drinking beer and looking toward the viewer. I'll have everyone at different angles to create visual movements through the space. It'll be some trick holding this baby together. The bike will be at a three-quarter angle to the picture plane. I'll have the Saint-Sulpice towers in the background. That big church has some feeling of a Harley-Davidson upside down, wheels spinning, anyway.

THE WHEELS OF HEAVEN SPIN IN SOME
MONSTROUS GAME OF CHANCE. PUT YOUR
LIFE WHERE YOUR MOUTH IS.

I'll have them up here, one at a time, to work in the portrait parts. I'll do sketches of Sweik's bike right there on the Place Saint-Sulpice. This painting will make "Guernica" look like comic-book art.

I spend another week transferring my drawing to the canvas. I buy one of those little glasses that make everything look far away. I can't actually get more than ten feet back from any part of the painting as it is now; have no way to tell how the damned thing really looks. I'll probably need to finish it off out in the alley.

. . .

It's a stupid thing to do, a painting like this. It's going to take over a month and nobody will ever buy it; nobody could even pay for the materials; nobody has a place to put it. This is a pure chunk of self-indulgence. It's wonderful not hustling for money. God bless you, Bert and Jan, volume buyers of fine paintings.

SOMETIMES AN ENCOUNTER HAS THE THRUST
OF INSIGHT, THE COMING TOGETHER AT ANOTHER
LEVEL, TANTALIZING TOUCH OF SUPERNATURAL.

I start by working up the entire painting in black, browns and whites, a genuine old-master-type cartoon affair; Leonardo and me. I get Sweik in first. I do him on a separate canvas, a 20F. Do him straight on, not the way I'll have him in the big one, where he'll be leaning over the bike. I just want to see him. What is it that gives him his spaced-out affectionate look, like a muscular Buddha? Blue-agate eyes wide apart, thick lips, bumpy skin—not pimples, bumps. He goes into some kind of trance while I'm painting him. When he talks, he talks mostly about Sandy. Since Spain they've been seeing each other.

He sits there and hardly blinks, the way the witch I painted in Spain did that time.

I get it all in one sitting. I'll paint him into my big painting when he isn't here. I want to paint everybody not so much the way they look but the way they are to me. I'm the lowest common denominator, the something that's in all of them. It's the way they are in this book, all partly me. And me, I'm partly them, the way they want me to be. The people and objects in this world only *seem* separate. In the big picture we're all the same thing, one greater being.

GRAVEL OF TIME DROPPING WITHOUT END,
POUNDING WITHOUT MOVEMENT. THE MEMORY
OF SAND, MAGIC OF CEMENT. WE CHASE IN
DEMENTED CIRCLES THE CONCRETE OF REALITY.

Generally, I get them in to pose one at a time. Painting Duncan, he says he's decided to marry Pierrette.

"Pregnant?" I ask hopefully.

"Nope," he says in his kind of inner-concentrated mind-drifting.

"Why do it, then?"

A moment's pause.

"Pierrette'd like it."

I keep painting, trying for the fadeaway in his cheeks; it can't be done with a line or a plane, has to be done with color. I can't get it too cold or he'll begin to look dead. I've got to keep it warm and make it go back. Good problem. Duncan's got high, side-moving cheekbones, makes for deep shadows. He'll be painted head straight on, looking out, a skull head to get something of the danger in bikes.

Holy Moses! I'm getting literary here. My mind goes in crazy circles when I'm painting. Writing about painting is like trying to kiss with a mouth punched full of novocaine. You know you're doing something; everything's in the right place but you can't feel it. I look up; Duncan's staring off into space.

"I've never been married yet; I'm thirty years old; thought I ought to try it out."

That's good a reason as any, but marriage without kids is a bread sandwich: two slices of bread; nothing inside, except maybe some butter or margarine.

I pull off one of Sandy I like. I do her very tough: arms folded, wearing her "What the hell" look. I miss the dolphin somehow; oil and water don't mix. I also get that asking look in her eyes; asking and telling at the same time. I try to paint what I feel for her: the powerful grandfather-granddaughter three-generation incest, the way she makes me feel—open, soft, vulnerable—but I can't get that either. We talk a lot about Sweik. I have his portrait and Duncan's on the wall behind me.

Dale's very uptight. She keeps backing away. I paint her like a bad Tampax ad; very *Rebecca of Sunnybrook Farm.* There's a tightness around those pop-up eyes of hers. In the painting she looks like the kind of girl who spent her teens in teeth braces and "A" cups. That must be a hard time for a little girl, when she's wondering if she's ever going to make it as a woman. A girl needs lots of help from everybody then; it's a giant leap. Too many never make it, stay girls. There aren't enough women in this world, at least the world I know; not many men either, for that matter.

Tompkins is a natural. I get the spiral-helix torque of physicist-poet. His eyes are open, soft, amazed at the world. His mouth is bearing into it. He has a twisted jaw, malocclusion; probably grinds his teeth at night. Donna sits there while I paint him and he stays on while I paint her. I don't think she trusts me. When Donna looks at me, big zeros register across her face; really zero; no negative numbers, total null.

Unfortunately, I get too much of that zero in the portrait. It looks as if she's watching a Western on television at two in the morning. It might well be the worst painting I've ever done; it even looks like her.

I try getting her to concentrate on Tompkins while I'm painting; turn up the flame a bit, but nothing happens. This is a very private woman. I decide I'll have her drinking from a bottle of beer, face half covered; those double-zero eyes looking over her hand.

My best painting is Lubar. I forgot he was coming that day. He had to struggle his way out of his office at IBM and cruise over on his BMW at lunch break. He catches me in but I don't have a blank canvas. So I paint him over an old canvas—dumb, poor practice technically and any painting is worth the twenty bucks in materials. Also, I don't trust my short-term judgment: too close; I'd probably paint over my best work.

I get Lubar sitting with his little bird head sticking out of his overwhelming leather jacket. The jacket has zippers all crisscrossing like scars. I paint his close-together eyes and bird-beak nose lapping his thin-lipped mouth in a snide half smile. The jacket's open showing white shirt and tie—modern man in disguise. The IBMW man.

He tells me his wife and he are finally divorced, she has the little boy; it doesn't seem to bother him. That part of life doesn't mean much to some men.

Lubar's migratory, sleeps around, no regular nest. One night he slept on our living-room floor, rolled his jacket under his head and zonked out, not even drunk. My Kate almost climbed a wall. She's not enthusiastic about people treating our nest as a flophouse.

Lubar's practically a pure migrating bird type. I'll have to try some birdseed on him. Has asthma, too; asthma's definitely a bird disease. People who are birds can't get the right kind of air on the ground. They all ought to live on tops of mountains.

I'm not having Lubar work on the bike and he's somewhat upset by that: other people using *his* tools! But he does bring his toolbox full for me to paint in the picture. I just couldn't let Lubar work on that lovely bike. He even has a hard time getting his contact lenses in. Sometimes he walks around without tying his shoes. It would be sacrilege, might work some kind of black magic and ruin the machine.

AN AWKWARD STUMBLING THROUGH LIFE,
TRIPPING ON HIDDEN TRUTHS WE ALL TRY
TO IGNORE: ANOTHER WINDOW, ANOTHER DOOR.

I'm having so much fun I begin worrying that I'm not serious enough about this painting. I'm painting and giggling; laughing too much and I'm not at all sure *why* I'm laughing. Still, I must say, some of the best paintings I've ever done have been the most fun.

Altogether, I do eight portraits. I'm putting myself in behind Sandy, looking over her shoulder with my back to the picture plane. Velázquez and me.

I spend three days painting Sweik's bike on the Place Saint-Sulpice. The last day, there's an enormous crowd around me. The flics come over from the station house to ask what I'm doing. I tell them I'm painting a portrait of a motorcycle, seems obvious. They want to know if the motorcycle is mine. I tell them no; I'm only an *admirateur.* The two of them stand beside me for a while, then head back across the Place to the station. Five minutes later they come with another flic; this one has extra braid on his shoulders and a flat hat. Here we go.

The square-headed flic with the braid asks me again if the motorcycle is mine. I stand stiff and salute with my brush. When I'm really bugged, I can get ridiculous.

These flics around the Place know me. We lived just up the street for nine years. Once they busted me because I was roller-skating around the Place with my kids. I'm giving our two eldest, Annie and Jim, roller-skating lessons. The cops tell me to get off the skates, stop. I tell them I won't. They take me by the arms and roll me into the station while I'm waving to the kids, telling them not to worry.

In the station they look all through their books: no law against roller-skating in public; no law against roller-skating on the Place. I think it just bothered them seeing a bearded man on roller skates laughing. If everybody were like me, we wouldn't need cops, so they know I'm a big threat to their jobs, subversive. Joy just might be catching.

Wintertime, when the water froze, the kids and I ice-skated around in the fountain itself. The cops watched us go round and round but didn't say anything. The whole police station of cops is standing outside their door freezing, watching us; lost their nerve. Terrific skating, like a miniature ice-skating rink. We rested by sitting on stone lion's paws. It got to be the thing to do; most of the kids in our neighborhood joined us. Paris is a good place for that kind of fun.

LIONS LURK UNDER SILVER-LEAVED TREES
AND THE FOUNTAIN POURS ROLLING STONES
IN ITS BED. STOP AND WAIT. THE
SUN IS SETTING WITH US.

Now they're wanting my papers. I give the top cop my passport, my *carte de séjour.* He stares.

Square-head asks if I have permission to paint the motorcycle. I tell him about Sweik. He wants to know where Sweik lives, has out his little book. I give him the address of a dentist I know in the sixteenth arrondissement. They'll never check. I snap off my brush salute, go back to painting and the head cop drifts away.

One of the young flics asks why I'm painting a motorcycle. I look at him; seems like a nice guy, really interested. I tell him about the big painting; invite him over to the studio; give him my address.

A NEW FACE IN AN OLD PLACE,
A NICE TOUCH, LITTLE OR MUCH.

This flic actually shows up the next day; looks almost human in civilian clothes. He's wowed by the painting. I get up nerve and show him our picture from the AMA magazine. There we all are standing in front of the cop motorcycles with the cop station behind us. They actually printed that picture we sent them, full-page spread. This young cop laughs his head off. He's never going to make it as a flic; cops *don't* laugh. Traude comes down from upstairs. She hears a young, laughing male voice, so naturally she comes down. I introduce them; his name is Clement and they go off together for a cup of coffee.

. . .

In the easel painting of the motorcycle I did out on the Place, it looks like a piece of pop art. In my big painting it's double life size; seems almost ready to roll off my canvas.

We have the gearbox open and the clutch spread on the ground cloth. That's the job they're doing in the painting, "clutch job." I think I'll call this painting "In the Clutch."

I work another week on the background. I get beautiful distance, fine air feelings between and behind the figures. The Hotel Récamier is on the right side of the painting and the Rue Férou closes off the right edge; a bit of the Luxembourg Garden shows at the end of Férou. The left side looks up the Rue Saint-Sulpice. The painting has a wide-angle-lens effect.

I take a day off to study the big Veronese painting in the Louvre called "The Marriage Feast at Cana." I try to establish the same relationship of thrust between foreground figures and background. Naturally, my background is pushed back with some subtle scumbling. I scumble white over the Saint-Sulpice towers against the sky, the sky wrapping itself around the towers: spinning Harley wheels. I keep trying to design movements and points of emphasis in both two and three dimensions. With a big painting you need to. If you're not careful, everything can fly off in all directions. This sucker's twenty-five feet across.

VARYING BACK WITHOUT THOUGHT, I
CRASH THROUGH SPACELESS TIME, CARRYING
IN SPENDED TROTH MY OWN LOST TRACKS.

Finally, it's finished enough so I need to take it out in our alley for the last touches. I cut a slit in the side wall; remove a board so the canvas can slide out without being removed from the stretchers. Sweik and Tompkins help me. We get it set up at the end of the alley.

Lord, is it ever impressive! It looks more real than anything real out there. It's like looking at a great Cinerama movie screen, only in broad daylight. I rig a cover over it with some rusty corrugated roofing tin.

I work another two weeks, running up and down the alley to get distance; those old-time painters of big paintings must have kept in terrific shape. I run off about five more pounds of gut; wasting away to a shadow, thick shadow. I'm using cans of paint I buy at a wholesale paint store; any size tube would be woefully inadequate. I spend more than two hundred bucks on paint alone. With a big surface like that, you need real texture if you want the apparent texture to look honest.

I take two days doing the last glazes and scumbles. By this time, there's a crowd every morning when I get there. By midday, the alley's full. People are lined up down our alley eating lunch standing up. One guy even has one of those periscope things for watching parades. There are some old geezers who come back day after day. Two girls are making sketches; it's a poor man's outdoor version of the Louvre. Motorcycles, coming in for a peek, clutter the streets for two blocks around. They make a tremendous racket blowing out pipes, racing each other, accelerating, booming away.

And, of course, the ever-loving flics arrive. They don't do anything, don't even talk to me, but they set up a guard. To be perfectly honest, I'm glad they're there. I leave a little light shining on the painting at night. It looks beautiful down the length of the alley, glowing, with everything dark. The gate to the alley is locked at ten o'clock by the concierge, so nobody can get in. Also, the blacksmith who lives next to the studio keeps an eye on things for me. Still, it's nice having flics sitting out there all night; there are all kinds of crazies. I'm half expecting the flics to present me with a bill, like when you hire the Garde Républicaine for a wedding party, or have the lights turned on the Eiffel Tower for an hour. Nope, it's all free. They're protecting the public interest.

CAN YOU SAVE ME FROM YOU—OR ME?
JUST WHAT ZOO IS THIS?

So then it's done; nothing more to do. I decide to have a party, celebrate. I get permission from the concierge to have my party in the studio; I know it will run over into the alley. It'll be a people's *vernissage.* I buy two fifty-liter barrels of wine, with spigots. I buy twenty bags of potato chips, a block of pâté, a wheel of Brie; cook popcorn for half a day.

I tell the cops I'm having a fête. In France, you're allowed one noisy party past ten o'clock a month. I tell any neighbors who might hear us; invite them to come. I get the affair for a Saturday night. Friday night the motorcycle people up on the Bastille hear about it.

Nearby, there's an American commune group living in a loft; call themselves the Skunk Patch. They're coming too. They've just driven down from Amsterdam in a psychedelic painted bus; on their way to New Delhi for a spiritual conference. They say they'll give a free show for the party. It's going to be a regular carnival.

Kate politely tells me she'd just as soon skip my people's *vernissage*. Says all she's worried about is the paintings getting hurt in the fun and frolic.

She looks me straight in the eye with her kindergarten withering look.

"Do you know *why* you're doing this? Why are you putting on this circus? It's costing a lot of money we could use and taking up too much of your time."

I know Kate's right; she usually is. I've asked myself some of these questions, not just about this *vernissage* but about a lot of things I do. I guess some of it's only simple showing off, playing the big shot. Another part's trying to convince myself I'm not dying, and *do* have some control of my own life. Doing something, anything, for no reason at all, playing, is one of the best ways, besides painting, to keep me from feeling pointed, aimed.

"I don't really know, Kate. I want to celebrate finishing the painting. I want people to see it before I have to take it off the stretchers and roll it up."

"Nobody's ever going to buy that painting, dear. It might be a good painting, probably is; but no one's ever going to buy it, so why put on this big show?"

We don't usually have these kinds of conversations. It's a decision we made at the beginning. Jane, my first wife, was always wanting to *talk* things out. We spent whole nights in bed sometimes, *sharing* our feelings, our hostilities, *ironing* things out. Then what good did it do? When something big happened, when I really needed her, she wasn't there.

I think talking's like drawing. You can talk your feelings away until there's nothing left to live, no mystery, no excitement, no romance, no spontaneity. As I said before, you can draw until there's nothing left to paint. It's the same.

But Kate wants some talking now. I'm not sure what to say. I know I don't want to say anything. I don't like looking inside myself any more than I have to. Part of being an artist is being able to surprise yourself. The best part of my paintings come from some secret inside places I don't know about. I think Kate surprises me even more than I surprise her; it's a big part of why I love her. I don't think I could live with a predictable, boring person. Kate's waiting. We're in the kitchen and I'm making popcorn.

"I can just call the whole thing off, Kate. It's probably a dumb idea anyhow. Why am I, the great gallery hater, giving a *vernissage?*"

"You know you don't want to do that, dear. All I say is just ask yourself what you're doing, think about it. Some of the things—the way you've been behaving the past months makes me wonder just what's the matter with you."

With that she goes out of the kitchen and the popcorn starts popping. I'm happy we don't go any deeper into things; I'm not ready yet.

SQUEEZING PIMPLES, A TOOTH
PICKED TO BLEEDING: FINDING OUT
IS NEVER QUITE THAT SIMPLE.

The party's already rolling before dark. It's a beautiful night: clear sky, big moon. Even though it's early summer, there's the feeling of a Halloween party. Mobs of people are on both floors of the studio; I'm hoping the whole place won't collapse. I set up the wine barrels downstairs; cover Claude's statues with burlap sacks. They look like corpses or mummies. The place has a spooky, mysterious look, lit only with candles.

There must be two hundred motorcycles lined up on the street outside our gate, mostly overpowered four-cylinder bastards. Guys with fluorescent helmets, full leather suits are coming down the alley like medieval knights. Their women are wearing fluttery Afghanistan jackets, sweat shirts. They're all loose-titted, swinging in the dusk.

The Skunk Patch crowd comes on at about eleven. They keep pouring in; there must be thirty of them. Leg-wrestling contests get started on the floor. The floor's already covered with spilt wine, some broken glasses. The driver of the Skunk Patch bus is the leg-wrestling champ. He's throwing people across the room with a twist of his leg. The place is beginning to smell heavily of grass. Holy cow, if those cops come in, they'll bust us for sure. I'm dancing like mad with all the wildest women. We're working up an ugly semi-orgy.

I FLAY VALIANTLY THROUGH UNCUT SKIES,
TESTED TANGENCIES VECTOR ME TO DESCENT.
I CLING HELPLESSLY TO A PROMISE OF MAGIC
IN THE PRIVATE INCANTATIONS OF DESIRE.

The painting's an enormous success. People are standing around it outside. I have it well lit with three spots. The motorcycle freaks are turned on by my painting of the machine; an old Ariel like that is a regular Mona Lisa to them. Sweik is there with Sandy. I can't believe it; she's wearing a dark blue suit, stockings and heels. She's even wearing a white blouse with a round tipped collar. She looks like a nun in mufti. She's leaning on his arm; he's standing straight, no back problem. It's nice to see them together. They spend most of the time looking at the painting, then leave about midnight.

That's when the Skunk Patch decides to do its trick. They wrestle in a huge plastic bag filled with yogurt. I don't know where they got all the stuff. Then one gal, one who's been dancing around in circles all evening—one hand, then the other, waggling over her head, like a confused Indian—strips and climbs into the bag. She lowers herself slowly into it. The other Skunk Patchers tie the top of that plastic sack tight under her armpits. She wiggles and squirms inside the sack, one hand, then the other, over her head. This woman must be six feet tall. She's like a giant slug with a woman's head, or a potato with a potato worm sticking its head out.

The bus driver–leg wrestler, called Billy, starts passing out straws to everybody; then he punches a hole in the side of the plastic with his straw and starts sucking out yogurt. Everybody joins in; the whole mob's bent around with straws and the woman's head is rocking back and forth over them. She's yelling "Suck, suck!" "Oh yeahh!"—things like that. Everybody starts taking turns on the straws. There's got to be fifteen kilos of yogurt in there.

They get it half sucked out so the yogurt is down to just below her tits, yogurt-covered tits and tight, slick plastic wrapped like pure pork sausages. I'm ready to get a flashlight pen and sketch pad to start drawing when the bag breaks.

Yogurt spreads slowly to the floor. Some women begin throwing off their clothes and rolling around in it; they start rubbing yogurt in each other's hair. The R-complex part of their brains is taking over. It's all getting very ritualistic. Guys begin licking yogurt off the tall woman, who's still spinning in her Indian dance. Round and round she goes, lick and lick and lick they go. They're licking her all over, looking for good spots. Other women start dancing in their own little circles. Everybody is licking everybody else off, with or without yogurt. Guys are getting covered with yogurt, so they take their clothes off, too. Now it's a true old-time full-screen orgy. Yogurt's all over the place; it's sticking to my Styrofoam ceiling. The burlap on the statues is saturated, sexy-looking. There's a mixture of laughing, screaming and slurping, licking noises.

I detach the water hose going to my studio upstairs; I'm afraid to go up there and look. There's hardly enough space on the floor to walk; more slurping, smacking sounds.

Kate knew what she was missing somehow. Maybe my mind doesn't think far enough ahead. Short-minded like shortsighted, that could be it all right; but then if you look too far ahead you get so paralyzed you never try anything, forget how to fool yourself.

MENTAL BLIND SPOTS SHIFTING
IN A VISUAL FIELD, NEVER SEEN
AND, IN NOT BEING SEEN, VISIBLE.

I turn on the water spigot outside in the court and begin spraying around with the hose. I'm washing yogurt off the gladiators. Maybe it'll cool the party off some. I spray around, putting out joints. Everybody's screaming and flopping over each other. I keep squirting, great fun. It looks like one of those summer New York pictures they always put in the newspapers on hot days where somebody's opened a fire hydrant and kids are jumping around in gushing water.

Now we have about six inches of floating yogurt on the floor. The water's draining slowly.

I turn *up* the music. They're beginning to tire out. There's a confused search for the right clothes, people helping each other dress, then helping them undress again. Clothes all wet, people wringing out shirts, pants, coats. Some of them go outside and wash themselves off at the spigot in the alley. Cézanne would've loved to paint this scene. The yogurt-soaked girls are lying flat on their backs on the cobblestones in front of my painting, slipping yogurt-soaked tight jeans over their slippery legs.

Just then, the flics come up the alley. I don't know what took them so long. I go out and tell how a plastic bag of yogurt we were going to eat for dessert exploded. We're all washing off. They don't believe me, nobody would, but the story's too good. They could never figure any other way to explain this scene anyway.

These are very nice flics. They tell me to cut down the noise; I turn the volume lower on the stereo. They say some of the bikes have to be moved: blocking traffic. I announce that. I invite the cops to come in, join us, but the chief is sitting out in the wagon waiting.

After they go, I go outside and look at my painting. It's inviolate: not a drop of yogurt or anything. It's beautiful standing out there, some more frozen time. People keep asking what I'm going to do with it now. I can practically cry looking at this beauty; like watching a daughter getting married. In the morning, I'll dismount it from the stretchers and roll it up. I really should wait another month to avoid crushing the texture and having it stick, but what the hell; there's not enough room in the studio to leave it up and still work. It blocks all the light. I've already had complaints from a couple of Italian guys whose garage door is blocked in the alley.

FORGIVEN TEMPTATIONS FALL EVENLY
WITHOUT CONTEMPLATION UNDER WATER-
WARMED ROCKS; ENEMIES WAIT SILENTLY.

These two Italians have a little factory where they fake Chinese lacquer ware. I visited the place once. They've worked out a fast dryer and heating system to get a many-layered effect. They make imitations of the Ming period, can make a dozen or more original Ming vases in a week. They're very good craftsmen; the best antique dealers buy from them. They've probably made more Ming vases than the Chinese. Our whole area here is filled with people faking everything from Louis XIII furniture to old brass. The center of the world's best fakes.

Well, the party starts dying off at about four. It goes on slowly, people sleeping, loving it up in different corners, smoking, dancing, until the morning light begins to make the candles look lonesome. I snuff them out, then dash over to a bakery and buy croissants. Some woman I don't know has volunteered to make coffee upstairs with the butane cooker. I don't know what's happened to Traude. Maybe she got mad and left or maybe somebody stole her.

We pass out coffee, croissants. I encourage people to go home. With some people, you open the door and they move in for life. Finally, I push the last bunch out the door and lock it. The coffee-making woman is moving around with a broom sweeping up. She's very efficient. I figure she's a waitress by the way she gathers up glasses, carrying a dozen at a time, slipping them into a bucket full of water.

I'm scooping up coal shovels of dirty yogurt and throwing it through the sewer grate. Our rats down there must think their luck has changed.

We get it all fairly well cleaned by seven. I begin to feel let down. I can't decide whether to go upstairs and flop out or go home. I know Kate's going to be too nice about it all. I can't face that.

I decide to climb upstairs and sleep it off in Traude's nest. The coffee-making girl follows me. She's not a girl at all; she's a woman, maybe thirty-five; first-class woman at that. We lie down together close and go to sleep. Nothing said, just sleep. What a nice way to end a party.

Later, I find out her name is Vascha, or Vrashca, Russian-sounding name. She's doing her doctorate at the Sorbonne in sociology, works as a waitress to stay alive.

Here we have another tremendous wife going begging. She'd have fine, close-to-the-ground kids with quick hands. I wish sometimes I had nine lives like a cat. I'd have a wife to go with each life; nine kids with each wife. Be-nine, benign, not malignant, benign; I think I hope! Or—better yet—I'd trade in those whole nine lives for just one life as a woman, an honest-to-God mother.

If I could be a woman, I'd have as many kids as possible, each by a different man, by as many different kinds of men as possible, from pygmies to Watusi, from Scandinavian blond giants to Semitic desert people. I'm convinced we're on the brink of destroying our species, maybe all species, if not the whole damned planet. During that war I sat out in prison, we killed over fifty million people with ordinary weapons; just think what we can do with atomic weapons!

I like humans, despite what that psychiatrist in the prison might say; I'd like to think of our species staying around for a while. To me, the only answer seems to be making a *new* kind of people, people who don't want to destroy themselves, or, if we can't manage that, at least having enough different kinds and blends of people around so there's a better chance for a few surviving and carrying on, staying alive, getting things going again after everything goes KAFLOOEY!

TWINKLE, TWINKLE LITTLE MUSH-
YOU DIDN'T LEAVE US MUCH ROOM!

XVIII

FIREMEN'S BALL

On Monday, I roll the big painting and store it under the steps where Duncan keeps his stuff. Duncan paints part-time. He does big abstract things on fiberboard. He has no place to store them in the little apartment where he and Pierrette are living, so he keeps them at my place. We stack them under the ladder going up to Traude's.

I stand my rolled-up master-monster painting in the corner there.

The storage of paintings is always a big problem for working artists; usually, nobody wants what we do but they seem too important for us to let go, forget.

SO HERE I AM, I'M A PAINTER.
AND THERE YOU ARE: A PERSON,
A BOTTLE, OR A WHITE CLOTH
WITH A BLUE SHADOW.

YOU'RE A MOUNTAIN, BLUE AND GREEN
OR A TABLE IN TWO-POINT PERSPECTIVE.
SO HERE AM I. WHERE ARE YOU?

I'm overflowing the attic at home, so I decide to make some storage for other paintings here at the studio. I buy piano wire and string it on staples, up and down, tight from floor to ceiling in that place under the steps. I space the wires about two inches apart. I string more than a hundred wires up and down; it's like a giant harp. When I strum it, there's background music for *Star Wars.* I suspend a platform in the middle and have storage for two hundred paintings. That should take some strain off the attic. My paintings will stand up against the wires but not touch each other; perfect. I'll haul stuff over from the *grenier*-attic a little at a time, using my wooden handcart.

I bought the handcart from a carpenter down the alley; got it for a hundred and fifty francs. It's one of those antique jobs with big wheels and a sliding tailgate. I move all kinds of things in it; it's also great for saving a parking place till Kate comes home from school. Parking is hellish in Paris.

I used to give our kids rides in the cart, too. Once I pulled Sara and Mike all the way over to the Jardin des Plantes zoo. Downhill going was OK, but tough coming back. The cart makes a loud, crunching noise on the streets because the wheels have metal rims. The kids loved it, good exercise for my old legs and heart, too; better even than running around the dining-room table.

I've always known exactly where to look from our place in case of fire at the studio. That whole damned alley is a firetrap. Those buildings are wooden and there's woodwork going on with machinery, paint, solvents. Also, there's Le Forte with his blacksmith shop. But worst of all are those cockeyed Italians with the Chinese Ming-ware factory. One cigarette in that spray room and everything goes swoosh. I have a special fear for fire.

One morning, about a week after the party, I'm running around our apartment bare-ass, sweeping, dusting, straightening up, when I look out the window and there it is, just in the wrong place. Black smoke's rolling up. I jump into clothes and scoot downstairs. I rev up the Honda and I'm there in three minutes. It's the Chinese Ming place; thunderous flames are shooting out. A few people are standing around with stupid looks on their faces. I pick the most intelligent-looking one and tell him to run to the restaurant and phone the fire department. He's an Arab, doesn't speak much French; we don't get anywhere. A little black girl is listening; she understands. I give her a franc, point to the restaurant and she runs like hell.

I dash up our alley. The Italian guys are beating at their fire with burlap bags. I pull out my water hose and try to squirt the fire, but the hose isn't long enough and I don't have enough power. The fire's starting to roar now. Huge, thick clouds are blotting out the sun. Brings on bad memories of my house burning in that California brushfire; eighty-two of us went down and I got the lining burned out of my bronchial tubes: spat black for six months. To this day, I can't stand eating in a restaurant with people smoking. If the ticker doesn't give out first, I'll probably die of throat cancer. That's how Sisley went; terrible death for such a fine painter.

I start spraying water onto the roof of my studio and

on my walls facing the fire. It's already getting too hot to stay there. I keep listening for fire engines. I spray myself and try getting closer but it's hopeless. I leave the water running and dash in for paintings. I drag down all the portraits for the motorcycle painting. I go back. I get out two of Duncan's big ones. There's still time for another trip. I'm heading back to get my motorcycle monster masterpiece when two flics grab me by the arm.

I try explaining about the painting. My French abandons me. They hold on to me tighter. Jesus! What'd happen if I punch out two cops? Who am I kidding? I couldn't punch my way out of a Big Mac Styrofoam carton. But they see it in my eyes. They hold me by the arms. I try putting my tongue in order, let the left half of my brain take over; explain slowly.

I ask them to spray some water on the roof of my studio and on the wall while I get some more paintings and maybe some sculpture out. No, they say, I have no permission to wet the building, neither do they. That's the work of the *pompiers*.

They want to know if I'm the *propriétaire*. I tell them I'm the *locataire,* the renter, but my paintings are in there. The buildings are going up in flames and we're being legalistic! They'll let the whole thing burn down so they won't have responsibility for any damage.

Two cars and three trucks are parked in back of the alley. There's still time to get them out; I tell the flics this. One strolls in and tries the door of one of the cars: locked. He shakes his head and comes back. He's going to let them burn because he won't force a car window. They'll most likely explode, blow gasoline over everything.

The corner of my studio is burning now. All we need do is spray it with my hose. The flic turns off the water at the spigot; I can't believe it!

People are hanging out windows, almost as much fun as watching the crazy painter paint.

SENSING THE BEGINNINGS OF NONEXISTENCE, OUR
SOULS TREMBLE, YEARN FOR THE FIRE OF ANNIHILATION.

The fire department finally arrives. They come running up the alley with ass-backward hats and axes. Yep, fellows, it's a fire! Yessiree, paintings, sculpture are burning up; isn't it a lovely day for a fire?

I hurry to move the paintings, the ones I did get out, off to the side so these firemen won't tromp on them. The only thing more destructive than a fire is a French fireman. They start stringing hoses down the alley and get a good burst of water going on the Italian place. Nothing's going to be saved there. They need to spray water on the houses around, on my studio, on the cars, the trucks. The tires are already burning on the trucks and one car. My studio roof is beginning to burn seriously. I point this out to a fireman but it's like talking to an enemy soldier. His eyes are gleaming. This is why he came into the fire department. All those days sitting in a little room, or practicing on a hot, dry courtyard, are finally paying off: noise, fire, excitement. Why should he put out the fire? This whole area is condemned anyway, has been for fifty years. This fire's a good way to flush out the squatting rat nesters.

They push everybody out the alley now; want it to themselves. I look down the alley: milling crowds, it's like the days when I was painting my big one. Only fires don't last as long as paintings; no time for periscopes. Then again, paintings last only as long as one fire.

I'm hauling my paintings back down the alley. Another fireman stops me. He thinks I'm stealing them, pillaging. The fire is blazing behind us while I'm pulling out identification and pointing to my signature on the paintings. He OKs my paintings but won't let me take Duncan's. I try to explain. No way. Duncan's paintings are big, kind of hard-line abstract expressionist. They're not the kind of thing a fireman thinks of as valuable but he won't let me out with them. There's nothing to do; he's treating me like some kind of fat, bearded child nut. I tuck the paintings out of the way as best I can; then the firemen push me clean up the alley.

People are on the street with television sets, mattresses, vacuum cleaners. One even managed to get out an electric washer. The poverty of most people's lives is unbearable. It's terrible to see them in the street, sitting on the things they think worth saving. I'm sure they think I'm a loon standing there surrounded by pictures of people. I ask the same little girl who called the fire department to stay with my paintings while I go get the cart. I come back and fill it up. I realize right then I've left my painting of the Spanish witch in that fire. It's upstairs in Traude's place; it's the one painting she asked to hang. HOLY JESUS! TRAUDE! It's only ten o'clock in the morning! She's probably still asleep.

I drop the cart handles, run full steam, break through the police line, past the police! They're all chasing me up the alley. I get to the firemen squirting away with the hoses. The head fireman grabs hold of me. The whole studio is burning; there's no way I can get in. I try to explain how there's a woman sleeping in there. He looks at the blazing studio; shakes his head; asks if anybody saw a woman come out. Christ! I should've thought of it. I should've gone up to check if she were still there. She sleeps tight, could sleep through it; sleep through the whole thing.

The fire chief begins asking questions. Is it my studio? Was someone living in there? I can see the net closing in. Nobody's supposed to live there. He pulls out his notebook. My lease is strictly illegal, between Sasha and me; we're all in trouble. I start backing off.

I was confused. They misunderstood me. It's only a painting I was talking about; painting of a beautiful woman is getting burned in the fire. The firemen look at each other, then at me, as if I'm crazy. The chief puts away his notebook. He asks about my insurance; I only have liability. It costs an arm and a leg but I need to have it by French law. I hate spending money that way; I'm my own insurance.

MY PASSPORT TO EVERYWHERE REVOKED
I WAIT UNDER RENTED SKIES WITHOUT A KEY.
MY HEART A TRANSPLANT FROM ONE STRANGER
TO ANOTHER. I SHIFT FROM FOOT TO FOOT WAITING
FOR AN END TO WAITING.

There's no way to save Traude but I've got to find out about her. It's a blazing inferno in there; firemen are all smiling. I go back through the police line; one tries to give me a bad time. I'm not in the mood, pull myself away. I start running. Another cop grabs me by the arm. I look up, about ready to let fly. It's Clement, the young Saint-Sulpice cop. Standing beside him is Traude!

I grab hold and dance her around in my arms. Thank God she isn't burnt in there. Thank God I don't have to die with such a terrible thing on my soul. You're so goddamned lucky, Scum; another sure strike curved at the last minute and called a ball.

The young flic is not too enthusiastic about me dancing in the street with his woman. It turns out she's spent the night at Clement's. She was coming back to get her clothes and things; going to move in with him. She's been looking for me, to tell me. They're very lovey, all over each other; nice to see. Traude doesn't seem to mind much losing her stuff. I tell her about the witch being burned. That's when she breaks down, actually cries, tries explaining to Clement in Dutch French. Traude is a very good woman; going to raise a large family of big-assed Girl Scouts and cops.

A MAN FOR A WOMAN, EACH TO
EACH OTHER; MOTHERING FATHER
FATHERING MOTHER.

I pull the cart home. I pull it the way a horse pulls, between the rails. I haul my paintings into the *grenier.* It's so crowded up there now you can hardly find place to squeeze through. Thank God I hadn't started moving any of my paintings to the new storage place: one time inertia paid off. I stand in the dark of my attic surrounded by paintings and think of that hot fire turning my gigantic harp into glowing red lines of hot wire. I'd like to have seen that. I look around at my paintings, my life, and think how it could all go up anytime. You convince yourself you're doing something more or less permanent and then a fire can eat everything up in a few minutes. What the hell can happen to them in four years, four hundred years; thousands of fires?

I go down to our apartment and phone Pierrette at work. I tell her most of Duncan's things burned. I tell her about the ones still in the alley so Duncan can go get them. Pierrette's shocked; she's been with Duncan while he created some of these.

Later I find out Duncan doesn't even go get the ones I saved. He says the fire convinced him painting's a dumb bag. He decides to have kids with Pierrette and get himself involved with real life.

I call Claude's wife. I have to talk with her in French, hard to get across what I want to say. She's very cool, say's she'll call Claude in Italy. I guess she agrees with all the rich friends, Claude's only playing with his giant stone building blocks. I tell her I think the stone pieces are OK but all the wooden ones probably burned. I'm wrong. Most of the stone ones are pulverized by the heat. Quite a fire.

So there goes about one third of my total income from rats' nests. Shot down—I mean burned down. I'm lucky I still have five of the original thirteen thousand left. I'm going to need it.

NESTLESS, I FEEL RESTLESS, LEACHING
OUT OF MYSELF, SEEING NEW BURROWS,
SCAMPERING, SCUTTLING, SCURRYING, SCRAMBLING,
A SQUIRREL WITH A NUT TO BURY.

XIX

A PIERCING THOUGHT

Talking about that vanishing thirteen thousand bucks, let's go back a few steps again.

Two weeks after he bought my paintings, I went with Bert to Les Amis des Artistes, an art store in Montparnasse, to select frames. Bert doesn't spare anything; buys the best frames they have. We have one painting with us to get an idea of what'd look good. After he decides, he orders thirty-six frames.

Old Monsieur Deslanges's smile almost slips through the floor. He keeps repeating "*trente-six*" and multiplying the sum out to see if Bert really knows what he's getting into. I know how he feels.

I manage to hustle a fifteen-percent reduction for volume and a promise of delivery in ten days. Bert wants me to pocket the fifteen percent, but I need to draw the line somewhere. Now I'm wishing I hadn't drawn the line so close. Da dum.

A week later, I come in with Jan, who orders another seven frames of the same kind. Poor old Monsieur Deslanges thinks I'm the biggest man in the Paris painting world.

A PANG OF REGRET FOR THE PAIN IN
GETTING. WAITING IS BETTER.

We see a lot of Bert and Jan after that. They are the nicest damned rich people I've ever known, not just because they bought my paintings either. We have great times together and, on top of that, they take us to restaurants we've only heard about. And let me say here, you can really pay through the nose for vittles in this town. Some of it's good, some not so good.

Generally, the fancy big-name places don't serve enough food. They pass out what looks like children's platters. I couldn't figure it at first, not till I looked around.

Most people who can afford to eat in those high-class eateries are old. They've got old stomachs, worn-out teeth, dried-up bowels, holes in their intestines, flaky livers. They can't eat a *real* meal anymore. They eat this super food in tiny portions. It reminds me to eat everything before my own insides start slipping out from under me.

Kate and I'd come home at night from restaurants where the bill'd been three hundred dollars for four and raid the fridge; we're still hungry.

QUANTITY OVERCOMES QUALITY
YES, INDEED, BUT MY PANTRY
SEEMS EMPTY, NOT EVEN A BONE.

When Bert has his paintings framed, he hangs and stacks them all around their apartment. He has them four high along the walls and down the halls. It looks like our place; I feel at home there, could move right in. I show Bert how terrific paintings look through binoculars. They fill the whole field of vision. You're looking at them up close and there's nothing else. I always bring binoculars to museums; get truly close and alone with paintings. They become the real world; everything else is cut out. People walking by think you're super-nearsighted.

We sit around a lot in their living room passing the binoculars back and forth. It's almost like looking at somebody else's paintings. I'm even more in love with them. If I had the money, I'd buy them back. Fat chance. Nicest people in the world to have them, Bert and Jan, almost: we're the nicest.

Bert's still pissed about the New York buyer who got the seven paintings. I have them stored at my place in our bedroom, along with the frames Jan bought. I've stacked them in my clothes closet, hanging my own things in Kate's closet; no place for my shoes. There's something hurts about having the paintings go all at once; almost as bad as a fire. I don't imagine there's *any* way to satisfy me.

Bert keeps playing the old game.

"Look at this one, Jan, the one of the shoemaker. How the hell could that stupid bastard've let a painting of that quality get away?"

He goes on like that: great for my ego; tough on Jan. Once in a while she strikes back.

"But, Bert, he did get the one with Saint-Sulpice in the background and the lady carrying laundry."

Bert mumbles under the binoculars.

"Bastard!"

FUN QUIBBLES, LITTLE GAMES TO
KEEP THE BLAME FROM LIFE.

We decide to have a surprise birthday party for Bert at our place. Jan plans it all. She's going to make Bert dress up and she's going to put on her best finery. She'll have him take her to Maxim's, then say she doesn't want to go there; then the Grand Vefour, same thing. Finally, the plan is she'll lead him to our place, our little hole high on a wall in the Bastille furniture district.

A NEST IN A NICHE
I'M A SON OF A BITCH!

Kate and Jan shop for two days. Our kitchen begins to look like Fouquet's. Nothing but the best will do. They buy a luscious venison tenderloin roast; fresh string beans from Africa; Pommard wines, at fifty dollars a bottle, and a cordon bleu cru for champagne. To finish off, she's having a favorite of Bert's shipped from Maxim's, no less than a soufflé Grand Marnier. This will arrive at ten o'clock.

That night, Bert comes in all shook up.

"Something's gotten into Jan, damn it! She usually makes up her mind like a knife, but tonight she's dragged me all over Paris and it's my *birthday*. My feet hurt and I'm hungry."

I lure him into our back bedroom to show him a new clock I've just bought out at the Clignancourt flea market. Kate and Jan are running around madly setting up the party. Jan's been cooking all day. The paintings are ready to be brought out and put on the walls. Everything's hot and steaming in the kitchen. We've farmed out our kids with good friends on the same block, other Americans. In the back room, Bert's getting bored; wall clocks aren't his thing. I get the signal from Jan just in time.

We start back to the living room. Candles are burning. We all begin singing "Happy Birthday." I think we really surprise him but you'd never know with a psychiatrist. When he sees the paintings on the walls, his mouth drops open. Jan has a little blue ribbon pinned to each one.

"Jan, how the *hell* did you do it?"

He turns to me.

"And why the fuck did you give her the name when you wouldn't tell me?"

We all laugh. I walk over to Jan.

"Bert, I'd like you to meet my New York buyer."

"You smart bitch."

He grabs her, lifts her off the floor and kisses her while swinging her feet out.

"I'll be damned!"

He walks around looking at the paintings. He starts laughing.

"Jesus, Jan, when I think of all the things I've been saying about that 'New York buyer.' I must say, he made some good choices."

He stares at the paintings. Bert seems to drink paintings. It's a nice thing to see, especially when they're your paintings.

"You're still a damned fool, though. You should've bought the whole series when you had first shot like that."

The meal is terrific, far better than any bought meal we had together. We're all half crocked from wine when the soufflé arrives in a Maxim's truck.

Our concierge can't believe it. These guys arrive in tuxedos with a little silver table. This is after Bert and Jan have already arrived, dressed to kill, in a taxi. A *taxi's* a rare event on our street. The Maxim's boys are just as astounded by our world, too; but they light the soufflé and serve. We drink champagne and are all beautiful by candlelight. We try offering some champagne and soufflé to the Maxim's contingent but no go: form and all that, I guess. Jan must've paid a fortune to get these sleek cats here to our little *passage* on a *passage* in a slum.

NOT TO BE PASSED, THE
LAST BASTION OF SNOBBERY.

When the caterers have left, we get talking about the secrets of being rich. I need to get myself ready: big seller of paintings. Most rich people I've known have been miserable. I want to find out what Jan and Bert do to beat the game.

Jan says the first thing is to remember you can only eat three meals a day and sleep in one bed at a time. That's a big part of life taken care of. If you try getting around that one, you're in trouble. Bert says health and freedom to arrange your own life are ten times more important than money. They both agree that privacy, anonymity, is the hardest thing to hold on to when you're rich.

They make a big point about being careful of what you buy. You can physically, mentally invest yourself in only just so much crap. Legal possession is nothing. Jan grew up in an enormous house where the servants truly owned the place. They knew it, loved it, took care of it. Her parents were kept people, always like visitors. They traveled all over the world, running away from their own accumulations.

Jan says when you start having people living with you to take care of the people who take care of you, you've gone over the line; you're managing a hotel. If you run a house with fifteen bathrooms, you'll have at least one toilet or sink or bathtub on the blink all the time. Then you need a plumber in the house. If you're going to have a chauffeur, gardener, houseman, valet, a couple of maids and a cook, then you're going to need fifteen bathrooms and therefore a plumber. It's a matter of diminishing returns. The cook is cooking your food and serving it to twenty people, only five of whom are your own family. And they all hate you for having money in the first place. No fun living around people who hate you.

WE ARE PARTLY WHAT WE HAVE.
WE HAVE WHAT WE ARE. INVEST
IN THE OUTSIDE AND BECOME EMPTY.

The party breaks up at about three. When they're getting into the taxi, Jan discovers she's lost an earring. Bert asks the cab to wait. We start searching through our courtyard and up the stairs. Bert takes Jan by the arm.

"Now, look, Jan, if we find this, will you promise to get your ears pierced? I guarantee a total anesthetic."

"OK, Bert. OK, I promise."

It turns out Bert designed these earrings and had them made for Jan as a twentieth-anniversary gift.

We search for more than ten minutes; find it slid down in the back of our couch. We dash for the taxi. On the way down, Bert reminds Jan she promised to have her ears pierced. She's backing off now. Bert turns to me and says in a low voice, "Those damned things cost forty thousand dollars and this has to be the tenth time she's almost lost one of them."

What a numbing idea, a twenty-thousand-dollar earring caught inside the fifteen-franc couch I got at the flea market. It's all crazy. Christ, forty thousand dollars jangling on your ears.

That's what I'd call a piercing thought.

XX

MIRACLE OF THE BELLS

Another thing I do in Paris besides rats'-nest and paint is collect clocks. The French were crazy for clocks back in the nineteenth century. A home then wasn't really alive unless there was a big clock somewhere, ticking away seconds, minutes; ringing away hours. Now everybody's switched to digital wristwatches and digital clock radios: easy time, fast time.

I'm a nineteenth-century Frenchman that way; I like to have a clock running in our home. I especially like what the French call a "Westminster." These clocks ring on the quarter hour: bong, bong, bong, bong. They add four bongs each quarter hour, different order, different tune, till at the hour there's a regular symphony. I like to hear this in the middle of the night. All's well, nest safe; I'm listening to everyone breathing.

I keep a low amber light burning twenty-four hours a day in the middle of our home: vigil light. I like to think of our home as alive at night, only sleeping; heat down, heart beating, vigil light burning away the darkness.

A SMALL PULSATION, INVISIBLE,
SIXTY TIMES A SECOND, A PROOF OF LIGHT,
OF A SUN TO RISE AGAIN.

I've been keeping my clocks in a loft I rent up on Vaugirard, near Métro Convention, almost out to the Porte de Versailles. Vaugirard is the longest street in Paris. It's one-way the wrong way going there. Going up, I need to jockey around with all kinds of little streets and I'm usually carrying a couple clocks on the rack of my Honda. Coming back is easy, just straight down a long street. Paris is that way; some places are easy to get to, hard to come back. I decide I'll convert that loft into a few nests—make up for the burned-down studio.

I talked to old Sasha the week after the fire. He was insured and he's truly sorry about the paintings and the sculpture. Great guy, I hope he lives a hundred years, has five more kids; fill up the world with life lovers.

RECAST A LIFE, BRING THE CRUNCH
OF SPRING INTO THE SLUSH OF WINTER.
MAKE ICE CONES WITH COLORED FLAVORS.

I'll move my clocks into the big room in my tunnel under Saint-Germain-des-Prés. I've got that place fixed up fine now. I ran electricity along the tunnel and into that room to light it up. I went in, swept and dusted off all those coffins. I found a gigantic seven-by-nine-meter fake Persian rug at the flea market in Montreuil for two hundred francs. I spread that in there, along with a table and some chairs. The rug has a deep worn spot in the middle but I put the table over that part.

This'll make a terrific place to store clocks. There's a constant temperature and it's not damp like a cellar at all. I've even built a trapdoor and a ship's ladder down into the hole from Lotte's place.

She's still hanging in there on the ground floor. I've built a vestibule and a wall where I come in, so she has privacy. Women can get me to do anything. Lotte knows she has a good deal and isn't about to move. It surprises me how she isn't interested in my tunnel.

VARYING INTERESTS. LIFE DIFFERENT
FOR EACH. WE SEARCH SPECIAL SHELLS
AND STONES ON PRIVATE BEACHES.

I rig a harness and pull my cart over to that loft with my Honda. I'm using it to move the clocks. This is a good trick; slowing down and stopping are rough. I have a stiff tongue nailed to the deck of my cart and tied to the rack on my bike. It's hard maneuvering through traffic on those back streets. Two flics stare at me as I roll past the Gare Montparnasse but they don't stop me. Moving takes a whole day, eleven trips. It's the first time I've counted my loot. I own seventeen grandfather jobs, twenty-seven wall clocks and fifteen mantel clocks. And I've got them all in working condition; mostly eight-day, windup. I haul the whole bunch down the steps and into my tunnel room. I store them helter-skelter down there, except I stand my grandfathers between coffins.

GRANDFATHER COFFINS, TELLING NOTHING,
TOLLING LOST TIME IN THE DARKNESS.

I need to fix up the Vaugirard place before I can really arrange things. I've got to start some cash flow moving; tuition time is coming soon.

The Vaugirard place is in the mansard of a five-story building; used to be a row of *chambres des bonnes,* maid's rooms, an artist friend of mine bought. He tore down the walls between rooms and put together a studio. He only stayed a year, then went back to the States. He sculpts in plastic; makes molds of things in plaster, molds of old shoes or a radio or somebody's face, then pours fiberglass into the molds, sticks these together in different arrangements and paints them. He makes a reasonable living that way; has a fair-to-middling name in the Middle West as a Paris painter-sculptor.

When I found he was leaving, I rented his place from him for practically nothing. I'll have to give it back if he ever shows up again, but he's been gone three years now; got himself married to a rich widow, a little girl thrown in with the deal. I'd like to buy his place, but not if I don't have to.

This loft has three different hall doors left over from the *chambres des bonnes.* I divide it back into three sections, back to the old maids' rooms. I use a frame system with light fiberboard. I rig a plastic hose from a water faucet at the head of the stairs and divide this line into two parts. On one I put a butane water heater and run that line to an outlet in each room. I run the other line straight in as cold water. I get three sinks at Montreuil for fifty francs apiece and hook those in. I need to hang them high because the drains come out into rain gutters running along an edge of the roof. It's illegal as hell but only somebody cruising along in a helicopter could ever see it. The concierge hasn't been up these stairs in ten years. I give her a hundred francs every Christmas. There's a john at the end of the hall, so that takes care of that. In an emergency, on a cold dark middle-of-the-night, you could stand on a chair and pee in the sink. My mother always suspected male bachelors of doing that anyway, even when there is a toilet. I'll bet women do, too: pee in sinks; OK, suspect, too.

MUTUALITY OF CONFESSION, SOME THINGS
TRANSCEND AGE, SEX, RACE OR PROFESSION.

I'm off to the flea market again. I buy some used beds—without fleas, I hope—a gaggle of little tables and chairs. I carry these upstairs, spread them around and I'm in business.

I go down and put notices up at the Alliance Française and the Institut Catholique. I'll rent them out for six hundred francs per month.

I have the three places filled by the end of the week. One's a Swede; there's an English girl and a little American with much Southern accent. They're all cute as bugs, unbelievably young. I could spend my days talking to them, fixing up the nests, playing father-grandfather. These are like three little birds' nests up against the sky.

SWOOPING AROUND, BACK AND
FORTH, IN AND OUT, LIVING IN
THE BRIGHT NEW SKIES OF NEW EYES.

I go back to my Rue du Four tunnel place. Lotte's home and stops me as I'm going down the steps. She's wondering what I've been doing; what's the running back and forth? I talk her into coming down my stairway and through the tunnel to my new clock room. I love showing people my clocks, and now I have a great place to store them. Lotte's never been down before. With electric lights all along the tunnel, it's like a miniature Métro *correspondance.* Maybe I can sell advertising space on the walls.

Lotte's impressed with the clock room but she's *fascinated* by the coffins. I've pried one open, just to check, and there's a skeleton inside all right, skull and all. This turns Lotte on. She's holding on tight, leaning into me. I'm getting worked up a bit myself. There's something about this entire situation: the skeleton, the clocks, the deep quiet; dark, frozen time.

It makes me want to lie with Lotte on that Persian rug, surrounded by clocks, coffins, stones and darkness; to share the only truly life-making, death-defying act; the one and only.

I know if we do it, Lotte'll get pregnant for sure; probably have twins, triplets, bunches of babies like bananas. I exert my last vestiges of willpower. I feel, I know, Lotte would do it with me, mother those babies. Sometimes humans will do impossible things just to prove the unprovable. We need to do something drastic, break the black-magic spell.

I start spreading my wall clocks along the walls at the feet of the coffins between the grandfather clocks. Lotte helps me. Clocks are more her kind of thing than motorcycles.

For somebody who doesn't pay more than three hundred francs for any wall clock, I have a beautiful collection. They're going to be worth a fortune someday; probably already worth a small fortune in America.

The French are spending big money for American faded blue jeans and university sweat shirts with "UCLA" written on them. Americans are buying French antiques. Nobody wants what they have. I guess that's what's called the spirit of life.

SOMETHING ELSE, SOMETHING NEW.
DOESN'T MATTER IF NEW IS WORSE;
ALWAYS CHANGING FOR NO REASON:
THAT'S OUR BLESSING AND OUR CURSE.

We get all the clocks distributed along the walls, between coffins, on the floor and on the table. Then I search out keys and start winding. I set all the clocks at quarter to twelve. It takes over an hour to get them wound and set. Then I start them. I know by listening just when a clock is balanced so it'll keep running.

MECHANICAL HEART SURGEON, I HOLD
THE TICK AND LISTEN FOR THE TOCK.

I grab Lotte's hand and we run out the tunnel, up the ladder, out her door, across Rue du Four, across Boulevard Saint-Germain and into the big church of Saint-Germain-des-Prés. I might well be giving my whole nest away, but some ideas are too important to ignore.

We sit four rows from the altar. There are a few tourists wandering around staring at the columns or vaulting, paging through guidebooks. There are the usual ten or twenty old women in black; some are telling beads, some just sitting and one is lighting a candle at a side altar. A priest or deacon is arranging flowers at the foot of a statue by the main altar.

Lotte and I know what we're listening for, so we hear the first notes. The sound is softly muted and, for some strange reason of acoustics, sounds as if it's coming from the vaulted arches where the nave and transept cross. The ringing tones accumulate, increase in volume till there's a cacophony of reverberating, hollow sounds: as close a thing to celestial-sphere music as anyone will ever hear.

The nice old lady drops her candle and stares into the vaults. The women in black on the benches stare up, mouths open. Our candle lady drops to her knees beside her burning candle on the church floor. The priest arranging flowers runs three quick steps to the front of the altar, shades his eyes and gawks up into the vaulting. He runs a few more steps down the aisle past us, staring up all the time. Then he runs back to the foot of the altar, genuflects deeply and scoots across out a side door.

By this time, the whole din has begun to drop off; the old women look around at each other. The one on the floor pushes herself painfully onto her feet and picks up her candle, still burning. The old women surge together. We're having a communion of saints, miracle of the bells.

Lotte and I hurry out. I'd better get back and stop those damned clocks. If they strike like that every fifteen minutes for eight days, either somebody's going to catch on or they'll change Paris into another Lourdes and that'd be one hell of a note.

MIRACLES DO HAPPEN. JUST BEING BORN OR BEING HAPPY. BUT WATCH OUT FOR CRAPPY HALOS OR POUNDING TALK IN A TENT.

XXI

AUTO-DA-FÉ

It's a rainy day, warm rain, early summer day. I'm home working on a still life of potatoes spilling from a paper bag, all earth colors and white. It's getting close to six o'clock, bank-closing time, so I pack up the box. We need a stash of cash day-to-day living money; cash flows through us like some kind of multinational corporation.

I take the checkbook and don't bother to change from my painting clothes; there's not enough time. I drive my Honda over to the Bank of America on the Place Vendôme. The streets are slick with light rain so I'm wearing my helmet. I've taken my name off it; some flic might stop me and turn in the escaped prisoner.

I go into the bank, dirty, wet, paint-smeared, wind-blown. I must admit I probably look like Jesse James; I write out my check for cash. The girl looks at me and asks for identification. I have a signature card on the bank, don't usually need identification. I drove over without my wallet, just the checkbook. There's a big consultation. They're not sure of the signature; I'm erratic in everything, even the way I sign my name. In the end, they refuse to give me my *own* money.

I could spit. Here I've gone all the way across town in the slippery rain for nothing. I leave the bank feeling like a panhandler shown to the door. It's raining harder.

MONEY KNOWS NO LOVE, RAIN SLIDES
OVER IT AND DEAD SEEDS DON'T GROW.
IT'S HARD TO CHEW OR EVEN BITE.

I get home and the concierge hands me a letter: official-looking affair, air mail special delivery. I hate opening letters like that anytime, and I especially don't want to look at one just now.

Upstairs, I pour myself a shot from my bottle of

homemade Cointreau. I bake the orange skins myself, then add eau-de-vie at eighteen francs per liter. It's drinkable. I open the letter.

It's from some real-estate investor in California; says he wants to buy my forty acres. I skip down to the bottom. He's offering me eight thousand dollars an acre, three hundred and twenty thousand U.S. bucks! I can't believe it. I read it again. There it is; this is an official bid on the property. Holy mud, I'm a rich man! I'm going to go out and buy myself a house with fifteen bathrooms, take up plumbing. I'm going to get me an apprentice girl Friday to run around after me, cleaning up my palette when I'm finished, stretching canvases, show my paintings for me, writing letters. I'll be a big international painter, like Sandy Asshole or something.

I sock down three more fake Cointreaus, reading and rereading the letter. It *looks* legitimate. I don't know anybody who hates me enough to pull a joke like this!

I bought that forty acres as the ultimate hideout. The only way to get in there is to hike about two miles uphill, or go in on a trail bike. It's the top of a high ridge and covers all the sides down to the bottom, including a dry stream on one side. It's down by that stream where I built my nest with the rocks and the corrugated plastic roof. I have branches growing all over that nest so nobody could ever find it, not even a rattlesnake. This is the place I dream about on the worst nights. When it all seems too much, things feel as if they're sliding out from under me, I dream about sneaking down there in the night.

I've got canned food buried, a shallow well and water storage. There's an old butane-run generator and six bottles of butane gas buried there wrapped in plastic. We could hide out in that nest for a year; nobody'd ever find us. When you've spent three years in prison, a private place like that is worth everything.

One kind of freedom is knowing you can get away if you have to. I don't want *social* security: that's just government robbery, plays on people's simplest kinds of fear. They take over thirteen percent off top and give a lousy four or five hundred or so a month when you're sixty-five. If I get that far, I don't even think I'll apply for it: old people's dole. I've got my own social security: rats' nests, clocks, paintings, kids.

LEANING BACK, ROCKING-CHAIR MIND
HOPING FOR PEOPLE TO BE KIND TO YOU.
GOVERNMENTS AREN'T CIVIL LET ALONE KIND.

And now, holy dog turds, I'm into three hundred and twenty thousand dollars. The IRS bastards are really going to make out if I sell. No way to hide a thing like that. Damn! They'll get their fat fists into it all right. They'll come out with about eighty thousand for doing absolutely nothing, taking no risks. They'll use the money to kill all kinds of people I don't even know—little children, maybe. They'll build more nuclear bombs so they can kill everybody in the world ten times more often. They'll make a bunch of creeps rich; people I don't like and don't want to know. What a pisser.

YOUR OWN HARVEST FLOWERS
BOMB OTHER LANDS
PASSING TO OTHERS, RIPPED
HARD FROM YOUR HANDS.

We bought this forty acres more than twenty-five years ago, bought it for six thousand. We started paying taxes at a dollar an acre, about right. The taxes have been sneaking up every year, getting to be an expensive hideout. For years, our biggest hump has been getting together enough money to meet those taxes. Now I can't keep up with them, just holding on by my teeth. Tax collectors are on my heels, barking after me to get our land, our nest.

NIBBLING, QUIBBLING, BITING AT
BUBBLES, MANUFACTURING TROUBLES.

California's where we moved when I got out of prison. We were living on a hill, in a shack, in a place called Topanga Canyon when we bought that forty. I wanted to get as far as I could from home, couldn't get a passport yet, even. If I could, we'd've gone to Mexico or Greece—anywhere, to put as much space between me and America as possible.

When I was in prison, nobody wrote to me, not my wife or even my mother. Nobody is writing to the draft-dodging, yellow-bellied Nazi lover. In prison mail is more important than food.

Then I start getting unsigned letters every day. They come for three years. I don't know who it is but I write back, write long letters, send drawings, trying to hold myself together.

When they finally let me out, after the cockeyed

war's over, she's waiting for me at the gate, turns out she's a former student of mine. By then we're already in love. I fell in love with Kate before I even knew her name. She tells me she's loved me since she was seventeen. I didn't even remember her as a student; had a hard time telling her that.

Anyway, with our second baby, Kate wants a more normal house, not a rats' nest. She wants electricity and sewers, streetlights and a place you can park a car. Kate *never* enjoyed riding on the back of a motorcycle. Sewers and things like that get to mean a lot when you don't have them.

Kate's my big love and I want her to be happy. She's probably the only woman in the world who could stay with me and be reasonably happy at it.

I keep asking her if she wants out. Anytime she wants to go, everything's hers: paintings, clocks, rats' nests, the works. So far, every year she's opted to stick it out. We always spend New Year's Eve in bed, stay up to hear midnight, drink champagne, have a private party; usually these days it's at the mill.

STAY TOGETHER, SOUL GLUE, NOT INERTIA, OUR
OWN DYNAMIC, TWO THRUSTS FORMING NEW VECTORS.

So back in California we go down to a nowhere place called the San Fernando Valley: flat, covered with people boxes. We buy an acre there in a walnut grove, ten evenly spaced diseased walnut trees growing on it. I'm teaching at a private school, so we have money. The way we live, a teacher's salary is big. I promise Kate I'll build her a real house.

I start designing. I begin by getting a bulldozer and plowing up little hills and valleys to give some character to that acre. Everything's so flat around there you're afraid to open your eyes; might just see clear off the end of the world. One of the troubles with California, generally, is that on a clear day you can see so damned far.

The skies are too high, the houses too low. You look out and you're liable to see anything, maybe something a hundred miles away. The smog helps scumble the world somewhat, but it kills you.

So I plow up my little hills to block the view, especially the view into my neighbors' view windows. This acre of mine begins to look like a miniature golf course or a poor man's Disneyland.

After I've built my landscape, I pick the location for my house, the spot with the most privacy. It's like trying to hide on a tabletop. I invest in trees and bushes, start the landscape-gardening part.

All around where the house is going to be, I plant trees that are supposed to grow fast with thick leaves. Then I design tree- and bush-lined paths between the hills from the street toward the house. There are four paths: three lead to dead ends; only one goes to the actual place for the house.

There's an agricultural college near us called Pierce College. They have a horticultural section. At night I steal exotic and interesting trees, plant them on my acre.

The neighbors around me have built expensive fake ranch houses with wood-shake roofs, or Normandy farmhouses with asbestos-straw roofs, exposed Styrofoam beams, all kinds of fancy gewgaws. These neighbors are watching me build my hills and plant my garden. They start getting worried looks on their faces; then they begin asking questions about what kind of house I'm going to build.

I tell my neighbor on the left, the one with the Tudor-style two-story house and the Bentley, how I'm building the whole house underground, with one long cone up into the sky to catch pure air and pipe it in. I tell him I'm putting a high fence around my acre and importing wild animals so it'll be like real nature. He asks about airspace. I tell him I've checked and I own up to two miles over my acre: approximately eight trillion bushels of smog.

I tell the next jocko, the neighbor on the right, who lives in an imitation Cliff May house with ten different kinds of colored pebbles all over everything, how I'm building a six-story house with one room on each floor, with an outside elevator and a penthouse on top. I tell him I'm a radio ham and I'm going to put up a huge antenna that'll be the highest in the west San Fernando Valley. I'll put this on top of the penthouse and be able to get China and Moscow. I invite him to come listen if he wants. He asks if it'll interfere with his TV reception.

The cowboy across the street, with the ranch-style house and straw hanging out a fake window over his three-car garage, stops by. He drives a pickup truck pulling a horse trailer with no horse. I tell him I'm building a completely round house of Duralumin. All the floors in the house will be slightly tilted so the place can be cleaned just by squirting a hose. All the furniture will be plastic and waterproof. I tell him my wife hates housecleaning, was brought up in China where she always had at least ten servants.

But worst of all is the lady who comes over while I'm watering my avocado trees and passionflowers. She asks where I got my hose. I tell her Sears; actually I got it at the Salvation Army Thrift Store. She sneers Sears and backs away.

I know I'm not going to make it. I'm an insult to these people, everything they believe. I don't want any more trouble. I go to a realtor and put our acre up for sale, as is. It's sold in a week and we make a good profit. I bought it for twenty-five hundred, sell it for thirty-three. The crazy place is worth fifty thousand now: fancy residential area called Walnut Acres—after those old diseased trees, I guess.

I take my money up into the hills to an artist friend, a ceramist who dabbles with real estate. I tell him I want a place where we can be alone. He tells me to get my boots; we hike up to this beautiful forty acres. I buy it right there; go home to tell Kate I've traded our one acre for forty. I feel like Jack who sold the cow for a handful of beans.

ONLY SOME KERNELS NOW:
NOT WORTH A COW.

The next day, I coax Kate onto the motorcycle and cruise as near as I can get. We hike in the rest of the way. From the top there, we can see the ocean in one direction and out over the San Fernando Valley in the other. There's nothing but natural canyon all around us. We can look as far as we want in any direction without being afraid of seeing anything, if you know what I mean.

Kate starts crying. She's standing on top of the mountain, looking out into all that emptiness and crying. She doesn't want to live up here. It's worse than where we live now. She's not going to live like a mountain goat!

I promise Kate I'll get electricity into the place where we're living. I promise to build an addition. We'll use our main room for a bedroom. I'll build a big room for the new living room and have a real kitchen. I promise her all the things she wants in a house. I even promise to doze in a road to the door and cut out a parking place.

It takes me five years' work but I get it done. I finish just in time for the big fire to eat it up with a whoosh!

The morning after the fire, we both go up there; everything's still smoldering and we look out over a black-and-white landscape. God, it feels good. We're free from all those crappy things, too good to throw away, not good enough to satisfy us. It's all gone. That's the kind of stuff gums up life. It's all gone.

BLACK IS WHITE AND SMOKE BECOMES
INCENSE, BLESSING US WITH FREEDOM,
RELEASING OUR NATURAL DESIRE TO FLEE,
FLY OVER ALL THE STILL WORLD AND THEN
ALIGHT TO OUR OWN LIGHT.

During those years from 1945 to 1960, life has been getting worse and worse in America. We don't want to raise our kids in the middle of all the competitive-comparative bullshit, but we're stuck.

Now Kate surprises me. She'd bought fire insurance without saying anything and that money helps spring us. I finally get a passport; we take off a month later and have only been back to visit. It's the best thing ever happened. Our kids never locked onto Channel 4; don't have standardized sesame-seed minds. Our life's been hard sometimes, but fun. Even Kate's learned to like being outside things, edge-playing, I think. A good part of being alive is staying alive on purpose.

PLAYING IN THE DARK, IN OUR OWN BALL PARK
NOT MUCH OF WINNINGS BUT HAVING OUR OWN
INNINGS.

So here I am, in Paris, France, sitting with this letter about the forty acres in my hand. What'll it do to us? What'll we do with all that money besides pay taxes? I know we won't buy any stocks and bonds; we'd be pure hypocrites if we did a thing like that. We still have some extra money, maybe a couple thousand. What could we do to make life any better?

I know I don't want any sports car. We've got all the food, all the shelter, all the loving we can handle. The blood-sucking money would probably be bad in the long run for our kids. The toughest thing in the world for *anybody* is to live in a nest that's so comfortable you get used to it, actually *need* it. You spend your life struggling to match what you've always had. There's not much sense of attainment in treading water. We won't do that to our kids.

Kate really likes her work here teaching. It's an important thing helping little ones hold on to the joy of learning, thinking, and she's damned good at it.

Since we can't have any more of our own, it's a shame to let all those fine mother juices go to waste. I think it also makes her feel good bringing in the bacon, making money. She gets paid a good salary for what she does and deserves it. And now three hundred and twenty thousand bucks staring down our throats like this makes any salary seem a joke. No, we don't need that.

Here I am, the maniac, always bitching about not having enough money, chasing my ass ragged, fixing up rats' nests, painting umpteen paintings a year, and suddenly I decide I don't need money, don't want it.

I feel struck down. It's as if something awful has happened: like having a parent die, or a child, or having a heart attack, or finding out you have inoperable cancer. The bottom's dropped out of things.

I sit there all afternoon mulling it over. I try not to slug too much of my phony Cointreau, just keep sipping away. I'm floating in oranges.

A PLUG PULLED, MORE SEEPAGE, A SENSE
OF ENDING, THE FAINT BREATH OF OBSCURITY.

One thing I work out. It's a big new idea for me. I honest to Christ did not know it before.

Considering everything, I'M HAVING THE BEST FUCKING LIFE I KNOW ABOUT! CAN'T EVEN IMAGINE ANY WAY TO IMPROVE IT!

I don't want to change my life.

It's a bit disappointing. I've always lived with the idea I was doing things to make the old life better. Maybe I can still dink around, doctor it up a bit, but sure as hell not with money.

It's an unforgivable, arrogant thing to do but I do it

anyway. Sometimes we're driven to things we can't explain away to anybody, especially ourselves.

I write a quick answer to the real-estate investor people saying we're not interested in selling. Then I have the joy of building a tepee of sticks in the fireplace and using their letter to start the fire. I quickly run downstairs to a bakery. I buy some tuiles, apple rolls and chocolate éclairs; run back. I fix up a tasty tea and put more wood on the fire. I'm ready for the family when they come home.

Maybe it's not fair but I need more time to think. Something like this changes too much. I'm not ready. I've got to talk with Kate in private, find out what *she* wants.

CONSULTATION IN A WHIRLPOOL, SWIM WITH AND
HOPE TO BE FOUND OUT; OR SWIM AGAINST THE
TWISTING DOWNWARD THRUST. WHAT TO TRUST?

XXII

23 SKIDOO

It's almost two weeks after the fire, not the studio fire but the little fire where I burned the forty-acre three-hundred-twenty-thousand-dollar letter. I'm at home trying to work out some storage for the paintings. I have no real studio now, no place to work.

With this weather, most of the time I'm out on the streets. Still, I need a place for stretching, preparing canvas; grinding paint, making varnish—all the technical stuff. But right now I mostly need space for storing paintings; as I said, my attic's chock-full.

THE MOUSE RUNS DOWN THE CLOCK. I CLIMB
IN MY HALF ATTIC, SEARCHING FOR A SPACE,
A PLACE TO BURY MY WINTER FOOD. SHELTER.

I'm considering converting one of the lofts in our apartment to painting storage. It's the loft where the kids used to leave up their trains or slot cars when they were little; nobody's using it now. Jim and Annie are gone and Mike will be off to UCLA in September, Sara has a private room for her stereo. Tim's still between toys and stereo; he reads.

I'm climbing around up there; it's only a little more than a meter high so I'm crawling on my knees. I've been out painting all morning, still in the Marais. Now I'm up there, cleaning out and stuffing things into the blind storage I built over our kitchen. There's a knock at the door.

I figure it's probably some salesman, or maybe the electric or gas company wanting to read our meter. Also, I'm afraid it might be the guy from Switzerland with the studio downstairs. We're always leaking our dirty water through our floor and his ceiling into his impeccable white studio, onto his black-on-black paintings. It's already happened three times. We're probably the most careless people who ever lived in a French building. We can't even remember to turn off faucets. The last time, he haughtily said to me in English, German-accented English: "Sir, your floor is my ceiling, remember that!" I thought about this afterward and it seemed pretty funny.

I climb down my ladder, open the door and it's Sandy. I almost crap my pants! The outside world doesn't usually come into this, the inner nest. I let her in. I'm wondering how the hell she found out where I live, probably asked Sweik or Lubar.

Soon as I close the door, she's in my arms. Oh boy! This is all I need, the chickens coming home to roost. I untangle and lead her to a chair at the big table. If anybody comes in, we're perfectly respectable. She looks at me; I'm sure she can see I'm all shit up a creek; my hands have started shaking.

"Matt gave me your address; he didn't want to but I made him. I want to talk with you in private."

Who the hell's Matt? I remember; that's Sweik's first name. How did she make him? OK, I think; I'm listening. But could we get it over and said in less than two hours, please? That's when the family will be coming home.

I'm feeling guilty. I feel guilty easily. It's as if there's some terrific crime I committed in the past and I don't remember what it is. I do remember.

I dream sometimes I have a body in the trunk of a car and I'm driving around trying to figure how to get rid of it.

THE TIMELESS WEIGHT OF FLOATING FEAR,
FEAR OF KNOWING THE UNKNOWN. FEAR OF
FINDING THE UNKNOWN IS SO BECAUSE IT ISN'T.

I smile and wait for Sandy to go on. I think of getting up and starting tea. Drinking tea would make us look even more respectable.

I wasn't feeling particularly guilty when Jan was up here; something big definitely happened between Sandy and me; no matter what I say, no matter how I try, it's there. Those kinds of things can't just be pushed into corners because they're inconvenient.

Sandy's wearing a dress again; I try not to peek at her knees when she crosses them.

"I'm pregnant."

"Hello, I'm pregnant." "I'm George, pleased to meet you." Those thoughts run through my scummy mind just as she pauses, not really stops, only pauses. The mind has to be the only thing faster than light.

"Do you know where I can get an abortion in Paris?"

Let me recommend *my* dentist, he's *conventionné,* it won't cost you a cent. But my mind is slowing down, the spin is letting up. I look at Sandy. She's being brave but she's scared. Hell, do *I* know an abortionist? If I did, I'd want to talk with him, find out what *he* thinks is important; what makes his mind work. What he feels about vacuum cleaning vaginas all day, every day.

"Are you sure?"

Familiar question; my originality is limited.

"Just passed the second furlong and turning the corner into the back stretch."

She smiles. I catch myself looking. Is there really another human being under that brown corduroy dress? I wish *I* could be in there. They say the first months you swim around, like a tadpole in a goldfish bowl. Imagine swimming and not having to breathe, in the dark, in a fluid, warm as you are, and supportive: the original hot tub.

She's waiting for me to say something. Does she actually want me to tell her where an abortionist is or does she just need to talk with somebody, anybody?

"You're the only one I could think of who might know."

Who *me,* lover of life, of babies, know an abortionist? It's amazing the idea people get of you from the outside. I guess Sandy has me pegged for a worn-out Romeo, inept seducer of lost girls.

IMAGE BENT BY WARPED LENSES, THE SIMPLE
SENSES BENDING TO REFLECTED LIGHT.

Holy heaven, it's a responsibility for women, the whole reproduction thing. Like everything else valuable: fire, atom power—if it's worth having, it can be hard to handle. Even Shakespeare, a man you'd think would have a good grab on life, at least from his plays, disowned his own daughter because she had to get married during Lent, although he and Anne Hathaway were pregnant when they married. Ah, hypocrisy! Poetic hypocrisy, yet.

Everybody flies apart at the seams when somebody

has a baby if the entire format of the culture isn't nailed down. But think about it. No man can have a baby and mostly only women between twenty and forty can; that's about an eighth of the population. A lot of these either don't want to or can't, so maybe we're down to one tenth. We should cherish that tenth, give them all the support possible, help them have their babies, shower them with gifts, aid from us all. The truly most valuable product of this planet is people, loved people.

Still, nobody should have a baby they don't want. Probably one of the worst things in this world is being born to somebody who doesn't want you. Once, someone compared it to coming into a room with a passel of hostile strangers. Thank God women have some control over these things today. I have to ask.

"Didn't you take care, Sandy? Aren't you on the pill or something—anything?"

Sandy looks down at herself—checking, maybe. Her lips come up in her sneering smile, smiling at me and sneering at herself, or the other way around. I don't know.

"I'm so irregular. I never thought I'd ever get pregnant. How old do you think I am anyway?"

I hadn't thought about it. When you get to my age, anybody with more than ten teeth is young. She's young-looking, very young-looking.

"I don't know, maybe twenty-one or two. How old are you anyway: eleven; going to break the world's record for the youngest mother?"

She smiles a real smile.

"I'm twenty-nine. You didn't know it but I've spent four years in and out psychiatric wards. I'm one of the walking wounded; cracked wide open in my junior year at Holyoke. I used to call it the Holy Hoax. Lubar knows, so does Dale, and now Matt. I didn't think they'd tell you."

"Nobody let me in on the big secret, Sandy. What's your specialty—fits, murder, arson, Napoleon acts?"

"Suicide. Three tries. My analyst tells me I didn't really want to since I failed three times, but I sure as hell had myself convinced."

She folds her arms the way I painted her in the portrait.

"Maybe *you* won't believe it, Scum, but my hang-up is

men; I'm afraid of sex with men. I was eighteen years old before I had my first period. I'd get the shakes if any man touched me, and my father didn't seduce me, I've never been raped; I have no excuse. The shrinks have run me up and down that course maybe a hundred times. There's just an unreasoning fear, floating anxiety, the hardest kind to get a handle on."

She needs to talk all right. I'm not sure if I'm up to it. I take these things too seriously; and I still need to work out a place for storing my paintings. I look over her shoulder up on the loft where I was climbing around. God, we'll be lucky to get out of here in two hours at this rate. I'm wondering, too, how long we'll both keep up the heroic Gallagher-and-Shean act, if we'll actually get down to talking. We were so close it scared me and now I'm afraid it might start up again. I'm not ready; I'll never be ready. It's so real and at the same time so much of "Let's Pretend."

To be honest, if that's possible, the whole motorcycle business stinks of "Let's Pretend." It's probably a good thing that big painting got burned. There wasn't much sincerity in it; something of a laugh at the world, a desperation kind of last laugh, not good to hear.

"Sandy. I don't know any abortionists. Are you sure you want an abortion? I don't want much to do with killing a little baby. It's an undefendable peculiarity of mine.

"I know a French doctor who's a pediatrician; she's also a psychiatrist. She wrote her doctorate at the Sorbonne on babies who were born after the mother requested an abortion officially and was refused. These babies when they grow up have a sad record of crime, alcoholism, suicide—the works. I'll give you Monique's number and you can go talk to her."

I hope I've said it straight enough. I hope Sandy doesn't think I'm only trying to duck out. She looks me in the eye; I try to keep my eyes level with hers. It's like playing stare-down in junior high school again. I still have that eerie feeling she's a junior-high-school high jumper; it's hard to think of her as pregnant with a real live baby.

As I'm looking into those eyes, tears start welling up, the way water seeps into the bottom of an old wooden boat; you can't see where it comes from, it just appears. God, I feel awful; I don't know what to do.

"That's the thing of it, Scum. I never thought I'd ever get pregnant, be a mother. The doctors told me I've never developed properly inside, that I have the uterus of a little girl. Now I'm pregnant and I just can't believe it. It's weird; something in me's glad to find out I can actually do it."

She stands up. I stand too. She pulls that corduroy dress across her stomach with thumb and fingers outstretched, both sides, in the classic gesture. There could be a little bulge there all right. She looks at me and she's smiling.

"I see it but I can't believe it. I feel different too, inside quiet when I should be more scared. I'm not scared enough."

We move toward each other. I take her in my arms. I try to feel her little baby belly pushing against me but I can't, too much of my potbelly between us. I'm pregnant with years. I hold her tight and try not thinking too much till she's stopped sobbing. All I need is for everybody to come home early.

"Don't worry, folks. Sandy here's just come to tell me she's pregnant and we're working things out, heh, heh!"

I hold her tighter. She's squeezing me tighter too; it's easy to forget how strong a woman can be. We've all got these preconceived notions. Of course, I need to say the next thing. The Scumbler has to say it.

"Why don't you have your baby, Sandy? Maybe you'd be happy being a mother. It could be the best kind of experience for you, give you something to build around."

She squeezes me tighter yet but is shaking her head back and forth against mine. We stay like that without saying anything and my back's beginning to break. Some of her hair is against my nose and making it itch. She's saying something into the side of my neck.

"Matt's asked me to take an apartment with him. I want to. I'm so happy being with him and I really want to."

My mind's spinning. So, wonderful, it all works out. I'm happy for Sandy, for Sweik. Let's break out the champagne, celebrate. Let's get *out* of here before the family comes home!

She shakes her head some more. I stick my head out sideways to get away from her hair. I hunch up my shoulder to scratch my nose.

"I can't do it to him, Scum; it isn't fair. I know he'd feel trapped and it wouldn't be right. I couldn't live with myself—I think I'm *in* love with him and it's wonderful; I don't want to spoil anything."

I'm ready to leave it at that. I did my best, little

chum; you probably weren't meant to make it this time around; better luck next time.

"OK, Sandy, you know best. Don't do anything you'll feel wrong about."

I begin untangling myself carefully. I move off into the kitchen and start tea. There's still more than forty-five minutes until zero hour. I'm feeling depressed, deflated, let down. My nerves are what seem to be failing me first.

I think—with me, at least—senility is hitting first in the nerves. I can't take the kind of flak I used to. Now, my knees are wobbling; my hands are so shaky I can scarcely dribble tea into my teapot. A little Twining's Earl Grey should be about right for the situation; it's Kate's favorite.

We sit and talk some more, sipping tea, trying to be rational. Sandy says she'll go see the doctor; I give her the name, address. I don't want to talk about it anymore; makes me feel too much the accomplice. We finish our tea and I clear the table, hoping she'll get the idea. She's a sensitive, smart person and takes the hint. She stands at the counter and looks over while I wash the dishes and dump tea leaves from the pot. I look up and she's giving me the double whammy again. I stare back with what little I have left. I'm afraid we're about to start the whole show a second time. I'll never make it.

"You didn't ask."

I go through my mind wondering what she's talking about. I've asked everything I can think of.

"What didn't I ask?" I ask.

"You didn't ask who's the father."

That's right. I didn't. I assumed it was Sweik; what's the difference? Honestly, I don't want to know who the father is if she's going to kill this little one off, sort of doubles the crime. Who the hell knows who a father is anyway? I thought I was father to my first kids; the American people said I wasn't, took them away. I've never heard a word from either of them; they're in their late thirties now. My son was a captain in the Vietnam War, Green Berets. Somebody else had to tell me that. My son a killer. Even de Maupassant couldn't've come up with anything more ironic.

I walk around out of the kitchen and she starts moving toward the door. I sneak a look at the clock; there's still almost half an hour.

"OK, who *is* the father, Sandy?"

"It happened down there in Spain. I know just when it happened because I don't have that much to do with men. First it was Lubar outside the cave in the sand at night; that was just because I was mad at Dale, trying to get back at her."

I feel my heart turn over. She can't think it's me. You can't get somebody pregnant through the eyes, the hands, the tongue, the mouth, the toes, the fingers, the heart. I stand at the door, waiting for what she's going to say. Maybe it's some kind of "con" game. I try not letting my mind lead up that particular blind alley.

"And then, Scum, you and I were together. For the first time, I was with a man and wasn't afraid. You really turned me on as a woman to a man for the first time."

She pauses.

"After you left, Matt and I *fell* into each other. At first *I* made love to *him,* because of his back; at first I was pretending he was *you.* Then, as his back got better, he made love to me and it was a whole new world."

My first thought is, I don't know why she needs to tell me all this. What good does it do? I stand, waiting for her to leave. She lingers in the doorway watching my face. I don't look away but it's tiring.

"You know, Scum, this should have been *our* baby."

She smiles, reaches out a hand, touches my beard, kisses me lightly on the lips, then starts tripping carelessly down the stairs. I have a hard time restraining myself from telling her to take it easy; after all, she *is* pregnant. But that doesn't make sense, even to me. Not much of anything is making sense. Can the world really be as senseless as it seems sometimes?

WILLFUL, LAST-DITCH WANDERINGS,
UNFILLED PROMISES LIE HEAVY IN MY SOUL.
BRAIN-FILLED EYES NOT SEEING, NOR KNOWING
THE BLUE OF CLEAR AND CLOUDLESS SKIES.

I sit around our apartment all that evening mulling it over. My family is accustomed to living with the mad artist, so they leave me alone when I'm moody. I hate being like that but sometimes can't help myself. I've tried several times explaining it to Kate and she still doesn't understand, but she puts up with it most times.

I keep thinking of that little baby, maybe a Sweik-Sandy baby in there, with no idea of what's about to happen. Maybe it's a Lubar-Sandy baby, a wild combination, but I'd love to see what it would grow up to be. Maybe half bird, half dolphin. I hate to think of Sandy under the knife of some French butcher. Our civilization certainly does get us into the craziest binds.

MY FLOWER BEGS BEES TO INVADE AND TASTE
ITS POLLEN, SWOLLEN STAMEN, EXPECTANT IN
THE SUN. A SMALL TRAGEDY, MY SEEDS NOT TO
BE BEGOTTEN, NOR GERMINATED FOR A COMING
YEAR. NON-FOLIATE, PRISTINE, INSECTLESS,
I TWIST MY FACE SLOWLY TO THE STERILE SKY.

We're in bed when Kate kisses me and asks what's the matter. I'm about ready to put her off with something general but I want to talk with her. At first I'm afraid to, but then I work my way sideways into the story. I tell about Sandy, how she's one of the ones who came down to Spain. I tell how she came to the house today.

This is dangerous territory; Kate doesn't care too much about the people I kick around with in the streets but definitely doesn't tolerate them mucking up her nest. Witness when Lubar came and slept on the floor. Kate enjoys a sense of normal progression; the ragged twentieth century is definitely not for her. I tell how Sandy is going to have a baby and came to tell me about it this afternoon. I tell her most of what Sandy said, minimizing my part in it all. The line between honesty and hurt can be hard to draw.

There's a silence. I wait. Then I let it all out. I'll *never* learn when to stop. I always expect too much of people, especially the ones I love.

"Kate, I know it's crazy, but I can't think of that baby being killed. Would it be all right if we offer to pay the hospital bills and help with the baby till Sandy's ready to handle it herself?"

This has got to be one of my most crackbrained ideas. I wait there in the dark on my back. I'm expecting anything from a nightlong silence to a quiet departure.

Kate lays a hand across my eyes.

"Are you the father?"

It had to come. It's a good question, a natural question. Kate always knows the right questions.

"No. I'm not, but I know within two who is."

She keeps her hands over my eyes. I lie perfectly still, waiting.

Kate's quiet a long time, then she kisses me. She takes her hand from my eyes, looks down from over me; I can just make out her face in the dark.

"Too bad, in a way; it would've been nice having half of one more like you around again. But no, I don't want to help bring this baby into the world. We don't have that kind of money and, from what you say, this girl doesn't sound stable enough to mother a child. We could wind up with it ourselves and we're too old."

I'm pretty sure Kate can only say that first part because I'm *not* the father. She knows I might not tell her everything but she also knows I don't lie to her. I stay still trying to put it together and at the same time to let go. I'm feeling torn apart. I pull Kate down to me and hold her tight, search her mouth for a hard, strong kiss. Then we share the blessed act by which we've all become.

BECOMING AS ONE WITH ANOTHER.
BEGETTING IS FORGETTING.

As we curl into each other, I know I need to tell her my other big secret; it's been burning holes in my mental side pockets.

"Kate, there's something else I have to tell you."

Quiet again. I can feel her body tighten inside mine.

"You really are the father, aren't you? You lied to me!"

"No, nothing to do with that business at all—not directly anyway."

So I tell her about the eight-thousand-dollars-an-acre, three-hundred-and-twenty-thousand-dollar offer for the forty acres.

Gradually Kate untangles herself from me; she turns and gets up on her knees in bed.

"You mean you've known about this for weeks and you didn't say a word?"

"I'm sorry, Kate. I'm so afraid of that money. It could ruin everything, the kids, us, the way we live, our life, the way you feel about teaching. I know I couldn't think of one thing I wanted to do with the money and so much of it would go in taxes to build more atomic bombs to kill more people. I needed time to think about it."

"So you kept it to yourself. I know *you* bought that crazy

mountain but it was *our* money. You have no right not to tell me, to make a decision like that yourself without even mentioning it. How do *you* know what *I* want? Maybe I want to take a leave from teaching, go back to America, live in a *real* house, be near my mother for her last years."

"I never thought of those things, Kate. You never said anything."

She's still on her knees. In the dim light I can see her fists clenched on her knees at the ends of her stiff arms.

"You never think of anybody but yourself. You treat everybody and everything as if we're all part of one big painting, a painting of *your* life, a self-portrait, a *selfish* portrait, and we're all only background. I'm sick and tired of it!"

Kate slides down on her stomach with her head turned away from me. Even I know sometimes when to keep my mouth shut. Even if I opened it, I wouldn't know what to say.

Kate will never agree to helping Sandy; I'll have to do that on my own.

There are all kinds of ways to kill. The most obvious is to do it yourself, the second is to force someone else to do it for you, like Stalin, or Johnson. Then there's the black-angel way, to encourage another. But the most common way is the teddy-bear way, letting somebody else die when you can help, by ignoring or panicking or pretending it doesn't matter. I guess by that last one I'm living with a killer. Since apparently my own son's a killer already, I should relax. I get in my own way too much.

But I will offer money so Sandy can have that baby if she wants. I can't stand by and see a thing like this happen just for economic reasons.

I lie there in the dark beside Kate, stiff and wake, breathing, thinking about this baby, our baby, Sandy and (should've been) me together. She probably won't take the money anyway. How close could you come to being born and get sideswiped?

YET, TO RESENT NON-BECOMING POLLUTES THE FOUNTAIN AT ITS SOURCE. THERE IS NO FORCE MORE THAN KNOWING OF KNOWING. THE SLOW FALLING SNOW IS MORE VISIBLE THAN THE DRIVING RAIN.

My mind is spinning in twenty directions. Ideas are bubbling in every combination imaginable. I'm being father, brother, uncle, mother, sister, aunt, grandmother and grandfather to that baby. I'll never get to sleep.

I think over what Kate's said. She's right, I'm always trying to design my own life. Life is so important to me it has to be lived on purpose with purpose. Most people seem to be just slipping along, sneaking through life without waking themselves. I can't be that way.

At the same time, I've got to quit designing everybody else's life. God, I'm pushing Sweik into Lotte's arms, Sandy into Sweik's, Traude into Clement's, even poor Sasha into his Arab bed. I'm like an old-time Jewish matchmaker.

Then there are all my nests: birds' nests, rats' nests, nature nests, family nests, artists' nests. I'm trying to design everybody's life, how they live, where—everything.

I don't really know how I got started being the way I am. I might be one of the only people who was expelled from kindergarten. I don't think I was a troublemaker, anyway; I never wanted to be. My usual way then, and I guess even now, has been constantly to try smoothing things out; or, if that didn't work, to run away.

I'd run away from home five times by the time I was sixteen; then I took early graduation from high school and left home for good.

The strange thing is that I had loving, wonderful parents and I loved them. I loved my brother and sisters as well. The problem is, when you're a child, people—even, maybe especially, good loving people—think they have a right to run your life for you; that they know what's best. My sweet, beautiful mother would always say, "Yes, but *I'm* the mother," and that was supposed to be a good enough reason for her to run my life.

I slowly shift my weight and ease myself to the side of our bed. Something big is happening inside me and I feel I might break out bawling any minute. I sit there with my bare feet on the floor to see if Kate is going to say anything more; I can't tell for sure if she's asleep or not.

. . .

My getting through college was a classic case of the upside-down way I've lived my life. I started a laundry for the students at the University of Pennsylvania. I bought a beat-up old truck and developed a pickup route. Mostly only rich kids went to college in those days. I found a broken-down store I rented for fifteen dollars a month. Down at the shipyards I bought some old used boilers as scrap metal and hauled them to the store. I fired up those boilers with a wood fire from wood I'd pick up at building or demolition sites.

That first year I washed those clothes old-style, stomping them with my bare feet. My only cost was soap and the electricity I used for my iron. I'd iron all day and sometimes all night. My store was in a solid black neighborhood of southwest Philadelphia; this was 1937 and I was all of seventeen years old. But I was making it, making it on my own, and that's just about all that counted to me then.

I carefully ease myself off the bed and stand up. I walk through the kitchen and into the bathroom. I close the door and turn on the light. I stare at myself in the mirror. God, I look awful! I don't even look alive. I look like a corpse nobody cares about enough to bury. I'm definitely more frazzled, worn-out-looking than usual; my face is so gray, along with my white messed-up twisted beard, I look like a black-and-white photograph of myself. I look like the face in a group photograph in a newspaper clipping with a circle around it to indicate the person who's just been killed in a plane crash.

By the time I was nineteen, I had two real laundry machines, three pickup trucks, five employees and was enrolled at Penn on a scholarship, living illegally in the attic of the physics building. I'd gotten into the sex part of life early and met my wife just before I graduated as an engineering student. In 1939, everybody with any brains at all was supposed to be an engineer.

I was married to Jane and became a father the first time two days after my twenty-first birthday. It was the way I wanted it. I was already designing my own life like a madman. I wanted at least ten kids and I wanted them all before I was thirty-five. I wanted to *play* with them. Jane was still going along with me in those days; I don't imagine I gave her much chance. I wasn't listening to *anyone* else. I guess I'm still not.

I look at my hands. They're filthy with paint and with just plain dirt from climbing around up there on the lofts arranging painting storage. Sandy upset me so much with her story I even forgot to wash before I went to bed. I sniff my armpits; I stink. Not only do I stink, but I stink like an old man, a stale alkaloid kind of smell, the smell of something live becoming inorganic. My sweat used to have a good animal smell, like a clean cage for a tiger in a zoo, but not any more. I guess the old metabolism's changed.

I really don't know how much longer Kate will put up with it; it can't be much fun living with a decaying animal. The only compensating factor I've had to offer her all these years has been vitality and now there isn't much of the vital "vita" left. That is, except for the paintings, which are probably slipping along with everything else.

Much of what I am, most of the way I live, what I do, is an insult to everything she values, the whole rest of her life.

I know it sounds like sour grapes, but, usually, the so-called cultured people I've met love art, whether it's painting, music, sculpture, literature, what have you; but they don't want anything to do with real live artists. The only good artist to them is a dead artist, like Indians—and look at all the Indians we've killed in the name of civilization; makes Adolf look like a raging humanitarian. Of course, there are always "good artists," "tame artists," like good, tame Indians, who will slip on some feathers or a beret and do tricks for the people.

No, I guess today the public artists are supposed to wear designer jeans with patches, or overalls, and split tennis shoes. They're supposed to take up drugs, alcohol, politics and give up working, sleeping, washing. But they don't count; they're just part of life, decoration to hide the cracks in things, amusement-park people, merry-go-round people.

I should take a shower but it'd make too much noise and wake everyone. Besides, I don't think I have enough energy to climb up and balance myself in our elevated shower.

It's truly amazing the things Kate has to put up with just living with me. I wonder how I can possibly suggest to her she's free to go off on her own, without hurting her feelings or just doing some more "life designing" again. Then what about Sara and Tim?

The psychiatrist in prison said I was a psychopath. He insisted I was masking as a benevolent psychopath but there was no such thing. I'd laugh in his face and he'd go on insisting my pacifism was actually based on a deep hostility and distrust toward all people. He said I separated myself, insisted on my uniqueness and had a strong disrespect for human beings. He told me this was typical of psychopaths; in fact, probably the definition. This alienation, separation, sense of superiority, is what makes psychopaths so dangerous.

God, I thought that was ridiculous then. I'd try to tell him how all I wanted to do was live my *own* life my *own* way and I definitely didn't want to hurt anybody. That's when he laughed and brought up the divorce and how I'd hurt Jane and the kids, my parents, that whole business. He's the one who put psychopath on my record so I had a terrible time getting a job teaching again after I got out of prison. That's what the U.S. government calls rehabilitation.

But now I know, how, in a way, that psychiatrist was right all those years ago. I *have* hurt a lot of people just by being alive and trying to be myself; I'm still hurting them. I don't want to hurt anybody but I'm doing it all the time. I think I hurt people by living; that my maniacal insistence on living my own life is in itself a terrible violation of everybody else; that I'm denying an important part of the human condition, human expectations, by aiming my life at unpredictability.

I suspect I've spent the greatest part of my life in a flight from boredom.

Now, I know that dependability, reliability, consistency are all part of that ultimate positive value for almost any society: responsibility. If life scares you, then any sudden unpredictable change is trauma, hence evil. The unpredictable person is ostracized, classified as pariah for the good of the group.

Perhaps unpredictability is the nature of the creative personality. I'm not necessarily talking about being an artist or a scientist, any of the creative activities, but just the way one goes about living. A creative human has a desire, an almost inhuman yearning, for uniqueness. This urge is probably the source material for most of our mental institutions. Also, it must drive everybody else crazy being around these characters who won't relax and accept things the way they are, are constantly trying to change, juggle everything so it's different, or, worse yet, if they *can't* change things; they're reconstructing, reinterpreting the so-called REALITY to make it *fit.*

I know that's what my paintings are. I don't exactly make them up out of whole linen and, at the same time, I don't even try to paint things the way they seem. I paint the world the way I *want* it to be.

And this story, this book: sure, there are people like Sweik and Lotte, Kate and Sandy; sure, there are tunnels under Paris and clocks, ugly orgies, motorcycle clubs, all of it; but I didn't tell it the way it was-is. I'm not a reporter, a recorder. I'd be bored out of my mind writing an accurate account about a whole bunch of mere facts, events, things, happenings, people. It'd probably bore *you* too, so you wouldn't even be here with me in my mind for the end of this tale. Maybe you aren't. Too bad.

But these *feelings* I've written here are true, true as I know how to be. They're *my* feelings.

Now the scum that should float on top has sunk to the bottom, become sediment. Maybe sediment *is* culture. I'm afraid that's what happens if you scumble too much. I should have known.

I turn the water on and fill the sink. My hands are shaking. Sandy upset me with all those babies; possibles, impossibles, probables, improbables. Then there's just been that whole shoot-out with Kate. I'm definitely running down; something like running away.

. . .

I reach for my old standby, 23 SKIDOO. I start rubbing, grinding it in. The combination of smoothness and built-in fine grit is comforting. I rub, scrub, scour, rinse, till the paint and dirt are gone. I dig with a nailbrush and nail file until the worst is out from under my fingernails. I pat my hang-nailed hands dry, then walk out into the living room.

I sit there alone in the quiet of the night, rocking in my rocking chair, listening to my favorite wall clock tick; trying to synchronize my rocking to the swing of the pendulum; trying to slow down the angry, tired pumping inside. I want to calm myself, make it go away. I try a few Kee Rings. Keeeerinng-Keeeerinng; I think I hear bird wings flapping.

There's only my amber vigil light burning, glowing in the dark. I'll sit up till my clock strikes one more time. One more time might just be quite enough.

FIN

XXIII

THE ULTIMATE NEST

But my God! If some fool's willing to give me three hundred and *twenty* thousand for that forty acres; think of it! I could surely borrow three hundred thousand. What a nest I could build with that! Just imagine!

First I'd sink a thousand-foot well, a shaft of steel casing deep into the earth, pulling up silver water free to that dry, open air. I'd tap hundreds of underground rivers, go almost down to sea level.

I'd bring it up with a gigantic multicolored, transparent plastic vaned windmill. It'd rise thirty feet off the ground with vanes fifteen feet long. Those rivers of water would just spurt into the air.

Then I'd build more windmills to catch the soft ocean breeze blowing over my mountain. I'd turn that breeze into electricity and store it deep underground in rows of batteries hooked in parallel—hundreds of them, drinking in my electricity, *holding* it for me.

I'd have so much energy I wouldn't use even a fraction of it. I'd get one of those two-way meters installed by the electric company. I'd pay them for any electricity they gave me, which would be nothing; then they'd pay me for all the electricity I'd pile back on them, and I'd really pour it into those lines.

I might put in solar panels, too, photon-platinum catalytic types, like on the satellites, as well as ordinary heat collectors. I'd put up windmills all around the outside edges of the property where they wouldn't get in the way of things. I'd have the vanes on these windmills just the right balance of different transparent colors so when they spin fast enough, they'll blend to a shining, glowing white, like flying saucers or halos. Imagine seeing them all swing together, with changes in wind direction; it would look like a bird dance.

LIGHT DISKS, SPINNING IN THE SUN,
GLOWING, TWISTING IN MYSTICAL ASSONANCE.

The next thing, I'll fence the whole forty, not so much to keep people out but to protect the animals inside. I want to stock my mountain with peace-loving animals: rabbits, deer, squirrels, guinea pigs, chickens, ducks—animals that will live a practically free life but you can pet if you want, they wouldn't really be wild.

I'll build this nest on the very top ridge; on that flat part there. I'll build it sort of like that nature nest the kids and I built down there in the Morvan, only on a COLOSSAL scale.

The center pole will be a column cast in bronze and more than thirty feet high. It'll be three feet in diameter and hollow in the center like a miniature Bernini column. Water will flow up pipes in the center to the top. Then some of that water will flow gently down the outside of the column, twisting, spinning, trickling down. This column will have all sorts of paths, and hollow places and little pools, miniature mountains and waterfalls, spurtings and drippings with different sounds to the water, according to how far it falls, how it hits the metal, how thick the bronze is. Smooth parts will become golden down to the bronze where the water runs over it; other parts will be all shades of green, with moss growing on some places.

There will be thousands of different combinations as the water flows down that center pole until it reaches the pond at its base.

This pond will be at least twenty feet in diameter and with more than a thousand ways the water drips into it. It'll be filled with fish and with little fountains inside, squirting, reaching up to meet the water coming down. Lily pads, water flowers, goldfish and all other kinds of tropical fish will be sprinkled by silver droplets of constantly falling water.

It'd take several lifetimes just sitting and watching that column and the pond filled with fish and flowers.

TIME INVISIBLE, INTEGRATE TO ME, NOT
PUSHING OR PULLING. JOYFULLY FLYING
SHADOWS OF DEEPEST GREEN SHADOWS.

Other water going up the center of my column will flow over a multicolored stained-glass pyramid like a circus tent. This will be the glass roof covering our entire patio. The nest will be built around this patio, with my column, the falling water, the pool, the fountains in the center.

The glass of this patio roof will be of many colors and thicknesses, in all changing patterns so you can make up any pictures from them you want in your mind: moving colored clouds. It will be like looking at the windows in Chartres or the Sainte-Chapelle on a sunny day with your eyes half closed. But it will be ten times more exciting because you'll be inside, part of it. Also, this glass will seem as if it's alive, because water will be trickling over it continually, making runnels of thickness and thinness, always varying without being predictable, causing millions of light patterns and spectra over everything under it.

The water will flow over the glass, then over the roof of the house and down to catchment basins and out to the pool-moat.

INSIDE A KALEIDOSCOPE, BENDING LIGHT,
A LUMINOUS SCULPTURE, TIDEWAY OF TIDINGS.

My nest won't just be round or square or any geometric figure known to man; it'll be totally irregular, forming at least twenty different kinds of triangles, all pointing their apexes up high to the top of the column; it'll look like a free-floating-all-glass cathedral.

Some of the water up there on top will gush like a geyser as high as Yosemite, or the fountains in the gardens of Versailles, or maybe even as high as that big geyser on the lake in Geneva. It'll spout different heights according to the wind or sun or the time of day or year, but all blended to natural schedules so it's never the same. It won't spout in the rain but it can spout so you can have your own rain shower whenever you want, even on the hottest, driest day.

Around the outside of my nest will be wonderful green lawns, dichondra or Bermuda grass, or some ground cover so they won't need to be mowed; I hate the sound of a lawn mower almost as much as that of a vacuum cleaner.

THE MUSIC OF NEAR SILENCE,
LIVE AIR, INSECTS BUZZING, WATER
FALLING, THE CLEAN BREEZE BLOWING
THROUGH CHAPARRAL, BUCKTHORN AND WILD LILAC.

Then, twenty feet farther out from the nest, will be the swimming pool-moat. It'll go all around the nest but will be only eight feet wide. It'll have most of the same angles as the house but still be different. Nothing will be monotonous; everything will always be a surprise in this nest, even if you live hundreds of years there.

You'll be able to swim all around that pool and it won't be deep anywhere: only four feet at the most; just for swimming, no diving. Around my nest, there will be flying but no diving.

In this pool-moat you can swim for almost a quarter mile without repeating yourself; you can swim along there and be looking out on one of the most beautiful views in the world: the entire Santa Monica Bay, the Santa Monica Mountains, rough and natural, with the simple Topanga Village below.

Off in the distance—just the right distance—on clear nights you can see the San Fernando Valley with lights of all colors, like long strings of jewels, glowing in the dark. You can swim naked in clean, safe, warm water up there, too.

The outside of my moat will be a wall, because the land drops away from the exact top of the mountain where my nest will be located; the nest will be wrapped in beveled angles around its patio. So nothing but beautiful rolling green and gray hills, alive, like a sleeping earth giant under a muted patchwork quilt, will be between you and the edge of sky.

The water in my pool-moat will be warm because it will have come down over the glass, over the roof of the house, where it will have soaked up all the heat. This will make the house always cool inside, not too dry and not moist either. There will be no glare in the house, even on the hottest days, and all the walls will be natural wood or rock except for the door-windows. The panes of glass in the outside sliding door-windows will be polarized. There will be double door-windows, one polarized vertically, the other horizontally, so you can slide the two doors over each other and block out all light and heat, or have one door alone blocking only heat or both doors open to let in heat and light. It will always be comfortable in my nest.

At night, extra heat from the pool will flow through tunnels beneath the floors where there will be volcanic rock to absorb this heat and radiate warmth; on warm days or nights this heat will be used to generate energy and run quiet, natural coolers. The temperature will always be just the way you want it.

And can you imagine swimming in water where there's no end? It'll be like swimming in a loving ocean. Even someone like me who's afraid of water could relax in that pool. It will be caressing, soothing, nothing of fear: just wonderful weightlessness.

All the rooms in my nest will open inside onto the patio. The windows will be like Japanese windows on the inside, with small panes and not polarized. They'll slide on silent ball-bearing rollers so you can close off the patio or push them open all together and let the patio come into the rooms: privacy or openness according to what you want. Sometimes you won't be able to tell the difference between the patio and the nest; the patio will be part of the nest, the deepest inside part.

In it will be birds flying free, a wonderful place for birds to fly, a huge semi-tropical environment, year round. There will be thousands of different flowers, blooming all the time, with oranges, lemon and grapefruit trees, avocados, mangoes, guavas, persimmons, lychees, arbutus and bananas. The birds will be mostly canaries, because they sing, but there will be exotic finches, also some nightingales and parrakeets. How my canaries will love singing with the symphony of water, bathed in flickers of color. Their wings will whisper wind songs as background to their own music.

Each bathroom will have sliding panels out onto the lawn so we can shower or bathe as if outside in nature. The bathing tubs will be smooth rock pools surrounded by greenery; the water will flow in over natural rocks. The wall around the moat will give privacy.

We might not even wear clothes in this nest, except for decoration sometimes: some nice fabric draped over a shoulder or wrapped around a waist, something to match the colors and lights of a particular day, or the music or the smells. Everything will be totally in tune, all running together but continually different, like good music or good painting or some good poetry.

. . .

There will need to be a road up to this nest for bringing in supplies once a year, or for letting in a few guests who can't fly; but mostly the gates will be locked and the road not used.

The only real way to visit this nest will be by air. The only kind of plane able to land on our landing place will be ultralights or hang-gliders, no helicopters. Helicopters are worse than vacuum cleaners and lawn mowers for noise.

Imagine how beautiful it will be seeing the flashing bright Dacron colors of hang-gliding friends coming up with air currents and veering to land, or the put-putting up of an ultralight, like a flying motorcycle, circling, then settling onto the deep green of our special airstrip surrounded by multicolored flowers.

Finding a place to park our ultralights in the world down below can be a problem. Perhaps we'll never go down, just cruise over the hills or out over the ocean. Or I might be able to make a deal with some schools allowing children to come up for a visit, opening the gates for them to walk up from the Topanga Village. I'll trade this off for landing rights in their parking lots or football fields when they aren't using them. I know the kids would enjoy visiting this nest.

One special thing will be I'm going to hang my paintings everywhere on the inside walls. There will be space for at least two hundred paintings, all beautifully lit so each one will be a special world of its own. It'll be a private museum, like the Getty or Frick, but more personal; all these paintings will be me. Boy, it'd sure be wonderful seeing all my paintings at once, like looking back over my entire life, seeing, feeling, smelling it all happen again.

I'm sure kids would love to see something like that, and besides they could watch the birds and fish, pet the animals outside. They'd probably like swimming around in the pool-moat, too. I'd set up a current so they could float around on little boats or just float out on their backs. With only four feet of water none of them are going to drown. It'd all be safe and I'd keep an eye on them.

Of course, all this would cost much more than a mere three hundred thousand dollars, but then again, I'd be getting rich from my "energy farm"—all that electricity I'm pumping back to the electric company. Besides, this place will be getting more and more valuable as I build it; I could float other loans, go for a second, third, fourth mortgage. This sky nest would be so beautiful nobody would ever let anything happen to it. It'd be proof of how incredibly wonderful, exciting this life can be if we want it to and we let it happen to us.

I wouldn't be worried about fires. With that moat all around and the water shooting up over everything like a veil of protection, there'd never be any danger of things burning. There could be a roaring forest fire all around and we'd turn up the rain a little bit and sit there on top of that hill, covered by mists of water making steam clouds all around, and just watch. We couldn't be safer.

Also, with our moat, no snakes or tarantulas or scorpions or even spiders would be able to get in. Kate might come live with me someday. Maybe even one day the kids could move in, then their kids. Maybe even my first kids, the ones I've never known, and even Jane could join us. We could all live together like a happy family for a long time up there.

Around the outside of the pool I'd build a jogging track, just the right firmness and softness to absorb shock. It'd be banked to keep too much weight from being put on one side or the other. This'd be even better than running around the dining-room table in Paris and I wouldn't have to make up different places to pretend I was running. I'd be running exactly in the place where I am, in the place I choose.

The whole hill down from the jogging track, thirty feet or more, would be planted in that kind of tiny succulent with fluorescent red, purple and pink flowers.

From down below, looking up to the top of our mountain, it will look as if the mountain has garlands of color around its neck and is wearing a huge, colored, pointed dunce cap. It'll be nice for everybody to look up and know we're happy there.

With a nest like this—quiet, relaxing; where I can paint and concentrate, swim in our moat-pool, do Yoga, meditate watching the water, birds, fish, little animals playing—have fun with my family, it would be like heaven. I wouldn't have anything to fight or worry me. I could probably live twenty more years—maybe even a thousand.

This'd be my ultimate nest.

A NOTE ON THE TYPE

This book was set in Univers 45, a type designed in the late 1950's by Adrian Frutiger and one of twenty-one variants he worked in this face. In this typeface the monoline is not rigidly adhered to; the ghosts of stress and serif have returned to lend their aid to the apparently unstressed and serifless letter. Univers, with its perfect fit, produces evenly colored pages, firm, unbroken lines, and coherent words, all based upon clear, legible letter-forms. The typeface was chosen by the author, who would have preferred that the book be set entirely in capitals (as the poetry extracts are).

Composed by Dix Type, Inc., Syracuse, New York.
Printed and bound by The Haddon Craftsmen,
Scranton, Pennsylvania.